Also by John David Anderson

Sidekicked

Minion

The Dungeoneers

Ms. Bixby's Last Day

Posted

Granted

One Last Shot

FINDING ORION

ORION

John David Anderson

WALDEN POND PRESS

An Imprint of HarperCollinsPublishers

Walden Pond Press is an imprint of HarperCollins Publishers.
Walden Pond Press and the skipping stone logo are trademarks and
registered trademarks of Walden Media, LLC.

ISBN 978-0-06-264390-2

20 21 22 23 24   PC/BRR   10 9 8 7 6 5 4 3 2 1
❖
First paperback edition, 2020

To my loving family. Stay quirky.

"Mostly it is loss which teaches us about the worth of things."
—Arthur Schopenhauer

"Lector, si monumentum requiris, circumspice."
—Epitaph marking the tomb of Sir Christopher Wren

WELCOME TO THE CIRCUS

The night we found out about Papa Kwirk, I had a jelly bean for dinner.

Not jelly *beans*. *A* jelly bean. One.

Strange as it may seem, I was used to it. Jelly beans were often the appetizer du jour at the Kwirk residence.

We sat around the glass table, so recently Windexed that you could still smell the ammonia. My older sister, Cass, wearing purple lipstick and hum-rapping songs from *Hamilton*. Younger sister, Lyra, pigtailed and perusing the pocket dictionary in her lap, no doubt discovering new words to show off with (like *perusing*). Mom and Dad sitting shoulder to shoulder, as if they were required by law to be within kissing distance, a sort of reverse restraining order.

And me, elbows on the table, hands pressed to my cheeks,

staring at the lonely piece of candy on my plate and thinking surely I was adopted.

It's a fantasy I come back to time and again: my parents sitting me down, showing me the papers, reciting the long-hidden history of my true origin. The orphanage where I was left. The day my so-called mother picked me out of the dozen or so slobbering tots. Or maybe something mysterious. Something more basket-on-the-doorstep-in-the-dead-of-night. Maybe I was rescued from a pack of hungry wolves in the middle of a dark forest. Or I crash-landed on Earth and they found me sucking my thumb in the middle of a crater. Though that would make *me* the alien, and I'm pretty sure that's not the case; if anyone in this house is from another planet, it's not me.

I know. Everybody's family is a little nutso. But there's nuts . . . and then there's the Kwirks.

I poked at my dinner, mottled beige and brown, a tiny thing sitting in the center of a big white plate like a weed sprouting in the snow. I wasn't going to be the first to try it.

"I have to admit, I've really outdone myself this time," Dad said, pushing his glasses back to the top of his nose.

Dr. Fletcher Kwirk. Conductor of the Kwirk family crazy train. Owner of a cow-patterned lab coat with the words *Science Is Udderly Awesome* sewn on the front and two dozen tacky, uber-colorful bow ties. A geek and a dork and a nerd all rolled into one, a true triple threat. My father knows the words to every cartoon theme song from the 1980s and sings them constantly, begging me to sing along. Ever heard of a Snork? Sounds like something that might happen if you drink warm soda too fast, but it turns out it's a race of annoying underwater creatures with bendy straws sprouting from their heads. Their theme song is the worst piece of music ever created, and Dad can belt out every word. *Tailspin* and *Gobots*. *Muppet Babies* and *Inspector Gadget*. He knows them all. He says it comes from too many Saturdays spent glued to the TV, but I suspect it's because he never bothered to grow up. Or maybe grew up too fast and is trying to get back there.

Which might also explain why he makes candy for a living. Dad is the chief flavor chemist at Kaslan's Candy Factory here in town. He has a PhD in organic chemistry and can tell you the exact compound necessary to make watermelon Jolly Ranchers taste the way they do (i.e., nothing like actual watermelons). If you'd like, he can even explain the chemical connection between Silly Putty and McDonald's french fries, thereby ruining something you love for the rest of your life.

But mostly he makes jelly beans. Kaslan's pride and joy was its Hundred-Flavor Mystery Jelly Bean Pack, and Dad can take credit for concocting twenty-seven of those flavors. Hence the appetizer on my plate.

My older sister rolled hers back and forth like a dead bug she couldn't identify. "It's not garlic again, is it? Because I honestly feel like you perfected that last time."

I nodded emphatically. Dad's garlic jelly bean tasted just like real garlic—which, in jelly-bean form, is pretty disgusting.

Just because you *can* make a piece of candy taste like something doesn't mean you should.

"It's not garlic, I promise," Dad assured us.

"Is it armpit?" Lyra asked, which is not a question a ten-year-old from any normal family should ever pose at suppertime. Not with a straight face, at least, and my sister's face was straight as a ruler.

"No. It's nothing bad. You'll like this one. And, to be honest, we're having some trouble isolating exactly what armpits taste like. The chemical composition is proving difficult." My father frowned. It had been several weeks since my family— minus one conscientious objector—sat around this same table with their shirtsleeves scrunched to their shoulders, craning their necks and licking their own armpits and describing the taste while my father took notes. "Musky" was one. "Salty" came up. "Not entirely unpleasant" was Lyra's response. Of course, she hasn't hit puberty yet; I'm guessing armpit doesn't get better with age.

I wouldn't know. I refused to lick my pits in the name of science *or* candy. Not until they make cinnamon-flavored deodorant, which my father could probably do.

"That's all right, though, 'cause this blows armpit right out of the water!" Dad was practically bubbling up out of his chair, waiting for us to try his latest creation.

Naturally Cass was the first. Always ready to don the mantle of eldest, bravest child. Without even pinching her nose, she popped the whole thing in her mouth and chewed slowly, her face scrunching. Not a great sign. "Wow. Is that . . . ?"

"It most definitely is," Dad answered, eyes bright, expectant.

Cass chewed a little more, swallowed, her eyes bulging. "Dad, it's brilliant!" she said at last. I waited for it to come right back up, certain she was bluffing, trying to get us all to dig in so we could share in her misery. I shifted a little in my chair, just in case her barf went projectile and sailed over the plastic flower centerpiece (Mom is allergic to pollen). "Come on, guys, you have to try it," Cass prodded.

Reluctantly I pinched the bean between two fingers and brought it to my lips, which instinctively curled inward. We'd been down this road before, my lips and I. Limburger cheese? Check. Curdled milk? Of course. Pickle. Patchouli. I had betrayed my taste buds too many times, and now they'd partnered with those lips to form a formidable first line of defense. In this family, you always have to be on your guard.

My tongue recoiled inside my mouth.

"Come on, Rion, just eat it. It's good," Lyra goaded, having gulped hers down. "Don't be a chicken."

Everyone at the table snickered. Alarms triggered inside my head.

"What? What's funny? It's terrible, isn't it? That's why you're laughing. It really *is* armpit. It's an armpit-flavored jelly bean!"

"No," Mom assured me. "It's not that at all. Trust us. It's fine. Try it."

I tentatively touched the jelly bean to the tip of my tongue. Had either of my sisters said it, I would have refused, but Mom was different. I trusted her. Closing my eyes, I bit down. My glands gushed as all those artificial flavors manufactured in my father's lab were unleashed.

And I suddenly got the joke.

Chicken. It was a fried-chicken-flavored jelly bean. And it was totally funky.

I mean, it *tasted* fine—tasted *just* like fried chicken, in fact— but it was still a jelly bean, and chewing a jelly bean is not at all the same as sinking your teeth into a piece of golden-crisp KFC. Yet the flavor was unmistakable, that salty, succulent sensation that somehow tricked my brain. I chewed slowly and swallowed.

"Huh," I said.

It was remarkable. My dad *is* kind of a genius.

Then again, so was Victor Frankenstein.

"See. What'd I tell you?" Dad said. "We've finally perfected the compound that approximates savory foods. I mean, bacon's been around for a while, of course. And the Slugworths think they've got the formula for sausage down, but frankly their sausage just tastes like dog food. This, on the other hand . . . this could be a real game changer!"

"The Slugworths" was Dad's name for Kaslan Candy's biggest rivals—the slew of blank-faced, heartless, soulless, scheming scientists at Garvadill Food Supplies. At least that's how he describes them. Garvadill concocted artificial flavors and then sold them to food manufacturers all across the world. Unlike Dad's company, whose recipes were strictly used in-house for Kaslan's famous confections, Garvadill catered to large corporations. They were global, big-business, blood-thirsty pirates, only in it for the money, as opposed to my father, who worked nine hours a day just to put food on our table and a smile on every kid's face—at least until the sugar rotted all their teeth and they had nothing left to smile with.

Dad claimed that Garvadill was notorious for stealing formulas from the competition, though nothing had ever been proven in a court of law. He was exaggerating, of course—this was *candy* we were talking about—but Dad was convinced that the Slugworths were out to get him. As a result, he treated his flavors like nuclear launch codes. Ultra top secret. The fried-chicken jelly bean I'd just eaten had probably been tasted by only one or two other people before it ended up on my plate. You'd think that would make me feel special, being one of the first. Except next time the flavor would probably be asparagus or cottage cheese.

Dad couldn't stop gloating. "Those chumps at Garvadill would *kill* for this recipe. I mean, we still have some kinks to work out regarding replication, but the possibilities are endless. With this we should have no trouble making pork chop jelly beans, brisket jelly beans, smoked turkey, rump roast. Who knows? We could someday have a jelly bean that tastes exactly like filet mignon. Wouldn't that be something?"

It would definitely be *some*thing. You know what else would be something? *Actual* dinner.

"It's amazing, Dad. Really," Cass said. "You nailed it."

"Yeah, Dad," Lyra echoed. "The taste is uncanny in its verisimilitude."

She and Cass gave my father a round of applause, and he took a bow over his plate. Sometimes living with my family was like being part of a freak show. One of those old traveling circuses. All we'd need is a clown. And maybe a parade of elephants.

Dad looked at me, waiting for something, and I realized I hadn't said anything yet. For some reason, he needed the whole family's approval. For everything. He was always asking us if we liked his tie or what we thought of the latest Kaslan's Candy commercial. He actually looked disappointed if you didn't laugh at one of his corny jokes. I usually just humored him. It was easier that way.

"You know . . . what she said." I pointed at my little sister. "Uncanning versus millipedes."

Lyra groaned at me for botching her fancy words, but I ignored her. I knew she thought I was mocking her, but most of the time I had no idea what she was saying. Across from me, Cass went back to rapping *Hamilton*, so I had no idea what she was saying either. It was like every member of my family spoke a different language.

My mother stood up and kissed my father on his starting-to-thin brown hair. "I'm so proud of you, sweetie," she said. "It was fantastic. Unfortunately, *I* made manicotti for our second course, so if you've suddenly got a craving for fried chicken, you're out of luck."

Actually, I was kind in the mood for fried chicken. I could still taste it. Dad leaned back in his chair, arms crossed triumphantly, face alight with satisfaction. "Filet mignon," he whispered. "This is going to make Kaslan's a fortune, you just wait and see."

Across the table, Cass started rapping again.

"There's a million things I haven't done. But just you wait!"

I wadded up my napkin and threw it at her to get her attention. "No show tunes at the table," I said, invoking a rule that had been in place for the last year or so, though admittedly it was more of an ongoing request than an actual rule, and I was the only one who tried to enforce it.

"No throwing things at your sister," she snapped back, taking my crumpled napkin and tossing it back at me. Just to annoy me, she continued to rap even louder. I tried to kick her under the table, but I missed and hit the table leg instead, stubbing my toe. Dad was oblivious, lost in daydreams of a fried-chicken-flavored fortune.

I was about to start making up my own rap, about an annoying sister who won't shut up, when I heard a knock at the door.

My sisters and I all scrambled out of our chairs and down the hall, but I was the first with my hand on the knob. Maybe, just maybe, it was a private detective hired by my real family to hunt me down because they felt bad for abandoning me and sending me to live in this nuthouse.

It wasn't a private detective, though.

It was, in fact, a clown.

The circus was complete.

"Mo-om, there's a clown on the porch," Lyra yelled over her shoulder, which might have beaten out "Is it armpit?" as the oddest sentence of the evening.

The clown gave us a weak smile. He had twin triangles of orange hair spiked out like horns and a bright red smear of a mouth to match his obnoxious nose and oversized flappy shoes. Rosy cheeks bloomed on a painted white face. His outfit was patterned in multicolored stars, a rainbow galaxy that clashed with a polka-dotted bow tie that looked a little too similar to one my father owned. The tag on his clown suit said his name was *Chuckles McLaughsalot*. Everything about our visitor screamed hijinks and happiness.

Except for the pained look on his face.

"Is this the Kwirk residence?" he asked.

We all nodded.

"Your parents home?"

I glanced over my shoulder to see Mom and Dad coming to the door, my mother wiping her hands on a towel. "Hi. How can we help you, Mr. Clown?" my mother asked.

"It's Mr. McLaughsalot," Lyra corrected.

The clown frowned. "You can call me Chuckles, ma'am. I'm here from Happy Times Message and Telegram Service to deliver a message to the Kwirk family."

Dad rubbed his hands together. "Wow. A singing telegram? I didn't even know they still had such things. Did my company send you? Is this about the fried chicken?"

Chuckles looked confused. "Fried chicken?" He stared at my father for a moment, then shook his head. "No, I don't think so." The clown released a deep sigh that made his nose squeak a little. "Listen, Mr. and Mrs. Kwirk, I feel like I should apologize in advance. This isn't really my thing. I normally do anniversaries, you know. Birthday parties. Occasionally I'll help with a marriage proposal. But this . . . this is a first. To be honest, I'm not entirely sure I can go through with it."

"Performance anxiety can be debilitating," Lyra informed him.

Chuckles looked down at Lyra like he'd just seen her there. "Uh-huh. Right. Okay. You know what? I'm just going to get it over with." The clown produced a pipe from some hidden flap in his puffy rainbow suit and blew out one shrill note, humming after it. "Ooohhhh," he began.

"Hang on," Cass said suddenly, one finger up. "Can I go get my phone so I can post this? My friends in musical production will love it."

"Honestly, that's probably not a good i—" Chuckles started to say, but Cass had already dashed back into the dining room, leaving the rest of us staring at the clown standing slump shouldered outside our door. I glanced up and down the street to see if any of the neighbors were outside, watching. "There's a clown talking to the Kwirks," one of them would say.

"Doesn't surprise me in the slightest," another would answer. It wouldn't be the strangest thing they'd ever seen happen at our house.

My sister returned, her phone held out in front of her. "Sorry. Please continue, good sir."

Chuckles hummed once more, getting his pitch before launching into a familiar tune, though I couldn't place the name of it. Sort of folksy, almost like an old nursery rhyme. The clown tapped one oversized red shoe as he sang.

> *"Oooooh, Papa Kwirk, he made life grand.*
> *He laughed big laughs. He made big plans.*
> *By all accounts, a superman.*
> *But Papa Kwirk has kicked the can."*

Chuckles hesitated, just for a second, scanning our faces. I wasn't entirely sure I'd heard him right. Or maybe I had, but I was waiting for something else. A punchline. An explanation. An actual chuckle from Chuckles. I stole a look at Dad, who was standing behind me, but he looked just as confused as I was. Our collective stunned silence only seemed to spur the clown on.

> *"Yes, he's met the maker. He's at the gate.*
> *He's pushing up daisies. He's found his fate.*
> *He's belly-up. He bit the dust.*
> *He's counting worms. He's gathering rust.*

He bought the farm. Cashed in his chips.
Went on that never-ending trip.
Took a deep-six dirt nap underground.
And now he's finally homeward bound.

And that is why I'm here today,
To tell you that he passed away.
But he doesn't want you feeling down,
And that is why he sent a clown

To say that even though he's gone,
His love for you goes on and on.
Yes, Papa Kwirk was a grand old man,
But Papa Kwirk has kicked the can."

Chuckles finished the song by shaking his white-gloved hands, showbiz style, before stuffing them awkwardly into his oversized pants pockets.

"Um . . . that's it," he said.

The clown stared at us. We stared back, paralyzed. A clump of speechless Kwirks crowding the entryway. An entire minute passed, which doesn't sound like very long until you are staring at a man in an orange wig and size-twenty shoes who has just informed you that your grandfather is dead. Then one minute seems like a million.

My father was the first to speak.

"Are you joking?"

Chuckles raised a bushy blue eyebrow. "Do I *look* like I'm joking?"

There was no good answer to this question.

"Listen, you seem like a nice bunch of folks, and I don't mean to upset you," the clown continued. "I just do what I'm told. I don't write the songs, I just sing 'em. Maybe it *is* a joke. But if it's not, then . . . you know . . . I'm really sorry for your loss."

My parents looked at each other, my mother's forehead creasing, my dad's mouth opening and closing wordlessly. Cass looked like she'd been told she'd lost the leading role in the school play. Lyra looked skeptical—but that's pretty much how she always looks.

And I just kept thinking the same thing over and over.

This can't be for real. Papa Kwirk can't be dead.

Chuckles McLaughsalot removed one hand from his pocket and held something out to us. A trio of rainbow-swirl circles on sticks.

"Lollipop?"

IF SANTA RODE A HARLEY

It would come as a shock to anyone, I guess, having a clown show up at your doorstep in the middle of dinner to sing to you about how your grandpa had passed away. Most people would inform their family with a phone call.

Then again, my grandfather wasn't most people.

Even delivered by a clown, the news still struck me like a cannonball to the gut. I'd just seen Papa Kwirk less than four months ago, over Christmas break. He seemed healthy enough. No indication that he was about to "cash in his chips." He still made fart jokes, told war stories that I was pretty sure weren't appropriate, and cussed up a storm when my parents weren't in the room. He still chewed black licorice by the pound, producing it from some bottomless inside pocket of his cracked leather bomber jacket. I suspect he chose licorice because he knew none of us liked it and he wouldn't

15

have to share, though it meant he always smelled like cough drops. My grandfather's mediciney breath is usually the first thing that comes to mind when I think of him.

He and my great-aunt Gertrude had come to visit like they always did—their requisite four days over holiday break—riding down on Jack Nicholson's back through the flittering snow. With Papa Kwirk's bushy white beard and Aunt Gertie precariously perched behind him and the sidecar holding one suitcase and a trash bag full of wrapped packages, they looked like the Hell's Angels version of Santa and Mrs. Claus. You could hear them coming from three blocks away, thanks to Jack's obnoxious growl. Jack Nicholson was grandpa's favorite actor, so naturally he had named his motorcycle after the man.

When he'd heard Jack's rumbling this last time, my father looked at my mother and said, "Here we go again."

"It's only four days," she said with a sympathetic look. Mom and Dad always got a little tense during the holidays. With Mom you could tell it was just the stress of having every-thing done in time: packages wrapped, tree trimmed, turkey stuffed, house spotless. With Dad, though, it seemed to be all about my grandfather. He tried not to show it, of course, but you could tell, and this last Christmas had been no different.

The moment they pulled into the driveway, Papa Kwirk started handing out our presents, insisting that we open them right there in the snowy front yard even though it was only Christmas Eve and twenty-eight degrees outside and my fingers were too stiff to undo the ribbon. Lyra got a calligraphy set. Cass got a creepy ventriloquist dummy that looked like it might come to life and murder me in my sleep. My package turned out to be a tactical combat knife with a hollow handle to store matches and fishing gear—"In case you ever find yourself stranded behind enemy lines," Papa Kwirk said. Then he proceeded to explain how I could use the hook and fishing line to suture a shrapnel wound, complete with a graphic description of what a land mine does to a body ("blows your leg clean off"). The knife went right into the attic, next to the junior crossbow Grandpa had gotten me when I was eight. Mom said I could have them both when I graduated high school.

"Why not just let the boy have it?" my aunt Gertie protested. "It's not like he's going to *stab* anybody."

As my great-aunt pleaded on my behalf, Papa Kwirk leaned down and whispered to me, "But if you have to, get 'em between the neck and the shoulder. They'll go down quick and easy that way." My grandfather was full of practical advice.

He also had a knack for gift giving, even the ones Mom didn't confiscate until I was old enough to join the army myself. Slingshots and fireworks. Tie-dyed rabbits' feet and shark's-tooth necklaces and oversized beer steins that I was only allowed to drink caffeine-free soda out of. Poker chips and posters of old horror movies like *The Thing* and *The Creature from the Black Lagoon*. He once got me a chipmunk that he'd stuffed himself. A real-life dead chipmunk. Because he "knew I liked chipmunks" (I didn't) and because "you're never too young to start an interest in taxidermy" (also not true). *That* gift went into the trash after they left. I wasn't sad to see it go.

That was the thing about Papa Kwirk, though—or at least one of the things, one of the *many* things: you never knew what was going to be in the box. The old man was full of surprises. Dad said I didn't know the half of it—in a way that suggested I'd rather not know the other half.

But this last surprise—the one that came in the form of a clown on our front porch—topped them all.

I couldn't recall Papa Kwirk ever being sick. Sure, a bag of black licorice every day couldn't be good for your blood sugar. And then there was the ritual cigar. Every evening during his visit, my grandfather would go outside to smoke, making little clouds that cast his face in a circle of fog. In the morning he would cough half a lung into the sink, but I was used to hearing it, just like I was used to him guzzling six cups of coffee a day and opening glass bottles of soda with his teeth.

That couldn't be enough to kill you, though. Not enough to kill him, at least. Papa Kwirk was tough. From the scars on his hands to the rough hide that covered his arms, he looked like he'd seen a century's worth of living and would live to see a century more. Dad once told me that Papa Kwirk "lived hard," which, I assume, was not quite the same as "having a hard life." I figured "living hard" just meant smoking cigars and riding motorcycles and adding to your grandson's arsenal every Christmas.

"He lived hard" was pretty much the most Dad ever said about his father. We didn't talk about Papa Kwirk much when he wasn't around, and he and Dad never said much to each other even during those Christmas visits. They hardly ever talked on the phone. When my grandpa called, which was rarely, he usually ended up talking to my mother, and even those conversations lasted less than five minutes: just long enough to relay a bit of news.

But he had still showed up on Christmas Eve, every year, for as long as I could remember. Licorice and cigars, cursing and coffee. Breath that could kill a chipmunk, and the skills to stuff it after. I just assumed it would always be so. That he'd ride in next Christmas, crush me in a bear hug, and tell stories about "dodging Bouncing Betty in the boonies" in Vietnam. He and my father would trade frowns for a few days, muttering more words under their breath than they would to each other. Then he'd ride away again, with my almost-as-crazy aunt Gertie straddling the back of Jack, waving goodbye. Because that's how it'd always been.

Which explains why I was struck speechless, standing there in the April evening chill with a sucker in my hand, staring at a grumpy clown who had just told me that there would be no more war stories. No more fingers to pull. No more potentially lethal Christmas gifts. No more trips around the block in Jack Nicholson's sidecar.

Because my father's father was never coming back.

* * *

The first call was to Aunt Gertie. For confirmation. And, hopefully, some explanation.

Aunt Gertie was the only other living relative on my father's side, at least the only one we were close to. Dad had some distant second cousins who lived out in Modesto who we always got a Christmas card from, but he just stuck it on the mantel next to the card from the family dentist. Aunt Gertie never had any kids of her own; she'd never even married. She claimed she couldn't find a man who could keep up with her—which I can believe—though she went through several dozen trying. To hear Papa Kwirk tell it, Aunt Gertie had more boyfriends than "a queen bee in a hive full of drones."

For a long time, Aunt Gertie lived out in New York City, lawyering, but then she retired from her practice and moved back to Illinois, into the same town as our grandpa, buying a house less than ten miles from the one where my own father grew up. Dad insists that she was the only person to ever move *back* to that town after leaving it.

Papa Kwirk and my great-aunt Gertie had been neighbors for the last decade or so, which seemed like a terrible idea to me. When I grew up, I was determined to live at least one country away from both of my sisters. Preferably with an ocean between us.

I stood right between them in the kitchen doorway, however, while Dad made the call with Mom behind him. We only got to hear half the conversation—Dad refused to put

Aunt Gertie on speaker—but the half we heard told us most of what we needed to know.

"Hi, Gertie, it's Fletcher. Listen, I called because . . . well . . . yes. Yes. As a matter of fact, he *was* just here. His name? Chuckles, I think. No, he didn't have a squirting flower. Aunt Gertie, did Frank . . ." Dad's voice quavered. The hand holding the phone started to tremble. Mom rubbed his back in slow, gentle circles.

Frank was Grandpa's first name. Technically Francis, though I never heard anyone call him that. My father always called him Frank. We all called him Papa Kwirk, which he said he liked better because there were enough stinking grandpas in the world already—even though our name for him was, as Dad put it, "a little Smurfalicious."

Aunt Gertrude called him Jimmy. It was a joke.

My grandfather's middle name was Tyler, making his middle initial a T. At some point when they were teenagers, Great-Aunt Gertie started to tease her brother by calling him James. As in James T. Kwirk. Or when she was feeling especially ornery, *Captain* James T. Kwirk. It's all right if you don't get it. I didn't at first either. It's a *Star Trek* thing, apparently. But Aunt Gertie thought it was hilarious and kept at it. Over the years, James gradually switched to Jimmy, at least for Aunt Gertie, but my father still just called him Frank, which sounded just as weird to me. I couldn't imagine calling my dad Fletcher. I couldn't imagine calling him anything but Dad.

Of course I also spent more than four days out of the year with him.

Dad nodded solemnly as he listened to what Aunt Gertie had to say. "Uh-huh. Uh-huh. And when did this happen? *What?*" Dad's cheeks flared. His voice rose. "And you didn't think to tell me until just now? By *singing telegram*? What do you mean? Whose idea was it, then?" There was a significant pause. I tried to imagine Aunt Gertie on the other end, trying to explain. She'd been a lawyer, after all; she could be persuasive when she wanted to be. "Oh. I see. Did he . . . you know . . . I mean, was it at least . . . peaceful? All right. Yes. No. I understand. You don't need to tell me what my own father was like, Gertie. I get it. I just wish you'd called me as soon as it happened. We could have come down earlier. We could have done something. No. I don't mean that. I understand. Well, yes, of *course* we will be there—he was my father. Yes, they're all here. Yes, I'll tell them. Yeah. Okay, let me call you back, all right? What? No, the clown didn't *do a dance*. What does that even mean, the deluxe package? Then call the stupid telegram company and ask for your money back. Fine. Okay. Call you later."

Dad hung up the phone and turned to look at the three of us wedged in the doorway, his face still pink as he let out a deep breath.

"That was Aunt Gertie," he said, as if we'd just apparated there and had no idea what was going on. "Apparently your grandfather passed away yesterday morning. Sudden cardiac arrest." He paused to let that bit sink in.

"Acute myocardial infarction," Lyra said, which I guess was another name for sudden cardiac arrest, which was just a fancy way of saying heart attack. "Infarction" sounded . . . naughty, somehow. Which meant it sounded like something my grandfather would do. Right after you pulled his finger.

"The memorial service is on Sunday. In Greenburg, of course. Gertie's already made all the arrangements, apparently." Dad looked over at my mother and snorted one of those half-hearted snorts that are one percent laughter and ninety-nine percent can-you-even-believe-this.

"He passed away *yesterday* and she didn't tell us?" Mom asked. "Why wouldn't she call?"

"Apparently this was how he wanted it. The clown was Frank's idea. Part of his last wishes, or something like that. I don't know. I never pretended to understand the man."

Dad looked like he might be ready to say something else, then he thought better of it, instead burying his chin into his chest, and then into my mother's shoulder as she gathered him in. Cass crossed the kitchen floor and put an arm around them both. Lyra followed, wrapping hers around Dad's waist, pressing her cheek to his back. It was a Kwirk family hug. I was the last to join, though I wasn't quite sure how to insert myself into the tightly huddled mass, so I ended up just standing next to Mom, laying my head on her other shoulder, wondering if I was supposed to cry.

I took my cue from Dad and just closed my eyes instead.

The town of Greenburg, where my father grew up and where both my grandfather and great-aunt lived, wasn't quite a four-hour drive. Which meant that we could have visited Papa Kwirk and Aunt Gertie pretty much whenever we wanted.

Except we almost never did. I could remember going there only twice—once for a week in the summer with my sisters while my parents celebrated their anniversary in Hawaii, and again when Papa Kwirk broke his leg Rollerblading. The doctor suggested Papa Kwirk take up a hobby more suited to a man of sixty years. He told the doc he was thinking of trying parkour.

Aunt Gertie often asked us to drive out for a visit, but whenever it was suggested, Dad had some excuse, citing his busy schedule at work or his philosophy that there were too many interesting places in the world to use precious vacation time on Greenburg, Illinois, a town he was much too familiar with already. I guessed there were other reasons; they just weren't things Dad wanted to talk about. The same reasons why, every Christmas Eve, Dad would sit in the recliner, grinding his teeth, waiting for the sound of Papa Kwirk's hog rumbling through the neighborhood.

Dad had no choice but to go back home this time, though, and we had no choice but to go with him.

The service was Sunday afternoon, so we could have planned to drive back that night, but Dad said I was probably still going to miss some school. "We might have to stick around a couple of days to get your grandfather's things in order." I wasn't sure what all that entailed—going through Papa Kwirk's stuff, rifling through his closets, cleaning out the garage, figuring out who got the leather jacket and the taxidermy kit. I imagined opening up his kitchen cabinets and seeing nothing but tubs of black licorice and cans of Folgers coffee.

Dad didn't seem thrilled at the idea of a long stay. Neither was I. For one thing, I actually liked school. I didn't like the learning, or the tests, or the homework, or the having to be quiet all the time, or how Simon Kazinski always kicked the back of my chair whenever he walked by. But I liked that school was not home. School felt normal. With normal kids complaining about normal problems and eating normal packed lunches, maybe with a piece of candy that didn't taste like horseradish.

It helped that I went to Willow Creek Middle School, which meant that I was in a completely different building from either of my sisters. Lyra was lording her vocabulary over the other accelerated learners over at Willow Creek Elementary, and Cass was hanging out with all her artsy-fartsy drama club friends at Mayfield High, so I didn't have to hear in the halls about how my one sister had made it to the finals of the county spelling bee or see posters of my other sister dressed as Cosette advertising the spring musical. For seven hours a day, five days a week, I could just be Rion, and I could choose to *not* correct anyone when they spelled my name the way any normal person would, with a Y and an A instead of an I and an O. I could just be the B-average kid who gets picked somewhere between fifth and eighth in basketball and doesn't have to worry about his father suddenly stopping to taste tree bark or his sister suddenly belting out some showstopping number from *Rent* or his mother screaming and running from a bumblebee buzzing around the playground because she's allergic to half the planet.

I mean, I understand that everybody's family is a little odd. My friend Jackson has a brother who will only eat plain toast for breakfast—no butter or jelly, just plain toast. And Amanda, who sits next to me in class, has an uncle who was fired from his job for wearing a toga to work. He'd somehow gotten it into his head that he was the emperor of Rome. The difference was that her uncle had a diagnosable mental disorder, which was soon being treated with medication and therapy.

My family was simply weird. And they don't make a pill for that.

My best friend, Manny, tells me that I'm overreacting. But Manny's family doesn't eat jelly beans for dinner or spend Tuesday evenings playing Shakespearian Scrabble, which is like normal Scrabble except you have to use "doth" and "thine" and "tis" instead of "does" and "your" and "its," while your sister calls you a poisonous bunch-backed toad for stealing her triple word space and then swoons all over the carpet like you stabbed her in the heart. Manny thinks it sounds like fun, but he doesn't have to live with it every day. His family eats at McDonald's and plays Frisbee in the backyard. His father doesn't own thirty bow ties or quiz him on the colors of the lions that made up Voltron. His mother doesn't Clorox every doorknob in the house every day of the year and twice during flu season. At least I don't think so. That's why it was Manny I turned to when I needed a dose of normality.

Like the night of the singing clown.

I didn't have my own phone yet—Mom was convinced too much screen time would stunt my imaginative growth—so I took the landline up to my room and shut the door. Manny picked up on the fourth ring.

"Get this," I said, interrupting his hello. "Chuckles McLaughsalot just told me my grandpa's dead."

"Um . . . okay. I was about to tell you that I just watched a fish stick explode in the microwave, but yours is bigger. Are you serious? Your grandpa? The guy with the hog and the ferret?"

"The one and only," I said.

Manny knew Papa Kwirk. He had ridden in Jack Nicholson before—only in the sidecar, of course, and just around the block like me. And he'd met the ferret too, the last time they'd come to visit. The ferret's name was Beelzebub, and it was Papa Kwirk's only pet. It liked socks, so much so that it tried to chew them right off your feet. Papa Kwirk would occasionally bring Beelzebub with him, somehow attaching the ferret's carrier to the back of the bike behind Aunt Gertie.

Dad's frown only grew longer when he saw Grandpa pull up with that carrier in tow.

"Who the heck is Chuckles McLaughsalot?" Manny asked.

So I told him. About the clown, and the phone call to Aunt Gertie, and the heart attack. "A cute myocardinal infartshun," I said, trying to sound as smart as Lyra.

"Huh. That really sucks. I'm sorry, Ri."

Of course that's what he had to say. That's what everybody says when someone dies. But Manny sounded like he meant it, at least. "Thanks," I replied, because I'm pretty sure that's what you're supposed to say when someone says they are sorry for your loss.

"He just had a heart attack? Just like that?"

"Yep. Just like that," I repeated, though it sounded funny to me. *Just* a heart attack. I know that's not what Manny meant— he meant that it came out of nowhere, all of a sudden—but the more I thought about it, the more it didn't fit. I'd always imagined my grandfather going out in a blaze of glory. Maybe a skydiving accident gone awry. Or mauled to death while wrestling a bear in the woods. Or trying to jump over some canyon on the back of Jack Nicholson. Heart attack seemed a little too *everyday* for the likes of Captain James T. Kwirk.

"Man. Jeez. How is everybody else? The rest of your family, I mean?"

That was Manny for you, always thinking of others, but I suspected he mostly wanted to know about Cass. The past

28

year or so, I'd caught him asking about her more and more, once even asking if she had a boyfriend yet, even though she's four years older than him, and my sister, and therefor completely off-limits.

"Well . . . you know . . . they're upset, obviously," I replied.

But the truth was, I wasn't sure how they were. After the phone call with Aunt Gertie, Mom stuck the untouched pasta in the fridge and then joined the others on the living-room couch. Lyra huddled close to Cass, who was steadily swiping away tears, neither of them saying anything. Dad sat on the end, making strange motions with his hands. He'd touch his fingers to his thumbs, like the first part of "Itsy-Bitsy Spider," except the rain never came down and the spider never got any higher; I'm not even sure he knew he was doing it. I sat in the chair and watched him, waiting for him to say something, but after ten solid minutes of near silence I grabbed the phone and ran upstairs. For all I knew they were all still sitting there.

"So you guys were, like . . . you know . . . close to him, then?"

Were we close to Papa Kwirk? We lived only four hours away. Four hours, and we still only saw him once a year. And even then, when we sat in the living room on Christmas morning, it was always the three Kwirk children on one side of the room, huddled around our parents by the tree, and Aunt Gertie and Papa Kwirk on the other side by the fireplace, almost as if my grandfather really was Santa and needed the chimney close by in case he wanted to make a quick exit. "Guess it depends on what you mean by close," I said.

"Well, you know, my grandmother *lives* with me. Like, literally, she sleeps on my couch and leaves her dentures in a cup on the bathroom sink. Have you ever had to pee in the middle of the night and looked over to see your grandma's teeth grinning at you? *Only* her teeth? It's spooky, man. I mean, they kind of glow in the dark they're so white. . . ."

He was trying to cheer me up. But it only made me wonder how different I would have felt if I had seen Papa Kwirk for more than four days out of the year. What would it have been like if he had actually *lived* with us? I don't think my mother could have put up with the cigar smell for that long. I'm not sure I could have either.

And Dad would never have gone for it.

Manny was still going on about his grandma's teeth when I heard a knock on my bedroom door. It startled me, and I nearly fell off my bed.

"I'll call you back."

I hung up, slid the rest of the way off the bed, and opened the door. Dad stood in the entry, still wearing his dress shirt and striped bow tie. One hand held a box of graham crackers. The other held a bottle of Gatorade. He still didn't look like he'd cried at all.

"Just came to check on you," he said. This wasn't unusual.

He was always coming upstairs to check on us, peeking in our doors as if to make sure we hadn't disappeared or to see if we needed anything. This time, at least, he had a good reason.

"I'm fine," I said automatically, then, realizing how terrible that sounded, added just as quickly, "I mean . . . I'm not *fine*, like, *good* fine, but I'm okay. I mean, I'll *be* okay . . ." I stopped yammering and looked at his hands. "What's with the Gator-ade?"

Dad looked down as if he'd forgotten he'd been carrying anything. Then he smiled a half smile. "Oh. Right," he said. "Milk and cookies."

I gave him my "Really Dad?" look, the one I'd perfected over several thousand opportunities: part eyebrow arch, part eye roll.

"Okay, so we were out of cookies," he admitted. "And I want to save the milk for breakfast tomorrow. So this was the best I could do. Red's your favorite, right?" He held the Gatorade out to me.

I nodded. Red *was* my favorite. And I wasn't opposed to the graham crackers either. After all, I'd had only one fried-chicken–flavored jelly bean for dinner.

"Mind if I come in?" Dad asked. I opened the door all the way, wondering if I should try to clear a path through the junk but then figuring on this, of all nights, it really didn't matter. We sat together on opposite ends of my unmade bed and Dad tore open a sleeve of crackers, splitting the first one down the middle and giving me half. The cinnamon sugar flaked off on my fingers. He waited until my mouth was full before talking again. "I know it can be hard," he began.

It. Losing someone, he meant. I chewed slowly, wondering why he said "can be" and not "is." Didn't *he* think it was hard? I grunted something close to "mm–hmm" and swallowed the lump lodged in my throat.

Dad turned his cracker over and over as if inspecting it for flaws. "I don't think I ever told you, but when I was little, younger than you, and I'd get hurt or upset, your grandmother would bring milk and cookies to my door."

My grandmother. Grandma Shelley. If there was anyone Dad talked about less than his father, it was his mom. She'd died when he was about my age, so of course I never got to know her, only what I could glean from the few memories Dad shared. That, and the glossy, glazed–over look Papa Kwirk would get in his eyes whenever *he* mentioned her, which was even less often than Dad did. I'd never heard anything about milk and cookies, though.

"She never came in, but I knew it was her. It was like this ritual. She'd knock three times, just like this . . ." Dad rapped his knuckles on my headboard. "And when I went to the door, they would be there, sitting on the floor, waiting for me. Like some milk–and–cookie fairy had paid me a visit. Always three cookies, and almost always Oreos. Sometimes I'd pretend to be hurt just so I could get them."

"Smart," I said, biting into a second cracker.

"Yeah," Dad said, still fiddling with his first. "When you're five, there's nothing that can't be cured with a Band-Aid and an Oreo."

I could get behind that. When I was little, it was usually Mom applying the bandages, not because Dad wasn't around, just because she had a ready supply. I don't remember there ever being cookies, though; our house was always full of free candy already.

Come to think of it, this marked the first time I'd ever eaten in bed. Thou Shalt Not Have Food in Thy Room was one of Mom's ninety-seven commandments. I wondered if she knew Dad was breaking it now.

"These aren't quite as good as Oreos," Dad said, holding up his graham cracker. "But they'll do." He finally took a bite, and the two of us sat and quietly worked our way through half a sleeve of them. After his third or fourth cracker, he sighed heavily. "You know, your grandfather . . . Frank . . . he was never . . . I mean, we didn't . . ." Dad's jaw worked back and forth as if he was chewing over all the words that might finish these sentences. Then, as if they'd all left a bad taste in his mouth, he slid another cracker out of its sleeve and handed me the rest of the box. He pushed himself up off the bed, turned, and looked me in the eyes. "This is good. This is what I needed. Thanks, Ri."

I nodded. "Sure," I said, though all I'd done was sit there and eat.

"We're downstairs if you need anything." He squeezed my

knee, then worked his way across my room, dodging the piles of dirty laundry.

"Dad," I called, catching him as he slipped out the door. He stuck his face back through.

I knew I should say something, I wanted to say something, but "I'm sorry" didn't seem like enough. Then again, probably nothing would be.

"Thanks for dinner," I said, holding up the box.

"Just don't tell your mother." Dad flicked off a crumb that had stuck to his bow tie and padded down the hallway, leaving the door open a crack.

TURNING ON THE SKY

It's hard, sometimes, reconciling the difference between what you really feel about something and what you think you're *supposed* to feel.

Like when you're sitting in the high school auditorium watching your sister onstage dressed like a freaky cat/human hybrid, singing and slinking around and licking her furry arms. And you know you should be proud of her, because she's your sister and it's one of the lead roles. And you are, sort of, but you're also really tired of sitting there watching this incredibly stupid musical where nothing makes any sense, and you wish the freaking Jellicle cats would just hurry up and get to the Jellicle Ball or maybe be run over by a Jellicle truck so you can go home and zone out with your PlayStation.

Or when you open your Christmas present and find socks and underwear. And you know you *should* be grateful, because you were down to only four pairs of boxers that fit, and you were occasionally going commando on the weekends because you forgot to bring your laundry basket down. But instead you think about all the other gifts you would have *rather* had, and why bother to wrap up socks and underwear in the first place?

Or when someone dies, someone close to you, and you know your heart should hurt, like it should be about to *explode*, but instead it's more of a dull ache in the background.

Don't get me wrong, I was sad that Papa Kwirk was gone. But I also felt like I wasn't feeling sad *enough*. Like there was a prerequisite amount I was supposed to be feeling, a kind of grief quota, and I was coming up short. I knew Cass had been up all night crying. I could hear her through the walls, could hear my mother's voice comforting her. But that was Cass. Some people wear their emotions on their sleeves. Cass made entire *outfits* out of her feelings and put on a fashion show. But even Lyra woke up puffy eyed the next morning, and she had the fewest memories of Papa Kwirk of any of us.

And I did feel *something*, a sort of hollowness, but I had to stop and think about it. And even then, it wasn't so much missing my grandfather as imagining what might have been, thinking about the Christmases to come and knowing that I wouldn't hear him roaring into the driveway or be able to smell the spicy cigar smoke from outside my open window above the porch. And though my stomach twisted and my throat tightened, I never managed to cry.

I wondered if Dad was struggling with the same thing. His forehead was slightly more furrowed, and he was a little quieter than usual, but he didn't seem to be overwhelmed with grief. Could you be *under*whelmed with grief? Was that a thing? And if so, what would it look like? Maybe it would look like my father, waking up early that Saturday morning, showered and dressed before any of us, clapping his hands and issuing orders, acting as if we were going camping for the weekend and not to our grandpa's funeral.

"Come on, Kwirks. Hop to it. We've got a busy day. I want to be on the road by noon, if possible."

We were scheduled to arrive at Aunt Gertie's that afternoon, which meant Saturday morning would be filled with cleaning and packing. Over a jelly-beanless breakfast of oatmeal with our own special toppings (slivered almonds for Cass, shredded coconut and sliced banana for Ly, good old-fashioned brown sugar for me) and the last of the actual milk, I overheard Mom tell Dad she had to run to work to get a few things sorted out. Cass and Lyra were arguing over whether or not coconut was technically a fruit or a nut, which was driving me crazy because who even *cares*, so I ambushed Mom and asked if I could tag along. It was better than listening to my sisters bicker or helping Dad straighten the house.

Besides, I knew she would turn the sky on if I asked her, and I kind of needed the distraction.

"Is your room clean?" she asked.

I was twelve. My floor was covered in at least three layers of comic books and clothes. "Pretty much," I lied, which seemed to satisfy her. She obviously had bigger things on her mind.

I crawled into the back seat of Mom's car, a Ford Expedition that we nicknamed the Tank. My mother never drove anything but the Tank. And she never let me or Lyra sit up front, even if we were the only ones riding along, because we were "statistically safer" in the back. I tried to tell her that it would take a collision with an *actual* tank to even put a *dent* in this thing, but she insisted. She wouldn't even pull out of the driveway until my seat belt was fastened.

Mostly my mother's constant worrying was an inconvenience. Like being the only kid who had to wear mittens in the winter because *technically* they kept your fingers warmer than gloves, even though it made it impossible to zip up your coat or tie your shoes. Or being the only kid at the pool who had to reapply sunscreen *every* time they got out of the water. Or not being allowed to even *try* the crossbow your grandfather got you for Christmas, even though knowing how to use it would come in handy during a dystopian government takeover. (She'd be sorry when the Reaping started and I didn't step up and volunteer as tribute in Lyra's place.) Of course she only worried so much because she loved me. At least that's what she said.

Twenty minutes of boring talk radio later, we turned into the entrance for the Verizon Planetarium, where my mother worked. Up until four years ago it had been called the Cannon Planetarium, named after famous astronomer Annie Jump

Cannon. But the university needed money for renovations and the telecommunications company didn't have enough buildings with its name on it, so the university renamed it. My mother still called it the Cannon Planetarium, though. It was her second home.

She parked the Tank by the back door and I followed her to her office, a tiny little room that sat next to the janitor's closet. The sign on the door read *Molly Kwirk, Director of Operations* and had a picture of her from back when her hair was long and curly. Inside, the top of her desk was spotless as always, and I couldn't imagine what work she could possibly have to get done. I looked around for anything out of place; it was kind of a personal challenge. My mother liked things tidy, and if I ever picked something up and put it back down right where I found it, she invariably came up behind me to make some minor adjustment.

Not that there was much to mess with. Only two things hung on the wall between the bookshelves: her college diploma and an autographed photo of Sally Ride. Mom was nine when Sally Ride became the first American woman in space, and from that moment on, Mom was smitten: with Sally, with space, with all of it. While my father was humming the opening tune to *He-Man and the Masters of the Universe*, Mom was out in her backyard in the hammock, staring up at the sky, wishing on stars. She wanted to be the first woman to walk on the moon.

And she might have tried, if she weren't afraid to fly.

Terrified, really. And if you can't even stand to be on an airplane, there's little hope of you blasting off in a rocket at twenty-five thousand miles an hour. Our family only took road trips, preferably in a giant SUV that could withstand a mortar attack.

So with no hope of ever becoming an astronaut, she did the next best thing: she brought the stars to her, getting her degree in astronomy and landing a job at the local university's planetarium, eventually working her way up to director, which meant she pretty much ran the joint. It made take-your-kid-to-work day tough. Go with Dad to the candy factory or with Mom to explore the universe. Cass and Lyra always choose Dad.

Mom placed her Bag of Holding on the desk. That was the name given to her purse (the Kwirks have a weird habit of naming things), a huge canvas sack with half a dozen compartments that contained pretty much anything you could ever need in an emergency: a packet of rubber bands, protein bars, an LED flashlight, a mini stapler, enough hand sanitizer to fill a bathtub. The bag probably weighed forty pounds. My mother's biceps were hard as rocks.

"I've got maybe twenty minutes of work. I'll try to be quick," she said. "Do you want to hang out here with me or would you rather—"

I nodded before she could finish the sentence. She really didn't need to ask.

The planetarium didn't open to the public until noon, and

the graduate students who ran it wouldn't show for another hour, at least, which meant I would have the galaxy to myself. I found my favorite seat, front row across from the exit, and tilted my chair back as far as it would go, staring up at the empty dome.

"You want audio?" Mom asked.

I shook my head. I didn't need Neil deGrasse Tyson or Morgan Freeman telling me about dark matter and gravity and cosmic expansion; I'd heard it all before. I just wanted the sky to light up.

My mother pressed a few buttons, and it did. Exploding. Instantly. Like the Big Bang. Like the dawn of everything.

"All right, kiddo. I'll come get you when I'm done."

I nodded again and watched her retreat to her office while the ceiling expanded at the speed of light, suddenly somehow containing the entire Milky Way. I let out a held breath and immediately began to identify the stars I knew, tracking them by the constellations they were part of. I pinpointed Venus. I traced the handles of the dippers and the path of the dog star back to his tail. The Great Square of Pegasus. The eye of the bull.

I don't know how many Saturday mornings I'd spent here, sometimes with my sisters but just as often on my own. It was nothing like the night sky outside my window, hazy and washed out by streetlights. In here, it seemed like you could see for infinity. Under the light of untold numbers of stars, billions of years could pass by, or time could stop entirely. I really had no idea. I just stared. And wondered.

But even with one of my favorite distractions, I still thought about Papa Kwirk. In fact, I might have thought about him even harder, lying there under the dome of stars. Papa Kwirk didn't understand the point of planetariums and often teased my mother about her job. Why bother with projections and pictures when you can go outside and experience the real thing for yourself? That's what he'd said. I'm sure he felt the same way about my father's work. All those artificial flavors. Trying to re-create something that already exists. You want fried chicken, go eat some fried chicken.

But what Papa Kwirk didn't seem to get . . . what I came to realize . . . was that sometimes the real version of things is disappointing. Occasionally a real cherry could taste bitter or rotten, but a cherry-flavored jelly bean tastes sweet every single time. I couldn't always find the North Star when I looked outside my window, but I could always spot it here.

Here, I could count on it being right where it belonged.

"Did you find you yet?"

Mom's voice tore me out of my trance. Surely it couldn't have been twenty minutes already, but there she was, clomping down the stairs in her boots and taking the seat right next to me, stretching out her long legs and staring up at the computer-generated sky. My mother's jeans were worn at the knees. All her jeans were like that. Seemed odd to have jeans with holes on the one hand and an office without a speck of dust on the other.

Silently I pointed at Betelgeuse on my right shoulder, Rigel in my left foot. I traced the stars along my famous belt—Alnitak, Alnilam, and Mintaka. The belt was the key. "Find the belt and you find the man," my mother used to tell me when she first started to teach me the names of the shapes in the sky. I'm so much easier to find than either of my sisters. It's one of the few things I get to hold over their heads.

"Your grandfather thought I was crazy, naming you all after constellations," Mom said, mentioning Papa Kwirk for the first time since we'd left the house. "He thought you should be named after him."

Francis Kwirk. That could have been me. Instead she named me Orion. Orion, Cassiopeia, and Lyra. Her three precious constellations. A lot of people think my name is cool. Kids at school with names like Mike and Andrew and David. They say they're jealous. But those people don't have to explain how their names are spelled all the time or get told that they come from outer space.

"How about it?" Mom asked. "Would you rather have been named Francis?"

I shook my head. There are probably a million other names that I would have chosen over Orion—like Mike or Andrew or David—but Francis isn't one of them.

"That's what I thought too."

Mom clasped her hands behind her head. She had seen this same sky a thousand times more than me, and yet she still looked at it with wide, wonder-filled eyes.

"When the Greek heroes died, the gods granted them a place among the stars," she said, channeling her own inner Carl Sagan, though I didn't mind it coming from her. "Orion was a skilled hunter. At least until he ran into that stupid scorpion."

Right. Scorpio. My archnemesis. I suppose Mom could have named me *that*. Then at least I could have made a cool costume and tried to take over the world.

"Your grandfather was a hunter, you know," she continued. "Like Orion. At least that's what your father tells me. Though, let's be honest, your grandfather was a whole lot of things."

I glanced at her, waiting for her to tell me *like what*, to fill in some of the gaps. I already knew Papa Kwirk was a biker. A smoker. An avid fisherman. I knew that he was a widower at the age of thirty-five. That he raised my father by himself after that. That he was a Vietnam War veteran and that he nearly died while he was over there. I knew that he also almost got arrested for peeing off the Great Wall of China and that his favorite snack was beef jerky and that he lived in the same Midwestern town for most of his life. I knew that he was a prankster, and he knew a million bad jokes but never flubbed a punchline.

And apparently, he liked clowns. Or at least trusted them to be the bearers of bad news.

I guess I actually knew a lot *about* him, but I didn't really feel like I *knew* him.

I waited, but my mother didn't have more to add to the

Papa Kwirkopedia. Or at least she wasn't about to volunteer anything. Instead she went back to the sky. She began tracing the patterns of constellations through the stars with the tip of her finger. "Sheesh. You really have to stretch your imagination to see some of these, don't you?" she said. "I mean, yours I get. And I can *kind of* see Leo. But how do you get a crab out of an upside-down Y? Honestly. It could be anything. They could have called it a horse or a bird or a tower. But a crab?"

I nodded my agreement. That's the way I felt about most constellations, Cass's especially. It's supposed to look like a queen, but it pretty much just looks like a toddler's first attempt at drawing a W. Of course, I didn't really get Cass either, and I'd known her my whole life. "I think people probably just look up there and see whatever they want to see," I said.

"Yeah. You're probably right."

We lay there for another minute, making shapes out of clusters of stars, and a question wormed its way up and out, one that I'd been working on all morning but had really been itching me since I'd been sitting there. I scooted a little closer to Mom. "Can I ask you something?"

"Always," she said.

"Do you really think that when we die, we go up there? I mean, not up there. But, you know . . . up *there*." I pointed. Past the dome. Past the building. Past the clouds that lay beyond it. I knew better, of course. We call them the heavens, but outer space is just outer space. It's hydrogen and helium and cosmic rays. But part of me liked the idea of Papa Kwirk still being out there. Somewhere. Watching over us.

Mom thought about it for a moment; she folded her hands over her heart. "Yeah. I think so," she said. "I mean, if you stop to consider it, we all come from stardust. Which means there's a piece of the very beginning, even the most infinitesimal trace of it, somewhere inside you. Inside everybody. And I think somehow, eventually, we all get back to it as well."

"Eventually. Like in a billion years?"

"Well, if we are being honest, I don't think anyone will be around in a billion years to know. But I do think the Greeks were on to something with their silly shapes. That our actions somehow outlive us and that we will all be remembered, somehow. Just maybe not through random connect-the-dots in the sky."

I nodded. It was a good enough answer for now. I'd have to think about it some more. There was another equally pressing question. "Can I ask you something else?"

"Shoot."

"Why a *clown*?"

My mother turned to me and shrugged.

"There are some mysteries in the universe that defy all rational explanation," she said.

The look she gave me suggested that my grandfather was one of those mysteries.

★ ★ ★

When we got home from Mom's office—after a quick stop at the Target to get me a nice shirt and a pair of dress pants—the suitcases were waiting for us in the driveway. Dad and Cass were barking at each other (not literally, of course, though with this family, you could never be sure). I could hear them through the open door, though I couldn't make out what they were saying.

"Wonder what that's all about," Mom said with a sigh, but by the time she got out of the car, Cass was already storming out of the house, pulling furiously at the ends of her frizzy brown hair.

"Dad says I can't take Delilah."

Delilah. Of course.

Delilah was Cass's pet python. Five and a half feet long and thicker than my arm (which isn't saying much, I suppose). Mom's allergic to cats and dogs and rabbits and guinea pigs—pretty much anything with fur. She's afraid of tarantulas, and birds had spooked her ever since she was a young girl and an owl stole her favorite knit cap right off her head. This limited our choices for family pet. But even if Cass had been able to pick any animal in the world, I'm pretty sure she would have picked a snake of some kind. It was the closest thing to having her own pet dragon, which was what she really wanted.

My mother tried to reason with her. "Sweetie. Delilah will be fine. She just ate last week, right? You can keep her warming rock on. She has plenty of fresh water."

"Yeah, but what about me? *I* need *her*, Mom."

I rolled my eyes. What sixteen-year-old girl *doesn't* need her pet python around all the time? Mostly, Delilah stayed in Cass's room, secure in her terrarium, and I didn't have to think about her, but there were evenings I'd come downstairs and find Cass in the recliner, book in hand, the snake wrapped around her neck, its thick diamond-shaped head pointed at the page as if it was reading along. Sometimes I wished it'd give her a good squeeze, just to see the look on Cass's face, but somehow my sister and that snake had an understanding. She would feed it dead mice, and in return it would humor her by not strangling her to death.

"It's only three days," Mom said.

"It's not like we don't have room in the car," Cass countered. "Besides. Grandpa liked Delilah. He would have wanted her to come. To say goodbye."

That was true. During his annual visit, Papa Kwirk would often take Delilah out and dance with her around the living room. They gave each other kisses. He sang her old rock-and-roll songs. I kept expecting the python to try and bite his knobby old nose off; it sort of looked like a mouse, after all—the hairs that shot out of it reminded me a little bit of whiskers, at least.

"Fine. But you absolutely cannot bring her to the funeral. I doubt reptiles are allowed in the church."

Cass hugged my mother and ran back into the house while I

helped heft the suitcases into the back of the Tank. Less than a minute later, Dad was standing on the porch where Chuckles had stood the night before, singing about counting worms.

"You said she could bring the snake?"

My parents seldom overrode each other, especially when it came to us kids. Ninety-nine percent of the time they formed a unified front. But on the rare occasion when they did disagree, my mother always won.

"Her grandfather died," Mom replied. "She's upset. Delilah comforts her. Just think of it as her bringing a favorite stuffed animal. Except instead of a teddy bear, it's a python. And instead of being stuffed, it's a living, breathing, cold-blooded killer."

Dad didn't seem convinced. He stood there with his arms crossed.

"Like it or not, Delilah's part of the family. And this is a time when our whole family should be together. Lord knows it doesn't happen that often anymore."

Mom was right. Between her and Dad's work schedules, Cass's rehearsals, my soccer practices, and Lyra's after-school clubs, we were lucky to even get around the dinner table at the same time most days—but that still didn't mean we needed to take the snake with us to Illinois. Not that I had any say in it.

Dad caved. "Fine. Just as long as she doesn't let it loose inside the car again," he said. The last time Delilah took a road trip with us, she had gotten stuck under the driver's seat, and we had to pull over at a gas station to get her out. The look on the face of the lady pumping gas next to us made it worth it, though. "I told Gertrude we would be there before dinner, so we should hit the road. Are you packed yet, Ri?" Dad added, looking at me.

"Pretty much," I said, once again meaning not in the slightest.

I ran upstairs, found an empty backpack, and threw whatever cleanish-smelling underwear and T-shirts I had inside. I also packed my deodorant, a toothbrush, a stack of comic books, and my 3DS. I threw in a bag of gummy bears (from Kaslan's Candy Factory, of course—all perfectly normal flavors), a water bottle, and three extra pairs of socks. Sweaty socks drive me bonkers.

I would have packed my new tactical combat knife if Mom had let me fish it out of the attic. I was going to my first-ever Kwirk family funeral, after all.

There was no telling what might go down.

THE SUPERFLUOUS SIDE TRIP

Twenty minutes later, Delilah sat in the back with Cass, and I was in the middle next to Lyra. Thankfully the Tank had three rows of seating—otherwise my sisters and I would have ripped each other's heads off before we ever got anywhere. At the very least I would have passed out from the fumes of Cass's body spray.

We hadn't left the driveway yet, though, because my mother was in check-down mode.

"Did you remember to turn off the coffee pot?"

"Yes, dear."

"Lock all the windows?"

"Did it."

"Did you lock the back door and put the door stopper in?"

Dad nodded.

"You unplugged all the computers in case of a lightning strike?"

"And the TVs."

"What about the fireplace? Did you shut off the gas? I read somewhere that this couple went away for two weeks and forgot to shut off the gas to the fireplace and when they came back their house had exploded because there was a leak that got triggered by the pilot light on the furnace. Did you turn off the furnace?" My mother had her fingers clenched around her giant purse.

"We don't need to turn off the furnace. Everything is going to be all right. We emptied the fridge of perishables. Shut off all the lights except for the one in the family room that makes it look like someone is home. Locked the back gate. Notified the credit card company." By the sound of it, you'd think we were leaving to spend the rest of the year in Costa Rica, not driving four hours to spend a long weekend with our great-aunt.

"And you're *sure* you turned off the coffee maker?"

My mom and dad stared at each other. Standoff. Finally Dad unbuckled, got out of the car, went to the door, unlocked both locks, shut off the alarm system, and went inside. He appeared in the doorway thirty seconds later with something in his hands.

The coffee maker.

He showed her the plug dangling from it like a dead snake (as opposed to the perfectly alive snake sitting behind me). He nodded as if to say, "Happy now?"

Mom gave him two thumbs-ups.

He set the coffee maker back inside, reset the alarm, and relocked both locks. He jiggled the handle, just to prove to her that it wouldn't open, then kicked the door repeatedly to prove that it wouldn't cave in from brute force. Not that my father was the best test subject. He was one hundred percent Banner, zero percent Hulk.

When he started buckling back up, my mother leaned close to him and put her head on his shoulder. "Thank you," she said.

"Love you," he said.

"Blech," I said.

Finally we managed to get out of the driveway. "We're off." Dad's voice held an unusual amount of enthusiasm for someone heading to his own father's funeral. "What should we listen to first?"

"BBC," Mom said.

"*A Way with Words*," Lyra offered.

"*Wicked*. Original Broadway cast recording!" Cass shouted.

"*Best of the Eighties* it is," Dad said.

In our family, the driver is the DJ, which is why I didn't even bother saying anything. Within seconds, someone Dad identified as Pat Benatar started telling us that we all belonged together. Stuck in the car for hours with my family, I had my doubts. In the house you could always get away, escape to the basement, sneak off to your room. Here we were literally

53

strapped in. No way out, unless you wanted to fling yourself from the speeding car—but even then you'd have to find a way past the child locks.

Might be worth a shot.

As we were about to turn off our street, Mom snapped her fingers.

"But did you remember to lock the *garage* door?"

Dad put the car in reverse.

Chomp. Smack. Chomp.

Flip. Giggle. Flip. Gasp. Sluuuurp.

Smack. Blow. Pop.

Flip. Sluuuurp. Flip. Giggle.

"De do do do, de da da da, is all I want to say to you."

Chomp. Chomp. Smack. Pop. Slurp. Flip. Gasp.

There's a story by Edgar Allan Poe about this guy who kills this other guy and then buries him under the floorboards. But the murderer mistakes his own heartbeat for the sound of the dead guy's still-somehow-beating heart and goes crazy and confesses to the crime.

Dad was still listening to *Best of the Eighties*, though it was turned down low enough that I could hear nearly every annoying sound my sisters made. And for some reason, I started to feel a little like the murderer in that Poe story.

"De do do do . . ."

Chomp. Smack. Scritch.

"De da da da . . ."

Flip. Sluuurp.

One look in the back of our SUV will tell you everything you need to know about my sisters. Cass in the way back, dressed in skinny jeans and combat boots, a bottle of SoBe green tea cradled in her lap (*sluuurp*), reading book four in her favorite fantasy series, the Vendar Chronicles, for what I assume is the five hundred and fortieth time (*flip, giggle, gasp*).

Button-nosed Lyra to my left, going to town on her sugar-free gum (*chomp, smack*) and skimming through *Webster's Tenth Collegiate Dictionary* (she left her eleventh edition at home because she didn't want to lose it), notebook in hand, jotting down new words to spring on us (*scritch*). Yesterday morning, for example, I was told that all boys were "infantile" and me especially. I responded by making farting sounds to drown her out until she screamed and left me alone.

And there's me, the normal one, head pressed to the window, staring at a cornfield that looks like it might stretch as far as an ocean. Amber waves of grain, except it was mostly green and brown and boring.

"Who could possibly eat this much corn?" I wondered to myself, unfortunately loud enough for my father to hear, even over the sound of the gum smacking and page flipping and terrible music.

"Oh—a lot of this won't be eaten. Not by humans, anyway," he said, and then he was off. My father felt obligated to make every moment a teaching moment, whether we wanted to learn or not. "Most of it will go to feed animals. Some of it will be used to make fuel. Corn byproducts are used in crayons and glue, and we use a lot of it in the lab to make candy, mostly as a sweetener. In fact, did you know that the ancient Aztecs—"

"Dad . . . . Dad . . . *Dad*." I had to say it three times to get him to stop. Kind of like summoning Beetlejuice. "It was a rhetorical question."

"Oh. Okay." Dad went back to his driving. I wondered if maybe I'd hurt his feelings. But really, it's corn. Nobody in their right mind would find it interesting.

I looked at the clock on the dashboard. We were only halfway there.

The page flipping was interrupted by a sniffle from behind, then another, followed by a whimper. I twisted and looked over my shoulder to see Cass with her book in her lap, staring out the window too, except she had tears in the corners of her eyes. At first I assumed it had to do with Papa Kwirk. Then I wondered if maybe she just found the endless fields of corn as depressing as I did.

"What?" she said, noticing me staring at her.

"What?" I said back.

"Why are you looking at me?"

"You're crying."

"Of course I'm crying!" she snapped. "Prince Teldar just sacrificed himself to the Arkfiend so that Zen and Elsalore could escape." She held the book up for me to see.

It took everything I had not to laugh. She was crying over

a *book*. And not even one of those sad books where the dog dies. She was crying over some shlocky fantasy novel. And *Elsalore*? What kind of name is that? Make up your mind: Elsa or Eleanor. Why do fantasy authors have to use such ridiculous names? My sister adored Elsalore, but she also had a major crush on Prince Teldar. As much as you can have a crush on an imaginary elf prince.

"Come on, it's not like you didn't see it coming. You've read that thing, like, twenty times." All right, maybe five hundred and forty was a little extreme. I felt solid with twenty though.

"It's still sad!" Cass snapped. "Just because you see it coming doesn't make it any less sad when it gets there. And this is only my *fourth* time, thank you."

"Four too many," I said.

"At least I *read* books."

"I read books," I snipped, pointing to the stack of comics sticking out of my backpack. Mostly old issues of the Avengers and a few Uncanny X-Men. Uncanny. Now that's a *good* kind of weird. I wouldn't mind being part of an *uncanny* family. Provided they could fly and shoot lasers out of their eyes. Cass could only roll hers dismissively. Which she did. Constantly. Including now.

"It's actually good for you," Lyra chimed in, coming to her sister's defense, like usual. "Scientists did a study and found that rereading the same book over and over lets you make an even stronger emotional connection to the characters and events, thereby intensifying the previous experience."

Intensifying the previous experience. My little sister often sounded like one of those guys who talk at the ends of prescription drug commercials and tell you the hundreds of side effects you'll experience trying to cure one thing.

"See?" Cass said, and stuck out her tongue at me. I was getting it from both sides now—standard sister flanking maneuver. I should have just kept watching the corn go by.

"Yeah. I'm sure you're making a real strong emotional connection with that dictionary," I said, pointing at the book in Lyra's hands.

"For your information, I read this to expand my vocabulary so that I can more intelligently converse with those around me," she huffed. "Though given that the person around me is you, it's probably superfluous."

"Yeah, it's superfluous," I said, wishing I knew what superfluous meant.

"The thing about Prince Teldar," Cass continued, "is that he loves Elsalore so much that he's willing to sacrifice his throne, his inheritance, even his own life for hers—a simple peasant girl with an amazing gift."

"Is it the gift of going on and on about stuff that nobody else cares about? Because if it is, then you two have something in common."

"For your information, we *do* have a lot in common."

"Yeah. You're both in love with the same guy," Lyra said with a snicker. My little sister had the working vocabulary of an English professor, but she still thought boys gave you cooties. Which meant when it came to the topic of romance, she and Cass didn't see eye to eye. I gave Lyra a fist bump, thankful to have her switch sides for once.

"Neither of you has an appreciation for literature," Cass concluded, and pressed her face more firmly into her book. Lyra went back to her list of words. I went back to the window to find—surprise!—even more corn.

Chomp. Smack. Flip. Slurp. Sniffle. This trip was going to take forever.

Out of nowhere, Mom asked Dad how he was doing. I shifted a little so I could see his face in the rearview mirror.

"I'm okay," he said, glancing back at me, at us. "We'll be there in no time."

"That's not what I meant," Mom said, a little more insistently. She was giving him a hard look. I tried to hide the fact that I was eavesdropping by keeping my eyes on the corn parade. Lyra still had her dictionary open, but her eyes were fixed on the back of Dad's head; she was just as interested in his answer as I was.

Dad let out an exasperated breath. "What do you want me to say, Moll? I told you last night. I mean, it's not a huge surprise or anything; Frank didn't exactly embrace a healthy lifestyle. Besides, he must have been anticipating it *some*how if he'd already written a song for a clown to sing about him after he died. I mean, who *does* that?"

It was the same question I'd asked in the planetarium, but Mom had a different answer ready this time. She put a hand on Dad's shoulder. "Maybe he thought it would make it easier somehow. Lessen the blow."

Dad snorted and stared straight ahead, following the thread of road that seemed to stretch on and on, past dilapidated barns and exit signs with promises of Waffle Houses open around the clock. "Since when did Frank Kwirk ever make anything easy on anybody?" he said.

That one she didn't have an answer to. Or maybe she thought it was a rhetorical question too.

Dad pointed out the window at a billboard. "Look, kids," he said, quickly changing the subject. "The world's largest mailbox. At the next exit. How big do you think it is?"

The way he said it, I knew we were about to find out. That's how he is. He gets his mind fixed on something and he makes it happen. Like when he left home to go to college all the way out in New York. Or put himself through graduate school by working two jobs. Or built his own solar-powered, automatic, self-guiding lawn mower—though admittedly Mr. Sunshine *did* take out Mom's azaleas on his first outing and was relegated to only tackling the backyard.

One word for that kind of personality is determined. Another is stubborn. You'd have to ask my sister for the rest.

Dad changed lanes and took the ramp. "It will only take a few minutes. Just a quick look-see. Besides, it will do us good to stretch our legs."

Maybe he really did want to see the world's biggest mailbox. Or maybe, now that we were on the road, he wasn't in such a hurry to get back to the town where he was born. Where his own father would be laid to rest. Maybe we were just delaying the inevitable.

I exchanged looks with Lyra.

"Superfluous means unnecessary," she said.

Admittedly, it *was* really big.

Maybe not the world's largest mailbox *ever*, though I couldn't imagine anyone wanting to build a bigger one. I mean, there was a stairway you had to climb to go *inside* it, and your voice echoed off the cavernous metal walls. If only the Tank had this kind of roomy interior.

At my mother's insistence, the three junior Kwirks had to stand inside the giant mailbox while she got a picture of us from down below. Then we had to walk up the block to take in the other ginormous things the town had to offer. A giant bird cage with a perch for you to sit on. (Cass actually made cawing sounds.) The world's biggest wind chimes. A pair of shoes fit for Jack's giant that my sisters and I had to pose inside for even more pictures. Apparently, this was what this place was known for—its collection of grossly oversized objects, all made by the same guy, and all on display in a town so small that it had only one McDonald's and no Starbucks.

It took us about thirty minutes to see everything the town had to offer.

Afterward, we stood beside a pencil that was longer than our car while Mom took more pictures. Lyra and Cass seemed fascinated, but Dad was clearly disappointed. I could see it in his drawn face. I'm not sure what he was expecting; it was exactly as advertised. The giant wind chimes even worked, though I'm guessing it would take a tornado to get them to produce any sound, as heavy as they were.

"I don't know," he said, staring up at the mailbox across the street. "I just don't see what the big deal is."

My mother and sisters laughed. I shook my head. Dad's jokes were cornier than all those fields we'd passed.

"Some people want to make their mark on the world," Mom replied. "You make jelly beans. This guy made a giant mailbox. We all want to leave something behind. This is his legacy."

"Legacy," Dad repeated. "I wouldn't call it a *legacy*. *Einstein* had a legacy. Darwin had a legacy. Marie Curie. Louis Pasteur. These are more like . . . trophies."

"Still got *us* to pull over," I said. Dad looked at me and frowned.

I took in the giant pencil he was leaning against. Make your mark. That was one way to go about it. Dad made his mark with his candy. Mom taught busloads of elementary school kids about the cosmos. Cass would probably grow up one day and be on Broadway. Lyra would go on to win *Jeopardy!* And I . . .

I didn't know what I would do. Hard to tell what your legacy is going to be when you don't even know what you're good at. What sets you apart.

I thought about Papa Kwirk and everything he left behind. His son. His sister. His grandkids. A Harley. A ferret. And what else? There had to be more. So much more. I mean, there were a lot of things I didn't know about my grandfather. Things that Dad wouldn't tell me. Stuff that I never got a chance to learn.

I'd find out, though. Sooner rather than later. After all, I was on my way to his hometown to remember the kind of man he was. I was bound to uncover a few new things about Papa Kwirk.

Sometimes it sucks being right.

A TREASURE TROVE OF TOOTHBRUSHES

"Ouch!"

I was rudely wrenched out of a nap by a slap across the head from my sister, and in the middle of a fabulous dream, no less, about rescuing my entire family from a horde of intestine-chomping zombies using the crossbow and combat knife that Papa Kwirk had given me. I was their hero. They owed me their lives.

"We're here," Cass said. She looked at my shoulder. "Is that drool?"

Sisters are trained to point out your faults. I wiped my mouth and looked out the window. We were off the interstate now, bouncing along a shabby dirt road.

Welcome to Greenburg.

The road led up to a gravel drive, which led to my great-aunt's house. A colonial-style two-story with a huge wraparound porch and a balcony. Not big enough to warrant the world's largest mailbox in her yard, but still bigger than our house back in Indiana—and we stuffed five of us in there, plus a snake. Aunt Gertie lived all by herself, and she was basically the size of a broom handle. Not the whole broom, even. Just the handle.

Most people when they grow older want to downsize, but not Aunt Gertie. Since moving from New York she'd come to appreciate wide-open spaces, she said, which was why the house sat on four acres, far enough from neighbors that you would have to hop in your car to borrow an egg from next door. Five bedrooms. Three bathrooms. A kitchen that you could run laps in. "This is what thirty-plus years of big-city lawyering gets you," Aunt Gertie remarked of her little mansion on the prairie, her mixed accent half humble Midwest farmer's daughter, half Jersey Shore spitfire.

Dad pulled up to the house, and all three of us in the back scrambled to get out of the car and away from each other as quickly as possible. It was starting to stink back there. Probably my fault—I forgot to put the deodorant on before putting it in my backpack—but I blamed Cass anyways. Aunt Gertie called to us from her porch. "You're late," she said.

"Sorry, Gertie," my mother said. "We took a slight detour."

My great-aunt strode across the lawn to greet us, hugging each of us in turn—a rib smasher that you wouldn't expect from a woman so skinny. Probably something she learned from Papa Kwirk. She'd gotten her hair cut since Christmas. It looked very no-nonsense. She put a hand on my head after she hugged me. "I think you've gotten shorter since I saw you last." It had been four months, and in that time I'm pretty sure I'd grown at least an inch, but Aunt Gertie liked to give everyone a hard time.

"And I think you've gained weight," I said. "Did you eat a whole french fry or something?" My aunt was notorious for her dieting, which only partly explained why she weighed less than her twelve-year-old grandnephew. She also exercised religiously. Really, we didn't have a whole lot in common.

"Funny guy," she said, and pinched my cheek. Her eyes shot back to Cass, who, with the help of my father, was pulling Delilah's terrarium from the back seat. "Are you freakin' kidding me, Cassiopeia Kwirk? You brought *that* thing? I already have the godforsaken ferret and now you bring the snake? What is this? *Wild Kingdom*?"

"Beelzebub's here?" Lyra exclaimed. She was the only one of us who actually liked Papa Kwirk's slinky little weasel. She thought it was cute. I mentally gave myself bonus points for packing extra socks.

"Yeah. He's in the house somewhere, probably crappin' all over the carpet. Jeez, that thing is huge." Aunt Gertie tapped on Delilah's glass as Lyra dashed into the house to find the ferret. "What do you feed it? Live chickens?"

"Mice," Cass said. "Small ones."

"Whatever. It stays in the garage. And I don't want to hold

66

it, so you don't even need to ask."

"Thanks, Aunt Gertie."

Dad got a second extra-long hug from Aunt Gertie, who whispered something in his ear. His eyes narrowed and he frowned, but he nodded and followed her across the lawn. "Come on in and make yourselves at home," she said to the rest of us, waving us through the door.

It was still familiar from the last time. The porch. The big trees. The frog lawn ornaments playing flutes and banjos by the bushes. The couple of times we'd come to Greenburg, we'd stayed with Aunt Gertie. Never with Papa Kwirk. I wasn't sure why. I assumed it was because she had the right number of pull-out couches and empty beds. And because Dad insisted.

"I made a whole list of places we could order from for dinner. As usual, just ignore the clutter," Aunt Gertie trilled.

Clutter was Aunt Gertie's name for the enormous piles of stuff that sat on every table and shelf in every nook, corner, cranny, and crevice of her house. Despite its enormity, there was surprisingly little space to set your stuff down.

Aunt Gertie was a *collector*. That's what she called herself. Dad called her a pack rat. Mom preferred the word "hoarder." She never said it out loud, of course, but my mother hated staying at Aunt Gertie's, you could tell. It probably took everything she had not to start throwing things away, or at least shoving them into closets so you'd have more room to walk.

I kind of liked it, though. You sort of felt like an archeologist uncovering some pharaoh's dusty tomb when you walked through Aunt Gertie's front door. After all, there was bound to be *something* priceless stashed away among all this useless junk.

"I see you've been busy," Mom said, stepping past a stack of boxes in the entryway with sloppy Sharpie scribbles on the sides. *Bedroom. Family room. Attic.* Several boxes were labeled *Pictures.* One was labeled *Ferret Crap.* I assumed it wasn't really Beelzebub's poop stored in a box, though with Aunt Gertie you could never be sure.

"Oh, that's all Jimmy's stuff," Aunt Gertie said casually. "At least, the little things. The big stuff is already in storage, except the motorcycle, of course—that's in the garage. This is mostly just personal items. Sentimental junk. We can look through it all later, if you'd like. Come relax and tell me about the trip."

Aunt Gertie and my parents immediately found spots in the living room—the least messy room in the house—and started talking about completely mundane stuff. Road construction along the interstate, the weather, the new color of paint on Aunt Gertie's walls (mint green and hideous). It was almost as if they wanted to talk about anything other than my grandfather, the whole reason we were all here. For her part, Aunt Gertie looked like she always did. No dark rings under her eyes. No nose rubbed raw and red from too much tissue wiping. She did not look like a woman who had recently lost her brother and best friend. She *was* wearing a lot of makeup for someone dressed in yoga pants, but that was Aunt Gertie for you.

It didn't take the Kwirk kids long to split off and go our separate ways. Cass was still out in the garage getting Delilah settled, and I could hear Lyra banging her way through the rooms upstairs, opening and closing doors, looking for the ferret—"Be-ellll-ze-bub. Where arrre you?" After I'd answered the required battery of questions from my aunt (School? Good. Soccer? Good. Friends? Fine. Girlfriend? Nonexistent, but thanks for asking), I interrupted a riveting conversation on the construction of the new roundabout in town to ask Aunt Gertie if she'd gotten any new toothbrushes since the last time we were here.

I hadn't forgotten about the toothbrushes.

"You bet your sweet bippy," Aunt Gertie said, and pointed to the stairs. "Up in the vault. In fact, there's one up there I got just for your dad. See if you can find it. And take your time. Your parents and I have some catching up to do."

That's when it dawned on me. They weren't talking around Papa Kwirk. They were talking around *me*—the only kid left in the room. I nodded and headed for the stairs, wondering what a bippy was and why I would bet it.

"Watch your step," my mother warned, no doubt worried that I would trip over some pile of Aunt Gertie's junk and get swallowed by the clutter, never to be seen again.

I started up the stairs, pausing for just a second to look at a picture on the wall of Aunt Gertie and Papa Kwirk, all dressed up. Maybe it was for the retirement party that we didn't make it to.

It was the first time I'd ever seen my grandfather in a suit.

Tomorrow, I assumed, would be the last.

The carpet in my great-aunt Gertie's house changes with almost every step. Sky blue in one room, pine green in another. Gold to maroon to a sort of brownish gray that looked like dirty snow. Every doorway was like a portal to another colorful dimension, though in some rooms it was hard to tell because you could barely see the floor at all. Not that I had a right to criticize.

I'm not sure what qualifies one as being a hoarder, but Aunt Gertie sure did have a lot of stuff. There were dolls sitting on shelves and books stacked in corners. Every room had at least one table with a lamp on it, even though all the rooms had overhead lights and none of the lamps had bulbs. There were towers of boxes scattered throughout, like the ones downstairs in the entryway, except these weren't even labeled. The house wasn't dirty, not even that dusty (though not spotless like my mother's office)—making me think that Aunt Gertie actually moved all this junk around to clean behind and underneath it, which made it even more of a wonder that she kept it. The last time we visited, Cass and I, in a fit of boredom, invented a game of trying to catalog all the strange stuff Aunt Gertie had accumulated. We wrote it down on a sheet of paper. Things like:

- Nine vacuum cleaners (five of them operational)
- Four toasters (plus one toaster oven, which she insisted was a completely different appliance)
- At least four boxes of ancient *National Geographics*, dating back to 1937 (admittedly these were kind of cool to look through)
- A giant pickle jar full of paper clips
- At least five hundred balls of wadded-up aluminum foil in two giant black trash bags (she said she was going to make a sculpture out of them one day)
- One unicycle, broken

Dad said it probably came from living for so long in a one-bedroom flat in Manhattan. That once she got a house with all this space, she insisted on filling it with *something*, and having no husband and no kids and apparently way too much money, she filled it with whatever she could find.

- A backpack full of old bottle caps from the seventies that my father secretly coveted
- A collection of salt and pepper shakers shaped like farm animals
- Thirty-two porcelain cats (can you still be a crazy cat lady if the cats aren't real?)
- A set of golf clubs, even though my aunt has never golfed once in her life (she claimed they were for self-defense)

Most of *this* stuff she kept upstairs in the Vault, one of three spare bedrooms and the only one that didn't have a spare bed in it. Probably because there was nowhere to put one.

That's the room I found myself in, looking for the large cedar chest, much like what I imagine pirates used to bury treasure on desert islands. I spotted it in the corner by a pile of shoes, knelt down beside it, and flipped the latch. It opened with a satisfying creak.

There it was. Aunt Gertie's most prized collection.

Her toothbrushes.

It was no secret that my great-aunt had a thing for proper dental hygiene. Her house was a wreck, but her teeth were perfect. Even at the age of sixty-seven, she still had her original set. But the treasures in this chest weren't ever used for brushing teeth. They were more like a monument to the awesomeness that is toothbrushing in general. A tribute to the glory of oral health.

There were at least a hundred of them. Imagine any kind of toothbrush, any shape, any material, and Great-Aunt Gertie had one. She had toothbrushes made of ivory and silver and wood. She had toothbrushes with foot-long handles and giant bristles. She had toothbrushes shaped like famous monuments (the Leaning Tower of Pisa was a personal favorite; it had a suction cup angled at the bottom so that it actually tilted when you stuck it to the sink) and celebrities (a Marilyn Monroe–patterned one was Aunt Gertie's pride and joy). Double-sided toothbrushes for getting your uppers and lowers at the same time. Toothbrushes with screwdrivers in the handle. Tooth-brushes that sang to you, that shot toothpaste out, that folded in half. Toothbrushes shaped like naked people—male and female; no doubt those would be a big hit around the lunch table at school. She even had one that concealed a tiny knife in the handle so that you could stab somebody *and* have fresh breath.

I scanned the top of the chest, looking for new additions. A lot of them looked unfamiliar. I didn't recognize the Super-man one. Or the battery-operated Justin Bieber (I resisted the urge to press the button, knowing I would regret it). I picked up a plastic frog that looked out of place and gasped when its head fell off, revealing a toothbrush protruding from its stubby neck. What kind of little kid would want to brush his teeth with a decapitated frog?

On second thought, I knew Manny would get a kick out of it.

I found at least a dozen new brushes but didn't see anything that screamed "Dad" until I noticed something on the floor. I guess it hadn't made it into the chest yet. Or maybe she'd left it out so that she could remember to give it to him when we came. The moment I saw it, I knew it was the one.

A ThunderCats light-up talking toothbrush, complete with Lion-O stand. Dad was going to love it. ThunderCats had been one of his favorite shows growing up. I pulled the handle free and pressed the big white button on the side.

"Thunder . . . Thunder . . . Thunder . . . ThunderCats. Hooo!" the toothbrush said.

"What the heck is *that*?"

I spun around, still holding the lion-man-shaped tooth-brush, to find Lyra standing in the doorway, her dirty socks in her hands. I expected Beelzebub to be pressed up against her, writhing and nipping and struggling to get free, but apparently she hadn't found him yet. Ferrets are good hiders, and lord knows there are plenty of places in Aunt Gertie's house to hide. Lyra had taken off her socks as a precaution. Or maybe as a lure.

"Is it for Dad?" She'd heard our father recount his weekday afternoons and endless Saturday mornings sitting cross-legged in front of the TV too. She could also name all the Smurfs *and* the Fraggles. I nodded and skootched so that she could sit beside me and admire Aunt Gertie's bizarre collection. "They aren't used, are they?" she asked, wrinkling her nose.

I forgot that Lyra was only five the last time we visited Aunt Gertie's. She hadn't gone on the cataloging quest with Cass and me. She'd never seen the treasure chest before. "Some of them," I said.

"Ew. That's disgusting. Why does Aunt Gertie collect used toothbrushes?"

"You collect words," I said.

"That's not the same at all. Words are indispensable. You can't do *any*thing without them."

"You could brush your teeth," I said. "Provided you had a toothbrush."

74

"Dubious," Lyra replied. "Without words, human civilization wouldn't exist and we wouldn't have even *invented* toothbrushes."

Now she sounded like one of Aunt Gertie's *National Geographic*s. "I bet you're wrong. I bet cavemen had toothbrushes. Probably made of bone and woolly mammoth hair or something." I was pretty sure Fred Flintstone had a toothbrush. Of course, he also had a car and a dinosaur crane.

"That's revolting," Lyra said. She picked up a toothbrush that appeared to be made out of Lego, obviously meant for little kids. Her forehead furrowed. "Why does Aunt Gertie have such a big house and no family?"

"She has family," I said. "She has us." *And she had her brother.* At least until recently. The two of them had been really close, I knew. I guess Papa Kwirk didn't feel the same way about sisters as I did. Or maybe he did when he was younger and managed to grow out of it. Was such a thing possible?

"You know what I mean. How come she doesn't have any progeny of her own?"

I stared at my little sister. "Progeny? Really? You can't just say 'kids'? You're ten."

"Almost eleven," Lyra corrected. "And progeny sounds better. Anyone can have kids. When I grow up, I'm going to have progeny."

I tried to imagine what a world full of Lyra's *progeny* would look like. A gaggle of pigtailed Boggle champions ready to take over the world. I shuddered. It's not that I wished she wasn't so smart; I just wished she did a better job of keeping it to herself. "Maybe she thought they'd be too much work," I said.

"Kids aren't too much work."

"*I'm* not *any* work," I told her. "*You*, on the other hand, are a chore."

Maybe that's why Dad never had any brothers or sisters either, I thought. Why Papa Kwirk never had any more kids. It must have been hard enough raising one on your own. Once Grandma Shelley died, it had just been the two of them. Dad never said much about those years either, when it was just he and Papa Kwirk.

Lyra twirled the Lego toothbrush around and around. "I sort of miss Grandpa already. Is that weird? Can you miss someone after only one day? When you wouldn't have seen them anyway?"

"I don't think it's weird at all," I said. I knew what she meant. There was something strange about being here, in Aunt Gertie's house. Something that brought Papa Kwirk's absence so much closer. This was his town. The place he lived and worked and fished and played cards. The place where our own dad was born and raised. The moment Papa Kwirk came back from the war, he married my grandmother and they settled down here in Greenburg and never left. *He* never left. Not like Dad, who hightailed it out of here the moment he graduated from high school, only coming back when he had to.

Like now.

I could almost feel Papa Kwirk's absence in the close air of the overstuffed room. If it felt strange to us being here, I thought, imagine how Dad must be feeling right now.

"Here," I said, handing Lyra the ThunderCats toothbrush stand. "Let's go show this to Dad. And then *maybe* I'll help you look for Beelzebub." I'd learned long ago to always add a maybe anytime I suggested I'd do something for either of my sisters.

It was always a good idea to have an out.

FORTUNES AND FELONS

When we got downstairs, the others had moved from the living room to the dining room in search of tea and coffee. Aunt Gertie was a coffee fiend. Six mugs a day, bare minimum. You could get a caffeine high off her breath. Mom and Dad sat on one end of Aunt Gertie's old wood table, scrunched close together as usual. At the other end, Aunt Gertie was telling a story to Cass about Papa Kwirk, which I guess meant that it was okay to talk about him again. It was a story from before my dad was even born, though it probably led to that moment eventually.

After all, it was about my grandma Shelley.

"Ah," Dad said when he saw Lyra and me. "You're just in time for another one of your grandfather's harrowing adventures." Judging by the tone of his voice, he could just as easily have said, "Ah, you're just in time for your root canal."

Aunt Gertie ignored him and continued her story, speaking mostly to Cass, who sat, riveted. "So it was their third date, and your grandfather was determined that he was going to ask your grandmother to go steady with him."

"Wait. Why would she want to study on their third date?" Cass asked.

"Not stuh-dee. Steh-dee. That's what we called it back then."

"She means 'going out,'" Mom clarified, though that just seemed to confuse Cass even more.

"Whatever you want to call it," Aunt Gertie continued. "Jimmy wanted to make Shelley Harper his girlfriend, so he took her to the carnival, where he was hoping to woo her."

"You mean make out with her," Cass said.

"That's not what 'woo' means, sweetie," Mom said.

"It's sort of what 'woo' means," Dad offered.

"Can I please tell this story?" Aunt Gertie interjected. "So your grandmother asks Jimmy if he could win her one of those giant stuffed bears—the ones that are almost as big as Lyra over there. And he figures his best chance is at the duck-shoot game. Jimmy had been hunting lots of times. He knew how to shoot real ducks, so metal ones that couldn't even fly should be no problem, right?"

Nobody had to answer. Whenever something *shouldn't* be a problem is precisely when it becomes one. Especially in this family.

"He tried seven times to win that bear for her. *Seven* times, at a dollar a pop," Aunt Gertie said. "Spent most of the money he'd brought along and barely had enough left over to buy her a soda. Of course your grandmother insisted she still had a nice time, but Jimmy wouldn't have it. He was just like that: get an idea in his head and there's no shaking it."

Yeah. I knew somebody like that. I glanced at Dad, who appeared to be scratching at a nick in the wood table with his fingernail, only half paying attention. Maybe he'd heard this one before.

"But Shelley Harper wanted that bear, and she was going to *get* that bear," Aunt Gertie continued. "So in the middle of the night, your fool grandfather wakes *me* up and tells me he needs my help. And because I didn't know any better, we sneak out to the fairgrounds where the carnival's shut down for the night, and he uses my shoulders to help him scrabble up over the metal fence. He whispers at me to keep guard and to make a sound like a duck if I see anybody. So I just stand there, waiting for what feels like an hour. And it's cold and I'm getting scared and I've got to pee, but as I head for a bush I hear dogs barking. So of course, I start quacking as loud as I can. And then I see your grandfather come tearing around the corner with the giant stuffed bear draped over his shoulders like a wounded soldier, huffing and puffing, face purple as a turnip. It takes him three tries just to throw the thing over, and I'm panicking, yelling at him to hurry, wondering how he's gonna get back over to my side when he needed my shoulders the first time. Then these two Rottweilers round the corner, flashing their big teeth and growling for blood—and your grandfather jumps higher than he ever jumped in his life, getting his hands on the top of the fence and pulling himself up, those dogs tugging at his pant cuffs, trying to drag him back down so they can have him for breakfast. Jimmy heaved himself over, landing on top of that giant, cushy pink bear just as a shotgun blast cracked the sky. *Kapow!*"

Aunt Gertie slammed her hands on the table and both Cass and my mother jumped high enough that they probably could have cleared the metal fence as well.

"Jimmy grabbed that bear, tossed it over his shoulders again, and we ran for our lives, all the way back home."

"Then what happened?" Cass asked.

"What do you think happened?" Aunt Gertie said. "The next morning, your grandmother-to-be woke up to find that giant bear sitting by her back door with a little dried mud on its fur and a note pinned to its belly. The note said, 'There's nothing I wouldn't do for you.' Your grandma got her bear. Your grandpa got the girl. And I got in trouble for making too much noise and waking your great-grandparents up in the middle of the night sneaking back into my room." Aunt Gertie shook her head. "The crazy things we do for love."

"If that was their third date, I wonder what the first date was like," I said.

She gave me a sly wink. "That's a whole 'nother story."

"Wait a minute," Lyra said. "You mean Grandpa *stole* the bear? Doesn't that make him a criminal?"

"And a trespasser," Dad pointed out.

"Well . . . yes," Aunt Gertie hedged. "If you look at it *that* way. Though the guy running the game probably made a fair bit a money off Jimmy that night too. And the game *was* rigged. They used to bend the barrels of those guns so they didn't shoot straight. There isn't anyone a hundred percent honest in this world."

"It's still illegal," Dad countered. He looked at Lyra. "Just because somebody wrongs you doesn't automatically justify wronging them back. Your grandfather had a habit of doing whatever he pleased, regardless of the consequences."

"Well, the consequences of this were that he made Shelley Harper fall in love with him," Aunt Gertie said. "And if *that* hadn't happened, you wouldn't be around now to criticize, would you, Fletcher Kwirk?"

Dad looked down at the table and resumed scratching at the wood.

Sensing a sudden shift in the room's temperature, I grabbed the ThunderCats toothbrush stand from Lyra and held it out.

"Look what we found upstairs," I said. "It still works." I pressed the button, and the toothbrush stand called the ThunderCats into action again. The toothbrush itself lit up blue and orange. Dad looked at Lion-O crouched, ready to knock the plaque right off your teeth. I expected his eyes to light up too, expected him to press the button himself. To at least tell Aunt Gertie thank you. Instead he pushed his chair back with an ear-grating creak.

82

"I think I'll go for a walk."

"I'll come with you," Mom offered, but Dad shook his head.

"No. That's okay. I'll be back in a bit."

Cass and I looked at each other, wide-eyed. When, in the entire history of Fletcher and Molly Kwirk, had one *ever* refused the other's company? There were gravitational forces that held them in orbit around each other. They even gargled their morning mouthwash together.

Dad went out the back door, banging it shut, my mother frowning after him.

"Is Dad okay?" Lyra asked.

Mom nodded and put an arm around her. "Your father's fine," she said. My mother was a terrible liar. She just didn't have it in her.

Aunt Gertie sighed. "Been meaning to get that door fixed," she said. "It slams every time."

I figured that wasn't true either.

I had never heard that story about the stuffed bear before. Maybe Mom and Dad didn't want Papa Kwirk telling it to us for fear that we would all grow up to be hardened criminals—though I couldn't think of a single girl I'd risk getting attacked by dogs for. Then again, Papa Kwirk had told us plenty of stories that didn't model good behavior. It was always understood that we were not to follow in our grandfather's footsteps when it came to most anything.

Or maybe I'd never heard it because it was also a story about my grandmother, and no one in my family talked about her much either. Occasionally Dad would mention something— like the thing with the milk and cookies. He could describe what she looked like, the dresses she wore all the time, kind of like Lyra. The sweet, earthy smells she brought home from the nursery where she worked selling flowers, or during the holidays, the nose-tingling scent of freshly cut Christmas trees.

I knew that her name was Michelle but everyone called her Shelley. I knew her father ran a hardware store here in town and that she never got to see the ocean. I knew that she was supposedly the most "drop-dead, knock-your-teeth-out, catch-your-pants-on-fire gorgeous woman in Greenburg, Illinois," because Papa Kwirk said so. To hear Papa Kwirk tell it, Shelley Harper was the brightest star in the whole universe.

I can sort of picture her, but only from the photo that Dad keeps on his nightstand. One of the two of them, when he was younger than Lyra, sitting side by side on a park bench, feeding pigeons. It's the only picture of her we have. At least it's the only one I've ever seen.

I know that my grandmother used to knit blankets. I have one, given to me when I was a born. It was my father's once. It has the words *Precious Little Boy* stitched into it, otherwise Cass probably would have gotten it instead. It's up in my closet now, tucked away in a corner, out of sight. The last thing I need is Manny to come over and see it; I'd be "pweshus widdle boy" for the rest of the rest of my middle school career.

Dad said he kept that blanket the whole time he was growing

up. It was pretty much the only thing he took with him when he went away to college—the rest he left for Papa Kwirk to throw away. He remembered how sometimes he would curl up underneath it with Grandma Shelley, and they would read books together in his bed, even when he was old enough to read them himself. She would wrap her arms tight around him, and he would drift off in the protective shell she'd made, only to wake up in the middle of the night to find she had somehow slipped away without him knowing.

The habit must have rubbed off on him, because he used to read to me too. Every night without fail, right up until a few years ago.

When I finally begged him to stop.

Dad returned from his walk just in time for dinner, delivered from the only Chinese restaurant in a ten-mile radius. Aunt Gertie adored her house out in the middle of nowhere, but it meant she had to tip big when the teenager finally showed up with giant containers of mu shu pork, General Tso's chicken, and what seemed like a bucket of fried rice.

"Thanks, Paul. Tell your father I said hello."

"Will do, Ms. Kwirk," the delivery guy said. My aunt was a regular customer of the Lucky Dragon, apparently. I suspect everybody in town probably knew who she was, though. Some people have that kind of personality.

"Know what I miss most about New York?" she said as she handed me the bags with orders to set the table. "The food.

Out here the only thing people really know how to make is hot dogs and macaroni and cheese."

"*And* fried-chicken-flavored jelly beans," Lyra said as we sat down.

"Fried chicken!" Aunt Gertie exclaimed, unwrapping chopsticks that she was the only one skilled enough to use. "I don't think I've heard of that one. Something new in the works, Fletcher?"

Dad stared at his chopsticks doubtfully, then put them down and grabbed a plastic fork. "It's really not that big a deal," he mumbled.

I nearly choked on my bite of rice. *Not a big deal?* Less than twenty-four hours ago, he was acting like he'd just discovered a new planet. Now it was nothing?

"Don't be modest," Mom chipped in. "It's remarkable. He's been working on it all year long. He says Garvadill is not even close to unlocking anything like it."

"And it *actually* tastes like fried chicken," Cass seconded.

Dad grinned. "It *is* a breakthrough," he admitted finally. "But don't tell anyone. We want to keep it under wraps for as long as possible. If we're lucky, Garvadill won't even know about it until it hits the shelves." There it was again, Dad's paranoia that the Slugworths would get their hands on his Everlasting Gobstopper.

"Fried chicken. That's amazing," Aunt Gertie said, taking a bite of chicken herself. "Now if you could only make one that tastes like cheesecake . . . I mean actual New York cheesecake, not that frozen crap you find in the grocery store, pardon my French."

"None of that was French," Lyra informed her. Aunt Gertie poked my sister's belly with her chopsticks.

"And they already have cheesecake jelly beans," I added. Though I doubted they would live up to Aunt Gertie's expectations. Sort of like all the men she'd ever dated.

"You kids know that eating too much candy will rot your teeth," Aunt Gertie said. "Especially those sticky jelly beans."

I froze, a piece of pork half chewed in my mouth. Here it comes. There probably wasn't a kid in the world who *didn't* know that, but Aunt Gertie felt the need to tell us every time we saw her. Not surprising for a lady with a treasure chest full of toothbrushes, but still.

And every time she said it, Dad's face would redden.

This time he let out a long nasally breath. "Those jelly beans are our livelihood, Gertie. They help put a roof over our heads," he said. "They help pay for groceries. They will help pay for college someday." As he spoke, a funny image popped into my head: my father standing in the checkout lane of the grocery store, counting jelly beans into the clerk's hands, then driving home to a house made of candy, just like the witch in a fairy tale.

Aunt Gertie looked taken aback. "I didn't mean to offend you. Honestly, Fletcher, I think it's wonderful. You work hard and you love what you do. And like you said, you provide for your kids. What more could you ask for?"

"Better than making the kids provide for themselves," Dad mumbled loud enough so I could hear, but I was sitting next to him.

"What was that?" my aunt asked.

"Nothing," Dad said.

"No. If you have something you want to say, please, feel free to say it. We're all family here." Aunt Gertie stared at my father and he stared back, as if their eyes were having a conversation we weren't a part of.

After a few seconds, my mother turned to Cass. "Why don't you tell Aunt Gertie how your acting is going?"

Cass was all too happy to oblige. "Okay. Get this. . . ."

The next ten painful minutes were spent hearing about how Marissa Innes was a terrible Belle because she couldn't fake cry and her voice wasn't strong enough and how she was only picked as the lead in the musical because she had naturally big eyelashes and looked good in a yellow dress. Then, to compound the torture, Aunt Gertie requested a serenade, and Cass broke into song right there at the table, flailing her arms around until she knocked over Lyra's glass of milk.

From there it was typical Kwirk chaos. Lyra called her a "foozler," which sounded like something out of a Dr. Seuss book, and threw a piece of chicken, which got stuck in Cass's hair, causing her to scream so loud that Dad jerked, banging his knee on the bottom of the table while Mom swabbed frantically at the milk with her napkin, desperate to keep at least

88

one part of the house clean. Aunt Gertie said it wasn't worth crying about, I assumed in reference to the milk, though it could have been the flung chicken or the banged knee or something else entirely, though nobody was actually crying. Not at the moment, anyway.

For my part, I just sat and watched, thinking, *Yup. Totally adopted. No doubt in my mind.*

When the mess was finally cleaned up—and after Lyra apologized for calling Cass names—Aunt Gertie dug the fortune cookies out of the bottom of the take-out bag and handed them out. At her insistence, we all took turns going around the table reading our little slips of paper out loud. Most of them were terrible. Things like **The greatest risk is not taking any** and **To love your life you must live the life you love.** Mine was **Be happy. You can read and you get a cookie**, which was hard to argue with. Aunt Gertie's was strangely specific: **You will find love on Thursday.** She said that was good because it gave her a few days to get her nails done.

When it got to Dad, he shook his head, then balled up his fortune and tossed it into the middle of the table, where it almost landed in the still-half-full carton of rice.

"I'd rather not," he said. Then he thanked Aunt Gertie for dinner and excused himself to the family room. Mom followed closely behind, their personal gravity working this time. I could hear them whispering to each other but couldn't tell what they were saying.

As soon as they were both out of the room, Cass and I both reached for Dad's crumpled fortune, but I got to it first.

Apologizing is hard. Foregiving is even harder.

Lyra leaned over my shoulder and pointed. "They spelled 'forgiving' incorrectly."

"Maybe spelling is the hardest," I joked, but neither of my sisters laughed.

Aunt Gertie cracked a smile, at least, but I got the impression she was thinking about something else entirely.

That night after Cass and I washed, dried, and put away the dishes under Mom's direction ("at least this will be *one* thing back where it belongs"), I gave in and tried to help Lyra find Beelzebub. But the ferret—like the chemical formula for the taste of armpits—proved elusive. We ended up back in the Vault, where Lyra discovered the boxes of *National Geographics*, and we spent the next hour side by side, flipping through them, mostly looking at the pictures.

At one point, Ly leaned over and showed me a photo of the aurora borealis overlooking some glaciers near Greenland. Iridescent waves of light with wispy edges, purple and green, stretching toward a dark horizon, like fingers reaching for something nobody could see. It was pretty amazing. And it made me wish I was in Greenland instead of Greenburg. Though, to be honest, just about any place could have made that list.

"I bet that's what heaven looks like," Lyra said in a singsong sighing voice.

But before I could say "That would be nice," she had turned the page.

PARRY AND RIPOSTE

The morning of Papa Kwirk's funeral, I woke to my older sister shoving a stick up my nose.

There are worse ways to wake up. Say, if you were knocked unconscious by a group of cannibal hillbillies and came around to find yourself smothered in barbeque sauce and strapped to a spit above a stack of smoldering logs. But on a day that already had one huge knock against it, my sister challenging me to a duel at dawn didn't help my mood.

"En garde," she said.

"What time is it?"

"Time for you to defend your honor."

I pushed the stick out of my face and squinted at the sunshine seeping through my window. "No, really. What time is it?"

"Really. It's time for me to practice. Dad's taking *another* walk, and Aunt Gertie's making breakfast. And you know how Mom feels about physical violence."

I knew. My mother was generally not in favor of people thwacking each other with sticks. Not without extra padding, at least, which we actually had back at home but hadn't bothered to bring with us. Probably because we'd come to Greenburg for a *funeral*, not a sword fight. "What about Lyra? Go bother her for a change."

"She's still asleep."

"I'm still asleep," I grumbled, closing my eyes and turning over, only to be poked in the side.

"Not anymore. Besides, Ly isn't tall enough, and I'm supposed to practice every day. You know that."

"So go beat up a tree or something."

"Trees don't fight back."

In that moment, I imagined a giant oak falling on my sister, pinning her to the ground. It made me smile.

"Rion. C'mon. I need something to take my mind off . . . you know. And I finished my book last night. Will you *please* just do this one thing?"

I let out a long, low groan, muffled only slightly by the pillow I was half-heartedly trying to suffocate myself with. I knew she wouldn't leave until I either said yes or called for Mom to come drag her away, and I didn't want to bother my poor mother. She was probably busy straightening the house behind Aunt Gertie's back. "You're so annoying," I said.

Cass tucked her stick under her arm. "That's a yes. See you

downstairs in five. And put some pants on. I can't possibly duel you in your Batman underwear."

I peeked down to see that I'd kicked the sheets half off the bed and was wearing only my black boxer shorts with the little yellow bat symbols all over them. Perfect. Sure, she had seen me in less, but not since I was a toddler. Once you get past the age of two, there are rules. Or at least there should be.

But in this family sometimes the rules just didn't apply.

The main event wasn't until the afternoon, and short of a few last-minute phone calls "to make sure everything was in place," Aunt Gertie insisted that there was nothing any of us could do to help.

Which meant I didn't need to put on my fancy pants yet, so I made do with yesterday's jeans. I ambled down the stairs to the kitchen, still wondering why I'd let my sister talk me into this. She needed a distraction. That made sense. So she chose beating me up. I guess in her mind, that probably made sense too. Maybe she should have brought another book. Where was Prince Teldar when you needed him?

Aunt Gertie was the only one I passed on my way to the back door, squinting at the directions on a package of pancake mix as if they were written in hieroglyphics. "Hrmm," she said, doing some kind of math with her fingers.

"Good morning, Aunt Gertie," I said without thinking, instantly wishing I'd gone with something less chipper. The morning of her brother's funeral would be anything but good, and my cheery tone, while fake, probably didn't help.

Surprisingly, Aunt Gertie stopped her squinting and offered me a warm smile. "Morning, Rion. Did you sleep all right?"

I nodded. "At least until something annoying woke me up."

She knew what I meant. "Yes. I think your sister's waiting for you in the backyard. But don't worry, breakfast should be ready shortly. I'll come rescue you before you lose *all* of your limbs." She went back to the box, her brow furrowed. "What's half of three quarters plus two and a half?" she asked.

"Two point eight seven five," I said. That one was easy, even for early Sunday morning. But Aunt Gertie apparently didn't like my answer.

"I'll just make the whole box," she said.

I closed the screen door gently behind me so as not to wake anyone else up, which *I* knew was a rude thing to do. Cass was there in the backyard, twirling her stick around like that swordsman from *Raiders of the Lost Ark*. If only I had a pistol. Instead I had to find my own stick.

"Over there," Cass said, pointing to a three-foot branch that she'd already picked out for me, leaning against Aunt Gertie's porch swing. It was a little crooked, but at least it was thick enough that it wouldn't break on my sister's first hit. Cass chose her weapons with care.

At home she had a real sword. A few of them, in fact, hanging over her bed. Last summer, after weeks of badgering, Mom gave in and let her go to fencing camp so that she could improve her stage fighting. She came home with something called an épée, one of those helmets that made her look like an extraterrestrial beekeeper, and way too much enthusiasm for the art of stabbing people. Since then she'd been taking classes every Tuesday after school with a guy named Eduardo, whom, I suspected, she was also in love with, given how she talked about him: "So graceful. Just gorgeous to watch. Ahhh . . . Eduardo."

Blech.

Some people might think it's cool to have a sister who's a fencer, but they would be wrong. It just made me mad. Of course *Cass* gets a sword, but I have to keep my knife that was a gift to me from my grandfather in the attic. Plus she even gets to wear her sword out in public. Not all the time, of course, but for one weekend a year when we go to Ren Faire.

That's short for Renaissance Faire. Which is, itself, short for Ye Longe Boring Day, most of it spent sitting on hay bales watching drama queens and kings parade around pretending like it's the 1400s and nobody has cholera. Imagine a bunch of people in knee-high boots and frilly shirts slogging through the mud, drinking beer out of ivory horns, and saying "Forsooth" a lot. Sprinkle in the smell of horse manure for full effect. There's a Ren Faire that happens in July less than an hour away from our house, and every year my parents drag me along for the entire weekend so I can watch my sister pretend to be some kind of fairy pirate handmaiden or something.

Don't get me wrong. Parts of it are cool. The jousting and the archery contest and the guy who eats fire. But after a while you start to feel like you're an intruder, and the people who are dressed up in flower crowns and billowy pants are having a lot more fun than you are because they know something you don't.

Come to think of it, I get that feeling a lot.

I gathered my stick and joined Cass in the backyard. The morning dew was cool and slick on my feet.

"Remember what I taught you," she said as I approached. "Salute. En garde."

Even dressed in her zebra-stripe flannel pajamas, Cass looked like a pro, striking the pose I'd seen a zillion times: branch out, leg extended, one arm back. I held my stick droopingly out in front of me with both hands like an apathetic Jedi. It wasn't how I was supposed to stand, but I didn't ask to be dragged out of bed this morning.

"Are you going to take this seriously or not?"

"When last we met, I was but a learner. Now I am the master," I replied.

"I take that as a no," Cass said. Then she shouted "Allez!" which is French, I assume, for "Prepare to have me beat you senseless," and she lunged, swiftly knocking my stick out of the way and jabbing me in the belly. I collapsed, clutching my stomach with both hands, moaning and rolling from side to side.

"I think you punctured my spleen," I groaned.

"I barely touched you. Now will you please get up and *try* this time, you big baby?"

I stood up and brushed myself off, only to be skewered again. And again. And again.

That's how it went for the next half hour or so. En garde, allez, and then Cass somehow disarmed me or knocked me off-balance before stabbing me in the heart, the liver, or the lungs. I did try, eventually—mostly out of an instinct for self-preservation. The harder she poked me, the harder I tried, though it wasn't easy with her shouting at me all the time.

"Feint! Feint! Parry! Riposte! *Riposte!* After you parry, why don't you ever riposte?"

"Because I never posted in the first place!" I said, which earned me an eye roll and another jab. "This is stupid. Stop poking me!"

"You know, it wouldn't hurt you to try something new every once in a while. Just because *I* like it doesn't mean you automatically won't."

No. But it made it highly probable. "What's there to like about you stabbing me?"

"You know what I mean."

I guess, maybe, I knew what she meant, but I was still tired of being beat. I tossed my stick into the line of trees behind Aunt Gertie's house with a grunt and turned back toward the door. Cass called out behind me.

"You can't quit now. We're just getting started."

I ignored her.

"You know Papa Kwirk always tried new things. And he never did anything halfway."

And see where that got him, I almost said, but I didn't. In fact, I instantly felt bad for even thinking it.

It seemed like something my father would have said.

By the time I'd washed my hands—Mom refused to let you join the table without sniffing them to detect a lingering presence of soap particles—everyone else was seated. Dad was back from his walk and was already wearing his suit and reeking of aftershave. He owned at least twenty colorful bow ties, polka dots and fancy stripes and even a black one with little gold stars that Mom said was her favorite, but the tie he wore today was of the straight and skinny variety, simple and boring, patterned black and gray. I had never seen it before and wondered if he kept it in the back of his closet just for occasions like this—though our family hadn't had many occasions like this. He looked strange with his hair slicked down and his shirt cuffs buttoned. Not at all like the dad I was used to.

That set me to wondering if Papa Kwirk would look just as weird to me when I saw him today. Except for that one picture on Aunt Gertie's wall, I'd always only ever seen my grandfather in a short-sleeve buttondown, the top two buttons loose to show off his patch of curly silver chest hair. I wondered if they would trim his bird's-nest beard. Wondered if he would look like him or like a wax replica, like something you would find in a museum. Maybe I could avoid going up to the casket to say goodbye, just so I wouldn't have to look, but then it would seem like I didn't care, which wasn't true at all. I just wanted to remember Papa Kwirk the way *I'd* always seen him. Leaning against Jack Nicholson, or snoring in our La-Z-Boy, or sitting on our stoop with a piece of licorice dangling out of his mouth.

"Eat up," Aunt Gertie said, setting a plate of pancakes on the table. She had, indeed, made the whole box, the stack threatening to topple over. We worked through them, though—it kept our mouths busy chewing. Unlike yesterday, when it seemed preferable to talk about anything other than Papa Kwirk, today it seemed wrong *not* to talk about him, so nobody said much of anything. Not until Lyra, who had only taken one bite of her breakfast, pushed her plate away.

"You okay, honey?" Mom asked.

My little sister shook her head, lower lip bulging. "I still haven't found Beelzebub."

"*That's* what's bothering you?" Aunt Gertie said, sounding relieved. "No worries, dear. He's got to be around here somewhere. His food bowl's half empty, and there's a big wet spot in the litter box, so I know he's not *dead*."

Dad choked on his pancake.

"Sorry, Fletcher," Aunt Gertie said.

"It's all right," Dad said, wiping his mouth with his napkin. He looked at Lyra. "I'll try to help you find him after the funeral, okay, sweetie?"

"Funneral," Aunt Gertie said, pronouncing it with a short U sound, like in "gun."

There was a pause, the room so quiet I could hear the

grandfather clock in the living room ticking.

"Sorry, what?" Dad asked, his fork hovering over his plate.

Aunt Gertie just kept eating, though, speaking with food in her mouth. "Jimmy always said that the problem with funerals was that they were no *fun*. So instead we're calling it a fun-neral."

I waited for the wink, but Aunt Gertie was all business. She didn't flinch.

"You can't be serious," Dad said.

"Serious as a funeral," Gertie replied. "Which is why today is going to be something different."

Mom suddenly looked uncomfortable, squirming in her chair like she'd gotten an itch in the middle of her back. "So what exactly *is* the difference between a funeral and a . . . um . . ." She cleared her throat as if the word had gotten lodged there. "*Fun*-neral."

"I guess you'll just have to wait and see," Aunt Gertie said, her eyes flashing. She shoveled a forkful of pancake into her mouth with a smile of relish.

Wait and see? Now I was nervous. Were people going to jump out from behind the coffin? Would there be streamers? Those little cone-shaped horns you blow at New Year's? My experience with funerals was limited, but I sort of knew what to expect from them. Black clothing. Speeches and prayers and lots of sniffling. Everyone with their hands in their laps. Hugs and flowers and organ music. What did Aunt Gertie have planned?

"Will there be more clowns?" Lyra asked, saying out loud what I only dared to think to myself.

"It's a funeral, not a birthday party for a five-year-old," Dad told her.

"Funneral," Aunt Gertie repeated in a carefully measured tone, fixing my father with her eyes. "Jimmy gave instructions for how he would like to be remembered. It was all outlined in his will. And as executor of that will, I intend to honor his final wishes." The tone of her voice was oddly authoritative all of a sudden. Like she was giving us a warning. Or an ultimatum. "It should be well attended, though," she continued, her voice softening. "Most of Jimmy's other family will be there."

"His *other* family?" I asked. I could have sworn that my grandfather's entire family was sitting at this table. I looked over at Dad, but he seemed to still be hung up on the difference between funeral and funneral. He rubbed at his forehead with one hand.

"Your grandfather lived in this town most of his life," Gertie explained. "Almost sixty years. You don't drop anchor somewhere for that long and not get barnacles on your boat. There are quite a few people here who knew and loved him. I think of them as family."

"Not my family," Dad said.

"Well, it's not your funneral," Gertie replied shortly. "When you die, you can make the guest list."

I could sense Lyra wanting to point out the logistical

problem with this statement, but she popped a strawberry into her mouth instead, chewing slowly.

"Your grandfather was a fixture in this community," Aunt Gertie continued, looking at me now, I think maybe to avoid looking at Dad. "Did you know he used to volunteer sometimes at the high school, talking to troubled teens?" I shook my head. Just as expected, I was learning new things about Papa Kwirk already. "Well, maybe if your dad had brought you around more, you would have," Gertie said.

The sound of Dad's fork clattering to his plate startled me.

"*Around?* You want to talk about being *around*? How about you tell the kids how often Frank was around when I was their age? Ask them if they knew where he was when I left for school some days? Or when it was time to make dinner? I'm sure they'd love to hear how *around* he was."

Aunt Gertie frowned and set her fork gently on the table. Mom looked up to the ceiling. Cass shifted in her seat. Mealtimes at Aunt Gertie's were starting to follow a familiar pattern.

Lyra swallowed her strawberry. "Did you guys know that the aurora borealis can be seen from outer space?"

Everyone looked at her, except for my father and my great-aunt. Normally this would be the point when Dad would jump in and say something about charged particles and magnetic fields and start to explain away the mystery of the whole thing, taking some of the beauty with it.

Instead he said, "I think I'm full," and stood up. "Thank

you for breakfast. I'm going to go finish getting ready for the . . ." He paused, and I could sense that whatever came next could trigger an explosion at the kitchen table. "For today," he finished. I watched my pancake soak up the last of my syrup as he tromped upstairs.

"Do you really have to make this more difficult than it already is?" Mom snipped at Aunt Gertie, before standing and following him.

I was starting to wonder if either of them would ever finish a meal the whole time we were in Greenburg.

"What was *that* all about?" Lyra wondered out loud.

"I'm afraid your dad and I don't always see eye to eye when it comes to your grandfather," Aunt Gertie said with a sigh. "But we will by the time this is all over. At least that's my intention."

I was pretty sure by "this" she meant the funeral, or funneral, or whatever it was called. I had no idea what we were in for. None of us did.

Only Aunt Gertie knew for sure.

SHAKING THINGS UP

I'd only ever been to one other funeral in my life. A few years ago, friends of my parents lost their six-year-old son to leukemia. His name was Ferran. He'd been born with thick black hair as a baby. He enjoyed riding his bike and baking cookies. He spent the last few month of his life stuck in a bed.

My dad worked with Ferran's dad, and though our families never hung out together outside of company picnics, I knew what the Amaris had been through. The treatments and the extended hospital stays, the expensive medications and the steadily worsening prognosis. The year before his passing, the community had a Festival for Ferran to raise money for treatment, a pitch-in street fair complete with kissing booths and pool-noodle swordfights. Naturally my family ran the mystery jelly-bean challenge booth: identify all five flavors correctly and get a prize. In total we raised eight thousand dollars, enough to pay for a few months of meds, maybe. They didn't stop him from dying, though. All the kisses and jelly beans in the world couldn't have done that.

Ferran's funeral service was held in a big Catholic church, filled to the aisles. The priest led the congregation in prayer after prayer, some of them in Latin. There were songs and poems. Ferran's older sister stood up and sang an a cappella version of "Stand by Me," but she couldn't make it through the chorus without breaking down, which choked me up, because crying can be contagious. I remember that the sun was brutal that day, sneaking through the haloes of the saints in the stained-glass windows, beating down on us later as we stood at the gravesite. I remember my mother holding my sweaty hand the whole time as they lowered little Ferran into the ground.

Papa Kwirk's *memorial*, as my dad insisted on calling it, wasn't going to be held in a church. Not because Papa Kwirk didn't believe in God—I knew he did, because I'd asked him once. We were standing by our Christmas tree looking at an ornament, given to us by a friend, showing Jesus in the manger. Papa Kwirk was telling me how he'd once had to sleep in a barn too, "though no camel-ridin' kings showed up with bags fulla gold for me." That's when I asked him.

"Hell yes. I believe in all of 'em," he told me. "I wouldn't've come back from 'Nam otherwise."

Papa Kwirk believed, but he never went to church, at least not that I knew of. Maybe he couldn't find one in town that would let him worship all of 'em at once. Or maybe he had too many other ways to spend his Sundays. On Sunday God rested, or so I'm told, but resting wasn't really Papa Kwirk's style.

Which all helped explain why his memorial service was being held at a neighborhood park instead of a church. That, and the fact that Papa Kwirk would have liked the idea of being surrounded by trees rather than walls. That's what Aunt Gertie said, and she was the one calling the shots.

We arrived at the park early at my father's insistence, following the little yellow flags and parking the Tank in the one space marked by a white sign that read *Immediate Family*. That was us. Immediate. The clouds sported angry gray bruises that threatened rain, so Mom pulled two giant umbrellas from the trunk that she kept there, just in case. She wasn't allergic to rain (though she *was* afraid of lightning); she just didn't want to get her nice black dress wet.

I scratched my armpits where my fancy fresh-from-the-package dress shirt was itching me. The pants itched too. When I complained about it out loud, Aunt Gertie told me that being uncomfortable was the price you pay for beauty and pointed to her own high heels. She then told the girls that they looked gorgeous in their dresses. "Don't your sisters look pretty?" she said, poking me with her elbow.

"You really don't want me to answer that," I told her.

The *park* was pretty, though. A patch of emerald studded with elms and evergreens and yellow and orange flowers, like flickers of fire, sprouting from pockets of mulch. A playground could be seen in the distance, peppered with kids running and swinging. I had to remind myself it was Sunday afternoon and there was no school for them either. They were all dressed in shorts and T-shirts, lucky jerks.

"You'll ruin your outfit," Mom said, noticing me staring longingly at the playground. "Besides, it doesn't look like we're that early after all."

In the center of the park sat an amphitheater, which Aunt Gertie said was used for summer concerts sporting local musicians. Today it was packed with white plastic folding chairs, already filling with people. Lots of people. "Quite a crowd," I said.

"I told you, your grandfather had a big family," Aunt Gertie said. "Everyone in town knew him. And most of them even *liked* him, which is to their credit." She grabbed my hand—hers was surprisingly rough for someone who had spent most of her life in New York City conference rooms negotiating business contracts—and walked with me, all the way down to the front row, her heels clicking on the paved steps. There, on a small metal stage, sat Papa Kwirk's casket and a few chairs, but little else. No flower bouquets. No wreaths or flags. A podium with a microphone stood next to an easel, on which sat the only other evidence for why we'd all gathered here: a portrait of the man himself.

Except it wasn't a portrait, exactly. It was a caricature. One of those silly drawings you can get at the zoo or at Disney World for twenty bucks, where your head is twice as big as your body and everything's slightly out of proportion. Grandpa's caricature was especially overblown. His ears were much too big and his inky eyebrows too bushy. The artist had drawn him sitting astride Jack Nicholson, smiling, missing tooth and all. That missing tooth used to drive my great-aunt crazy.

The casket was closed, thankfully. Which meant that instead of seeing Papa Kwirk's waxy face, layered in makeup, with a forced, tight-lipped smile, I would get to remember his giant gap-toothed grin. I thought it was better that way. Obviously so did Aunt Gertie.

Dad felt differently.

"Closed casket?" he asked, pointing up at the stage. His suit must have been itchy too, because he'd been squirming in it ever since we left the house.

"Jimmy's wishes," Aunt Gertie said. It was the fourth or fifth time I'd heard her say it already this morning. Every time Dad would ask a question, Aunt Gertie would deflect it or say it was a surprise and then follow it with "Jimmy's wishes," which only frustrated my father even further.

He looked about ready to self-combust now, staring at the sparse scenery onstage. "And that's the best picture of him you could find?"

"That's the picture he wanted," Aunt Gertie replied. I could tell by the vein now visibly throbbing above Dad's pinched brow that he didn't approve. Of any of it. The closed casket. The park. The picture. I could also tell by the expression on Aunt Gertie's face that she didn't much care whether he approved or not. "Now if it's all right, I have some people I'd like to introduce you to," she said.

"Yes. Of course," Mom answered for us, trying to keep the peace.

The next thirty minutes were spent shaking hands and taking hugs from people I didn't know: a parade of strangers coming up and putting their mitts on my shoulders, telling me all about myself. "Oh, you're Frank's *grandson*," they'd say, as if I needed a reminder. "He used to brag on you all the time. You still play soccer? He always said you were almost as good-looking as he was." They gushed over Cass and Lyra too. "So beautiful. So grown up." I didn't realize Papa Kwirk talked about us that much. And to the entire town too. It seemed like they all wanted to meet us.

And yet nobody said what they were supposed to say. Nobody said, "I'm sorry." It was as if they were specifically instructed not to. That's what you say at *feeyoo*nerals, of course, and this wasn't one of those, though it wasn't all that much fun, either. Instead they told us how they'd come to meet my grandfather. What they remembered most about him. Little snapshots from Papa Kwirk's past accumulated with every handshake.

A man named Howie, from the American Legion, who once challenged my grandfather to an oyster-eating competition that ended badly for both of them.

A woman named Georgia who said Papa Kwirk once saved her cat from being eaten by a coyote.

Papa Kwirk's postal deliveryperson, a boulder of a man with huge hands that swallowed your own, who admitted that Papa Kwirk always left him a snifter of brandy in the mailbox on Christmas Eve.

A waitress at one of his favorite restaurants, who said Papa Kwirk always tipped five bucks whether the meal was ten dollars or thirty. "Even if he just came in and ordered a cup of coffee, he'd leave a five under the saucer. What a sweetheart."

The processional marched on. Dad seemed to recognize some of them. A librarian who had been working at the local branch since Dad was a kid and reminded him that he once returned a book that was five months overdue. Another ancient-looking lady from the neighborhood who lived in the condo next door to Papa Kwirk and would bake him white-chocolate macadamia nut cookies "because they were his favorite." A dentist. A barista. The owner of a bowling alley. They all had some connection to Papa Kwirk, which seemed to them to mean they had some automatic connection to us. But they were all strangers to me.

They were mostly adults, too, closer to Aunt Gertie's age. There were a few other kids, but they kept their distance or hid behind their parents, which was exactly what I would have done, which was what I *wanted* to do, but it was my grandfather who had died, so I was required to stand there and smile-frown-nod.

One girl had the courage to come right up and introduce herself, though.

"Hi," she said, extending her hand to me.

After a nudge from Cass I said hi back. Apparently because this girl was about my age, I was the family's designated first responder.

"You're Frank's grandson?" she asked.

I nodded dumbly. I didn't expect another kid to call my grandfather by his first name. I was also having a little trouble forming words. The girl had black curly hair, dark skin, brown eyes. Her braces had turquoise bands that made it look like she had a mouth full of jewels when she smiled. She wore a blue sundress with bright orange flowers that for some reason made me think of Hawaii. Or at least of Hawaiian Punch. That made me thirsty. Or maybe my mouth was just dry.

"He was a strange bird," the girl said, shaking her head.

"He was?" I mumbled. He was. Of course he was. But to hear this girl say it, this girl I didn't know . . . it felt weird somehow. Like breaking the rules. Were you allowed to come to a funeral, or even a funneral, and tell the grandson of the deceased how weird his grandfather was? Who was this girl? Had I met her before? Had she come over to the house once while we were visiting? Did Grandpa introduce us? I swear I didn't recognize her.

And I didn't think I would have forgotten.

"Sorry," she said, which was the first apology I'd heard that afternoon. "I didn't mean strange in a bad way. I just mean he was unique. He had his own beat. Which is cool. Because who wants to be the same as everyone else, right?"

"Yeah," I said, though I wasn't really sure. There was such a thing as too different, wasn't there? Too out there?

"You're pretty lucky, you know," the girl continued, her hands folded in front of her.

Lucky? Did she mean to have Papa Kwirk as my grandfather? I hadn't really thought about it. I mean, he did give me a dead chipmunk once. I was about to ask how she knew him when Aunt Gertie interrupted.

"Oh. Hi, Ms. Kwirk," the girl said brightly.

"Hi, Tasha. You've met my great-nephew, I see? Rion, this is Tasha Meeks. She's a friend of the family. Your parents are here, aren't they, dear?"

"In the back." Tasha pointed. "I just thought I would come up and tell you that I'm ready. And to thank you again for the opportunity."

Ready? What was she ready for? Was this one of the surprises that Aunt Gertie kept warning us about? And why was I sweating so much all of a sudden?

"Well, in that case, let's get this party started, shall we?" Aunt Gertie said.

"It was nice meeting you." Tasha waved as she walked up the aisle to the back of the amphitheater, her flowery dress swishing with each step.

"Such a sweet girl," Aunt Gertie said, pulling my attention away from the swishing. "It broke her heart when Jimmy passed, though she's too tough to admit it." Then, before I could ask why, Gertie turned to the rest of our family and said we should all take a seat.

Given what we'd already seen, I thought that was probably good advice. Whatever was coming, whatever surprise Papa Kwirk had in store for us, it would be better faced sitting down.

The crowd quieted on cue when my aunt walked up onto the stage, and I wondered if they all knew her just as well as they'd known my grandfather. I'd heard somebody say once that funerals were for the living. Maybe the big crowd that had gathered had less to do with Papa Kwirk and more to do with comforting his family, particularly his grief-stricken sister. Though Aunt Gertie didn't appear grief-stricken. She looked cool and composed as she tapped on the mic.

"This thing on? Guess so. Well, all right. Hello, everyone," she began. "So nice of you all to make it out here this afternoon to honor Jimmy's memory. I know if he were here, he would probably look out over this huge crowd and say, 'What a lousy bunch of moochers! We're not *feeding* them all, are we?'"

Laughter rippled through the crowd. I looked over at Dad to see if we, as a family, were supposed to find this funny, but his look was stern, his jaw rigid, so I kept a straight face too. Though it *did* sound like something Papa Kwirk would say.

"My brother Jimmy—or Frank, as most of you know him—had a saying," Aunt Gertie continued. "'That which doesn't kill us will only try harder next time, so you might as well make the most of the space in between.' Actually, Jimmy had a lot of sayings, but that's the only one that isn't R-rated. And it's also the one that sticks out to me the most, because I really think he believed it."

I glanced around, taking in the faces of the crowd, all eyes fixed on Aunt Gertie in her sleek black dress with its fancy white scarf. I looked straight behind me and saw Tasha, in the back row, looking serious as Aunt Gertie continued her eulogy.

"Those of us who knew him knew that Francis Tyler Kwirk was a salty, sharp-tongued, son-of-a-you-know-what, but my brother also had the biggest heart of anyone I ever knew. And whether his foot was in his mouth or halfway up your rear end, you knew that that big heart of his was in the right place. I think just about everyone in attendance today can reach back and think of something kind my brother Jimmy did for them. Whether he helped you build your deck . . . or fix your leaky faucet . . . or just bought you a drink at Bailey's, we've all owed him something at one time or another. Some of us *still* owe him. How much do you owe him, Larry?" Aunt Gertie called out, scanning the crowd.

"Sixty-five bucks," a man in the audience called out. "Plus interest." This caused another trickle of laughter.

"You keep it," Aunt Gertie said, smiling. "Take Cindy out to dinner somewhere."

I could only assume that Cindy was Larry's wife. I had never heard of either of them. Two more names tethered to me only by the memory of the man lying in the closed cherrywood coffin onstage. And yet *they* all understood. They laughed. They smiled. Some of them seemed to be dabbing at their eyes with tissues or shirtsleeves, but even still, this was nothing like Ferran's funeral, where everyone was a sobbing, stuttering wreck. Suddenly I felt out of place, like there was some big inside joke that all these people were in on and I would never get. Like I was back at the Ren Faire, the only one without a sword and a pair of leather pants.

On the other side of my mother, Dad started tapping his heel, his leg bouncing up and down like a jackrabbit. She placed a hand on his knee to quiet it. It worked for about three seconds. And then he started up again.

"I don't need to tell you all how Jimmy lived his life," Aunt Gertie continued. "How hard it was at times. The things he'd seen and suffered through. You all know. You've heard the stories. All I can say is that if the rest of us live twice as long as he did, we'll still only live half as much. He was a good brother, a devoted husband, a loving father and grandfather, and a true Kwirk. He was also my best friend. May he rest in joy, because I'm almost positive he'd find resting in peace too boring for words. Goodbye, Jimmy. I'll sure miss ya."

Aunt Gertie turned and blew a kiss toward the casket. Someone behind me blew their nose. It sounded obnoxious, too loud, like an elephant's roar. A little girl sitting in the aisle across from me giggled. It all seemed so strange.

And it was just getting started.

My aunt gestured toward the crowd. "Now I'd like to welcome to the stage some fellows most of you have heard of, and some of you have even *heard* . . . the Salty Shakers."

With that, three old men stood and made their way up the stairs with applause at their backs. I had never *heard* or heard *of* the Salty Shakers, and I doubted anyone outside of Greenburg, Illinois, had either. The Salty Shakers, apparently, were a musical group.

More specifically, they were a barbershop quartet.

Except they weren't a quartet anymore. Three mostly bald men stood around the one microphone on stage. They were dressed in red-and-white striped vests and matching red pants with shiny white loafers, making them all look like squat, fat candy canes. I had never seen these men before in my life and wondered how I hadn't managed to spot them in the crowd. They stuck out worse than Waldo.

"Hello, Greenburg!" the lead Salty Shaker cried out, earning him a cheer from the audience. In the next seat over, my mother had her hand cupped over her mouth, as if she was afraid something might fly out of it. My father just looked sick. Pasty white. With a tinge of green.

"We are the Salty Shakers." Another big hoot from someone in the back. "And this will be our last performance. In honor of one of our own. The dearly beloved Frank Kwirk."

Cass leaned over and whispered in my ear. "Grandpa was in a barbershop quartet?"

I shrugged. It was news to me too. At that moment, I tried to imagine what Papa Kwirk would have looked like in one of those too-short vests and those blinding white shoes, but before I could even wrap my head around it, the lead singer said, "Frankie . . . we know this one was your favorite. Hit it, fellas."

The guy on the left, who was skinny by comparison to the other two, started in with the *bum-bum-bum* of a bass line. Then the guy on the right launched into some kind of *do-do-do* melody, the tune of which struck me as familiar, though I couldn't quite place it. Until the guy in the middle started to sing.

"A well'a bless my soul. What'sa wrong with me?
I'm itchin' like a man in a fuzzy tree."

That's when I recognized the song. It was Elvis. I'd heard Grandpa crank it up on our family's ancient radio while sitting in the backyard at our house, gnawing on a licorice whip and telling me that they don't make music like they used to. I believe my response at the time was "Thank God."

Now the ghost of Elvis had returned at my grandfather's funeral. In three-part harmony.

"I'm in love. Unh. I'm all shook up."

The lead singer, a man with hardly a wisp of hair on his head but plenty of girth around his waist, started to wiggle his hips and thrust his pelvis. The crowd cheered. Cass covered her eyes. I didn't blame her. I kind of didn't want to watch, either, but I couldn't bear not to. All around I could see people bouncing their knees and tapping their feet. Even Aunt Gertie, standing off to the side of the stage, was wiggling her bony shoulders.

The three old men finished the song to rousing applause and another hoot from the back. "Salty Shakers! Yeah-aa! You guys *rule*!"

"Thank you. Thank you very much," the lead singer said. He glanced over his shoulder and pointed at the casket. "That one was for you, Frank."

Aunt Gertie wiped a tear from her eye as she clapped them off stage. "That was marvelous, gentlemen. Though it's just not the same without Jimmy's tenor, is it? And now, before we finish this part of our program with a prayer, I want to introduce a young lady who would like to share a few words with you all. Tasha?"

I still had the image of some old geezer in red pants working his pelvis burned into my retinas when the girl with the blue-and-orange dress marched down the center aisle and up to the stage, accepting a hug from Aunt Gertie before taking the microphone.

I'd never heard Grandpa Kwirk mention this girl. Not once.

And yet there she was, up on the stage, about to talk. And here *we* were, his son and daughter-in-law and his three grandchildren, sitting in the audience. None of us had been asked to say a few words, and yet this mysterious girl was up there, twisting the mic around in both hands, one foot knocking the toes of the other.

"Sorry. I'm a little nervous," she began. Then she cleared her throat and took a deep breath. "Thanks, Ms. Kwirk, for letting me be up here today. For giving me a chance to share with you . . . with all of you . . . how much Frank means to me. I realize I hadn't known Frank near as long as most of you, but I certainly knew *about* him. The motorcycle guy, I used to call him, because you could hear that big hog of his up and down Main Street every Saturday night. I used to be afraid of that motorcycle, actually. Just the *sound* of it made me shiver. It sounded dangerous. Like if it saw you, it might get a mind of its own and chase you. And the few times I saw its rider, I thought he seemed dangerous too, with his leather jacket and his cowboy boots and that missing tooth of his." She turned and looked at Papa Kwirk's obnoxious drawing, smiling a little. "He was an outlaw. A stranger. And definitely someone I should stay away from. But that was before I got to really know him.

"I didn't meet Frank until a few years ago, when my father had his accident. Most of you know what my dad was going through and how hard it was for him. What you might not know is that it was Frank who came to Dad's rescue. He helped my father recover. To overcome. And in the process, I got to know the dangerous-looking man on the motorcycle. In fact, I even got to ride along."

How could I have never heard about this before? Why hadn't Papa Kwirk mentioned it? I glanced over at my mother, but she was transfixed by the girl with the microphone spilling her guts up on stage.

"It was Frank who sometimes picked me up from dance practice when my mom was at work and Dad couldn't drive," Tasha continued. "Often taking a detour to the Tastee Freez for a chocolate-and-vanilla twist. 'Best of both worlds,' he'd always say."

Several people in the crowd nodded and smiled. Apparently the Tastee Freez was the place to go in Greenburg.

"Some nights he would come over to talk to my dad or to pick him up for a meeting. And when he'd come in, if I was hunched over my homework, Frank would sit down at the table beside me and ask if I needed help. And it seems like I always needed help." The girl paused, glancing over my head, over all of our heads, to the back row. "And I wasn't the only one. I remember one night in particular. Mom was working the late shift and Dad was gone. I was home by myself and someone knocked on the door. I looked through the peephole to see Frank with my father leaning up against him. 'Your daddy slipped,' he said. Frank carried my dad to the bedroom, and I peeked through the doorway as he laid my father down. He took off Dad's shoes and socks, tucking the one inside the other. Then he asked me when my mom was supposed to come home.

"That's the night I learned how to play Texas Hold'em. Betting with goldfish crackers. We played hand after hand until my mother walked in the door around midnight. I remember Frank asking her not to be too mad at my father. And also telling her that she'd better watch out for me, because I had a killer poker face. By the end of the night, all the goldfish were mine, though I suspect Frank was just letting me win."

Tasha paused, licked her lips. She looked like she was about to lose it, but after a deep breath, she regained control and kept going.

"I'm not sure what he means to all of you, but for me Frank Kwirk is all about motorcycles, and twist cones, and going all in, even if it means losing your crackers. And being the kind of guy who remembers to take your shoes off and stays with your scared little girl till midnight so she doesn't have to feel all alone. So I guess I just wanted to say . . . thank you, Frank. Thanks for helping my family. And for being there when it mattered most."

The girl handed the microphone back to Aunt Gertie. She got even more applause than the Salty Shakers. I heard a sniffle and looked over to see my mother tearing up. Dad, however, remained stone-faced, staring at Papa Kwirk's closed casket.

I couldn't even begin to imagine what was going through his head.

"Thank you, Tasha. That was lovely," Aunt Gertie said. "Now I'd like our good friend Pastor Mike to please come up and lead us in Jimmy's favorite prayer."

Finally, I thought, something you'd *expect* at a funeral, a pastor and a prayer—though the man huffing his way up the steps wore a beige wool sweater instead of a cleric's collar or a robe. I didn't know Papa Kwirk prayed that much. Not enough to have a favorite, anyway. I tried to think of the last time I prayed—probably last month when we got our midterm report cards. Somebody out there must have been listening, because I managed to squeeze out a B in social studies and avoid a lecture from my dad on the importance of good grades.

"Let us all bow our heads," Pastor Mike said softly.

The crowd went silent again, and I shut my eyes and tried to imagine God, all blinding halos and shining trumpets and oohing angels—or maybe just something like the aurora borealis—but all I could picture was Papa Kwirk in a too-tight Salty Shakers outfit. Sitting on Jack Nicholson. Eating a twist cone.

Any other time it would have made me laugh.

Five seconds of silence passed before Pastor Mike spoke. What came out next took half as long.

"Good friends. Good treats. Good Lord. Let's eat. Amen."

123

"Amen," the crowd repeated, except for Lyra, who said, "Hallelujah," because two syllables were never enough for her. And then, as if they had heard our collective prayer, the food trucks arrived.

THE BIG SURPRISE

I knew most funerals usually had a vehicle processional: a long black hearse trailed by a line of cars with flags and police motorcycle escorts that everyone was supposed to pull over for. Grief on parade. We'd been part of the one that took Ferran from the church to the cemetery. It stretched for three city blocks.

Papa Kwirk's processional was only three vans long and came *to* us rather than *leading* us somewhere. Instead of black flags, they sported deep fryers and menus plastered beside their windows. There was the Hummus Hut, specializing in pitas and gyros; the Traveling Taco, with its sizzling green and orange peppers painted on the side; and 'Wiches on Wheels, with a picture of an actual witch riding a four-wheeled hoagie instead of a broom. All three pulled up to the curb by the parking lot, and the Traveling Taco started playing music through a speaker on the roof. The spices tickled my nose.

Mom looked bewildered. Not horrified, just confused, as if she'd opened up her beloved Tupperware cabinet to find none of the lids matched the bowls. At a signal from Aunt Gertie, the crowd stood, half of them pouring out the back of the amphitheater toward the parking lot where the triangle of food trucks waited, the other half making a line to tell my family just how wonderful Papa Kwirk's service had been.

"Truly beautiful," a woman introducing herself as Papa Kwirk's one-time physical therapist said.

"Really?" Dad questioned, his voice catching, no doubt thinking of so many other words he would have used. The vein on his forehead continued to pulse.

"Your father sure knows how to make an exit," one of Grandpa's old war buddies told us. "Been to a lot a these, but I don't think I'll ever forget this one."

"And how could you?" Dad mumbled.

"Frank would have loved this," the lead singer of the Salty Shakers said, also shaking Dad's hand. Dad just nodded, then asked the man how long they'd been singing together. "Oh, about six years or so."

"Six years," Dad muttered.

They all seemed to say the same thing: that this was just what my grandfather would have wanted. And each time they said it, my aunt's smile stretched and my father's frown grew more pronounced, until they looked like those two masks that you see outside theaters. Comedy and tragedy. Finally the second round of handshakes and awkward hugs from strangers who smelled of too much perfume and cologne ended, leaving just our family standing by the stage.

Dad looked like a bundle of firecrackers with all their fuses twisted together, and Aunt Gertie looked like a kid with a book of matches.

Mom turned to my sisters and me; we were standing much closer together than we would have normally. Safety in numbers. "Why don't you guys run and get something to eat? We will join you in a little bit."

My brain did the easy translation: Dad and Aunt Gertie were about to have it out. Mom was going to stick around and referee and make sure no blood was spilled, but just in case things got heated, it might be better if we were off in the distance stuffing our faces with falafel. Cass took Lyra and me by the shoulders and led us toward the parking lot.

"Wow," she said when we were out of our parents' earshot.

"Yeah," I said.

"That was . . ."

"I know."

"Do you think Dad's all right? He looks . . . sweaty," Lyra asked.

My little sister could read at a high school level, but reading *people* was different. Dad's bright red face, stiff jaw, and grinding teeth were hard to miss, though. I tried to pinpoint exactly which part of the memorial service might have fried his circuits. "Maybe it was a little *too* fun," I guessed. "A little too much Elvis." I could just hear Papa Kwirk's voice inside my head. *Blasphemy, boy. There's no such thing.*

"It wouldn't have mattered," Cass said. "Dad doesn't agree with anything grandpa does. Or did," Cass corrected. "He wouldn't have liked it no matter what."

I didn't know if that was true or not. Maybe Cass knew more about it than me. Add it to the list of things she was better versed in, along with snooty French fencing terms and the words to all the songs from both *Annie* and *Annie Get Your Gun* (which, I've been informed, is not the action-packed sequel).

"I actually liked the singing," Lyra said. "It was mellifluous." I assumed that meant "appealing to old people."

We hit the food-truck lines and went our separate ways, Cass to the sandwich shop because she had a thing for witches and Lyra to the hut for a gyro. I went for a burrito, though I wasn't really hungry. I just didn't want to be left standing there with nothing to do. Not while everyone else seemed to be having such a good time.

And people really seemed to be having a good time. Everyone around me was talking and laughing and hugging and stuffing their faces. My grandfather's memorial service rocked harder than my last birthday party at the Roller Cave, and my parents had even splurged on the unlimited slushy bar. Part of me wanted to scream, "What is *wrong* with you people? Didn't you see the casket on the stage? Don't you even know why we're here?"

But I didn't. Instead I got in line and waited. That's when I felt a tap on my shoulder.

"Decided to go with the Traveling Taco too?"

I turned to see the girl who had spoken so movingly of Papa Kwirk, standing in line right behind me. My brain instantly went mushy. "Tacos good," I said, sounding like Frankenstein's monster.

Tasha Meeks smiled her aquamarine smile. She was flanked by a woman in a dark gray dress and a man wearing a navy suit, his hair buzzed close to the scalp. "These are my parents. Parents, this is Frank's grandson, Ryan."

"Ryan," Mrs. Meeks repeated.

"Yeah, but it's spelled I-O-N," I said, though I'm not sure why. "You know. Like the word 'ion.'" Tasha gave me a funny look, and the part of my brain that processes regret cursed the part that just says stuff impulsively. She probably thought I was a moron.

Mr. Meeks swallowed up my hand in his. He had a big smile, but not a flashy one. Just the warm, welcoming kind. "But it's actually Orion. Like the hunter," he said. "I know because your grandpa used to talk about you kids all the time. He called you his bright and shining stars."

Bright and shining stars? Really? I'd never once heard Papa Kwirk call us that. He called us lots of things when he came to visit: *Where are the little vermin? Where are the little brats?* He was only kidding. At least I always told myself he was only kidding. But bright and shining stars? That sounded more like something my parents would say.

Mr. Meeks's shadow loomed over me. He stood at least a foot taller than Tasha's mom, with a broad chest and big hands that rested on his daughter's shoulders. I could see scars all along those hands, woven in between his fingers, working their way up his wrists and disappearing into his suit cuffs. I thought about the accident that Tasha had mentioned, but this didn't seem to be the time or place to ask. Not while standing in line for a taco.

"Frank was a good friend of ours," Mr. Meeks continued. "If it weren't for him, I'm not even sure I'd be here today. He was quite a character."

I nodded. Papa Kwirk's arms had been decorated with lots of scars too, though his were all from the war. I used to point and ask about them, but he said he couldn't remember where they all came from. "Shrapnel," he'd say, then add, "probably." Mr. Meeks was way too young to have served in Vietnam, though. He was around my father's age. "You knew my grandpa a long time?" I asked.

"Not as long as I would have liked," Mr. Meeks said. Tasha took her father's scarred hands in hers.

I knew him all my life, I almost said, *and it still wasn't enough.* I was about to ask how Mr. Meeks and my grandfather met when another voice spun me back around.

"What can I get for you?" The lady at the window smiled down at me. "Everything's on the house—in honor of the dear departed," she added, as if she had known Papa Kwirk too. "The special today is Frankly Loaded Fish Tacos. Comes with just about every topping imaginable."

Frankly loaded—it seemed wrong to order anything else. Besides, I wasn't sure I was going to eat it anyway. I thanked the lady, who handed me two soft tacos wrapped in foil. As I stepped out of line, Tasha said, "Nice to meet you, Rion Spelled Like Ion. Maybe I'll run into you again sometime."

"I'd like that," I managed to spit out, though I seriously doubted it. After today, I imagined Dad would be ready to get back home as soon as possible, maybe never to return.

I wandered and wove until I spotted the rest of my family gathered by the Hummus Hut. It didn't look like either of my parents were eating, but Aunt Gertie had no such reservations. "This tabbouleh is delicious, isn't it, Lyra?" she said, shoveling something green and healthy looking out of a bowl.

"Scrumptious," Lyra said.

I unwrapped my tacos and offered one of them to Dad. He just shook his head. He looked like he'd cooled off a little. He'd stopped vibrating, at least.

"Jimmy loved these guys," Aunt Gertie said, pointing at her Styrofoam container. "He loved all kinds of food. Greek. Thai. Mexican. Though he said you could never go wrong with a big greasy burger."

"No beer truck, though," Dad muttered, side-eyeing Aunt Gertie. Clearly they hadn't fully worked things out while I was gone. "I figured one of those would have led the pack."

Beer at a funeral? No stranger than tacos and tabbouleh, I

suppose. It looked like maybe Dad could use a beer. Except my father never drank. Not that I'd ever seen, anyway.

"Well, that just goes to show what *you* know, Fletcher Kwirk," Aunt Gertie replied. Then she spotted something on the hill behind the amphitheater and looked at her watch. "Aha. Right on time."

"Right on time for what?" my mother asked.

In response, a deep boom echoed across the park. Not an explosion—though at this point that might not have surprised me—but the echoing sound of a big bass drum. We all turned to see a marching band come into view, cresting the hill and winding its way around the playground, heading our way.

It wasn't a big outfit—not what you'd see at the Macy's Thanksgiving Day Parade or anything—but they made enough of a ruckus that everyone in the park instantly took notice. The marchers all looked to be about Cass's age, and I wondered if Aunt Gertie had recruited them from the local high school. They wore maroon uniforms with gold tassels and shiny brass buttons. The drum line finished a riff, followed by three shrill whistle blows; then the band launched into a horn-blasting, tree-leaf-shaking version of "When the Saints Go Marching In."

Now, I have seen some odd things growing up in the Kwirk household. I've seen my sister dressed up like Captain Hook, complete with curly mustache, running from a stuffed crocodile. I've seen my father find something lodged between the couch cushions and give it a good sniff before putting it in a petri dish, hoping to later turn it into a piece of candy. I've seen my mother sitting on our roof with her telescope, her waist tied to our chimney with jump ropes because she was afraid of falling off, determined to catch a good glimpse of a comet. But watching those high school kids marching single file up over the hill at my grandfather's memorial service might have topped them all.

"Of course," Dad said as the band made its way around the amphitheater where Papa Kwirk's body was waiting to be laid to rest. "A marching band. Why not?"

Aunt Gertie set her bowl of tabbouleh on the ground and rubbed her hands together as the band circled the amphitheater, blurting and trilling and cymbal crashing their way toward the parking lot where nearly everyone was gathered.

I'm pretty sure that what came out of her mouth next had never been uttered at a funeral before.

"Conga line!"

She danced up to the band and put her sixty-seven-year-old hands on the sixteen-year-old bass drummer's hips. And like the rats of Hamelin, the crowd of people who had come to say goodbye to Papa Kwirk joined in right behind her.

Strangely, it was at that moment that the sun started to break through the clouds.

★ ★ ★

After their fifth song, something called "Louie Louie" that nobody really knew the words to but sang along with anyway, the high school band marched back over the hill and everyone cheered.

Or almost everyone. My sisters and I followed Dad's cue and stayed out of the dancing, despite my great-aunt's attempts to wave us in. Then, when the band had finally disappeared, Aunt Gertie borrowed the sound system on the Hummus Hut to thank everyone for coming. "Show's over, folks. May peace and happiness be with you."

That was it. The last hurrah. No more encores. Papa Kwirk, it seemed, was all out of surprises. The remaining crowd gathered with the Kwirks at its core, as everyone who had introduced themselves earlier felt the need to pay their respects one last time, talking as if they'd just finished a dinner party. Except this time they directed most of their comments at Aunt Gertie.

"It was splendid, Gertrude. Really."

"Frank would have been so happy to see this."

"The food was fantastic. Do you think the Hummus Hut does birthday parties?"

Admittedly, the food *was* pretty good. Midway through the marching band's rendition of "Every Teardrop Is a Waterfall," the smell of queso and roasted peppers got the better of me and I dug into my Frankly Loadeds. Even lukewarm, they were delicious, and I ended up scarfing down the pair, wiping my greasy hands on my itchy pants. Dad didn't know what he was missing, but I wasn't about to tell him that.

By the time everyone shuffled off to their cars and the food trucks closed their canopies and pulled away, it was late afternoon. The white folding chairs down in the amphitheater were empty. The cardboard trash bins overflowed. The kids on the playground had departed with the band, leaving only us Kwirks in the park—the seven of us, if you included Papa Kwirk, with his melon head and too-big ears looking over all of us from his easel.

The sudden quiet was a relief. I slumped into one of the front-row chairs, my shoulders sagging. All I'd done was stand and shake hands and listen to total strangers describe my own grandfather as if I'd never met the man before, and yet I was exhausted. I could tell Dad felt the same. It must have been harder on him than any of us. The Frank Kwirk he knew obviously wasn't the same Frank Kwirk everyone else seemed to remember. Frank the friend. Frank the war buddy. The gambler. The cat rescuer. The Salty Shaker. But only one person really knew the kind of father he was.

It still nagged me that I never cried. At my own grandfather's funeral. But hadn't Aunt Gertie said that was the point? She'd honored Papa Kwirk's last wishes. And we'd honored him by being here. By eating a taco in his name. Now, finally, we could go home.

Dad stood by the foot of the stage, staring up at the distorted sketch of his father. His eyes narrowed behind his glasses and his forehead wrinkled.

I'd seen that look before, mostly as he chewed over something—literally some morsel of food, trying to isolate each and every molecule of flavor, to reduce it to its basic chemical components so that he could re-create it in the lab later. That's what he did. He analyzed. Broke everything down into bite-sized chunks and then scrutinized them, because, I guess, that's the only way he could really understand them. His features softened as he seemed to come to some conclusion; then I watched as he started up the stairs to the stage, hands tucked into his pockets.

"Where are you going?" Mom called after him.

"To say goodbye," he said. "For real this time."

"Here we go," Aunt Gertie whispered under her breath.

I didn't like the sound of that. I felt my own body tense, every muscle from my ears to my ankles. My great-aunt was up to something. There was still one more surprise to come.

"He's my father," Dad continued. "And I'm pretty sure the last words I said to him face-to-face were 'Drive safe.' I don't care if he requested a closed casket or not, I'm going to look at him one last time and tell him how I feel."

Dad bounded up to the stage but hesitated once he stood in front of the casket. I couldn't blame him. It seemed like the whole point of the day wasn't to remind us that Grandpa had died, but just the opposite. Maybe that was the problem. It didn't seem as if Papa Kwirk was gone at all. There had been laughter but hardly any tears, lots of amens but no apologies.

It just didn't feel like things were *over*. Maybe that's what Dad was hoping for. That feeling.

Hesitantly, he lifted the top section of the casket. From where I stood, I didn't have the best view, but I expected to at least catch a glimpse of Papa Kwirk's face peeking out from the box. Dad just stood there, leaning awkwardly, almost as if he was using the lid of the casket to hold himself up.

"Aunt Gertie?" he called down finally.

My great-aunt grinned at us, that same grin your friend gives after they've slipped a thumbtack onto an empty seat and are just waiting for a victim to plop down. She climbed the stairs slowly. The rest of us followed behind, but I didn't even have to get up onto the stage before I realized what my father was looking at.

Rather . . . what he *wasn't* looking at.

That was the thing about Papa Kwirk.

You never knew what was going to be in the box.

My stomach wrenched, and I thought for a moment that I might unload my Frankly Loaded tacos right there on stage.

"Whoa." That was the best my little sister could do. Cass reached out and grabbed hold of Mom's arm. I managed to will my lunch to stay put as I stared at the casket.

The empty casket.

The one hundred percent dead-body-free casket with its quilted inner lining, soft as satin, pristine white. I peered down into the bottom half, irrationally thinking that maybe Papa Kwirk was somehow scrunched down there. Like he was hiding from us.

But he wasn't. Papa Kwirk was just *gone*.

Nobody else said anything at first. Just Lyra's "whoa," which seemed to sum things up. I couldn't begin to say what ran through everyone else's mind, but I suddenly started thinking about a book I'd had to read last year for ELA. *The Adventures of Tom Sawyer*. The book wasn't half as funny as Mr. Bendecker had promised it would be, but I did like the part where Tom attended his own funeral, listening to everyone talk about how the world was an emptier place without him before he showed up with a "Gotcha!" I looked around for some sign of my grandfather, maybe rustling around in one of the oak trees, spying on us with a pair of binoculars, laughing his butt off. "You should have seen your face when you opened that casket," he'd say, but I knew that couldn't be it.

Papa Kwirk was dead. He just wasn't *here*.

Dad's face made the shift from white back to crimson again. "What's going on here, Gertrude? Where's my father? And what is *this*?" He held up a scrap of paper, presumably discovered inside the casket when he opened it. I couldn't tell what was written on it. It was no bigger than the slip you'd find in a fortune cookie, like the ones we'd all read last night. He was waving it in front of Aunt Gertie's face, his hand trembling.

She reached up and took his hand in her own, though she made no attempt to take the slip of paper from him. She must have already known what was written there.

"That," Aunt Gertie said, "is part of your father's final wish."

Dad's mouth opened and closed, but no sound came out. Like a ventriloquist, Mom had to speak for him.

"Gertie, I think what Fletcher is trying to say is—where is Frank's body?"

Aunt Gertie shrugged. Then she pointed to the piece of paper in Dad's hand. The rest of us craned our necks to look over his shoulder as he held it up.

There was only one sentence, written in black ink.

TO FIND ME, START DIGGING IN OUR FAVORITE SPOT.

ASHES TO ASHES, AND LIGHTNING OUT OF THEIR BUTTS

I looked around for clowns, hidden cameras, but there was nothing. Just an empty casket. And a note from my late grandfather telling us where to dig.

This was the grand finale. The moment where the magician, locked in chains and submerged in a tank of ice-cold water, has surely been under too long . . . and then the black cloth drops to the floor to reveal the empty chamber, the picked locks and coiled chains in a pile at the bottom, the magician gone, and the audience left flabbergasted.

"Seriously?" I shouted, my voice carrying through the amphitheater. "This freakin' family can't even *die* normally!"

My sisters both gave me dirty looks. I didn't really mean to shout it. It just kind of slipped out. It was the kind of thing that should have gotten me in trouble, except my parents were too focused on Aunt Gertie, waiting for an explanation. "Why is Frank's casket empty?" my mother wanted to know.

"Well, for one, it's not really his casket," she said. "We're just borrowing it."

Even my aunt's explanation required explanation.

"Borrowing it? From *who*?" Dad asked.

"From whom," Lyra corrected. I kicked the back of my little sister's shoe. Now was not the time for Lyra Kwirk, Grammar Police. Now might, in fact, be the time for the *real* police. There was a body missing, after all. But not missing, exactly. Just not where it was expected to be.

"It belongs to the Danfields," Aunt Gertie told us, referring to the casket. "Friends of a friend. Their great-grandmother passed away last week, but the service isn't until tomorrow, so I borrowed it to use as a kind of centerpiece. I thought the stage would look too empty without it." Cass nodded as if this somehow made sense to her. It was a matter of stagecraft, apparently.

"Oh my god," Mom said, sounding horrified. "I think I met the Danfields. They were standing right here. *I shook their hands.*"

"Yes, well, you probably should have thanked them for lending us this casket," Aunt Gertie said, "Except, of course, you didn't know."

"*Know?* How could we have *known*? You didn't tell us!" Dad shouted.

"I didn't tell you because it's supposed to be a surprise. So . . . surprise!" Aunt Gertie opened her eyes wide as they would go and shook her hands. Just like Chuckles McLaughsalot, only less funny, if that was even possible.

"What is going on?" Dad blurted. "How did . . . why did . . . what kind of . . ."

Aunt Gertie put a finger to Dad's lips as if he was a three-year-old at the library who needed to be hushed. "I think we should probably wait and have the rest of this conversation back at the house," she said calmly. "I only have the space rented till four, and it looks like it's time to pack up."

She pointed to the parking lot, where a hearse from Reynolds's Funeral Services had pulled up. It was strange, seeing a hearse parked where the food trucks had been only moments before. Then I had to remind myself that the food trucks were the ones out of place. Everything was getting mixed up in my head. I watched as two large men got out of the hearse and started toward us.

It appeared the Danfields wanted their casket back.

The drive back to Aunt Gertie's was quiet as a cemetery.

Cemetery. Noun. That place you go to bury a dead body. That is, if you *had* a dead body. And a casket to bury it in. But we had neither. Not anymore.

What we had was a slip of paper with one sentence scrawled on it and an aunt who refused to say anything more until she was "back at home and finally out of these heels and pantyhose." The only break in the silence was the sound of the turn signal, like a mechanical heartbeat, and my father softly humming the theme to *DuckTales*. It was the show he and Grandma

Shelley would watch together every day after school, he told me once. It was their favorite.

When we finally got back to the house, Aunt Gertie didn't get out of her pantyhose. She had barely managed to slip off the heels before my parents cornered her in the kitchen.

"How could you do this?" Dad fumed. "Is this some kind of sick joke?"

"My job as the executor of your father's will is to carry out his last wishes," Aunt Gertie said evenly, refusing to match my father's pitch. "And this is what he wanted." She pointed at the slip of paper in Dad's hand, the one he hadn't let go of since he'd found it. "He wants you to go and find him, Fletcher."

"I shouldn't have to *find* him! He's dead!" Dad shouted. "He should have been in that casket. *A* casket. His *own* casket," Dad corrected, remembering ours had been a loaner. "For god's sake, Gertrude, my mother's buried in a graveyard less than ten miles from here. Why couldn't we have just put him next to her? He was a war veteran. He probably could have gotten a free military funeral somewhere. Instead you're telling me he wanted *this*?"

"That's what's in his will," Aunt Gertie said.

"Then let me see his will," Dad demanded.

"I can't do that either. The will states that you're not allowed to *see* the will until you've found your father."

I shook my head, dizzy from my aunt's convoluted logic. The *fun*neral was one thing, but this was a whole new level of bizarre. In death, my grandfather had out-Kwirked us all.

Dad threw up his hands. "This is insane. Somebody please tell her this is insane?"

I was more than willing to back Dad up on this one, but Cass beat me to it. "Wait, so you're saying Grandpa's body is *hidden* somewhere?" she asked. "And we have to go dig it up like some kind of buried *treasure*?"

"That's one way to think about it," Aunt Gertie said.

Lyra's eyes got googly. "That's actually kinda cool."

"There's nothing *cool* about it," Dad snapped. "It's demented."

"It's totally demented," I agreed. *And also a little cool,* I thought. In a demented sort of way.

"Can you even do that?" Mom asked. "Hide a dead body somewhere? Aren't there laws against that sort of thing?"

"Well, it's not his *whole* body," Aunt Gertie clarified.

My mother let out a startled-mouse squeak. Dad's jaw dropped.

"Wait a minute, you mean you cut Papa Kwirk into pieces and buried them somewhere?" Lyra exclaimed. "That's so *macabre.*"

"Oh, heavens no!" Aunt Gertie said, staring at my little sister, appalled. "I had him cremated."

I didn't know what "ma-cob" meant, but I knew what it meant to be cremated. Ashes to ashes. Dust to dust. It meant we actually needed an urn instead of a casket. Though apparently we didn't have either. Unless the Danfields had an urn they could lend us too.

"It was also part of his last wishes," Aunt Gertie added.

"Outlined in his will."

"The will that you're not allowed to show us," Dad muttered. "Well, we'll see about that."

Like a spinning top, Dad started whirling wildly around the kitchen, opening drawers and then banging them closed, throwing opening cabinets, rifling through papers. "It's around here somewhere. I know it."

"You'll never find it," Aunt Gertie said. "Not until you find him. That's the deal."

"What deal? There is no *deal*. This isn't a game, Gertie. This is my father we're talking about. You're telling me Frank's ashes are buried somewhere and we are supposed to go and *dig them up*?"

"Kind of defeats the purpose," Cass said.

"Totally superfluous," I said. Lyra gave me a thumbs-up.

Aunt Gertie stood on the opposite side of the room from the rest of us, watching my father spin around aimlessly, her expression unreadable, a poker face that Papa Kwirk would have appreciated.

My mother tried to reason with her. "Gertrude, I know you're only trying to do what you think is best and to honor Frank's wishes. And I think the service today, while unconventional—"

Dad snorted. Apparently not the word he would have used.

"While *unconventional*," Mom repeated, "was still very touching and in keeping with Frank's spirit. But really, don't you think it would be best for everyone if you just told us where he is so we can make arrangements to scatter his ashes somewhere appropriate?"

"Well, it would certainly make it *easier,*" Aunt Gertie admitted. "But Jimmy never believed in doing things the easy way. And this was important to him. I know it was. I know it's what he wanted."

"But he's gone," Dad snapped. "So it really doesn't matter what he wants."

Aunt Gertie returned Dad's chilly stare with one of her own. "I agree with exactly half of that," she said.

Dad ran his fingers through his hair, pacing back and forth through the kitchen like a tiger at the zoo. "You're being unreasonable."

Aunt Gertie shrugged.

"Why can't you just tell us where he is?" Cass asked.

"I'm not permitted," Aunt Gertie replied. "I'm not allowed to help you. That's part of the deal. You have to find him on your own. Like I said, it's all—"

"In the will," Mom finished for her.

"This is unbelievable," Dad muttered. "Absolutely unbelievable. You're almost as bad as he was."

"We all have our own way of saying goodbye, Fletcher. This is his. Take it or leave it." I pictured a young Gertrude Kwirk at the negotiating table in some high-rise New York office, staring down a row of men in dark suits, delivering her final offer, knowing they would buckle and she would get her way. But this was different. She'd been pushing Dad all day with one surprise after another, and she'd finally pushed too hard.

"Then I leave it," he said.

"Fletcher . . ." Mom reached for Dad's hand, but he pulled back, just out of reach.

"No. Not this time. It's always something with that man, Molly. You know that. He never knew when to quit. But I do. I'm done. Tomorrow morning, we are going home." He faced my aunt. "You know where his remains are, Gertie. You can get them and do whatever you want with them. Toss them in the garbage, for all I care." He looked at the rest of us, standing in a line. "Make sure you're packed up tonight. I don't want to stay here another day."

I swallowed hard and nodded alongside my sisters, all of us stricken silent by Dad's sudden outburst.

Aunt Gertie shrugged. "Do what you want, Fletcher Kwirk. But if you run away this time, I think you'll regret it."

If Dad heard her, he didn't respond. He was already on his way upstairs to pack.

Wherever Papa Kwirk was, it might very well be his final resting place.

There was no dinner that night. My stomach was still loaded, and no one else seemed interested in eating. Mom and Dad had shut themselves in the guest bedroom for hours, talking in loud whispers, but not quite loud enough to hear unless you pressed your ear to the bottom of the door, which started to hurt after a minute. Not to mention the risk of being caught if one of them opened it suddenly, so I stopped eavesdropping after a while.

Besides, it didn't take a super sleuth to figure out what they were talking about. It's not every day you open your dead father's casket to discover his body's missing, with only a riddle telling you where to find it.

Aunt Gertie was on the phone in the kitchen, taking calls from people who weren't able to attend the memorial but wanted to offer their condolences. "Oh. It's all right, Martha. Yes, it was quite a large turnout. You should have heard the band. No. Not the Shakers. They were good. But the marching band really whipped the crowd into a frenzy." When she saw me on the stairs, she waved and pointed to the table at a plate of brownies she'd set out: leftovers from 'Wiches on Wheels, according to the little paper sleeves they were wrapped in. I shook my head and went looking for my sisters.

It's not something I make a habit of. In fact, most of the time when Lyra or Cass enters the room, I find some excuse to go into another one. But at this moment, the last thing I wanted to be was alone.

I found them both in the backyard. Lyra was spinning around in the tall grass catching fireflies—of which there seemed to be a blue million, so many that you could put out your hand and have one land right on it. There were some advantages to living out in the country. The woods all around. The chorus of the frogs. That smell—crisp and subtly sweet like a ripe apple. And the sky. You could see the stars better from Aunt

Gertie's backyard than you ever could from ours. You could easily spot yourself in them, if you knew where to look.

"Hi, Ri."

Cass was sitting on the porch with her phone in her hand and Delilah coiled around her neck. I found it strange that she could take the snake outside and it never tried to get away. Maybe my sister's skinny shoulders were more comfortable than they looked. I sat down next to her, but not too close; even though she'd had that python for two years now and I'd never seen it eat anything but dead mice, I wasn't taking any chances. Delilah flicked her tongue at me. I stuck mine out at her.

"I think Dad and Mom are fighting," I said.

"Mom and Dad don't fight," Cass said back. She finished her text and set her phone in her lap so she could look at me. "They debate."

"I think Mom and Dad are debating, then."

"Whether or not to stay and hunt for Grandpa's ashes?"

"I guess," I said. "I really couldn't hear very well. Aunt Gertie has thick doors."

"Wait, you were spying on them? Good thing they didn't catch you. Dad's ticked enough as it is."

It was true. I'd never seen Dad so angry. I'd seen him frustrated or irritated—usually with himself, or something to do with work—but hardly ever mad. I'd never heard him slam a door or stomp up the stairs. He wasn't one of those fathers who shout themselves hoarse. Not until this weekend. Not until he'd found out his father had died.

"He's right, though. It's totally nuts, Grandpa wanting us to find his ashes," I said.

"I don't know," Cass said. "I actually think it's kind of epic. Like some ancient Greek tragedy. Or something out of *Scooby Doo*. 'The Mystery of the Missing Body.'" *Scooby Doo* was one of the theme songs Dad would sing to us sometimes. He would even make the Scooby sounds. *"Heroow, Wraggy!"*

"Too bad we don't have a big blue-and-green van to drive around," I said.

"Or a dog."

"A *talking* dog," I corrected. All we had was a python and a missing ferret. "Did you see the look on Dad's face when the marching band showed up?"

"Or how about when those old guys came onstage to sing? I swear I didn't know about half the stuff I heard today. Did you know Papa Kwirk was part of the volunteer fire department? Or that he saved that guy's life?"

She meant Mr. Meeks. The one with the scars and the daughter with the Hawaiian Punch dress and big brown eyes. "I never heard that story before," I admitted.

"That's because Dad never talked about him," Cass said. "At least not with me. Did he with you?"

I shook my head.

"I don't think that's normal. Do you?"

I almost asked what *she* knew about normal—a girl who sometimes spoke in rhyming couplets and had a crush on an imaginary elf. Instead I got to thinking about Papa Kwirk and how strange the whole day was. Not just because of the empty casket and the Hummus Hut, but because of the feeling I'd started to get. A sense of disappointment. It was sort of what Cass was saying. All the stuff she didn't know. Like my own grandfather was a stranger to me. After listening to everyone else talk about him, the people he'd spent every day with, the people he'd shared most of his life with . . . it felt like he belonged to them. And not to us.

But we were still his family. Just because we only saw him once a year, that didn't change the fact that he was our Papa Kwirk. Imagine if we had been called onstage instead of Tasha Meeks. Instead of the Salty Shakers. What would we have said? What would Dad have said?

What would *I* have said?

I looked at Cass, who was staring up at the stars, chin in her hands. "What do you remember most about him?"

"About Papa Kwirk?"

I nodded. "Yeah. Like, what's the first thing that comes to mind?" I wasn't sure she would even want to answer. My sister and I weren't the share-your-feelings-with-each-other sort, so my question probably took her a little by surprise. Like a lot of things today, I guess.

"I'm not sure," Cass said, mulling it over, the snake still happily curled around her neck. "I do remember this one time—you were still pretty young, and Ly was just a baby. It was Christmas, of course. And he and I were just watching TV in the living room. Papa Kwirk had the remote and was just flipping channels and I kept begging him to put on Sponge-Bob, but he wouldn't do it. And then, finally, he found *The Wizard of Oz*."

Ugh. I hated that movie. The ending was terrible. I mean, water? Really? That's how you kill a witch? Drop a house on her, sure; that will kill just about anybody. But water? You're telling me it never rains in Oz? Where the heck do all the flowers come from? And then to find out it was all just a dream? Lame.

Cass loved it, though—watched it every time it came on.

"It was the scene were Dorothy meets the Scarecrow," she continued. "The Scarecrow started singing, and Papa Kwirk started singing right alongside him. Then he jumped out of his chair and pulled me off the couch and we started dancing together." Cass smiled as she conjured up the memory. "He flung me around the living room, twirled me and flipped me upside down, going on and on about not having a brain. And I remember laughing and screaming so loud that Dad rushed in to see who was being murdered, only to find me giggling at Papa Kwirk, who was doubled over on the couch, trying to catch his breath."

I could totally picture it, my sister dancing with my grandfather. I could picture the look on my father's face as well.

"What about you?" Cass asked. "What's your best memory?"

I didn't even have to think about it: the first time I got to ride in Jack Nicholson. Stuffed down in the sidecar with my bike helmet on and a pair of Dad's lab goggles strapped to my head. We only went around the block—that was all Dad would allow—and no faster than thirty miles an hour, though I think Papa Kwirk clocked over fifty once we were out of Dad's eyeshot.

I'm sure I looked like a total dork with my hands thrust in the air as we whipped around each corner, but I didn't care. And even though I was probably perfectly safe, riding through our empty neighborhood streets, it still *felt* dangerous. Like we were just barely in control and could crash any moment.

"Riding on the motorcycle," I said. "Do you think we will get it? Jack Nicholson, I mean? Do you think Papa Kwirk left it to Dad?"

"Are you kidding?" Cass said. "No way would Mom or Dad let us have a motorcycle. Have you *met* them?"

Point taken. But somebody had to get it. You had to do something with everything that was left behind.

Lyra finally grew tired of her firefly catching and came and sat next to us, shoving herself in between us so that I had to scoot over. "It's too easy. What's the point if they're just going to land right on your hand?"

I thought about what Aunt Gertie had said to Dad right before he stormed upstairs. *Jimmy never believed in doing things the easy way.*

Of course, in some ways, neither did Dad. He never skipped a step. Never cheated or used a hack. Even when he helped with homework—and he *always* wanted to help with homework—he'd ask you to explain your answers rather than just tell you if you were right or not. *It's right,* he'd say. *But what* makes *it right?* That's why I tried to get my homework done before he came home, or just lied and told him I didn't have any. It went faster that way.

"They aren't even flies, you know," Ly added.

"What?" I asked, regretting it instantly. Asking Lyra to explain something was almost as bad as asking Dad.

"Fireflies. They aren't really flies. They're beetles. From the order Coleoptera. If you look at them closely, they look more like ladybugs. That's why 'lightning bugs' is a better name for them, because at least they *are* bugs. And they light up. But then they should be called lighten*ing* bugs, not *light*ning bugs."

Leave it to my nerdy little sister to care about the difference.

"That's funny," Cass said. "'When I was little, I actually thought they made lightning in their bellies. Little storms of it. Like something out of Harry Potter. But then Dad explained that there's no lightning inside them, that's it's all just a chemical reaction, and I was bummed."

"According to Dad, *everything's* a chemical reaction," I said. "But that *would* be cool. If they, like, actually zapped lightning out of their butts." I pictured a swarm of them descending on a city, electrocuting the fleeing masses in their bid to take over the world. "You would think with a name like that, they would at least sting or *something*. They seem so fragile." That was why I didn't like catching them myself; I was always afraid of accidentally smooshing them.

Lyra sighed. "That's how it goes, I guess. Some things you *think* are magical, but then you find out they're just ordinary after all."

"Welcome to the real world," Cass said.

"Yeah. Get used to it," I added.

We got quiet after that. I just sat there on the back porch with my sisters and watched the perfectly ordinary lightning bugs blink on and off like flickering stars. At one point, I noticed Lyra shivering and scooted closer to her until our arms touched.

That night I managed to borrow Aunt Gertie's phone long enough to call Manny. Everyone else was shut in their room, probably packing their bags per Dad's instructions. I would have to do that too—my clothes were strewn across the floor, to make me feel more at home and to help Aunt Gertie in her mission to leave no square foot of carpet exposed—but packing would only take five minutes, and I had a lot to tell my best friend.

"Okay. You're really not going to believe this."

"Is it better than the death clown?" Manny asked. He sounded like maybe I'd woken him up. I wondered if it was an hour later there, then realized it was technically a school night.

"Ever heard of the group the Salty Shakers?"

"Are they like the Red Hot Chili Peppers?"

"Yeah. Pretty much the exact *opposite* of that," I said.

I proceeded to tell him all about Papa Kwirk's funneral. The Shakers. The marching band. The food trucks. And, of course, the empty casket. The only thing I neglected to mention was Tasha, only because I knew he would have too many questions. Like what did she look like, and what did you say to her, and was she like *hot* hot, and speaking of hot, how is your sister? I finished by reciting the clue my grandfather had left behind and explained that his ashes were buried somewhere for us to find.

"Okay. *That's* a little strange."

"A *little*?" I pressed. I really didn't think he was taking this seriously enough.

"Yeah, I mean, who *buries* their ashes? Don't most people scatter them in the ocean or off a cliff or something?"

"You're thinking of *The Big Lebowski*," I told him, remembering one of the eight gazillion not-entirely-age-appropriate movies he and I had watched together in his basement. His parents had Netflix *and* cable and had, thankfully, never figured out how to work the parental safeguards. "I think most people keep them in a vase on the mantel in the living room."

"Right, because that's not creepy either," Manny said. "'Hey, everyone, say hi to Grandpa. That's him in the big metal pot on the coffee table. Try not to spill him.'"

All right. So maybe it was kind of odd keeping your dead relatives' charred remains sitting out as decoration, but it certainly wasn't any stranger than burying them like a chest of gold somewhere and forcing your family to go find them.

"It's called an urn," I said. "And honestly, I don't think it's going to matter. Dad's fed up. We're coming home tomorrow morning. Wherever Grandpa is, I think maybe he's just going to have to stay there." As soon as I said it, I felt a pang of guilt. This was his last wish, after all. And even if he wouldn't know the difference, it still felt like we were letting him down. Not that I had a choice in the matter. This was Dad's call.

Manny was still caught up on Papa Kwirk's empty casket and the clue he left behind. "Oh, man, when I die, I'm totally gonna make my kids do all *kinds* of crazy crap to come find me. Then when they do, I'm gonna have 'em toss my ashes in a volcano."

"Why a volcano?"

"I can't even believe you have to ask that question," Manny said.

Fair enough. Still, I seriously doubted Papa Kwirk's clue would lead us to a volcano. There were no volcanos in Greenburg. But that just made me wonder where they *might* be. After all, he'd passed away only four days ago. That wasn't a lot of time for Aunt Gertie to carry out the requests in his will, which meant he was most likely somewhere here in town. The same town where they both grew up. The same town where my own dad was born and raised.

"Hey. You okay?"

I realized I'd been sitting there with the phone pressed to my sweaty ear, not saying anything. "I guess I just don't get *why*, you know? Why make us go and find him?"

"Maybe he left behind some unfinished business," Manny suggested. "You know how in the movies, ghosts hang around sometimes because they've got some secret to spill? 'I see dead people' and all that? Maybe there's something you gotta do before his spirit can move on to the afterlife."

Great. Just what this family needs—the ghost of our crazy grandfather haunting us.

"Or maybe your grandfather was some kind of super spy, and he's about to lead you to evidence that proves the president is secretly an alien overlord," Manny suggested. "You gotta admit: it would explain some things."

I could maybe picture Papa Kwirk as a super spy, except super spies don't sing tenor in barbershop quartets. More likely Dad was right, and this was just Papa Kwirk getting the last word somehow, one final punchline so he could laugh at us from beyond the grave. So to speak.

"Whatever it is, I don't think I could leave without at least trying to find out," Manny added.

If you run away this time, I think you'll regret it.

"You're starting to sound like my great-aunt," I said. But there had to be a reason. Every riddle has an answer, and somewhere out there, Papa Kwirk was waiting for us to solve his.

Us. Not Larry or Pastor Mike or the mailman or even Tasha Meeks. Everything leading up to the moment Dad opened that casket seemed like it was meant for everyone else, but this . . . this was Kwirk family business. *Immediate* family. This last wish, Papa Kwirk had saved for us to fulfill.

And we were headed home instead.

"Forget the volcano," Manny said, interrupting my train of thought. "They're mostly full of ash anyway, so you'd just be all mixed in with the rest. No, I want my kids to blast my ashes into outer space. They do that now, you know."

"Yeah, I don't think we're going to find Papa Kwirk's ashes in outer space," I told Manny.

As it stood, *we* weren't going to find them at all.

FiSHiNg FOR ANSWERS

My memories of Papa Kwirk are scattered, like the last stray leaves on a tree in winter.

Or a dead person's ashes off a cliff.

They are happy memories, mostly. Snowball fights and dirty jokes. Playing gin rummy at the kitchen table with both of us cheating. Riding in the car with him and Dad, listening to the radio because it filled the quiet space between them. I could probably count the memories on my fingers and toes, but at least I had some, even a few that felt like normal grandfather sorts of things. Like feeling his scratchy beard on my bare neck when he bear-hugged me. Licorice breath and Old Spice cologne. I would always have those to hang on to.

I never even had a chance to know my grandmother, though. Dad says she always wore a hat when she went out. He says she was sort of quiet, like me, but with a laugh that surprised you, like the sound of a bleating goat. Her hands were always in motion; if she wasn't busy with anything else, she would pick up her knitting needles, just so her hands would have something to do. And she made the best homemade biscuits, apparently, which he used to slather in butter and honey both.

I would have liked to meet her. I would have liked to try one of those biscuits.

Dad says almost all of his early childhood memories are of Grandma Shelley, but he keeps most of them locked up.

He was only eleven when she passed away, a week before her very own birthday. One minute she was in the kitchen spreading strawberry jam on toast for Dad's lunch, the next she was lying on the floor—at least that's the story I got.

He was in the backyard hunting butterflies when it happened. Grandma Shelley kept a flower garden there, in the corner by the fence, protected by the shade of an old sycamore tree, with lavender and marigolds and a blueberry bush, all designed to entice the butterflies. Sometimes you could net one if you were quick enough, Dad said, though he never tried to keep them. Always catch and release.

He couldn't remember if he caught one that day or not. He only remembers walking through the patio door and seeing his mother on the kitchen floor, silent and still. He called 911, but the paramedics didn't get there in time; there was nothing they could do.

That's all I know about that day, because it's all either Dad or Grandpa ever said about it. I know a little bit of what happened afterward, though. I know Aunt Gertie flew in from New York and spent a month with them, but the demands of her job soon called her back to the coast, leaving the two boys to fend for themselves. Dad says he wished she would have stayed. That once she left, the house felt too empty, too quiet. But Aunt Gertie didn't move back to Greenburg until after Dad went off to college, and Papa Kwirk never tried to find someone else to fill the half of the bed where Grandma Shelley used to sleep.

Dad, for his part, found Mom. And then they had us. And our house was never quiet.

He says he likes it that way.

I couldn't sleep. Part of it was being in a strange bed with flannel sheets that smelled like Aunt Gertie had used eight gallons of flowery fabric softener. Part of it was the pesky barn owl that hooted every thirty seconds. Mostly, though, it was my revved-up brain recounting the crazy day. I could still hear the Salty Shakers crooning in my head. The saints marching in. Tasha Meeks spelling my name. I kept picturing the look on Dad's face when he opened the casket, Aunt Gertie whispering, *"Here we go."* Mom reaching for Dad's hand and missing.

And the gap-toothed cartoon grin of Papa Kwirk, mocking us all.

What was he thinking?

After an hour of kicking at my comforter, I gave up and

crept downstairs for something to drink. The light in the kitchen was on, which meant somebody else was up. I peeked around the corner, careful to take soft, noiseless steps.

Dad sat at the table, hands clenched into fists, staring into space. His glasses were folded beside him, and the skin under his eyes looked bruised. He was still in the clothes he wore to Grandpa's service, though he had at least taken off the boring tie, which was poking out of his pocket like a snake peeking out of a hole. A chocolate-crumb-covered plate sat in front of him, along with a half glass of milk. The clock on the microwave said it was three thirty.

My first instinct was to turn around, head back up the stairs, and get a drink of water from the bathroom sink. The dad sitting at Aunt Gertie's kitchen table wasn't the put-together one I was used to. This dad looked disheveled, haggard, confused. If I went down there, he would want to talk—he *always* wanted to talk—and I just wasn't sure what I would say to him. What I *could* say to him. I'd never had to comfort my own father before.

I started to retreat, but I must not have been noiseless enough, because he glanced my way.

"Rion?"

Caught. No going back now.

I came down the last two stairs and into the kitchen.

"Hope I didn't wake you," he said, his voice scratchy. "Couldn't sleep."

"Me neither," I said. I pointed to the stack of brownies

sitting in the center of the table, wondering how many he'd already eaten. "Milk and cookies?"

"Something like that," he said.

I went to the fridge and poured a glass for myself. I'd heard once that there was some chemical in milk that could make you tired, but Dad had informed me that you'd have to drink fifty-plus glasses to feel a difference, and then you would probably throw up or have to pee all night. The brownies probably wouldn't do much to make me sleepy either, but that wasn't going to stop me. I was here now. Might as well make the best of it.

I sat next to Dad at the kitchen table, listening to the frog song and cricket accompaniment (and that stupid barn owl solo) coming from Aunt Gertie's backyard. I took a bite of brownie, noted that there were walnuts in it, and promptly put it back on my plate. I'm not fond of nuts.

I waited for Dad to ask me how I was doing. That was how our conversations always started. *How are you feeling? Are you okay? Do you want to talk?* I suppose I could have asked *him* any of these, but that's not how it worked.

Then again, this day hadn't really followed standard protocol.

Dad was tight-lipped, staring at the far wall, where Aunt Gertie had hung a wooden plaque that said *Lord Bless This Mess*, so it took me a little by surprise when he finally spoke. "I didn't even know he could sing," he said.

He was talking about Papa Kwirk and the Salty Shakers. I

didn't know he could sing either, of course. It's not as if we went out caroling when he came to visit. I'd been spared that embarrassment, at least.

"You think that would be something you would know about your own father," Dad continued, "that he dresses up in striped vests and sings Elvis a cappella professionally."

I thought *professionally* was stretching it a little—they were the Salty Shakers, not the Barden Bellas—but I didn't say so. Dad must have sensed my disbelief, though, because he pulled out his phone to show me something. "See? They have a Facebook page and everything. Three hundred and forty-two likes. They're practically famous."

Famous was *really* stretching it. But sure enough, there was a picture of Papa Kwirk standing with the other three Shakers from the service. They were posing outside a nursing home. I'm not sure if they were performing there or if that was where one of them lived—could be both. "They were really good," I said, trying to sound convincing. "I bet Papa Kwirk was really good too."

Dad sighed, and I wondered if I'd said something wrong. "I guess we'll never know."

Something about the way he said it made my chest feel tight. He didn't sound angry or bitter—that uncharacteristic edge he'd had in his voice all through the funeral. He just sounded *defeated*. I'd never seen my father like that.

I glanced over at his plate, spotted with crumbs. Without a word I switched it with my own.

Dad looked at my nibbled brownie as if I'd just performed some fancy sleight of hand, making a partially eaten dessert appear from out of nowhere. Then he looked back at me and smiled.

"Thank you," he said.

"It has nuts," I said, as if I needed an excuse. Dad took a bite from the same end as I had, then let out another huge sigh.

"I don't know, maybe it was *my* fault," he said with his mouth full, chewing slowly. "I mean, I spent more than half of my life ignoring him, avoiding this town, doing my own thing. But the crazy thing is, if he'd just told me, if he'd ever once asked me to come and hear him sing, I would have."

Dad looked at me expectantly and I nodded, though in my head I was counting all the other invitations we'd turned down. Offers to come spend the weekend. To attend the wedding of someone my dad went to high school with. Easter dinners. The Fourth of July. Granted, most of those invites had come from Aunt Gertie, but Dad had still said no, each and every time. Would a Salty Shakers concert have been so different?

Or do you just see things differently when you realize you can't go back and change them?

"I don't know, Rion. I just can't make any sense of it," he said. "I just don't know what he wants from me."

Dad opened the fist not clutching a half-eaten brownie, and I saw, for the first time, the slip of paper he'd been holding. The note from Papa Kwirk's borrowed casket. He'd crumpled it up as if to trash it, but there it was, still in his hand. "I must have looked at it fifty times," he continued. "And every time I think, *No.* It's crazy. It's stupid. If he's already in the ground somewhere, then guess what? That's where he belongs! And I crumple it back up. Then three minutes later, I have to look at it again. It's like getting a song stuck in your head. And I'm afraid if we just up and leave, the song will be stuck there forever."

I think it would drive me crazy. That's what Manny said. I'd been thinking the same thing too. There had to be some reason Papa Kwirk wanted us to find him. And not just us, but Dad in particular. The note had been addressed to him, after all. *Our favorite spot.*

Which was probably why he was sitting down here at three thirty in the morning. The ghost of Papa Kwirk wouldn't leave him alone.

Which meant maybe Dad wasn't quite ready to leave yet, either.

"Can I see it?"

Dad handed me the ball of paper, and I spread it across the table, trying to smooth out the wrinkles. "It says *our* favorite spot, right? So it must be somewhere you visited together. Maybe a bunch of times, just the two of you. Something you two shared."

Dad grunted dismissively. "I'm not sure if you picked up on this, but your grandfather and I didn't share a whole lot. Growing up, we didn't even *eat* together half the time. I'd come home to an empty house and make my own dinner. That was all after your grandmother, of course."

I tried to imagine what that would be like, coming home to nobody. Some days I prayed for an empty house just so I could watch whatever I wanted on the big TV in the family room, but that wasn't the same. Some things that are nice every once in a while are not so great when they're all the time.

Still, there had to be *something*. I thought about all the things Dad and I did together, some with my sisters tagging along, but some just the two of us. The trips to Cincinnati to watch the Reds. Visits to the candy factory to test new products. Games of chess on the back porch. Would any of those qualify as *our* favorite? It would be hard to choose.

I looked at the clue again, getting stuck on the word *our*. "He was your father. You had to do *some* stuff together."

"Honestly, Ri, we didn't have much in common. Pretty much the only thing we *ever* did, just the two of us, was . . ."

Dad paused, a sudden light in his eyes, the same spark I dreaded during those back-porch games of chess when I knew I'd made a huge mistake. He snatched up the clue that I'd spread on the table and held it in front of him, shaking his head. "I'm such an idiot. I can't believe I didn't think of this before."

"You know where it is?" I asked.

Dad nodded, the gleam still in his eye.

"Where Papa Kwirk is buried?" I pressed.

He nodded again. "I think so, at least."

"Is it close?"

"It's close," he said, suddenly breathless. "We could drive there. We could go now. It would only take fifteen minutes."

I looked at the clock. It wasn't even four yet. It was still pitch black outside. Everyone else in the house was asleep. "We could?" I asked, suddenly doubtful.

"We *could*," Dad echoed, his voice also full of *what-if*s and *even-though*s. He raised his eyebrows at me, and it was almost like our roles were reversed, like I was the adult and he was asking *my* permission.

"We could," I repeated.

"Then we should," he said, slapping his hands on the table. It was like a switch had flipped inside him. Dad smiled as he put his glasses back on and pointed to the stairs. "Go wake up the girls and tell them to get dressed. But quietly. I don't want to disturb your mother."

"Wait, what? Why not?" I said, halfway out of my chair.

Dad shook his head. "You know how anxious she gets. She'd try to talk me out of it or convince me to wait. And I'm afraid if I wait, I'll change my mind."

Dad's eyes were huge and wild all of a sudden. I'd seen that look before too, but not on *his* face. It was the same look Papa Kwirk used to get whenever he started up Jack Nicholson, goosing her engine, ready to tear down our street in a cloud of exhaust.

I didn't know my father could get that look.

"And where are we going, exactly?" I asked.

"Home."

"Wait. But I thought . . . I mean you just said . . ."

"Not *our* home," Dad said. "*My* home."

Dad waited until we were all in the Tank before he told us the plan. I sat in the middle row with Lyra, still rubbing my chin from where Cass had "accidentally" slapped me, claiming I interrupted her in the middle of a bad dream. Lyra was much less violent, groaning and calling me a pest—that is, until I told her we were going searching for Grandpa's remains in the middle of the night. Then her eyes lit up just like Dad's.

Dad met us in the driveway holding a shovel he'd taken from Aunt Gertie's shed. He was still wearing his suit, which somehow made him look even more disturbing, like he'd just graduated from grave-robbing school. I'd had trouble recognizing the man sitting slump shouldered at Aunt Gertie's dining-room table binge-eating brownies half an hour ago, but this manic, wild-eyed version of Dad seemed almost as strange. He hurried us into the car, tossing the shovel into the trunk.

"Where are we going?" Cass asked as she buckled into the front seat. She was tallest and oldest, so shotgun was hers for the taking when Mom wasn't around.

"My old backyard," Dad replied.

Meaning the backyard of the house he grew up in. The same house that Papa Kwirk had lived in for over thirty years.

"So you figured out the clue?" Lyra asked. "What was it?"

"Fishing!" Dad said.

"Fishing?" Cass repeated. "But you *hate* fishing. We *never* go fishing."

That wasn't entirely true. I'd been fishing three times in my life, in fact—the three times I was sent to overnight summer camp. But Cass was right—the closest our family ever came to fishing together was going to the seafood buffet and seeing who could eat the most popcorn shrimp.

"That's because it's brain-numbingly boring and I'm terrible at it. But it's still the *one* thing Frank and I did together."

What does it mean that the one thing you remember doing with your father is something you can't stand?

Dad pulled out of Aunt Gertie's driveway slowly, keeping the headlights off. It felt like we were doing something criminal. I slunk down in my seat, though there wasn't a soul outside to see us.

"We used to fish at the pond near the woods behind the old house a few times each summer. Mostly it was terrible, but there was one part of the experience I liked. Well, two parts, really. The first was the red cream soda. Frank had a cooler, which he said was supposed to be for the fish, but the only thing we ever kept in it was soda and beer."

Dad seemed to lose his train of thought for the moment, pausing at the end of Aunt Gertie's driveway.

"And the second part?" I asked.

Dad looked at me in the rearview mirror and smiled. "The worms."

Worms. Something that fishing and dead bodies have in common, at least.

The Tank crept slowly along the dark dirt road. Once we were far enough from the house, Dad flipped on the lights so we could see where we were going. The trees outside my window looked ominous at four in the morning, shadowy and huge, with limbs like reaching claws. I was starting to doubt the decision not to wake up Mom.

"Frank said we had to get at least ten fat worms before we could go. And for some reason I loved hunting for them, sifting the soil through my fingers, putting them in the jar. And there was one spot that was better for digging than all the others. Underneath the rocks in your grandmother's garden."

"Your favorite," Cass whispered. Dad nodded.

"Hold on," I said. "You think Papa Kwirk had Aunt Gertie bury his ashes in your old *backyard*?"

"Makes sense, doesn't it?" Dad prodded.

"Not really," I said. None of this made any sense. Assuming he was right, why not just leave Papa Kwirk's ashes there? The backyard of his former family home seemed as good a place as any. Why go dig them right back up again?

"Wait a minute, doesn't somebody else live in that house now?" Cass asked.

Dad nodded again.

"Do you know them?"

"Nope," he said.

"And you're just going to take that shovel and start digging

172

up their backyard? In the middle of the night? Wearing a suit?"

"That's the plan."

"Okay," Cass said with a shrug. Dad reached over and gave her a pat on the knee.

"How in the world is this okay?" I asked.

"Don't worry," Dad said. "Nobody will be able to see us. We still have a couple of hours until sunrise. Though unfortunately, Aunt Gertie only had one shovel."

"If you've only got one shovel, what do you need us for?" Lyra wanted to know.

Dad glanced at us in the rearview mirror.

"Lookouts," he said.

That didn't make me feel any better.

"This *totally* seems like something Papa Kwirk would have done," Cass said.

That didn't make me feel any better either.

LiKE ASSASSiNS iN THE STiLL OF THE NiGHT

Papa Kwirk had sold the house four years ago. The same one my father was driving us to in the wee hours of the morning with a shovel in the trunk.

We only heard about it after the fact. That's how it was with Papa Kwirk. One surprise after another.

I had never been there, to the old house. When we'd come to visit, we'd stayed with Aunt Gertie, despite my mother's suggestion that we could just get a tidy hotel room instead. We never stayed in the house where my father grew up because he didn't want to. Too many memories. He never actually *said* that, not to me, anyway; that's just what I figured out.

And yet, when he heard that Papa Kwirk had sold the old house, Dad was furious. It was one of the few times I'd heard him yell. I'd seen Dad angry at my grandfather before, but it was always a teeth-grinding, sulk-in-a-chair kind of mad.

Quiet and contained. The day he found about the house was unforgettable.

It was also Thanksgiving.

Papa Kwirk and Aunt Gertie decided to make their annual visit early that year because they were taking a cruise together over Christmas to the Bahamas (another benefit of big-city lawyering). It was an odd Thanksgiving from the start. It was unusually cold, even for November, a feed-the-fireplace *and* run-the-heater kind of cold. Mom was making veggie lasagna instead of turkey because my then-twelve-year-old older sister had sworn off meat, which meant the rest of us had to suffer. There wasn't even a fried-chicken-flavored jelly bean to be had.

It was almost as cold inside the house as out. Grandpa had only been there a few hours, but I could tell he was already getting on Dad's nerves, the two of them room hopping so that they wouldn't have to share the same space. When one was in the family room, the other would hang out in the kitchen. Front porch and backyard. They watched the parade on two different TVs. But we only have the one dining room. They sat at opposite ends of the table, but it was still too close.

It was while he was spooning up some mashed potatoes (to complement the Thanksgiving pasta, of course) that Papa Kwirk let it slip that he'd sold the family home.

"You did *what*?" A limp bit of lasagna hung from Dad's fork, halfway to his mouth.

"Yep," Papa Kwirk said, snapping his fingers. "Went just like that. Made a good chunk o' change from it."

"You sold the *house*?" Dad repeated in disbelief.

Papa Kwirk shrugged. "Sure did. Just felt like the time was right, you know? Turkey is delicious, by the way," he said to my mother.

"I didn't make any turkey," Mom said, obviously taken off guard.

"I know," Papa Kwirk said, giving my twelve-year-old vegetarian sister a wink.

Dad was not amused. "Are you kidding me? That's my house!"

"Actually, *this* is your house," Papa Kwirk said, indicating the cream-colored walls of our dining room. "And it's a very nice house. You should be very proud. *That* house, on the other hand, was *my* house. It was in *my* name. I paid for it with *my* money. And now it belongs to the Burbages. Bursages?"

"Burgesses," Aunt Gertie said.

"Bur-somethings," Papa Kwirk concluded. The fact that he couldn't even remember who he'd sold it to just seemed to make Dad even angrier.

"How could you do that?"

"Honestly, Fletcher," Aunt Gertie interjected. "That house was too big for Jimmy all by himself. He found a nice condo in a little community only twenty minutes down the road from me. They mow the lawn for you and everything. It's perfect."

My father, the man who said "dagnabbit" or "holy Toledo" whenever he stubbed his toe, uttered a curse and started jabbing at his asparagus with his fork. He didn't seem interested in eating it, just stabbing it repeatedly. "When did this happen?"

"About two months ago," Papa Kwirk said.

"Two *months*! And you didn't tell me?"

"Like I said," Papa Kwirk replied calmly. "Not your house."

"But it's the house I grew up in! It's the house Mom—" Dad stopped abruptly and pointed his mutilated, speared asparagus at Papa Kwirk.

"You don't need to remind me about your mother," Papa Kwirk said, setting down his glass of ginger ale and leveling my father with a stern look. "If I'd thought you wanted it, I would've asked. But you hightailed it out of there the first chance you got and hardly ever came back, so what does it matter? Or were you thinking about moving back to Greenburg to be closer to us?"

Dad and Papa Kwirk glared at each other across the table. You could hear the football game playing on the TV in the other room. The Lions were getting creamed.

"That's enough," Aunt Gertie huffed. "You boys need to stop. You're going to ruin Thanksgiving."

But it was too late.

I sat between them—my sulking father and my stone-eyed grandfather—and quietly ate my yucky vegetarian lasagna, wishing it was turkey, wishing Thanksgiving dinner was over already, part of me even wishing that Papa Kwirk had just skipped this year's visit altogether.

And wondering, If Dad cared so much about that old house, how come I'd never even seen it?

Mom said she was going to hop into the kitchen real quick to check on dessert.

All three Kwirk kids decided to go help her.

I was finally going to see my father's old house. My palms were sweaty, even though it was cool in the car. I sat in the back, mentally outlining all the potential problems with Dad's plan. One being that the aforementioned "favorite spot" might not be there anymore. The current owners—the Bursomethings—could have redecorated, maybe moved the rocks around. There might not be an X marking the spot. All we had to go on was Dad's memory from childhood. And this was provided we even had the right answer to the riddle to begin with.

Add to this some other concerns, which I pointed out in as sensible a voice as I could manage.

Like "Isn't this trespassing?"

And "Don't you think it's going to look a little suspicious, the four of us sneaking around in some stranger's backyard, carrying a shovel?"

And "We are still out in the country. Don't people out in the country usually have guard dogs? And shotguns?"

And "Have you ever seen the movie *The Texas Chainsaw*

Massacre?" Though this was Illinois, not Texas. And the Bur-somethings probably weren't power-tool-toting cannibal murderers. But how could you be sure?

My concerns about shotguns and chainsaw-wielding psychopaths were met with more mumbled assurances from Dad. "It's all right. We'll sneak through the woods and slip through the back gate under cover of darkness," he said.

"Like a band of Zendali assassins!" Cass added, clearly feeding off Dad's strange newfound enthusiasm.

Yeah. Or like a quartet of trespassing, hole-digging wackos, I thought.

Dad shut off the lights again when he turned down his old road and parked in the grass, far away from any of the street-lamps. You could see the shadowy outlines of houses behind the rows of trees.

"I used to spend hours in these woods as a kid. I know them like I know the chemical composition of isoamyl acetate," Dad said.

"Oh, well in *that* case," I muttered.

Dad took the shovel from the trunk and led us, single file, to the edge of the woods. The same kind of woods where the bodies of kids who have been missing always turn up six weeks later. The kind of woods that, in the afternoon, would probably appear tranquil and inviting, but in the early hours of morning looked like the setting for a scene from *Slayaway Camp Seven.*

I felt the need to casually mention this, but Dad marched

right into them, shovel bouncing on his shoulder like he was one of the seven dwarfs headed to the mine. *Heigh-ho. Heigh-ho. It's off to dig up our grandfather's dead body we go.* "I told you. There's really nothing to worry about," he said. "Now, from here on out, try to use hand signals when possible and talk only when necessary."

I wondered what the hand signal for "This is stupid" was. I settled for circling my finger around my ear. The cricket chirps that had seemingly followed us all the way from Aunt Gertie's were loud enough to mask our footsteps, but I still watched every footfall, looking for roots that might trip me. Lyra walked behind me, pushing on me to hurry. I heard something skitter off to my right and wondered what kinds of animals hung out in these woods at night. Raccoons and opossums. Maybe a fox. Cougars? Were there cougars in Illinois? Whatever was out there, it probably had rabies.

"We're almost there," Dad whispered.

The trees thinned as we came to a line of gray picket fences, almost as tall as me. I remembered Aunt Gertie's story—the one about Papa Kwirk and Grandma Shelley's third date. How he barely made it back over that amusement-park fence before getting eaten alive by dogs. The crazy things we do for love. Except the fence we were facing had a gate. And the gate was hanging wide open.

Almost as if we'd been invited.

Dad walked through first and the rest of us followed, though we nearly crashed into each other when he stopped abruptly.

An image of an ax-toting serial killer riding on the back of a giant, rabid Rottweiler popped into my head, but it was just Dad pausing to take in his old backyard for the first time in ages.

He drew a deep breath, as if he could inhale the whole of it, the scent of every flower, every tree, every stem of grass. Smell and memory are deeply connected—Dad explained it all to me once in tedious detail: how a particular aroma could trigger all kinds of intense emotions, even flashbacks. I wondered if they were good memories or bad ones racing through Dad's brain. It was too dark for me to see his face, but I thought I heard him sniff. "It's just the same as I remember," he whispered.

While Dad took in the backyard with its soccer ball and plastic slide, I inspected the windows of the house, making note of the fact that all the lights in it were off. I prayed for them to stay that way.

"Dad?" Cass said, tugging on his arm. "Worms? Shovel? Favorite place?"

"Right," Dad said, and pointed to the back corner of the yard. There was the butterfly garden, pretty much just how he'd described. The sycamore still stood guard over the blueberry bush, which was still a ways from bearing fruit. Everything else was just starting to bloom. I tried to imagine it in the daylight, and I could almost picture my grandma Shelley, the woman I'd never met, bent over this patch of flowers, pulling weeds. She wore the same dress as she did in the picture on Dad's nightstand, the one of them sitting on the bench together. Her feet were bare and the bottoms were smudged with dirt. I don't know why, but for some reason I imagined her as the kind of woman who liked to be barefoot outside. Just like me.

At the center of the little corner garden stood a round rock just big enough for a boy of ten to sit on, his net draped across his lap, waiting for a butterfly to alight. That was the rock Dad knelt beside now, setting down the shovel and rubbing his hand along the stone's smooth surface. Maybe it was the same rock he'd been sitting on when she collapsed in the kitchen, so long ago.

"Give me hand with this, will you?" he whispered.

Cass and I bent down and dug in with our fingers, helping Dad roll the rock backward, revealing a patch of earth beneath. Even in the darkness I could see things crawling and squirming, taken by surprise by the sudden prickle of cool air. It gave me a shiver. I could see where this would be a nice spot for finding worms, though. I just hoped it was a nice spot for finding dead grandfathers too.

"This is so nefarious," Lyra said softly.

"It's not nefarious," Dad insisted. "We aren't doing anything *bad*. We're just honoring a dead man's wishes. Now hand me that shovel before somebody catches us."

Dad jabbed forcefully into the earth, stomping down with his fancy dress shoes and pulling up a huge clod. "Dirt's loose," he said, forgetting his own rule about talking as little as possible. "Somebody else has been digging here recently."

Dad attacked the ground. This same man who only hours ago had been shouting at us all to pack up so we could go home now grunted as he worked the shovel, wiping his sweat on his shirtsleeve, getting dirt all over his black trousers. Keeping the still-dark house at the corner of my eye, I watched him unearth one shovelful after another, working frantically. The hole he'd made was two feet deep at least— but all we'd found so far were the worms. Maybe Dad had gotten it wrong. Maybe Papa Kwirk had been thinking of something else, another spot, another favorite place. After all, it's not as if the two of them ever agreed on much of anything before.

"Dad. I know you *think* you know what you're doing—" I began, but as soon as I said it, there was a dull metallic clang as the blade struck something hard. Dad handed Cass the shovel, then dropped to his knees and starting digging with his hands.

In moments, those same hands appeared holding a metal tackle box. The kind you would use to hold fishing gear.

We'd found him. We'd found Papa Kwirk.

"I don't believe it!" Cass said, much too loud for any Zendali assassin.

"Is that really Papa Kwirk?" Lyra wondered in a whisper. "It's so *small*."

Dad shushed them both again and pulled his phone from his pants pocket, activating the flashlight. He handed it to me and I cupped my hand around it, focusing the beam on the box, worried that the sudden light might attract the attention of cannibals and cougars alike. With dirt-crusted hands that he'd absentmindedly wiped on his white dress shirt, Dad unfastened the box's latch. *Be careful,* I thought. This wasn't the first box he'd opened on this trip. We'd figured our grandfather was in the last one too.

Dad slowly lifted the lid and peered inside.

Then he let out a gasp loud enough to wake the dead.

"Where's Grandpa?" Lyra asked.

It's the kind of question you ask when you are at the mall, or maybe at the beach, and you notice that a member of your family has disappeared.

It's not normally asked while staring at a steel tackle box that you've just dug out of the ground in someone's else's backyard. I continued to shine the phone on Dad, who was still bent over, staring at the contents of his unearthed treasure and shaking his head.

These weren't the remains of Francis T. Kwirk. And it wasn't old fishing gear either, which would have made even more sense. Instead, the tackle box was filled with cards. Stacks and stacks of cards. Like trading cards, except they weren't of baseball players or Star Wars characters or Pokemon.

They were all of kids. Like, *gross* kids. Cartoon drawings of children oozing pus, or leaking snot, or gushing blood, some with holes in their skin or extra eyeballs or excessively hairy armpits. The one on the very top showed a corpse rising from a grave. Dead Ted. They all had names like that. Stinky Stan and Barfin' Barbara and Patty Putty. Whoever made these cards was a big fan of alliteration. And also demented.

Dad snorted and shook his head, like he couldn't believe his eyes. I didn't blame him.

"What are they?" Cass asked.

"They're Garbage Pail Kids," he answered. "*My* Garbage Pail Kids. My whole collection." He wiped his grubby hands on his shirt again before picking up a handful of cards and shuffling through them. "I assumed they were long gone. Figured he just threw them out. Frank *hated* these cards," Dad muttered.

I could see why: kids being beheaded and electrocuted, covered in spiders or boils or boogers or goo. Some were clever, though, like the picture of the kid in a karate uniform trying to chop a board and shattering his arm instead. His name was Bruised Lee.

I actually kind of liked them.

Dad riffled through cards, pushing them from one side of the tackle box to the other. "This can't be it," he said. He pushed the box into my hands, then bent down for the shovel again. "There has to be something else down there." He drove the blade back into the dirt, sinking it as deep as it would go.

I handed Dad's phone to Lyra and started sifting through the cards myself, skipping past Leaky Lindsay and Fryin' Bryan, digging through the contents of the box as Dad speared the ground. Then I spotted it. Taped to the bottom. A photo, the old Polaroid kind that spit straight out of the camera back in the dark ages. It showed Papa Kwirk and Dad standing by a pond, fishing poles in hand. Dad looked like he couldn't have been more than eight—younger than Lyra, at least. He was holding up a fish no bigger than my hand. On the white border at the bottom, somebody had written names, in all caps, just like on the other cards:

FISHIN' FLETCHER AND FATHER FRANK

"Dad. Look."

Dad left the shovel stuck in the dirt and leaned over my shoulder. Lyra angled the light so we could all see.

"Heavens to Murgatroyd," Dad whispered. He carefully pried the picture free from the bottom of the box, working at the tape with his dirt-crusted fingernails. "I remember taking this picture," he said. "I remember writing our names."

It was a little weird, seeing my father so young. No glasses. No bow ties. No gray hairs. And Papa Kwirk too, without his leather jacket and bushy beard, looking so clean-cut and carefree. I'm not sure I would have recognized them.

"There's something on the back," Lyra piped up.

Dad flipped the photo over to reveal something written in the white space, though it was different handwriting from the names on the front.

"'To find me you'll have to conquer Mount Everest,'" Dad

read aloud. His voice jumped a few decibels, well above a whisper now. "What's *that* supposed to mean?" I put my finger to my lips, to let him know he was being too loud, but it was too late. The light in one of the windows in the second story of the house where my father grew up blinked on.

We all stood there, frozen, waiting for the light to shut back off. For whoever had stumbled out of bed to give up and go back to sleep. But it didn't. Instead, the blinds started to raise.

"Hurry! Fill the hole!" Dad said, reaching for the shovel.

"No time!" Cass hissed. I slammed the lid of the tackle box closed and tucked it beneath my arm. Dad pulled the shovel free. "Go, go, go!" Cass gave me a push toward the gate, where Lyra was somehow already waiting, gesturing frantically for us to hurry, the light from Dad's phone flashing like a beacon. From the now-open window, I could hear a woman's voice shout down at us.

"Who's out there? What are you doing? Get out of our yard!"

What do you think we're trying to do, lady? I thought to myself.

"I've got a gun!" she added.

"See? Told you!" I said to Dad's back as we bolted from the butterfly garden where he used to dig up worms, into the woods where he used to play, stealing back a memory that he'd thought he'd lost and a pail full of garbage-y kids.

A frantic run through the trees and a short getaway drive later, Dad pulled the Tank into the parking lot of a CVS so that we could all have a moment to calm ourselves. Beside me, Lyra was taking long, slow breaths like she did right before each of her turns at the statewide spelling bee. Cass was giggling uncontrollably, her head pressed to the window. I was pretty sure she'd lost it, if she'd even had it to begin with.

Not that I could blame her. My heart was hammering, my shirt was damp, and I had scratches along my arms from the branches I'd scraped against running for my life in the dark. The last time I'd been this keyed up was when I'd prank called Principal Williams to tell him he'd won an award for World's Best Administrator . . . at Farting. Manny still owed me five dollars for that dare.

The good news was that we didn't get shot. The bad news was that we hadn't really gotten what we came for, either. Only a picture of Papa Kwirk—along with pictures of a hundred other kids, leaking various fluids out of their bodies. Grandpa's clue hadn't led us to his remains—just to another clue, which only confused me more. What kind of crazy cigar had he been smoking when he wrote out that will of his? Why couldn't I be part of a family that buried their dead in coffins instead of a family that buried pictures of puking kids in tackle boxes?

And why was my father mumbling the word "Easter" to himself?

"What?" Cass asked, glancing at Dad, her lunatic giggling finally subsiding.

Dad twisted in his seat to face the three of us. His glasses were smudged with dirt, just like his shirt and his pants . . . pretty much all of him was coated. He had a peculiar look on his face. It reminded me of the look Manny got whenever he tried to do subtraction in his head.

"You know how your mom and I hide your Easter baskets every year?" he asked.

We all nodded. Some kids have nice Easter bunnies who leave their baskets on the stairs or by the door. Not the Kwirks. Our Easter bunny was a sadistic prankster who liked to torture us. We had to *hunt* for our baskets, sometimes for hours. They were never just behind the couch or in the closet, either. Once I found my basket in the trunk of the neighbors' car. Considering they were only filled with candy that we could get for free whenever we wanted, the reward hardly seemed worth the effort. But then . . . there was something about the hunt itself that was exciting. The last couple of Easters I'd looked forward to the process of finding the basket more than eating the goodies inside.

"Well, I never told you this, but it's kind of a family tradition," Dad continued. "When I was little, your grandmother used to hide my basket too. But she would give me clues, written on these little scraps of paper, scattered all throughout the house."

"You never give *us* clues," Lyra complained.

"That's because you're smarter than I was," Dad said.

"And you have each other. But it was just me growing up, so Grandma Shelley would give me little riddles and rhymes that had me going from room to room, trying to find the next clue, and the next, until the last one led me to the dryer or the pantry where my basket would be."

"Like a scavenger hunt," Lyra said.

"Or a Dan Brown novel," Cass said. Her English teachers probably adored her.

"Something like that," Dad said. "But then, after your grandmother passed away, the clues stopped. That first Easter without her, my basket was just waiting for me on the kitchen table, and the year after that, there was no basket at all. We just sort of stopped celebrating, I guess."

That was terrible. Suddenly I felt guilty for complaining that my basket only ever held leftover candy from the Kaslan factory. At least I always got a basket, even if sometimes it took an hour to find it.

"Because of that, I always assumed my mother made the clues. That it was all her idea, and that Frank really could care less," Dad mused. "After all, she was the one who did everything with me."

"Not everything," I said, and held out the picture of Fishin' Fletcher showing off his modest catch.

Dad took the photo and stared hard at it in the weak glow of parking-lot lights—not at the clue written on the back, but at the faces on the front. He and his father, huddled together,

Dad looking straight into the camera, Papa Kwirk beaming down at his son.

Papa Kwirk hated those cards, but he held on to them. Dad hated to fish, but still he went.

The picture shook a little, but Dad's jaw tightened. "We can't go home. Not until we find him."

"We'll find him. We will," Cass said, reaching over and putting her hand on Dad's arm. "But first we should get back to Aunt Gertie's before Mom wakes up."

Dad nodded and handed the photo back to me before starting the car. Lyra looked at the back again. "Conquer Mount Everest," she whispered.

That was the next step. The next clue in our hunt for Papa Kwirk. Though I was sure that didn't mean actually climbing the *real* Mount Everest, it still hinted at something daunting. Maybe something even more dangerous than sneaking into a stranger's backyard and putting a hole in their flower garden.

But Cass was right. We needed to get back to the house.

Because my mother could be just as daunting and dangerous if she wanted to be.

ICE CREAM, POOP, WINKY FACE

I've never snuck out of the house before. I've never met a friend for a midnight rendezvous in the park, or had to smuggle a telepathic girl with a buzz cut out of my basement, or run away with a Reese's Pieces–eating alien. But I think I could do it if I had to. The getting out seems like the easy part—there are windows to climb through and trees to shimmy down. It's the getting back *in* that's tricky. Because you don't know what happened while you were away.

For instance, your mother might have woken up to find the other half of the guest bed at your great-aunt's house empty. She might have walked through the cluttered rooms looking for your father, only to find two notes on the kitchen table—the first from your great-aunt, informing everyone that she left early for crack-of-dawn yoga at the Y, and the second from your father, saying that he was running out to get something, that he took the kids, but not to worry, he'd be back soon.

Of course, if your mother is anything like my mother, asking her not to worry is like asking the sun not to rise, which was what it was starting to do when we pulled into Aunt Gertie's driveway and found Mom waiting for us on the porch wearing her nightgown and a face that Lyra was quick to find a word for.

"She looks consternated."

"Ew," I said. "That's disgusting."

"Not *constipated*, you dope, consternated. She looks worried."

"Oh." That I couldn't argue with. Mom was glaring at us through the Tank's windows. I thought I could hear her teeth grinding before I even got out of the car. We made a line, standing like captured soldiers facing the firing squad.

"I can explain," Dad began. This seemed doubtful but certainly worth a try.

Mom just stood there, taking in our muddy shoes, Dad's filthy dress shirt, the scratches down my arms, the leaves in Cass's hair. We looked like we'd just barely escaped from the deepest jungles of the Amazon. "I'm listening," she said. But her arched-eyebrow Medusa's stare must have paralyzed Dad, because he suddenly went mute, so we all jumped to his defense, each of us talking over the others.

"So we figured out the first clue . . ."

". . . came downstairs for a glass of milk . . ."

". . . woke me up and I slapped him, but then . . ."

". . . got in the car and drove . . ."

". . . in his old backyard under this rock . . ."

". . . through the woods by the pond, but the gate was unlocked . . ."

". . . used to dig for worms . . ."

". . . pretty sure they had rabies . . ."

". . . with Aunt Gertie's shovel . . ."

". . . found this box, but it turns out it wasn't Papa Kwirk . . ."

". . . like these cards, with pus, and pimples, and guys with their heads chopped off and brains leaking out all over the place . . ."

". . . this photo of Dad fishing with Grandpa . . ."

". . . and a *second* clue—this one about Mount Everest . . ."

". . . like a scavenger hunt . . . you know . . . on Easter . . . but with a dead body instead of candy . . ."

". . . light came on, and some lady started saying something about having a gun . . ."

". . . might or might not have been a serial killer . . ."

". . . ran as fast as we could back to the car . . ."

". . . and drove back here . . ."

". . . and it was a stupid, stupid, stupid thing to do," Dad finished for us, frowning. "I honestly don't know what came over me. I'm sorry."

"Yeah. Sorry if we worried you, Mom," Cass seconded.

My mother took it all in, judge and jury, dressed in her

floral nightie and flip-flops, listening to the accused desperately plead their case. We dropped our chins and stared at our filthy sneakers.

When she spoke, it was in *that* voice, that chilling robot-mom voice that's somehow even worse than yelling at you because it's dripping with parental disappointment, except her eyes were fixed on Dad this time. "You took the kids?"

"I know," Dad blubbered. "It was dumb. I just thought—"

"You took the kids?" Mom repeated sternly. "*Just* the kids?"

Then it dawned on me. She wasn't angry that we did what we did—okay, she probably was—but the thing that *really* stung was that we'd done it without her.

"I'm sorry, Moll, I just thought . . ."

"You thought I would have said no," Mom finished for him. "That I would have told you it was a terrible idea. That I would have tried to talk you out of it."

Dad nodded. Mom took a deep breath.

"You're right," she said. Then she reached out and took Dad's hand. "But I still would have gone with you. That's how it works, remember? We do it together. All of it."

"In that case," Dad said, smiling sheepishly, "how would you like to climb Mount Everest?"

I knew a few things about Mount Everest. I knew it was the tallest mountain in the world. I knew that it costs a gajillion dollars to climb and that more than three hundred people have died trying, which makes it one of the most expensive ways to kill yourself.

I also knew it was nowhere near Aunt Gertie's house. Eight thousand miles to get over there, plus another dozen death-defying miles by foot to get up. No way Papa Kwirk was on top of the *real* Mount Everest. Which meant it was another riddle. A code that needed to be cracked.

But we were the Kwirks. A father with a PhD in chemistry. A mother who read books on astrophysics. One sister who could recite soliloquies from *Hamlet* and another who knew how to spell the word "soliloquy" when she was six.

And me. I'd seen the movie *Everest* three times. Once in IMAX. That practically made me an expert.

Naturally we started by looking for a Mount Everest equivalent nearby. Trouble was, there are no mountains in Illinois. The highest point in the entire state is really just a mound—Charles Mound—which doesn't sound big or intimidating at all, and Greenburg itself is surrounded by soybean fields, the land flatter than a Coke that's sat open for three days. The closest thing I'd seen to a mountain since I'd been here was the tower of brownies that still sat on Aunt Gertie's kitchen table.

Which was where *we* all sat, trying to decipher Papa Kwirk's second clue. Mom, Dad, and Cass were on their phones. Lyra and I had to make do looking over their shoulders, telling them which links to click on. I looked over Mom's, because Cass had Delilah wrapped around her neck again. Apparently with Aunt Gertie off at yoga, the no-pythons-in-the-house rule didn't apply.

There was an Illinois Mountain, but it was in New York. There was a Mount Saint Mary's Catholic school, but Grandpa wasn't Catholic. There was nobody with last name of Everest in the Greenburg phone directory. There was an Everitt and an Everset, but neither of them had ever heard of Frank Kwirk, and both asked us to never call them again.

After what seemed like hours of fruitless searching, we'd gotten no further than when we started. Dad leaned back in his chair and rubbed his temples. "It's hopeless," he said. "What was the man even thinking?"

Maybe that should be the family motto. *The Kwirks: What Were They Thinking?* I imagined a coat of arms with a big question mark in the middle and the words in Latin circling the outside. Cass could wear it to the next Ren Faire.

"Maybe he's trying to tell us he was eaten by vultures," Lyra suggested.

"Yeah. Because *that* makes sense," I said.

"For your information, it *does* make sense," she shot back. "Mount Everest is on the border of Nepal and Tibet, and Buddhists in Tibet believe that after your soul leaves, your body is just an empty vessel that needs to be returned to the earth. So they chop you into pieces and put you on top of a mountain and the vultures come and eat you. I read about it in *National Geographic*."

"I don't think your aunt fed your grandfather to vultures," Mom said.

"Maybe she ate him herself, then."

We all stared at my little sister this time.

"What? It's called endocannibalism. It's practiced by the Yanomami tribe of South America. Or is it Yamonami?" Lyra's face scrunched, then relaxed. "The point is, when somebody dies, they mix the ash of the dead person up with mashed bananas and eat it. That way the soul of dead person is absorbed by the tribe and is protected from evil spirits."

"You're suggesting we search Aunt Gertie's trash for banana peels?" Cass asked.

My eyes instinctively went to the white plastic garbage can sitting in the corner.

"I really don't think your great-aunt ate your grandfather either," Mom said. "It has to be some kind of metaphor. A challenge. Something *like* climbing Mount Everest. Let's think. What's the hardest thing Frank ever did?"

I tried to remember all the stories that Papa Kwirk used to tell us. Some were about his childhood, growing up poor here in Greenburg. Dumpster diving and sneaking sweets from other people's lunch bags. Putting crawdads in Aunt Gertie's hair for fun. His teenage years, smoking cigarettes and listening to records—back when they were cool the first time (the records, not the cigarettes)—and trying to stay out of trouble at school.

But most of his harrowing stories—or at least the ones I remembered—were about the war. The going *and* coming back. Stories about venomous snakes and booby traps and practical jokes his fellow soldiers would play on each other. His favorite story—the one I heard the most—was about the night his unit got pinned down in the boonies. They were taking fire, finding cover wherever they could, when an artillery shell landed right next to him, practically in his lap. Turned out it was a dud; otherwise there'd be no story to tell. It just proved how lucky he was. "That was as close as I ever came to fillin' my britches," Papa Kwirk said, which was always the point when Mom declared story time over and tried to change the subject.

I wasn't sure what any of that could possibly have to do with Mount Everest.

Dad had an answer, though. And it had nothing to do with the war.

"It was me," he said. He put down his phone and rubbed his eyes. "Frank once said that the hardest thing he'd ever done was raising me."

"He actually *said* that?" I asked. Even if it was true, it wasn't the kind of thing either of our parents would ever admit. I could picture Papa Kwirk saying it, though. *Getting shot at in the middle of a booby-trapped, bug-infested jungle on the other side of the world is hard, Rion, but it's nothing compared to raising a kid.*

"I'm sure he didn't mean it," Mom added.

"No. I'm pretty sure he did. Though I can't imagine how hard it could have been. I pretty much raised myself after Mom died."

"But if you're Mount Everest, then where's Papa Kwirk?" Lyra asked.

We were stuck again. Mom and Cass went back to their phones. I grabbed the tackle box full of Garbage Pail Kids and sat on the floor, spreading them out. Maybe Brainy Janie or Drippy Dan could help us.

As I looked over the cards, I thought about how certain things run in families. How they get passed down. Like, I'm pretty sure Lyra inherited Dad's analytical brain. And Cass obviously inherited Mom's tendency to see every choice as a matter of life or death. And I'm pretty sure I inherited Papa Kwirk's salty sense of humor.

But we all liked to collect things. I collected comics. Dad collected Garbage Pail Kids and wacky ties. Lyra collected words. Cass collected quotes from her favorite books and movies, printing them out and hanging them on her wall. Aunt Gertie collected everything, from toothbrushes to vacuum cleaners. We all hoard something, I guess. Which made me wonder . . . what did Papa Kwirk collect? Maybe the collecting gene skipped him somehow.

Maybe he was the kind of guy who didn't hang on to anything for long.

Or maybe I just didn't know enough about him yet.

"I give up. I'm calling Aunt Gertie," Dad said finally.

"She's not going to tell you anything," Cass countered. But Dad ignored Cass's warning and dialed anyway, putting it on speaker. It went straight to voice mail.

"This is Gertie Kwirk. Let's be perfectly honest: I'm probably screening your call. But that should just make you feel even more special if I bother calling you back."

At the beep, Dad hung up and started to text her instead. "Found . . . the . . . second . . . clue," he said, narrating as he went. "Stuck . . . on . . . Mount . . . Ev . . . er . . . est. . . . Please . . . ad . . . vise."

"It's a waste of time," Cass reiterated in a singsong voice. "She can't tell you. This was part of Papa Kwirk's last wishes. It's all in his will, remember?"

"Then maybe we should try to find his will again," I said. "While she's not around to stop us." Though in this junkyard of a house, I wouldn't know where to start.

"That's cheating too," Lyra said.

"Do you have any better ideas?" I snapped.

Dad's phone rang.

"Aunt Gertie?" Mom asked hopefully.

Dad shook his head. "Riya," he said.

Riya Kumari was Dad's lab assistant at Kaslan's Candy Factory and, frankly, one of the best reasons to visit him at work, outside of the free jelly beans. She was smart and funny, and had worked with Dad on the mango chutney jelly bean, which proved to be an instant success. She also could touch her tongue to her nose, which I found impressive.

Dad went into the other room to take the call. Before he shut the door, I could hear his voice jump an octave. "What? When? Do we know *who*?"

"That doesn't sound good," Mom groaned.

"Trouble in Loompaland," I said. Something had obviously happened at the factory. I wondered if this meant we were going to have to leave early after all. Give up on finding Mount Everest. Give up on Papa Kwirk. I wasn't sure how I felt about the idea. Last night I had almost been ready to leave, but now that we'd started, it seemed wrong not to finish. We sat and waited for Dad to return. He was frowning when he came back into the room.

"Somebody hacked into the servers at Kaslan's over the weekend. We just found out this morning."

"Garvadill?" Mom asked.

Dad pointed to his nose, which I guess meant that yes, they were the most likely suspects. Either that or they stank. Probably both.

"Those jerks," Cass said. "What did they steal?"

"Nothing vital," Dad confirmed. "They managed to access our emails. Some sales reports. That's about it."

"No formulas?" Mom asked.

"Of course not," Dad scoffed. "We don't ever send those out over email. Whoever it was may know *what* we're working on, but they have no idea *how* we're doing it. That's all in here." Dad pointed to his head, and in that moment, I got a flash of what the inside of my dad's brain looked like. A bunch of Snorks and Mutant Ninja Turtles and GI Joe guys all wearing polka-dotted bow ties and spouting complex chemical equations at each other. "Our tech guys are going through everything now. They'll find out what was taken, hopefully trace it back to the source."

"That's gutsy," Mom said. "Just breaking right into your system like that."

"It's flat-out piracy is what it is."

Now I had an image of a bunch of scientists dressed in lab coats and eye patches, brandishing gummy swords and licorice whips, raiding Dad's office, looking for treasure chests full of jelly beans. The whole thing seemed ridiculous to me, but Dad was fuming.

"I told you, Molly. Those guys will do just about anything to try and get ahead. But we'll still beat 'em. The day Garvadill takes Kaslan's Candy under is the day I eat my—"

He was interrupted by another sound from his phone: Optimus Prime telling his fellow Autobots to transform and roll out. It was his text notification. "Aunt Gertie," he said.

"What's it say?" we all asked at once.

"'Maybe you need a break. Take the family out for a treat. There's an old-fashioned ice-cream parlor off West Street called Mallory's. It's the best,'" Dad read aloud.

"That's it?" Cass asked.

"Take a break? We're just getting started," Lyra complained.

Dad quickly started texting back his reply, talking his way through it, as usual. "Don't . . . see . . . how . . . getting . . . ice cream . . . will . . . help . . . find . . . Frank. . . ."

I stood up and huddled with the rest of my family around Dad's phone this time, waiting for Aunt Gertie's response. Ten seconds later, Optimus Prime gave his orders again.

Mallory's has a HUGE menu. So many flavors. It's impossible NOT to find what you're looking for.

The text was followed by a string of emojis. An ice-cream cone, followed by the poop emoji, followed by a winky face.

"Please tell me she thought that was chocolate soft serve," Cass said.

But it was the winky face, not the swirly poo, that did it.

My parents looked at each other. Then Mom told us all to go upstairs and get changed.

I was going to have ice cream for breakfast.

By the time we were ready (Mom insisted we shower off the dirt from our earlier expedition), it was clear that it would be closer to lunch. We piled in the Tank, and Dad followed the GPS into the center of town. He'd never been to Mallory's before. Apparently the building had housed a Mexican restaurant when he was growing up, but that was almost thirty years ago. It made sense that some places would disappear and others would rise to take their place.

And yet downtown Greenburg still looked a lot like it probably did thirty or even fifty years ago. Everything had an old-fashioned feel: green awnings and redbrick siding, bright blue mailboxes and old yellow fire hydrants. Wood placards listed store hours, and actual metal bells hung from doors to announce your arrival. There was even a phone booth. It didn't work, of course—it was just for looking at, but it was kind of neat seeing one out in the wild, and I had half a mind to jump in and rip off my shirt, Clark Kent style. Except there wouldn't be a Superman logo underneath, just my pale skin and the one annoying chest hair that seemed to have sprouted overnight.

Mallory's Ice Cream Parlor and Restaurant was situated next to an old-timey barber shop—the kind with a red-and-white striped pole swirling out front. It reminded me of the Salty Shakers. We were still twenty minutes early—the place didn't open until eleven—so Mom suggested walking around town a bit. Who knows, maybe we'd find a mountain along the way.

As we walked, Dad's voice rose and fell as he pointed out the places from his childhood. He didn't recall there ever being a coffee shop, but he did remember the antique furniture store on the corner and the place that sold soaps and candles next door to it. Cass asked if we could stop there. I knew if I objected I would just be outvoted, so I didn't even bother.

Flicker's Candle Shop smelled a little like Kaslan's Candy Factory, sweet and spicy and fruity all at once. It hit you right as you opened the door. I followed along behind Dad while the girls went to check out the froofy bath salts and anything made with milk and honey. Naturally Dad stopped by the row of candles that smelled like food.

"Eighty percent of taste comes from olfaction," he told me, his nose hovering over a candle that smelled just like fresh pineapple.

"Eighty percent of lectures come from know-it-all fathers," I said under my breath. If it had been Manny, I would have said something like "If it smells so good, why don't you eat it?" But that wasn't much of a dare for my father. I was a little surprised he hadn't licked the candle already.

"I used to come here all the time as a kid, you know," he said.

Right. Because who needs a toy store or an arcade when you can come to the candle store and sniff wax all day? Such a nerd. My father took another long snort. "Ethyl butyrate. They put it in orange juice sometimes." He handed the candle to me.

I took a little sniff. "It reminds me of the beach," I said, mostly because I didn't want to say what it really reminded me of, which was a certain orange-and-blue flower dress and the girl who wore it. Talking about girls to my father sounded even less fun than rubbing Aunt Gertie's feet. I put the candle back and watched as Dad moved down the line, smelling each and every one and muttering a string of chemicals to himself. Anyone who didn't know him would probably assume he was missing a few screws.

Lyra came over and shoved a bar of soap up my nose and demanded I smell it.

"Peppermint," she said. "And it exfoliates. Mom said she'd buy it for me."

What was it with my sisters shoving things in my face all the time? "Good for you," I said, hoping "exfoliates" meant "to make disappear," but I wasn't going to hold my breath.

"You could borrow it if you wanted," she added. "You've got a little pimple right there." Lyra pointed at a new zit on my chin. I swatted her hand away and she pranced off.

By the time we left the store, both girls were carrying little bags from Flicker's like they were souvenirs and Mom had a new lilac-scented candle stashed in the Bag of Holding. As we walked the rest of the way around the block, Dad continued to reminisce about growing up there. Just about every sentence out of his mouth started with "Used to."

"That used to be a Radio Shack," he said. "And I'm pretty sure that was a bank. And *that* used to be a music store. I bought all my tapes there." I considered asking him what a tape was, but I knew it would just be faster if I looked it up on my own later. Or just forgot about it entirely.

He stopped on the corner. "There used to be a doughnut shop over there that your grandmother would take me to on Saturdays after my Little League games," Dad said wistfully. "Didn't matter how many times I struck out, she'd still buy me two chocolate cake doughnuts. We'd sit on that bench and feed the crumbs to the doves."

Dad smiled as Mom tucked her arm through his elbow. It seemed strange to hear him talk like this. He always said how he couldn't stand this town, how happy he had been to get away. Yet there was the street he used to ride his bike down. And there was the little community theater where he saw his first play (Cass was desperate to know which one, but he couldn't recall). And here was the bench where he ate his chocolate doughnuts. I wondered if it was the same one as in the picture sitting on his nightstand at home, and felt a twinge of sadness. Grandma Shelley might have sat on that bench. We turned the last corner to see the wooden sign outside the ice-cream parlor had been flipped.

The bells on the door jingled as we walked in.

"Welcome to Mallory's. Take any seat. I'll be with you shortly," called a man's voice from the kitchen.

There were plenty to choose from. There were only three other people in the place. It looked like something out of an old movie. The floor was tiled blue and white, and the stools by the counter looked like they spun all the way around. A giant glass container held long paper straws. The walls were all decorated with metal-plate advertisements for sodas and sundaes, save for one wall toward the back, which was covered with photos, most of them in color but some in black and white. The whole place smelled like sugar and french fries, a winning combination.

We took a big booth in the corner and waited for our server, a young man with slicked-back hair. He looked like something out of the musical *Grease*; I know because my sister made us all watch it. I wondered if he always wore his hair that way or if it was required as part of the job.

"Hi there. I'm George and I'll be taking care of you today. Have you been to Mallory's before?"

Dad answered for all of us. "We're from out of town." It was the simplest explanation, I guess.

"Well then, welcome, first timers. Here are some menus," George said, handing them over. "Food toward the front, sweet stuff toward the back. Our soup of the day is cheesy potato. Our flavor of the day is You Mocha Me Crazy. I'll give you some time to look things over and be right back."

I flipped to the food, forgetting, for a moment, why were even here. The picture of the double bacon cheeseburger was taunting me. Sitting next to me, Cass hadn't even gotten to the food yet. She was still on the first page, the one detailing the restaurant's history. "It says here that this place was first founded by the Mallory brothers in 1952 and stayed in business until 1967, when the elder Mallory died and the younger one sold the property to pay off debts. The building went through several other owners until it was bought by the Meeks family and turned back into an ice-cream parlor three years ago."

The name caught my attention. Mom's too.

"Did you say Meeks? Didn't we meet them yesterday at the service?" she asked. "Wasn't she the girl who said all those nice things about your grandfather?"

Her name was Tasha. She had beautiful black hair and a great smile and pink lip gloss with a touch of glitter. She also had on earrings shaped like dolphins. *She was wearing white sandals and had painted her toenails to match her dress.*

"Yeah, maybe," I said with a shrug.

"Well, it says he here that the Meekses bought it with the express intention of restoring it to its former glory," Cass continued. "The new owners even went back to the Mallory family and got some of their original recipes. Several of the menu items are the same as those served in the 1950s, and even some of the pictures on the wall date back to when the parlor was first opened."

"That's great," Dad said, "But I really don't see how . . ."

"Um . . . Dad . . ."

As expected, Lyra had skipped clear past the food and gone straight to the dessert. She turned her menu so we could all see it and pointed down at the bottom of the Sundaes and Shakes page. To six words in a fancy rolling script.

A lump lodged in my throat.

We'd found it.

AN AVALANCHE IN REVERSE

<u>*Do You Dare Conquer the Mountain?*</u>

*Do you have what it takes to conquer the most
legendary dessert known to man? Twelve scoops of
Mallory's premium ice cream, towering high and topped
with chocolate, caramel, and strawberry sauce,
then smothered in whitecaps of whipped topping.
With or without nuts. The Mountain is calling.
Will you answer?*

There was no picture of this legendary dessert; that was left
to the imagination.

Dad turned to Mom. "You don't really think . . . ?"

"Don't you?"

George returned with five waters and a cheesy smile that

I'm guessing was also part of the uniform. "So, have you had a chance to look over the menu?"

"What can you tell us about the Mountain?" Dad asked.

George's cheesy smile somehow got cheesier. "Oh, yeah, it's pretty epic. You get to pick any twelve flavors you want, and it comes in a giant bowl. And if just *one* person eats it alone, then they've conquered it and get their photo on our Wall of Fame." George nodded over his shoulder to the back of the parlor, the one covered in the snapshots that I'd noticed earlier. "Believe it or not, we still have pictures of Mountain climbers up there from when this place was around the first time."

"Wait—you're telling me that one person can eat twelve scoops of ice cream in a single sitting?" Mom said.

"Sure. One person *can*. Most people don't. They share it. But it doesn't count as conquering the Mountain unless you go solo. And you don't get your picture on the wall. Or the T-shirt. You can't cheat your way to fame and glory, ma'am."

"I don't think I can eat twelve scoops of ice cream by myself," Dad muttered.

"I think I could," Lyra said.

George, our server, shook his head. "A lot of people come in thinking it'll be no problem, but then they see it and it's, like, 'Whoa! That thing is ginormous!'" George made a gesture with his hands to show us just how ginormous. Bigger than his chest, anyways. "Apparently back in the day, the Mallory brothers actually called it Mount Everest. That was back around the time those first guys—Hillary and Norgay—got to the top, so it was really big in the news."

The Kwirks exchanged another furious volley of glances. This *had* to be what Grandpa's clue was referring to. Aunt Gertie had led us right to it, even though she insisted she wouldn't help us. That she *couldn't* help us.

"Of course, now pretty much anybody can climb the real thing, so we just call ours the Mountain and leave it at that," George concluded.

"And you say it doesn't count if your whole family eats it? It has to be solo?"

"One climber. One Mountain," George confirmed. Then, noticing the nervous looks we were all giving Dad, he nodded. "Let me give you all a couple more minutes to think it over."

As our server escaped back to the kitchen, Mom frowned at her menu. "I don't think this is a good idea, Fletcher. That much sugar will send you straight into a coma."

"I work in a candy factory," Dad replied. "I think I can handle it."

"Eating a handful of jelly beans over the course of a day is not the same as consuming twelve scoops of ice cream in one sitting."

"Molly, the clue said to conquer Mount Everest. This is Mount Everest." He pointed to the description on the menu. "I don't see what choice I have."

"Surely you don't expect him to be waiting for you at the bottom of the *bowl*."

I shuddered at the thought of Grandpa's ashes being mixed in with the ice cream somehow. Like Yanomami mashed bananas. Just gross.

George returned a moment later, interrupting the debate. He was shaking his head.

"Okay, so get this. I talked to my manager, and he says he'll make you a deal. The whole family can conquer the Mountain together . . . *but* you have to triple it."

"Thirty-six scoops?" Dad asked.

"Yup. Twelve flavors, three scoops of each. Plus he says if you can finish it, it's free. But you still only get one T-shirt."

"How many scoops is that for each of us?" Cass wondered.

Everyone at the table looked at me.

"Seven point two," I said. The reality of the math settled over us.

"I can't do it," Mom protested. "There's just no way."

"Bring it on," Lyra taunted.

"Are we talking, like, big scoops or kid-size scoops?" Cass asked.

But it didn't matter what size the scoops were. Dad had made up his mind.

"We'll do it," he said.

"Excellent." George rubbed his hands together. "I'll go tell my manager while you head to the counter and pick out your flavors." As he walked back to the kitchen, George called out, "I think we're going to need a bigger bowl."

The challenge of conquering the Mountain started with the

five of us trying to agree on twelve different flavors. We stood at the counter, pointing out options, debating possible combinations, and making gagging sounds when one of us said something the others didn't like.

"Ew! You can't have mint chocolate chip *and* peanut butter chunk in the same bowl. That's like orange juice and toothpaste."

"Is it asking too much to have cherry cordial *and* strawberry *and* raspberry ripple?"

"Am I the only one here who likes pistachio?"

"I really don't think you can put chocolate sauce on top of cotton candy. That's, like, overkill."

"Dude, you can put chocolate sauce on top of *anything*."

"Maybe we should just get thirty-six scoops of vanilla."

"Why would anyone want to eat something called rocky road? That's a terrible name."

In the end, each kid got to choose three flavors, and Mom and Dad shared the last three picks because, as they put it, "We are adults and know how to compromise." I picked cookies and cream, brownie batter, and luscious lemon. I figured I'd try to save the lemon for when I was suffering from chocolate overload and needed something light and refreshing. We were headed back to our booth to await the arrival of our triple-sized Mountain when I heard a familiar voice call my name.

"Well, if it isn't Rion Like Ion."

I turned around slowly, thinking there was no way, not here, not now, but there she was, standing by the cash register, tying on an apron. Her curly hair was pulled back, and she was dressed in the same white polo shirt as our server. She looked better in it than he did.

"Um. Hey there," I said, heading slowly back to the counter, making sure I didn't trip over anything along the way. "You . . . uh . . . *work* here?"

"Didn't you read the menu?" Tasha Meeks asked. "My parents own the place. So, yeah. I work here."

"Yeah, but, like, don't you have school . . . and stuff?"

Me talk so good to girls.

"It's our spring break this week. Some kids get to go to Florida with their families and lie on the beach. I get to come wipe tables and wash dishes." She finished tying her apron and leaned over the counter on her elbows. Glitter lipgloss again. Not that I was paying that close attention.

"Wow. That sucks," I said. "Sorry."

"It's not so bad," Tasha said with a shrug. Same dolphin earrings, too. "Dad says it's teaching me the value of hard work, but mostly it's just made me sick of mopping floors."

My parents only made me empty the dishwasher at home. And even then, my mother would usually come behind and redo it. Apparently the plastic cups and the glasses had to stay on separate sides of the cabinet. "What about you?" Tasha asked. "Shouldn't *you* be in school?"

Yes. Probably, I thought. *Except my grandfather's body is still MIA.* "We're sticking around another day or so. There are some . . . loose ends we have to take care of."

216

Tasha Meeks's brown eyes narrowed. "I know why you're really here," she said, a sly edge to her voice.

I swallowed hard. "You do?" If she knew about Papa Kwirk's last wishes, she must *really* think we were nuts.

Tasha nodded. "Of course. You came for the ice cream. That's all anybody ever comes to Mallory's for. I mean, the food's decent, but it's really just an excuse to get dessert."

I let out a sigh. "Right. You got me."

"Don't worry. I'm not going to judge," Tasha continued. "Personally I prefer soft serve in a cone. That's what your grandpa and I used to get sometimes . . . but I guess you already know that."

Motorcycles, and twist cones, and going all in. "Yeah. That was a great speech, by the way," I said. "You really touched me. . . . I mean, *it* touched me . . . but, like, in a good way. . . ."

I scratched my suddenly hot cheek, thankful that my sisters weren't standing here listening to me make a fool out of myself.

"Yeah, I was pretty nervous," Tasha admitted. "But I wanted to do it. To honor him, you know? For everything he's done for my family."

I still wasn't sure what all Papa Kwirk had done. Only that he gave her a ride sometimes and taught her how to play poker. That he was there when she needed him. "So your dad and my grandfather . . . ," I began.

"I know. Doesn't seem likely," she said. "They were both war vets, so they sometimes talked. But then when Dad had his accident . . ." Tasha paused, chewing on her lip, studying me as if she expected me to know the whole story. "But of course you're not from around here. It was a pretty big deal. Three cars. Drunk driver swerved into oncoming traffic. Nobody died, thank God, but several people got hurt."

That explained the scars, at least. "That really sucks," I said.

"Yeah, well. It *really* sucks when your dad was the one who'd been drinking," Tasha said, frowning.

I wasn't sure what to say. I wanted to ask her what happened, exactly. And how it was that my grandfather saved her dad's life. And if her dad was better now.

Or maybe, judging by the frown, I should just change the subject and ask her if she liked living here in Greenburg. And what it was like working at an ice-cream parlor. And did she have a lot of friends. And were they mostly girl or guy friends. And if they were guys, were they like, cute, athletic guys with perfect teeth and noticeable muscles, or was she maybe sort of *over* all the guys in her hometown and looking to trade emails with strange boys with unexfoliated chin zits who she'd only just met but whose grandfathers used to take her riding on the back of his motorcycle?

I didn't get a chance to ask any of those things, because George chose that moment to ring a cowbell. He was standing beside our table and had the attention of the now six other customers in Mallory's.

"Is that necessary?" I asked, covering my ears.

Tasha rolled her eyes. "Whenever somebody attempts to

conquer the Mountain, we have to make a big deal of it. Besides, George is studying theater in college, so he makes a big production out of everything."

"Sounds like someone else I know," I said, looking at Cass.

George put the bell on our table. "Ladies and gentlemen," he said in a voice better suited for a circus ringmaster. "For the first time in the history of Mallory's, an entire family will attempt the improbable. A gastronomic feat neither for the faint of heart nor for the hyperglycemic. Brains will freeze. Shirt buttons will pop. Someone will probably end up passed out on the floor in this ultimate test of the human body's ability to process the most glorious marriage of sugar and fat known to man. In this corner, hailing from—where are you from again?"

"Indiana," Mom said.

"Hailing from the far-off land of Indiana, we have . . ." The server paused.

"The Kwirk family," Tasha called out from beside me.

"The Kwirk family!" George repeated, louder and more obnoxious.

There was a smattering of applause from the other patrons. I could feel my ears burning, and I wasn't even sitting at the table with the rest of them. Unlike Cass, I didn't like being the center of attention.

"And their opponent: weighing in at nine thousand eight hundred calories and sporting thirty-six scoops of pure creamy awesomeness with enough whipped topping to fill an

Olympic-sized swimming pool . . . it's been called the Behemoth, the Belly Bulger, and the Last Dessert. It's your pancreas's worst nightmare . . . the one, the only . . . Mountain."

With that, a third member of the Mallory's crew, presumably the cook, emerged from the kitchen wheeling a cart, upon which was placed what looked to be a giant metal salad bowl. The applause was bigger for the ice cream than it was for my family, but I could see why: thirty-six scoops piled high and dripping with sauces and giant crowns of whipped cream, each one a miniature version of the dessert's namesake. A dozen cherries were scattered over the top like mini red boulders, but thankfully no nuts. The server who had wheeled it out set it on the table as George handed out plastic bibs to every member of my family.

"You should go get a bib," Tasha said. "It'd be embarrassing if you got chocolate sauce on you."

Right. Because it's *not* going to be embarrassing wearing a bib and trying to eat what amounts to a trash can full of ice cream?

"Seriously, go. Your family needs you," she said, and she gave me a shove. The playful kind, where her shoulder pushed into mine. Not the kind Mike Vaughn used to give me on the playground that ended with me spitting mulch out of my mouth.

"All right. But if you see me pass out, call the paramedics," I joked. She promised she would, but in a voice so serious that I wondered if it had ever happened before.

I took my seat next to Lyra and reluctantly put on my bib. It said *You Missed Your Mouth* in upside-down lettering, so that you could look down and read it yourself.

Hilarious.

"I don't even know where to start," Dad muttered, spoon held at the ready.

"You can't tell what flavors are what, there's so much topping," Lyra marveled.

Admittedly it was a masterpiece. The Mona Lisa of ice-cream sundaes. One of the seven wonders of the dessert world. There was absolutely no way we could finish it. Not unless we were allowed to sit here all day into tomorrow morning.

As if reading my mind, George looked at his watch. "Oh, and did I tell you that you have exactly thirty minutes? Starting . . . now."

I took one last look at Tasha, who gave me a nod of encouragement. Then, armed with our long-handled spoons and guided by the spirit of our dear departed grandfather, who, for some unknown reason, wanted us all to gain ten pounds in his honor, the Kwirk family dug in.

Whenever you set out to climb a mountain, there is risk. There is the chance that you won't make it to the top. There is even the chance that after you summit, you won't make it back down alive.

Cass was the first to go.

This came as no surprise to the rest of us. In a family that earned half of its livelihood from a candy factory, you learn who can handle their sugar, and Cass had the fewest sweet teeth of all of us. She believed carrot sticks were an actual snack and not projectiles to throw at your friends during lunch, and she was the only one of us who would ever go to a restaurant and order just a salad for dinner.

"Oh my god, I'm so stuffed," she said, slumping melodramatically in the booth beside me, a dribble of chocolate sauce in the corner of her mouth like a trickle of sticky blood. She had eaten maybe three scoops. Any other time, that would have seemed impressive for her, but now it just meant more for the rest of us.

"You can't be done already," I said.

"Tell that to my stomach," she protested. There was no point in arguing with her.

Mom dropped next, claiming she had eaten close to her seven required scoops, though it couldn't have been much more than four, judging by the dent on her side of the bowl. "I can't make it," she huffed, arms cradling her belly. "You guys . . . go on . . . without me."

"You did great, sweetheart," Dad said, and reached over to rub her shoulder.

"Don't touch me," she warned him. "I literally might burst." She put a napkin to her mouth and groaned.

That left Lyra, Dad, and me, though it was obvious that my sister and I were doing most of the grunt work, as Papa Kwirk would say. Dad was too busy isolating flavor compounds, making what Mom called his tasting face (head cocked, one eye half closed, lips pursed together), cataloging each bite like a connoisseur. "Butter pecan, but with notes of goat's milk and just a touch of praline."

"Don't analyze it. Just eat it." I went in for another spoonful.

"It's about the journey, Rion, not just the destination."

The journey. Right. It had been nearly twenty minutes, and already most of the ice cream was half melted and mixed together. I couldn't tell you if I was eating moose tracks or chocolate monkey. We had less than half of the Mountain left to climb, but I was starting to feel sluggish. I'd already battled my way through two table-pounding brain freezes. My tongue was numb, not just from the cold but from so much sugar at once; my taste buds were paralyzed from sensory overload. Worse than that, though, was the feeling I was starting to get in my stomach. The lurching, burbling, corkscrew motion it made. I belched, exhaling a breath that could knock out a diabetic, and looked over at the counter to see Tasha stifling a giggle.

She was watching me. Of course she was. I couldn't quit now. But wouldn't it be worse to upchuck all over the floor of her parents' ice-cream parlor? What if she was the one who had to come clean it up?

"It's impossible," I muttered, holding my spoon upright like planting a flag of surrender.

Dad leaned over the bowl and looked me in the eyes. He pointed his spoon at my nose. "'It is not the mountain we conquer but ourselves.' Know who said that?"

"Frodo Baggins?" I guessed.

"Sir Edmund Hillary."

I liked my answer better.

"It means if we put our mind to it, we can accomplish anything," Dad added.

Which was fine, except there was only so much room in my stomach, no matter how open my mind was.

Beside me, Lyra was busy fishing out pieces of cookie dough from the gloppy, melty mess. She'd easily outeaten me, though I had no idea how she managed to squeeze it all into her little body. On the other side of the table, Cass picked up her spoon as if she was ready to leap back into the fray, but after only one bite, she said, "Oh no. Bad idea. Baaaad idea," and put it back down. She set her head on the table, taking long, slow, deep breaths.

From the counter, I heard Tasha's voice. "Come on, Rion. You got this. Show that ice cream who's boss."

Great. Now I had my own cheering section. I flashed her a weak smile. This was not going to end well.

Lyra groaned. "I'm feeling a little nauseated. I think I should stop." She put her spoon down. I couldn't fault her. The girl had probably eaten her seven point two scoops plus another two, picking up our sister's slack. Lyra curled up in the booth, her head on Mom's lap. "Rest now," Mom cooed, stroking Lyra's long hair. "It will all be over soon."

That left only the two Kwirk men. And five, maybe six

scoops left, though "scoop" was pushing it. The Mountain was little more than a sickeningly sweet, lumpy, pink-and-brown stew, chunks of dark chocolate floating to the surface. Even knowing what it was, I could barely stand to look at it.

"Just don't think about it," Dad said. "Don't think about how sweet it is. Or how rich. Just imagine you're eating something light and savory. Like popcorn. Or rice cakes. Or slurping down air. Sticky, syrupy, stomach-churning air."

We had the attention of everyone in the place now, watching us, no doubt secretly placing bets on which of the two of us would bow out next. It seemed as if my arm and hand were working independently from the rest of me, a machine repeating the motion of dunking my spoon into the slop and transferring it to my mouth, where I reluctantly managed to choke it down like a kid swallowing cough syrup. Dad and I got into a rhythm of sorts, alternating our bites, him working from one end, me from the other, determined to meet in the middle.

"I'm never. Eating ice cream. Again," I groaned. I thought about the old white truck with the smiling ice-cream cone on top that came through the neighborhood during the summer. How Cass and I used to run him down, sometimes chasing him for blocks barefoot, waving sweaty dollars in our hands. From now on, whenever I heard his tinny song, I would tremble in fear.

I took another bite, swallowing a piece of cookie dough whole—I could not be expected to chew any longer—and noticed Dad pausing, looking at me. There couldn't have been more than two scoops of ice cream left.

"You don't look so good," he said.

I felt like strawberry syrup was flowing through my veins. Like any moment chocolate sauce would come streaming out of my eyeballs. I knew if I took one more spoonful, my body would revolt. I doubled over, pressing my hands to my pulsing temples. "I'm sorry, Dad. I tried."

"Don't be sorry, son," he said. "You did your best."

He offered me a proud smile. The same smile he gave me every time I came off the soccer field, whether I played well or not. I closed my eyes and thought about Papa Kwirk and the picture of him and Dad fishing. I wondered how many times he'd given my father that same look. Probably not near as often.

I heard something hit the table and assumed it was my father's face falling straight into the bowl, conceding victory to the Mountain. We'd done our best, but it was too much. Even for the Kwirks. I opened my eyes to see my mother instead, suddenly sitting upright, reaching for her spoon with a fierce look in her eyes. She and my father faced each other.

"Together," she said.

Dad clanked his spoon with hers. "Together."

And with renewed fury, my parents commenced to slurping. They hovered over the bowl like a two-headed monster, melted ice cream dribbling out of their mouths and back into the bowl, only to be scooped up in the next spoonful, shoveling it in as fast as they could. It was the most revolting thing I'd seen since catching my sister French-kissing Damien Moorehead last summer in the basement.

Two agonizing minutes later, Mom scraped together the last slurp of what had once been Mount Everest and fed it to Dad, who choked it down with the look of a man who has just been given a lethal dose of poison. The crowd erupted in applause—as much as a crowd of eight or so can. George let out a shrill whistle. Tasha shook her head, either impressed or grossed out, I couldn't tell.

Dad held up the empty bowl with both hands in a victorious salute. The Mountain had been conquered, fulfilling my grandfather's dying wish—or part of it, at least. Fletcher Kwirk smiled in triumph. Then he set the metal bowl back down and hurriedly squeezed out of the booth.

Bolting to the bathroom with his hands cupped over this mouth.

You *can* have too much of a good thing. Don't let anyone tell you otherwise.

After Dad's trip to the men's room, which he unnecessarily described to us as "sort of like an avalanche, but in reverse," George and Tasha emerged from the kitchen, him holding a blue T-shirt and her holding one of those old Polaroid cameras—the kind that spits out pictures of you fishing with your dad that he later buries in the backyard for you to find after he's dead.

"Behold, the conquering Kwirks," George proclaimed. "May their bellies be forever full of their victory."

"Too late," Dad said.

George handed Dad the blue shirt, which had the Mallory's logo on the front and *I Conquered the Mountain* on the back, complete with an outlined drawing of a stick man climbing a giant scoop of ice cream. I wondered if Dad had a bow tie that would match.

"We would like to get a picture of all of you for the wall. If you don't mind."

Tasha held up the camera and motioned us to get together. *Great,* I thought. Memorialized on the wall of gluttony. Something else I can be forever embarrassed about. We huddled together by our booth, Mom and Dad in the back holding up the bowl, me squeezed between my sisters in the front.

"Hold on a sec," Tasha said. She came right up to me and, with her thumb, wiped something from my forehead. The touch sent a chill straight down to my toes. "You had some whipped cream in your eyebrow."

Of course I did. Because I am just that talented.

My eyebrow twitched where she'd touched it. Tasha smiled and stepped back, reframing her picture with an even more red-faced version of me in its center. "Say 'ice cream'!"

"Oh god, no," Mom muttered.

"Just 'cheese,' then."

I tried not to smile too much. I didn't want to look like taking family pictures was something I enjoyed—rather, something that I stoically suffered through out of the goodness of my heart.

"And now you can add it to the Wall of Fame," George said, pointing to the back and the seventy or so pictures that were already posted there. While my dad led the way, photo in one hand, ceremonial thumbtack in the other, I lingered behind with the photographer.

"You did it," she said.

"Team effort," I told her. "Besides. It was only ice cream. Not like the *real* Everest."

"Well, it's something. Lots of people have climbed mountains. Not many people can say they've *eaten* them."

That was true, I guess. Just all the ones on the back wall where my family was now standing. Where, in fact, my mother had just shouted, "No way!"

"I should probably go check and see what that's all about," I said.

"Yeah. You probably should," Tasha prodded.

The rest of my family was jammed together, all staring at one particular photo. It was black and white and a little washed out, obviously one of the originals, from back before the Mallory brothers sold the place. It showed a guy and a girl. Teenagers. She wore a short patterned skirt and sweater, long hair pulled back in a ponytail with a ribbon. He wore a bomber jacket and a T-shirt with a dark stain on the front—maybe, *hopefully*, chocolate sauce. The empty bowl proclaimed his victory over what was then still called Mount Everest, though on the other side of him sat a bucket.

The picture was captioned underneath, in black marker, slightly smudged.

FRANK KWIRK WITH SHELLEY HARPER. SEPTEMBER 1966.

"This is it. This must have been their very first date," Cass said.

Aunt Gertie's voice echoed in my head. *That's a whole 'nother story.* For their first date, Papa Kwirk had brought Grandma Shelley to Mallory's and then tried to impress her by eating twelve scoops of ice cream in one sitting. How romantic.

George stood next to us. "Ooh. He's got the bucket. Not a good sign. But he's still on the wall. You just have to get it down, not keep it down."

"Like father, like son," Mom said.

Dad reached out and gingerly pulled the photo free. I hadn't seen enough pictures of Grandma Shelley that I could recognize her teenage self easily, but Papa Kwirk was obvious to me now, even so young. His beaked nose. His shallow cheeks. The thick head of hair that would eventually start to recede, or at least make the leap down to his face. I suppose somebody might think of him as handsome back then, in a rough-and-tumble way.

Grandma Shelley, on the other hand, was a hottie.

"She looks just like you, Cass," Mom said.

Okay, I thought. Forget the hottie part.

"But where's Papa Kwirk?" Lyra whispered up to Dad, careful so only our family could hear. "I mean, where's the *rest* of him?"

In the afterglow of our victory over the Belly Bulger, I'd almost forgotten why we'd even eaten it to begin with. Dad hadn't, though. Knowing now how the game was played, he flipped the picture over, and just as with Fishin' Fletcher, someone had written something on the back in blue ink.

LOOK FOR ME IN THE MAGIC TREE, HIDDEN AMONG THE LEAVES.

I groaned. I couldn't help it. Admittedly, most of it had to do with the ice cream sloshing in my stomach, but also the fact that, after all that, we'd only uncovered another clue.

Papa Kwirk was still out there somewhere.

Which meant the weirdest day in Kwirkdom was about to get even weirder.

SWOONERS, MULLETS, AND MAGIC TREES

With bursting bellies and raging sugar highs, we waddled to the door, Dad leading the victory parade, T-shirt draped proudly across his shoulder like a sash. I scanned the parlor for Tasha, hoping to at least say goodbye before we left, but she'd slipped away while we were studying our dead grandfather's third clue. George said she was in the back on the phone and asked me if he should go get her.

Papa Kwirk would have said yes. Heck, Papa Kwirk would have leaped over the counter and gone back to the kitchen to say goodbye himself. Papa Kwirk once jumped a metal fence and stole a stuffed bear to get a girl to like him. He conquered Mount Everest just to impress her.

Of course, then he tossed his cookies and cream. My stomach was already a gurgling volcano barely lying dormant.

Maybe better not to push it.

"Just tell her the charming guy with the whipped cream on his forehead said it was nice to meet her. And I hope we see each other again sometime. I mean, like, *again* again."

"Sure, man. Whatever." George started to walk away, carrying a stack of menus in one hand and his cowbell in the other.

"Maybe leave out the 'charming' part," I called after him, starting to doubt myself, suddenly thinking that Tasha was just being polite, talking to me only because she liked my grandfather, and because you can't be mean to a kid who has recently lost someone close to them. "And all the 'again' stuff," I added. "Know what? Just tell her Rion says bye."

I slipped out the door before I could make a bigger fool of myself.

Outside, Cass was repeating the last clue over and over. The girl could memorize speeches from Shakespeare, so a one-line riddle should pose no problems. Dad didn't ask if he could take the photo of our grandparents on their first date; Papa Kwirk had earned his spot on the wall, after all, and he deserved to keep it. Instead, my father just used the thumbtack George gave him to put our family picture right next to my teenage grandparents.

I wondered what he made of it—that photo. Obviously, Papa Kwirk was trying to tell us something. What did fishing, Garbage Pail Kids, ice-cream mountains, and first dates have in common? I would have asked, but Dad seemed just as puzzled by the whole thing.

Puzzled and a little green, as if he could be sick again any minute. Mom looked the same.

Lyra, on the other hand, bounced like Tigger as we walked back to the car, her pigtails flopping. "That was epic," she said, skipping circles around us. "We should totally do that again sometime."

"I think that's a terrible idea," Mom said. "Conquering Everest is a once-in-a-lifetime experience."

Cass slowed down to walk next to me. "Well, she sure is pretty."

"Who?" I said, playing dumb, hoping she'd drop it. I should have known better.

"Tasha, right? The one from the funeral—sorry, *funn*eral," Cass corrected herself.

"Yeah, I guess," I said, trying to sound disinterested. Never, *ever* admit to your sister that you think somebody's cute. Especially if your sister is anything like Cassiopeia Kwirk, Queen of Storybook Romances, Cataloger of Crushes Real and Imagined. She will ship you faster than FedEx.

"You *guess*," Cass repeated, grabbing hold of my arm with both hands. "C'mon. Admit it. You were totally into her. And when she wiped the whipped cream off your face? The *look* you got? *Sooo* smitten."

I shook off her hand and tried to put some distance between us, but it was too late. Like sharks sniffing out a bloated whale carcass, she was quickly joined by her own kind. "Who's smitten?" Lyra asked, her ears pricking, skipping up beside us.

"Ri was swooning over that girl at the restaurant."

"I was not swooning," I snapped.

"You were totally swooning," Cass insisted.

"I don't swoon. *You* swoon."

"Pfff. When have I ever swooned?"

"Are you kidding?" I spat. "You're like the world's foremost authority on swooning. You swoon when you see a pair of shoes you like. You swoon over characters in books. You swoon at movie previews. You're a total swooner."

"Swooner's not a word," Lyra informed us.

"Don't try to change the subject." Cass smiled her showbiz smile. "I *saw* you back there. It was total swoonage. You were one big swoonball."

"Swoonface," I shot back.

"Swoonhead."

"Swoonbag."

"Swoon-for-brains."

I got right up in her face. "Swoony McSwoonsalot who lives in Swoonsville and eats Swoonios for breakfast thinks she's so friggin' swoontastic that the whole swoony world swoons at her stupid swoony feet."

"I am rather swoontastic," Cass admitted, mock-admiring her nails.

I punched her in the arm, not near as hard as I could.

"Ouch!" she said, and punched me back. *Really* hard. A lot harder than I expected. Who knew my sister with her Pixy Stix arms had a fist like a sledgehammer? I resisted the urge to hike up the sleeve of my shirt, even though I was sure a bruise was already blossoming there.

"You two need to grow up," Lyra said. "So *juvenile*."

We reached the parking lot and all piled into the car, me rubbing my arm as I crawled into the back to get away from Cass, who was still batting her eyelashes at me. Up front, I overheard Mom ask Dad, "Do you even know where you're going?"

"You mean do I know the way to the magic tree?" Dad replied with a snort. "If it's the one I'm thinking of, I know where it used to be. But that was thirty years ago." He started the car, his fingers tapping on the wheel. The one he was thinking of? How many magic trees could there be in Bumtussle, Illinois?

"You know, there's this one group of people who live near Manila who bury their dead in hollowed-out tree trunks," Lyra informed us. "You even get to pick out your own tree before you die."

"That's nice, sweetie," Mom said.

"Better than being eaten by vultures," Dad remarked.

"Or by your own family," I added.

In the seat in front of me, Cass mumbled, "Oh, Tasha," pressed her hand to her forehead, and pretended to faint.

If I'm being honest, I wasn't that surprised by there being a third clue at the top of the Mountain (or the bottom, depending on how you looked at it). Disappointed, but not surprised.

I seriously doubted we would find Papa Kwirk at Mallory's.

For starters, an ice-cream parlor seemed an unlikely place to store a cremated body; surely it constituted some kind of health code violation—though then we could have said that he had been "ice cremated," which is the kind of joke my dad would make. Mostly, though, I'd seen enough movies to know that no quest is ever completed after only two steps. First the tackle box. Then the photo from his first date with Grandma Shelley. There was an equation here, but we didn't have all the variables yet. I wasn't sure what it would all add up to in the end, but I knew it couldn't be solved so easily.

No surprise, then, that he wasn't hidden in the salt and pepper shakers at Mallory's, but I *could* imagine Papa Kwirk waiting for us at a "magic" tree. I know there's no such thing, of course, except for the one in those books about the time-traveling siblings that I read when I was little. Jack and Annie getting chased by saber-toothed tigers and ninja assassins. Those books were so unrealistic; there was no way a brother and sister could spend *that* much time together and not kill each other. If I ever traveled back to ancient Egypt with Cass, I'd leave her there.

Dad insisted there was a magic tree in Greenburg, though, at a place called Polk Park. Mom fed him directions from her phone while I stared out the window and tried not to think about Tasha Meeks. Honestly, I could still feel the little jolt from where she'd touched my eyebrow, though not as keenly as I felt the imprint of my sister's fist on my arm.

It was probably better that I hadn't said goodbye. Sure, she liked my grandfather, but he'd been a part of her life. Besides, he rode a motorcycle and had war scars and tattoos and played poker. The rest of my family sniffed candles, kept snakes as pets, and gorged ourselves on ice cream. Not to mention— who manages to get whipped cream on their *forehead*?

"You're messing with your eyebrow again," Lyra said, staring at me. I put my hands in my lap and ignored her smirking until Dad told us that we'd arrived.

Polk Park wasn't very busy, though once I got a good look at it, I was surprised there was anyone there at all.

"I haven't been here in ages," Dad said.

It looked like the park had been *around* for ages. An ancient playground stood off to the right, with an old metal slide and four weathered swings, one of which hung down to the grass by only one hook and another had been twisted so much that its chain made an impossible knot. There was a balance beam, rusted, and a sandbox filled with weeds. The three smaller kids I spotted on the playground avoided all of these, choosing to share the rickety-looking roundabout that squealed when it spun. Their parents stared at their phones on nearby benches.

The place didn't look too magical to me.

The park had a huge field, at least, which seemed to be the only thing about it that wasn't in disrepair. The grassy area was studded with big oak trees providing pockets of shade, though nothing about them struck me as being particularly magical either. None stood out as being the tallest or grandest, or shimmering with some kind of glittery, ethereal glow. There were no Jack and Annie style tree houses to be seen.

But Dad seemed to know what he was doing. He walked purposefully toward the field, Mom and Lyra following on his heels. I stopped to read the bronze plaque that stood at the entrance, thinking maybe it would help if I knew a little bit more about the place. The plaque said that the park had been made in honor of James Knox Polk, the eleventh president of the United States. There was an engraved picture of Mr. Polk looking unhappy, though all presidents looked unhappy to me. Probably came with the job.

"Is that a mullet?" Cass said, coming up behind me.

"Yeah. Maybe," I said, bending down to inspect President Polk's hairdo. I didn't know presidents wore mullets, though maybe being president entitled you to have dumb-looking hair too.

"I've never even heard of this guy."

"Me neither," I said. He wasn't on a coin or a bill or Mount Rushmore. None of the schools I ever went to were named after him. But he *was* on a bronze plaque commemorating a patch of weedy grass in the middle of Greenburg, Illinois.

Lucky him.

Cass ran her finger along the engraved outline of Polk's face. "Don't you think it's funny, how you can be the president of the United States and still be forgotten by almost everybody?

I mean, more people probably know who Justin Bieber is than this guy."

My sister had had a crush on Justin Bieber when she was ten. T-shirts, posters, everything. It was sad. Even Prince Teldar was a step up, in my opinion.

Cass was right, though. This guy had been president—probably had his name on plenty of laws and libraries and stuff—and I knew nothing about him. It made you think about all the people in the world who won't be remembered at all after they're gone, who leave nothing lasting behind. Probably that's most of us.

I'm not sure if I'd ever had a more depressing thought in my life.

Cass poked me in the shoulder. "Hey, sorry about the whole swooner thing," she said, squinting in the sun. "That was uncalled-for."

I stood there and blinked at her, not sure I'd heard her right. Cass had apologized to me before, but always with a parent looking over her shoulder, making sure it was done with the suitable amount of forced authenticity. In those cases, I was usually expected to make the same fake apology back. Except Cass could fake being remorseful much better than I could. "Hold up. Did you just apologize? Like, for real?"

"I can take it back," she said.

I raised my hands. "Nope. Too late. Apology accepted."

We both went back to admiring President Polk's mullet.

"I'm sorry I punched you so hard," I mumbled.

"It wasn't really that hard," Cass said with a shrug.

"Neither was yours," I lied.

From halfway across the field, Lyra yelled at us to hurry up. Dad had apparently found his magic tree.

We arrived to find the rest of our family standing around a large oak, lording over its own little patch of wildflowers. It was one of the tallest of the bunch, with a thick, gnarly trunk and stocky branches that twisted and crisscrossed, creating a lattice that seemed perfect for climbing. The end of a mild winter had coaxed the tree's leaves out a little early, but you could still trace a path up the limbs with your eyes.

There were carvings in the trunk near the base. M.T. hearted J.S. Shawn B. was a jerk. Mike was here. But there were no initials we recognized. No *Frank loves Shelley*. No *Welcome to the magic tree*. No *This way to Egypt*.

"Doesn't look so special to me," Lyra said.

"No. Not to you," Dad said, putting one hand on it. "We used to come here on Sundays when I was little, while everyone else was at church. Mom packed a picnic, and we'd find a spot here in the shade, far enough from the playground that Frank could have some peace and quiet to read the Sunday paper. He and Mom would sit and do the crossword together."

"What makes it magic?" Cass asked, studying the tree.

"Your grandmother called it that because I used to climb up into it and disappear."

"Wait a minute," Mom said. "This is *that* tree?"

My sisters and I looked at each other. Clearly there was another story here. Another piece from the puzzle of my father's foggy childhood that he'd apparently shared with Mom but not with us.

"When your father was a little boy, he broke his arm falling out of this tree," she explained.

"I wasn't *that* little," Dad countered. "I was eight. And it wasn't my fault. A branch snapped. I broke both the bones in my forearm, right here." He pointed to a spot halfway between his right wrist and elbow.

"*You?* Climbed *that?*" I pointed to him and then to the big oak. I'd never pictured my father as a tree climber. It just seemed a little too daring for a chemist who only drove the speed limit and kept a stack of *Scientific American*s on the back of the toilet.

Dad nodded. "Probably a hundred times. Until the *one* time your grandmother wasn't watching. She'd gone back to the car to get something, and Frank was stuck in his paper. I was up there, calling down to him, trying to get his attention, and *snap*." Dad slapped his hands together, causing Lyra to jump. "I had to wear a cast for eight weeks. Got me out of PE, at least." Dad looked up at the tree and shook his head. "We still came back to this park every other Sunday or so, but that was the last time I ever tried climbing it."

"And it's *still* going to be the last time," Mom said.

"Come on, Moll. That's the whole reason we're here. This is *the* tree."

"But didn't you just say how you almost died the last time? And you probably weighed seventy pounds then. And now you weigh . . . what? A hundred and seventy?"

"One sixty-three," Dad corrected.

Mom shot him a look.

"Okay. One sixty-seven."

While Mom and Dad "debated," I circled around to the other side and found the lowest branch, which I could just jump up and grab. From there it was a stretch to get to the next, but after that it would be just like climbing a ladder. I couldn't see anything special from down here, but that didn't mean that there wasn't something hidden up there. Another clue, maybe. Some little bit of Papa Kwirk. I leaped and grabbed that first thick handhold, my feet scrambling up the trunk. My parents continued to jabber at each other.

"Let's just call the fire department."

"Really, Molly? You want to call the fire department and explain how we think my dead dad left a clue to his missing body hidden in the top of a tree in the middle of a public park?"

"Okay, maybe not. But I also don't think that at your age you should be climbing fifty-foot-tall trees either. You know how I feel about—" My mother stopped, suddenly realizing where I was . . . already fifteen feet off the ground. "Rion Kwirk! You get down from there right this minute!"

I pressed close to the trunk, methodically working my way to the top, branch by branch. "Don't worry, Mom. I got this,"

I called down. I looked around for something, anything. A message from Papa Kwirk. Maybe something etched into the tree itself. Another scrap of paper nailed into the trunk or a photograph nestled in the leaves. I circled around as much as possible, worried that I would miss something on the other side as I climbed. The tree was so thick, I couldn't even wrap my arms around it.

"I'm going up too," I heard Lyra say, followed by the grunts of her trying to jump up to the first branch, but there was no way Mom was going to let more than one of us break our neck. *Finally,* I thought, *something I can do that my sisters can't.*

Thirty feet up now. The branches were getting thinner, some of them bending underfoot. I knew I wouldn't be able to go too much higher.

"Be careful!" Dad commanded, somehow sounding just as panicked as Mom.

I was high enough now that looking down made me dizzy. More concerning, though, was that there was nothing up here. Maybe Dad had the wrong tree. Or we were thinking about the clue the wrong way.

That's when I spotted it, on the other side of the trunk. Something that clearly didn't belong: a ziplock bag impaled on an upturned branch, just dangling there like ripe fruit.

"I think I found something!" I stretched for another branch and pulled myself a little closer. "It's a book." I could see the cover through the plastic now. *"Bridge to Terabithia."* There was no immediate response from below. I glanced down to see the tops of everyone's heads, so far away.

Finally Dad's voice floated up to me. "Can you reach it safely? If you can reach it, just drop it, then come back down *slowly*." He even said the word "slowly" slowly.

"I think so!" I shouted. Provided I could wiggle it off the branch it was stuck to. My left hand had a death grip on a branch above, leaving me one free hand to work. I scooched around the tree and out on the limb, shuffling by centimeters. God, it was a long way down. I felt a leaf tickle my ear. Another branch poked me in the side. I managed a couple more inches, just enough to take hold of the bag. One good tug should do it.

"Rion, please be careful!" My mother was practically screeching now.

One. Good. Tug.

The bag ripped free, causing everything under me to shift. My foot slipped and suddenly I felt woozy, one leg hovering over nothing. The book slid out of my hand and heard it *thwip* and *thwack* as it tumbled through the branches below me. Not wanting to follow it down, I grasped madly for another branch to steady myself, finding a second, even skinnier limb for my dangling left foot to rest on.

I hugged the tree like it was a girl in a blue-and-orange dress.

"Rion!" Mom's voice. Dad's voice. Even Cass's voice.

"It's all right. I'm okay," I called down. "I'm coming down now."

I looked around for the easiest possible path when I noticed something else. Something I'd missed on the climb up, nestled between two branches. It looked like a giant Christmas ornament. Or like a cocoon, made out of papier-mâché. With a hole in it.

And something crawling out of that hole.

I heard a buzz in my left ear, followed by something landing on the back of my neck. I let go of the branch to swat it away.

Not my smartest move.

I am not allergic to bees. My mother is allergic to bees. But she is also allergic to dust mites and latex and mangos. Getting stung by one bee wouldn't have killed me.

Falling forty feet out of a tree, on the other hand . . .

I wasn't sure if the thing that landed on my neck was even a bee. All I know was that I panicked and slapped at it with the hand that had the surer grip. I felt the other branch snap off in my left hand, felt both of my feet slip out from underneath me, heard a bad word, a Papa Kwirk kind of word, slip from my lips, followed by my mother's shouting and the *fwip fwip fwip* of leaves brushing my ears. I felt the sting of smaller branches snagging my shirt, others bending beneath me, until I hit one big enough to stop me, my legs curling around it, hands groping for anything solid to hold on to.

I was hanging upside down, fifteen feet from the ground, my sweaty T-shirt falling over my face, blocking most of my view. I reached up, cursing my gym teacher for not making me do more sit-ups, trying to get one hand on the branch that had caught me, when I heard Dad's voice.

"It's all right, Rion. Just drop. I've got you."

I looked straight down, past my shirt, to see Dad standing right underneath me with his arms stretched out.

I shook my head. Fifteen feet was still a long way, and my father wasn't exactly a Master of the Universe. If it came down to it, I'm pretty sure Mom could take him in an arm-wrestling contest. There had to be a better way. "That's okay. I've got this," I said. I *so* didn't have it.

"I'm right here," he said, his voice suddenly calm.

He was right. But I had an image of my father lying in the grass, screaming and cradling his broken arm, Papa Kwirk running up to him, ten seconds too late. Saying you'll do something and actually doing it are two different things.

I could feel my legs slipping. I couldn't hang on. I looked back at Dad.

"I'll catch you," he said again. "I promise."

He promised.

I dropped.

We both hit the ground with a *whoomph*, Dad on the bottom sprawled across the grass, me an awkward bundle of splayed limbs in his arms. The air whooshed out of my lungs. I felt Dad's arms entwined with my legs, under my neck, my face pressed to his armpit, my elbow digging into his stomach.

He had caught me.

Mostly.

Dad started making strange sounds: a high-pitched whistling, heaving wheezing. It took a second to realize he was laughing, and struggling with it because he could hardly breathe with me on top of him. Mom was suddenly in my face, pulling me to my feet.

"Are you hurt? Can you see? Are you dizzy? How many fingers am I holding up? Oh my god, you're BLEEDING!"

I reached up to my cheek. There was a little scratch there from where a branch must have grazed me. "I'm all right, Mom," I said. "It's him you should worry about." I pointed at Dad, who still lay there in the grass, looking up at the magic tree with laughing tears in his eyes.

The tree that could make you disappear could also make you reappear. Suddenly. In your father's arms.

Ta-da.

Cass looked at me and shook her head. "Such a swooner."

Ten minutes later, we were on the playground. Cass and Lyra took over the two working swings while Mom broke out the emergency medical kit. The Bag of Holding came equipped with bandages, gauze, tape, antiseptic cleansing wipes, cotton swabs, a pair of gloves (latex-free), and a disposable poncho. Not to mention the bottle of Bactine that she was spraying the cuts on my arm with, even though they were barely bleeding.

"I'm okay," I tried to assure her.

"You're okay when I say you're okay. You have sticks in

your hair." She picked one out and showed it to me.

"Maybe we should go to the emergency room, then," I said. "We can have them surgically removed."

"Stop being such a smarty-pants. You almost gave me a heart attack." The moment she said it, we both glanced at Dad to see if he'd heard, but he was distracted. "Bad choice of words." Mom found the smallest bandage she could for the cut on my cheek and I let her stick it on, vowing to tear it off the moment her back was turned.

Dad was sitting two benches away, the torn plastic bag at his feet, the treasure it contained in his hands. I managed to escape from Mom while she was stuffing her traveling hospital back into her bag and took the space next to him.

"All patched up?" he asked.

I nodded. "Good as new. So what's this book that I risked my life for?"

Dad held it up for me to see. "*Bridge to Terabithia*? It's kind of a classic," he said, squinting at the cover. "This was the book your grandmother and I were reading together when, you know . . ."

Dad trailed off. *Were* reading. Not *read*. They'd had to stop in the middle. He didn't need to explain.

"Afterward, I just couldn't bring myself to pick it back up," Dad continued. "I tossed it on my shelf and ignored it. I assumed Frank just threw it out with the rest of my stuff."

Like the Garbage Pail Kids cards currently still scattered across Aunt Gertie's kitchen floor. Dad assumed Papa Kwirk had trashed it all, or sold it at a yard sale, or taken it to Goodwill, but that wasn't turning out to be the case. It seemed Papa Kwirk had held on to more than we thought. The question was *Why?*

"Don't see what I'm supposed to do with it now, though," Dad mumbled. "There are no photos tucked inside. Nothing written on the flaps. No dedication or anything."

I reached up to my hair and picked out a leaf that my mother had somehow missed, pressing it between two fingers, feeling how smooth it was, like the cover of Dad's book. *Look for me in the magic tree, hidden among the leaves.*

Leaves.

I snatched the book from Dad's hands, ignoring his shocked look as I started flipping through the pages. *Leafing* through the pages. It took only a second to find what I was looking for. On the fourth page. "Look," I said, pointing. The letter K in the word "kid" was circled in pencil. There was another one on page six. The O in "grasshoppers." Flipping through, I noticed more letters with circles around them.

"Quick. Ask Mom if she has a piece of paper and a pen." It was a dumb question. Odds are she had a whole pack of Bics and three spiral-bound notebooks in that purse of hers. Dad skipped the asking part and just starting digging through the Bag of Holding. My sisters, noticing the sudden commotion by our bench, left their spots on the swings and came up behind me.

"What did you find?" Cass asked.

"Letters," I said, taking the pad of paper and pencil Dad handed me.

"Wow. Letters. In a book, no less. You *are* a genius," Cass smarted off, but then she saw me copying the circled letters down, carefully flipping from page to page, making sure I didn't miss one. There were four in chapter one. Three in chapter two. Two in chapter three. My family huddled around me as I sat on the bench, methodically working my way through Dad's old book, shouting when they spotted one before I could.

Cass started to get excited. "This is just like the time Elsalore has to decipher the password to get into Lord Blackheart's fortress."

"Yeah," I said. "Just like that."

The last chapter had four more circled letters: N, I, A, and M.

I stared at what I had written in the notebook.

KOLOORFEMNIHETTOTBOMFOETHLEBOTTNOILLWOWDANNIAM

"What's that supposed to mean?" I looked at Dad, who shrugged.

Lyra leaned over me, her chin practically resting on my head. "Wait. There were only a certain number of letters per chapter, right? So don't try to read them all at once. Break them up the way you found them."

"Yeah, maybe," I said. It was worth a shot. I went back through each chapter, putting a slash in between the letters that marked the end of one chapter and the start of the next. When I'd finished, I read the whole thing out loud, stumbling over the unfamiliar sounds.

"Kolo orf em ni het totbom fo eth lebott no illwow dan niam."

"Well, that clears things right up," Mom said.

"What's a totbom?" Cass asked.

"Maybe it's Vietnamese?" I suggested. After all, Papa Kwirk had taught me a few Vietnamese phrases from his time over there, though most of them were dirty and I was sworn not to repeat them around Mom or Dad.

Lyra groaned and plucked the notebook out of my hands. "Come on, people," she said. "That's not Vietnamese. Don't you get it? It's a jumble."

"You're a jumble," I said, slightly miffed at her grabbiness, even though I'd done the same thing to Dad only minutes ago.

"No. See?" she said, and then she started scribbling in the notebook we'd taken from my mother's purse, rearranging the new groups of letters to make actual words. English ones. She worked quickly with her tongue poking out of the corner of her mouth and got hung up only once, on illwow, but then Cass, who was standing next to her, whispered, "Willow." The rest fell quickly into place.

Lyra held the notebook up proudly. "'Look for me in the bottom of the bottle on Willow and Main,'" she read.

Dad wrapped his arms around her, squeezing her tight. "You . . . are a genius," he said. Except, unlike Cass, he actually meant it.

And it was probably true. Lyra probably was a genius.

But if it wasn't for me, we wouldn't even have the book in the first place.

WHY I WILL NEVER GET IN A BAR FIGHT WITH MY SISTER

You fall, and they catch you.

I don't know a whole lot about parenting, being twelve years old and never even having kissed a girl, but I know that's a big part of it (the catching, not the kissing). They wait at the end of the slide the first time you go down. They stand at the bottom of the stairs. They hold your hand as you teeter along the icy driveway. You're going to fall. They know it. So they spend fifty-nine seconds of every minute watching, so that they can be there when your shoelaces trip you up, waiting to say, "I got you."

Except when they don't.

I learned to ride a bike at age eight. Later than both of my sisters. It was a matter of choice—at least that's what I told myself. I liked to run, and my two spindly legs could take me anywhere I wanted to go. But the truth was, I was scared.

It was only the frustration of watching my older sister zip around the block with no hands, mocking me with her stuck-out tongue, that persuaded me to learn. On a sun-drenched Saturday afternoon in the middle of June, while Cass was at art camp so she couldn't make fun of me.

I learned on her old bike—salmon pink with purple flowers and a white plastic basket with Dora the Explorer on the front. That bike was the *real* motivator. The moment I could make it down our street and back without falling, Dad said he would take me to the store to pick out something a little more my speed, meaning the red-and-blue Spider-Man bike that I'd had my eyes on for weeks.

But first I had to learn to stay upright. And Mom had volunteered to be my teacher.

The same woman who insisted we keep those plastic baby-proofing plugs on the unoccupied outlets in our kitchen permanently because one of us could accidentally slip and jam a butter knife into it and electrocute ourselves—she was going to teach me to ride a bike.

So she stood behind me, one hand next to mine on the handlebar, the other on the seat, pushing me, steadying me, doing all the work for me, until I started to pedal faster than she could push. And even then she was running beside me, huffing words of encouragement, refusing to let go.

And because she wouldn't let go, I never managed to pick up enough speed. I would wobble and panic and scream, and she would stop me before the bike tipped over. Time and time again.

"He just can't seem to get his balance," she said to my father, who had come out to check on my progress, which was effectively zero.

"Could have something to do with the knee pads you're making him wear," he joked. Then he offered to take over the lessons, suggesting that maybe my mother go read a book in the backyard or something.

"You don't want me to watch," she guessed.

"You don't want to watch," he insisted.

Three minutes later, I found myself at the top of our sharply slanted driveway, my knee and elbow pads in a pile in the grass, though my Spidey helmet (to match my future bike), was still snugly buckled to my noggin.

"Forty feet," Dad said, thumping me playfully on the top of the helmet. "The driveway is forty feet long, then it spits straight out to the street. You don't even have to turn. Just let gravity do the work, and when you hit the pavement, start to pedal. Easy peasy."

My father thought organic chemistry was easy peasy.

"I'm scared," I admitted. The driveway suddenly looked incredibly steep from atop Cass's sparkly, training-wheel-less bike. A veritable Everest. A one-way ticket to a fractured skull.

"It's all right," Dad said. "Nothing terrible is going to happen to you. I promise."

My father never promised anything he couldn't live up to, at least not to me.

I took a deep, determined breath and nodded.

Dad let go.

The bike quickly gathered speed as it rolled down the driveway, my feet slipping off the pedals that started spinning too quickly, all my concentration on just keeping the handlebars straight and not veering into the grass. And for a moment, it felt like I was flying.

Then the bike bumped off the curb and out into the street. I glanced behind me to my father, who was still standing at the top of the driveway, making pedaling motions with his hands. My focus lost, I felt the handlebars twist and frantically yanked them the other way. One foot slipped off the pedal again, the bike began to wobble, and I went down. Hard.

My Spidey head bounced a little. Tiny pebbles pockmarked my palms. My knee was barely scraped, but the rash on my arm just below my elbow was raw and already starting to spot over with blood. It hurt like a hundred beestings.

Dad was beside me instantly, it seemed, untangling me from the bike and pulling me into his lap as I started to cry, cradling my bloody arm. Dad gave it a good look, then inspected the rest of me before unbuckling my helmet and setting it beside my bike with its still-spinning back tire.

"That was good," he said.

Good? I thought. *How in the world was that good?* I'd barely made it those forty feet.

"You promised," I sobbed at him.

"I promised nothing terrible would happen," he corrected. "This isn't terrible. This is a scratch. And scratches are just reminders of what to do differently next time." He wiped my leaky nose with his sleeve and stood me up. "Come on. Let's get something on that before your mom sees."

He guided my bike—Cass's bike—to the top of the driveway with one hand, guiding me with the other. We snuck into the bathroom and got the bloody elbow cleaned off. Then Dad led me back out front. "This time, don't forget to keep pedaling. It's easier to stay balanced when you are moving fast," he said.

That didn't make any sense at all. It was harder to do things fast. Coloring. Using scissors. Solving Rubik's cubes. I shook my head. The man was crazy.

"You can do this, Rion." He patted the bicycle seat. I considered refusing, kicking the bike over, and running to my room, but I didn't. Partly because I wanted to learn. Partly because I wanted that Spider-Man bike.

But mostly because he said I could.

"Second time's the charm." Dad held the bike steady as I climbed back on. He made sure my helmet was buckled tight, and then he let go again.

He was wrong.

Second time was not the charm. Third neither. I fell four

more times that day, in fact, though none of the others was as bloody as the first, and after each fall, I just grew more determined not to fall again. Until I made it forty feet and forty feet more. Until I heard him cheering me on.

When Mom saw the dirty bandage two hours later, she still insisted on dousing my entire arm in hydrogen peroxide, which made me grimace, because I really couldn't stand the smell of the stuff.

It stank all the way to Walmart, so I just stuck my head out the window, smiling the whole trip.

They catch you or they don't. Sometimes it's on purpose. I guess because they know it's only going to be a scratch— nothing that a Band-Aid and a cookie won't fix. But sometimes they don't catch you because they can't, because they don't get there in time, or they had no idea that you were about to crash.

Or maybe because they were falling themselves.

I was a mess.

I had blood on one sleeve of my shirt from an oak tree's ragged claws, and a matching spot of strawberry ice cream on the other sleeve. I also had a mark where Cass had jabbed me too hard with a stick the other morning, and a bit of a bruise where she had punched me even harder. My nails were still caked with dirt, despite my shower, and my hair was going haywire. But I didn't care. I was running on two thousand calories of ice cream (estimated), and the rush that comes from tracking your dead grandfather through the streets of his hometown.

"'Look for me in the bottom of the bottle,'" Lyra repeated, still holding the jumble that she'd unscrambled.

"Sounds like the lyrics to a bad country song," Cass said.

"Name a *good* country song," I challenged.

Cass opened her mouth and then closed it. She only knew show tunes. And the Biebs. Nobody in my family had any taste in music.

Dad was quiet. He leaned against the Tank, arms crossed, looking across the parking lot at kids still spinning on the roundabout. They were different kids at this point, but they were going through the same motions, taking turns pushing each other, leaning over the edge, just far enough so they could imagine falling off. I wondered what thoughts were spinning inside his head. If he was thinking about Papa Kwirk or Grandma Shelley or about me falling out of that tree on top of him. Or maybe he was just trying to figure out where to go next.

"South Koreans sometimes turn their dead into decorative beads and then stick *them* in a bottle," Lyra informed us. "But that's mostly because they're running out of room to bury people."

"I think that's enough from *National Geographic* for now, Ly," my mother said.

"Actually, I read about that one in one of Dad's science magazines."

The dangers of keeping your reading material in the bathroom where your ten-year-old daughter can get to them.

"You don't really think Aunt Gertie put Papa Kwirk in a bottle, do you?" Cass asked. "I mean, wouldn't that be weird?"

"Yeah," I said, "*that* would be weird."

"'Willow and Main.' Is that a corner here in town?" Mom looked at Dad, who just frowned back at her. He had the same look on his face as this morning, when he'd heard about the computer hacking at Kaslan's.

"I know where it is," he said. He looked at the book in his hands, the story he'd never had a chance to finish. "I've been there before."

The area around Willow and Main Street was nothing like the picturesque blocks of downtown Greenburg. There were no cobblestone paths. No old-fashioned streetlamps. No fancy signs with gilded lettering telling you how long buildings had been around. Instead, the streets were potholed, the sidewalks littered with trash. We passed a series of chain restaurants and strip malls where every second building was a nail salon and every third building was for rent. We passed three different tire stores. I suspected the potholes kept them all in business.

The intersection itself had a drugstore, a jewelry store, and a bank. It seemed like a curious combination, just begging to be on the local news. You could buy a pair of pantyhose from the one to use as a mask while you robbed the other two.

And to work up the courage for your crime spree, you could

first have a drink at Bailey's Pub, right across the street.

That's where we were headed, Dad said. I nodded. Seemed like as good a place as any to find an empty bottle.

He pulled the Tank into the pub's parking lot and stared at the front entrance for a solid minute, almost as if he was waiting on Papa Kwirk to come strolling through. The neon writing on the darkened windows advertised half off cocktails during happy hour and karaoke every Thursday night. The sign said they were open from noon to midnight. According to the clock on the dash, it was well after four. We'd spent the entire afternoon chasing after Papa Kwirk, and we ended up at a bar, of all places.

"I think I've heard of this place," Cass said.

I thought I had to. At least heard of an Old Man Bailey. I remember once Papa Kwirk telling me that he wouldn't still be around if it weren't for Old Man Bailey, or, as he put it, "that old coot saw me through some pretty hard times." Of course, Tasha's Dad said the same kinds of things about Papa Kwirk. Maybe that's just how people talked in Greenburg.

"Home away from home," Dad mumbled, more to himself, I think, than to us. I had to lean forward from the back seat to hear. "Two or three nights a week, I'd hear your grandfather leave. He probably thought I was asleep. Heard the click of the front door and the car starting in the driveway. I'd get up and watch out my bedroom window as he turned at the end of our block. Some nights it would take me hours to fall back asleep. In the mornings, I'd ask him where he'd been, like he was some teenager breaking curfew. He'd just say, 'I was at Bailey's,' and that would be the end of it. He'd shuffle off to bed and be snoring before he hit the sheets."

I shot Cass a did-you-know-about-this look. She shrugged a news-to-me shrug. I knew that Dad had spent a lot of time alone after Grandma died, but I guess I never stopped to think about what that meant, outside of him knowing so many theme songs from hours of watching cartoons.

Now I knew: he was alone in the house because Papa Kwirk had been here instead.

I tried to imagine what it would be like, having your one parent—your only parent—leave you by yourself in the middle of the night to come to a place like this. No one to stay up and wait with you till that parent returned. Nobody to teach you how to play poker with Goldfish crackers. Nobody to slip off your shoes and tuck you in.

The Tank's engine continued to purr; Dad's hands still rested on the wheel. For a moment, I thought he was going to throw it in reverse and drive us back to Aunt Gertie's, but then he turned the key and unbuckled his seat belt.

"All right. Let's go."

"I'm not sure the kids are allowed," Mom said.

"It's the middle of the afternoon," Dad countered. "And there's no sign on the door saying otherwise. Besides, it's not like we're going in there to *drink*."

Our parents never opened a bottle of wine with dinner. When New Year's Eve rolled around and we had people over to watch the ball drop, my parents would take an obligatory sip of champagne and leave the rest in the glass while my sisters and I drank sparkling grape juice out of plastic cups. I'd never seen Papa Kwirk drink anything but coffee and ginger ale either, though. Of course, he and Aunt Gertie always left before New Year's.

I'd been in restaurants with bars before, but I'd never been any place that called itself a pub. I expected old, dark wood, gouged and stained. Cigarette burns in the seat fabric. Peanut shells and the smell of stale sweat, a dartboard missing half its darts, and maybe a pool table with a long, jagged scratch down the middle where a fight had broken out and a chip in the wood where someone had forcibly lost a tooth.

Instead, we basically walked into an Applebee's.

The fluorescent lighting was bright and warm, showing off clean tables and floors. An odd assortment of decorations hung from the walls, everything from old board-game boxes to airplane propellers to rowboat oars. There were three times as many booths as barstools, and the whole place smelled like steak sauce rather than BO. Instead of flashing neon advertisements for Budweiser, there was a giant chalkboard that said *New IPAs*. The same chalkboard said the soup of the day was tomato bisque. "What the heck *is* bisque?" I asked Lyra, but even she didn't know.

As soon as we stepped in, the bartender, a young woman with short spikey blue hair, waved to us. "Hi there. Welcome to Bailey's," she said, obviously thinking nothing of a family of five showing up at her door at four in the afternoon. "Dining in or carrying out?"

The thought of eating anything made my stomach clench. Eight scoops of ice cream were still taking a very rocky road through my plumbing.

"Neither," Dad said, shuffling up to the bar so he wouldn't have to shout to be heard. There were a dozen or so people in the pub already, scattered at different tables, perhaps enjoying the half-off cocktails. Nobody was paying any attention to us. "This may sound strange, but I'm actually here looking for my father, Frank Kwirk."

"Kwirk?" The bartender repeated. "All right. Hang on a second." She banged an empty mug on the bar. "Excuse me. Is there a Kwirk in the house?"

A handful of strange faces looked over at us. A few shook their heads.

"Ah," Dad said quickly, reaching for the bartender's wrist, maybe to stop her from banging again. "Sorry. I guess I wasn't clear. He's not, like, *here* here. And if he *is* here, I'm pretty sure he's not going to answer you." Dad half laughed to himself. "You see, he's dead."

The bartender yanked her hand away. "Okay. *Seriously* creepy."

Dad put his hands up defensively. "No, not like that. I don't mean like his *ghost* is haunting the place or anything. I mean his actual dead body could be here somewhere."

"Good job, Dad," I whispered. "That's much better."

The bartender with the blue hair took several more steps back. "Riiiight," she said, stretching the word as long as it would go. "Let me just go get my manager." She raised a finger before disappearing around the corner of the bar and down a hallway. I figured she was calling the police. Or she'd gone to get a baseball bat or a gun. I'm not sure what it was about this town that made me think everybody owned a firearm. Maybe I'd inherited some of my mother's paranoia.

Dad didn't seem fazed, though. He looked around at the tacky decorations and the digital kiosks on each of the tables. "It's not quite how I remembered it," he said, but before he could elaborate, the bartender with the blue hair returned, along with an older man dressed in a button-down shirt and jeans. He looked plenty big enough to throw us out without having to resort to using a baseball bat. The top two buttons of his shirt were undone, showing off a broad chest with lots of hair, just like Papa Kwirk. A pointed goatee framed his smile. He looked oddly familiar.

"Fletcher Kwirk?" he boomed. "Hi. Isaac Alvero. We met yesterday at the memorial service?"

Dad shook his head as he shook the man's hand. "I'm sorry, I'm afraid I don't remember. There was . . ." Dad struggled. "There was a lot going on."

"You're telling me. That marching band was somethin' else, wasn't it? Your aunt Gertrude really knows how to make an impression."

"She does at that," Mom agreed.

Mr. Alvero gestured to the closest booth and asked us all to sit. Lyra and Cass somehow managed to squeeze me between them, while the manager of Bailey's Pub pulled up a chair at the edge. "So, what can I do for you all today?"

The way he said it was peculiar, like all my teachers who already know the answer but don't know if *you* know it and are tired of just feeding it to you. I'm not sure if Dad picked up on it, though. He was too busy taking everything in. "This place sure is different," he said.

"That's how it goes. You gotta change with the times. We cater to a younger crowd now," the big man with the goatee explained. "Locally sourced lettuce on your free-range grilled chicken sandwich and all that."

"And how long have you worked here, Mr. Alvero?" Mom asked, probably just making conversation. Or maybe she was getting at something.

"Well, I've only been the *manager* here for five years, but before that I was a bartender for almost twenty. Back then this place was a real hole-in-the-wall. That's probably the Bailey's *you* remember," he said, looking directly at my father.

Dad shrugged. "I'd only been here once or twice," he said. "Frank was the regular."

"That he was," Isaac said.

"Wait, so you knew Papa Kwirk?" Cass asked.

The manager looked at us three Kwirk kids scrunched together on one side. "You kidding? I got to know your granddad pretty good over the years. We talked all the time."

The word "granddad" struck me as funny. Papa Kwirk was no granddad. Granddads drove Buicks; Papa Kwirk rode a Harley.

The front door opened, and a young couple came in and took seats at the bar. Mr. Alvero waved to them and they waved back. I tried to picture Papa Kwirk, about my father's age, sitting on one of those stools, telling jokes to a twenty-five-year-old Isaac Alvero behind the bar, both of them with their top two buttons undone. I wondered what all they talked about. Baseball? Money problems? The price of gas? If I had to guess, I'd venture that Isaac had heard Papa Kwirk's old war stories as many times as we had. Maybe more.

"Doesn't surprise me," Dad said. "He spent a lot of time here. Over a lot of years."

"You could say that," the manager said after a moment.

"Stayed right up until closing time most nights, didn't he?"

I could sense something sour seeping into Dad's voice. Like the aftertaste of New Year's sparkling grape juice.

Mr. Alvero stopped smiling. "Most nights. Yeah."

Dad nodded. He looked like one of those TV lawyers, pressuring a witness. He leaned across the table. "So let's be honest, because there's really no point in hiding it. What are we talking? Fifteen? Twenty hours a week? Just how much time *was* my father here?"

Isaac Alvero scratched his goatee, though he didn't flinch from my father's stare. "Couldn't tell you for certain," he said with a shrug. "Though we've probably got it written down somewhere, if you really want to know."

Dad laughed a strangled kind of laugh. "Did you hear that, kids? They kept track of how many hours your grandfather spent here. Now what does *that* tell you?"

I wasn't sure, but Isaac was quick with a response. "Don't know what it tells *you*, but it told *us* how much to pay him."

Dad's laughing stopped, his face pinching like he'd bitten into a spoiled-milk-flavored jelly bean.

Mom shook her head. "Wait. Did you say pay him? For what, exactly?"

"Busing tables, mostly," Isaac said with a shrug. "Sweeping and mopping. Tossin' out troublemakers. Occasionally he'd have to fill in on the grill, but he was a lousy cook. Man couldn't make a bowl of pretzels if you helped him open the *bag*. But you probably know that, being his son and all." The manager of Bailey's fixed my father with an amused look.

The image in my head suddenly shifted. No longer was Papa Kwirk huddled over an empty beer glass with his elbows on the bar. Instead he had his arms in suds up to those elbows, scrubbing out shot glasses.

Dad leaned back and shook his head. "No. I'm sorry, Mr. Alvero. My father didn't *work* here. He was a repairman all his life. He worked for the same heating and air-conditioning company for twenty-eight years. He just retired, what was it, three years ago?" He looked to Mom for confirmation. "I know. We sent him a card."

It was true. I remembered signing it. We were invited to

the retirement party, of course, but we didn't go because Dad had to work overtime in the lab that weekend. Aunt Gertie called and told us all about it, though. They gave Papa Kwirk a plaque to commemorate his years of service, plus free heating and air-conditioning tune-ups for life. Sort of like giving Michelangelo free art lessons as a thank-you for painting the Sistine Chapel.

"Well, sure, that was his day job," Isaac explained. "But then he was also here a few nights a week. I should know. I was here right along with him. Ol' Frank, he was good at cleaning house. Come three o'clock in the a.m., he'd start to herd the regulars through the door, but always in such a way that you didn't feel like you were being thrown out, you know what I mean?"

Dad shook his head. "No. You're wrong. I'm sorry, but you're wrong. Frank left me home alone after Mom died. He snuck out in the middle of the night and came home reeking, barely able to stand."

"I'm telling you, Mr. Kwirk, your father was an employee," Mr. Alvero insisted.

"And I'm telling you my father was a drunk!"

Dad's voice was suddenly loud enough that a few of the pub's patrons glanced our way. I sensed Cass tense up next to me, but she didn't make a sound. This was one of those sit-quietly-and-soak-it-in kinds of conversations. Dad gritted his teeth as the other customers went back to their own conversations.

Mom gave Mr. Alvero a sympathetic glance, but the pub's manager seemed to shrug and nod at the same time. "I can't say you're wrong," he admitted. "In fact, there were some nights I ended up kicking *him* out. But there came a point in Frank's life when I think he saw the road he was walking, and he knew he had to change. And it was about that same time that Old Man Bailey offered him a job. A chance to straighten himself out, and a little more money to give his son what he wanted."

"What *I* wanted?" Dad said, clearly trying to control his voice. "The only thing I ever wanted was to—"

"Get the hell outa Greenburg," Mr. Alvero said, snatching the words from the tip of Dad's tongue. "That's how Frank used to put it. 'Gotta save for college,' he'd say. 'Get my boy into a good school and away from his old man.'" Isaac Alvero shook his head. "He was always bragging on you, about how smart you were. Fletcher Kwirk. Science whiz. Figured you'd go somewhere with a great reputation. Definitely out of state. All the way to—where'd you go to college again?"

"Columbia University," Lyra piped up proudly, apparently not feeling the sit-quietly vibe that Cass and I were giving off. Dad didn't look proud, though. He looked like someone had punched him right in the heart.

"Columbia," Isaac repeated. "That's right. New York City. Nice school."

I knew "nice" meant pricey. Hard for a single father to afford only working one job as a repairman. Dad continued to shake his head.

"Kids are expensive," Isaac continued, looking over at my mother. "You know that, Mrs. Kwirk. I got two girls of my own. Between the clothes and the car insurance and the 'Can I have a few bucks for this?' and 'Can you give me twenty dollars for that?' And don't even get me started on college. My oldest wants to go to Oxford. *Oxford*. In *England*. Look at me. I manage *this* place. You think I got the money for Oxford?" Isaac Alvero laughed again. He had a husky kind of laugh.

The door opened, letting in the sounds of the street outside, and Dad started doing that thing with his fingers, the itsy-bitsy spider motions he'd made the night we found out about Papa Kwirk. "I knew he saved money . . . ," he said, looking down at his hands. "Between what he'd saved and the scholarships . . . but he never said anything about working *here*."

Isaac shrugged. "Wiping up whisky and scrubbing out urinals ain't anyone's dream job, Mr. Kwirk. Maybe he thought you'd think less of him if you knew."

"Think less of him?" Dad looked up. "Less than believing he was sneaking out of the house to get drunk?"

"Sometimes we don't want people to know how tough things are, 'cause when they do, they feel like they owe us something. And that can be a hard feeling to live with."

I pictured Papa Kwirk again, this time stumbling through the door at four in the morning, wobbly from exhaustion, desperate to kick off the work boots that he'd worn for twenty hours straight. No wonder he was still out cold when Dad woke up. Young Fletcher, fixing his own breakfast, packing his own lunch, seeing himself to the bus stop. Coming home to an empty house.

Starting to hate his own dad.

How does something like that slip by you? If either Mom or Dad had a second job, wouldn't I notice?

But this was Fletcher Kwirk. The scientist. For him, the simplest solution is usually the right one. And the simplest explanation was this: Papa Kwirk was an alcoholic. He went to the bar. He came home nursing a headache and smelling of beer. It was a good hypothesis, except Dad never bothered to test it. He'd just always assumed he was right.

"I'm not saying Frank wasn't what you say he was." Mr. Alvero looked my father square in the eyes. "I'm just saying that's not *all* he was."

The manager of Bailey's Pub said he had something he wanted to show us. Something he'd been hanging on to. It was back in the office—he just had to run and get it.

Dad was obviously shaken. I tried to think of something I could say to him, but all I could come up with was some sarcastic comment about me not wanting to go to Oxford. "I think I need some water," he said, and stood up to go talk to the blue-haired girl who probably still thought he was crazy. Mom got up to follow him.

"Sit tight," she said, leaving me smooshed between my sisters, too tight already.

"Papa Kwirk was an alcoholic?" Cass whispered when she

was sure our parents were out of earshot. "How come Dad never told us?"

I tried to imagine how *that* particular dinner conversation would have gone. "Made a new jelly bean at work today. Tasted terrible. Had to drink three cups of water to get the taste out of my mouth. Hey, speaking of drinking and terrible things, did you know your grandpa is an alcoholic?"

Of course, it wouldn't have been any worse than a singing clown showing up at our door to tell us Papa Kwirk was gone.

"Maybe Dad didn't want us to think less of him either," I said. I'm not sure anything anybody could say about Papa Kwirk would surprise me, but I did feel a tug of disappointment. Mostly it hurt to see the look on Dad's face. I thought about all the Christmases spent together, the two of them almost always in separate rooms, both of them acting as if they were still hundreds of miles apart.

"Dipsomaniac," Lyra said.

"What?"

"That's what they used to call people who drank too much. It was on my word-a-day calendar." The calendar had been my Christmas present to her last year. The same thing I'd gotten her for the last three years, which I guess meant I partly had myself to blame for how she turned out.

"Great. So our grandfather was a maniac," I said.

"A *dipso*maniac," Lyra corrected.

"It must have been hard on him," Cass said, though I wasn't sure whether she meant Dad or Papa Kwirk.

While Mom and Dad continued to talk by the bar, two more guys came through the door and were told by the bartender to find a seat wherever. They moved to the corner on the opposite side of the room. Cass stared after them. "Huh," she said.

"What?"

"Nothing," Cass said. "Just, I'm pretty sure I saw those same two guys at the park this afternoon."

I gave them a second glance, then a third. The taller of the two had a mongo mustache, big enough to completely cover his lips, top and bottom. The shorter one had bright orange hair like Chuckles, and clusters of freckles scattered over his face.

"You mean Freckles and Broomstache?" I asked.

"Broomstache." Lyra giggled. "That's a good one."

I couldn't be sure, but I thought I'd seen them before too. Maybe at the memorial service. Or maybe I'd also just caught a glimpse of them at the park. Honestly, there was too much going on to keep track of the parade of strangers who populated the town of Greenburg.

"Don't stare. They're looking at us," Cass warned, talking behind her hand and banging her knee against mine. Sure enough, Freckles looked at me and smiled. Then he turned his attention to his phone just as Mom and Dad squeezed back into our booth. Isaac Alvero followed behind them, holding an empty bottle with a white label. Jim Beam bourbon. He set it on the table with a pronounced *thunk*.

"*This* was Frank's favorite," Isaac said, admiring the bottle. "Same drink. Every night. He drank it neat. No ice. Two fingers a glass." Isaac demonstrated Papa Kwirk's preferred serving with one hand, keeping the other wrapped around the bottom of the bottle as if he were afraid to let go of it. "He drank this *particular* bottle of bourbon in one sitting. You know what night *that* was."

Dad nodded. I had a guess, but I wasn't sure. Not until Mr. Alvero started talking again. The manager turned his head and nodded toward the bar. "He sat right there and emptied the whole bottle without saying a word. I even let him pour himself, even though his hands trembled so much by the end he could hardly lift the bottle."

That Elvis song snuck into my head. The one from the service the day before.

Well, my hands are shaking and my knees are weak. . . .

"And after he emptied this one, he asked for another. The bar was practically empty by that point. I was about to give it to him when Old Man Bailey comes over. He was still running the place then. Bailey took your dad's empty glass away. Told him to go home. Said he'd had enough. Course, Frank started cussing and carrying on about how he was a paying customer and could do whatever he pleased and didn't we know what had happened to him, what he was going through? And Old Man Bailey looked him square in the eyes and asked, what would Shelley say if she walked through the door and saw him like this? Because she could, you know. She was watching him, waiting on him to come home. And that shut Frank right up. He still sat there for another hour, though. Not drinking. Just sitting. As if he couldn't bear to walk out that door."

Can't seem to stand on my own two feet . . .

"That was the night," Isaac Alvero continued. "There were others after it—plenty of them—but that was the worst. After we called your father a cab, Old Bailey told me to keep this empty bottle on the shelf as a reminder for your dad and me both that there's nothing at the bottom worth getting at."

From the bar, the blue-haired girl told Isaac he had a phone call.

"That's probably him now," Isaac said. "Ol' Bailey retired a while back, but he has to call every afternoon to make sure I haven't burned the place down." The manager looked at the bottle still in his hand. "I'll just leave this here for you." He stood up and carefully put his chair back at the table where it belonged before heading to the bar, leaving us with the bourbon that Papa Kwirk had drained in one sitting, thirty years ago.

"Look," Lyra said, pointing.

It had been hard to tell at first because of the way Isaac had been holding it, but now you could clearly see a scrap of paper resting in the bottom. Much like the one that had been waiting for us in Papa Kwirk's coffin.

Dad took the bottle in both hands and tilted it upside down. The paper dropped toward the neck but stopped, trapped. It must have been rolled up in order to slide it through the neck, but it had unfurled since. Dad tried reaching in with his pinky but couldn't get ahold. He shook it, swung it, and banged the bottom of it repeatedly with his palm before setting it back on the table with a grunt. "It's stuck," he said.

"Maybe we can still read it?" Mom suggested.

"Let me try." I started spinning the bottle around, slowly, trying to get the right angle to capture the light from overhead so I could, but the way it was still half rolled up, it was impossible. I felt the bottle pulled from my hand. I tried to snatch it back, but Cass held it up over her head. She had six inches on me and longer arms.

"Come on, people," she said with a huff. "Book Two of the Vendar Chronicles? The scene where Elsalore is surrounded in Dargol's tavern by a dozen Anthrokian bounty hunters and has no way to defend herself? I swear you all need to read more."

My big sister slid out of the booth and positioned herself where Isaac had been sitting only moments before, planting her feet and turning the bottle upside down, gripping it by the neck with both hands. She licked her lips. "I've always wanted to do this," she said.

"Cassiopeia Elizabeth Quirk, what on earth do you think you're—"

But Mom didn't get to finish her sentence.

I cringed and pushed back against Lyra, flattening her against the side of the booth as the bottle came down, violently striking the edge of the wood table, a percussive crash followed by the melody of shattering glass. Sharp shards skittered across the table, catching the light. The bulk of the bottle clattered to the floor in three jagged pieces, leaving only the neck, a wicked-looking glass dagger, in my sister's hands, perfect for gouging an Anthrokian bounty hunter's eyes out. Cass looked at it with a gleeful smile.

"Cool," Lyra said.

Everybody in the pub was staring at us now. A family of four. The couple at the bar. Freckles and Broomstache. I guess none of them had ever read Book Two of the Vendar Chronicles either.

Mom flashed Cass the Look of Ultimate Parental Disapproval, complete with Eyebrows of Extreme Archedness, and my sister gently set the deadly glass weapon she'd made on the table.

"Sorry," she said. She turned and waved to the people who had been quietly enjoying their half-priced margaritas and mozzarella sticks. "Sorry to bother you."

She sort of melted back into the booth, hands in her lap, but not before gingerly picking up a sliver of glass that she nearly sat on. There was usually applause whenever Cass finished a performance. This time she was just met with silence . . . until my mother started in again.

"Seriously, Cass, what were you *thinking*? You could have blinded us! You could have sliced your hand open! You could have lost a finger! Two fingers! Isn't that right, Fletcher? Fletcher?"

But Dad wasn't listening. He was on the floor by the table, on his hands and knees, in the midst of the mess that had once been his father's bourbon bottle, carefully pulling the slip of paper free from the heap of jagged glass.

The broom and dustpan given to us by the blue-haired bartender came with a dirty look.

"Here," she said, thrusting them into my father's hands. "And make sure you get all the little invisible pieces." I wanted to ask her how we would know whether we got them or not, but I was sort of afraid she might take the broom back and beat me with it. Instead, Dad gave the broom to Cass, who tried to give it to me, but I shook my head. I wasn't the one who just went Wild West in the middle of a wannabee Applebee's. Not that it hadn't been kind of awesome. Just that it wasn't my job to clean it up.

While Cass swept up the pieces she *could* see, the rest of us puzzled through what was written on the slip of paper Dad had recovered. Papa Kwirk's next clue.

WHEN YOU GET TO BE MY AGE, THERE'S ONLY ONE PLACE THEY CAN PUT YOU.

"Only one place they can put you?" Dad muttered. "The place *I* would have put him was the one place he *wasn't*."

I assumed he meant the casket. Except right now, old Mrs. Danfield was probably in there. Unless she had pulled a Papa Kwirk and made her family go hunting for her corpse as well. The Danfields were probably nothing like the Kwirks, though. Nobody was.

"Does he mean, like, a nursing home?" Mom pondered.

"Florida," I suggested. "Isn't that where they ship all the old people to?" Florida would have been loads better than Greenburg, Illinois.

"Duh." Lyra was shaking her head at all of us. "Obviously it's a *museum*. Papa Kwirk used to say this all the time. 'I'm so old, they're going to have to put me in a museum.'" Lyra tried to imitate our grandfather's raspy voice, but of course hers was too high and not phlegmy enough, so it came out sounding funny, like Mickey Mouse hitting puberty.

I couldn't remember the museum thing specifically, but Papa Kwirk did have a lot of sayings. Like being hungry enough to eat a horse. Or feeling like a one-legged man in a butt-kicking contest. Or not having the sense to pour piss out of a boot if the instructions were written on the heel. That was probably my favorite. They were a lot more fun than Dad's sayings, which were teacher-poster-type things like every journey starts with a single step and if opportunity doesn't knock, build a door.

"Is there even a museum here in Greenburg?" Mom asked, looking at Dad, the man who'd lived here for half of his life, but he shrugged.

Taking advantage of her being on her hands and knees under the table, I swiped Cass's phone from her back pocket and typed in the password that I'd secretly watched her key in a half dozen times: *elflove4ever.* Google soon informed me that the little town of Greenburg had not one but *two* museums.

"The Museum of Modern Warfare and the Kopfoben Wig Museum," I said.

"*Wig* museum?" Dad questioned. Maybe it opened after he went off to college. You couldn't grow up with a wig museum in your hometown and not know about it.

"Says here they have over four hundred wigs from all across the world. They apparently have a wig worn by Beyoncé *and* King Louis the Fourteenth."

"Like, the same wig?" Mom wanted to know.

I would have answered her, but Cass had finished her sweeping and snatched her phone back, giving me a dirty look.

"Well, I think it's pretty obvious where we should start looking," Dad said.

Papa Kwirk was a war veteran. And he clearly had a fondness for weapons, judging by the Christmas gifts I had stashed up in the attic. Plus, he'd never worn a hairpiece in his life.

"Except the Museum of Modern Warfare closes at five, and

it is now . . ." Cass checked her phone. "Four fifty-seven."

Three minutes. The only way we would get there in time was if it was right across the street. We could wait till morning when the museum reopened, of course. That's what people in their right minds would have done.

Which, of course, meant it wasn't even an option for us.

"We'll find a way," Dad said.

He could sense it. I could too. We were close. There was something about this last clue. *Only one place they can put you.* We would find him there. Or what was left of him, anyway. Then, finally, we could say goodbye and go back home.

"We're coming, Papa Kwirk," Lyra said to no one in particular as we pushed our way through the door of Bailey's Pub, leaving our mess on the table, along with a ten-dollar bill that my dad dropped for the disturbance we'd caused, even though we didn't even order anything.

My grandfather used to leave a five-dollar tip wherever he went, no matter what he got.

Leave it to Dad to one-up him.

THE KWIRKS GO TO WAR

The man who cracked open the creaky wood door at the Greenburg Museum of Modern Warfare looked like he might have seen every war in history. His pale, haggard face had been invaded by wrinkles, many of them marching down his forehead to the thick white eyebrows that he pinched at the sight of the five of us standing outside the redbrick building. The man's teeth were yellow like his eyes, and his breath smelled like cinnamon—the candy, not the spice. Dad had taught me how to tell the difference.

"I'm sorry," the old man said, frowning. "We're closed."

"I know, but—" Dad started.

"Our hours are posted right there on the door," the man interrupted. "Feel free to come back tomorrow."

The door creaked closed again, but my father put up both hands in desperation to stop it. We'd come through mountains and haunted woods. To the tops of bee-infested trees, to the bottom of the bottle and back. Through blood, sweat, tears, and an avalanche of ice-cream vomit, just to find our grandfather. It was hard to imagine anything standing in our way.

"So sorry to bother you, Mr. . . ."

"Oglesby," the old man said. "I am the curator of this facility, which, as I've already said, closes at five p.m." He pointed at the sign. No doubt he saw us as the kind of people who could not, in fact, pour piss out of a boot if the instructions were written on the heel.

"I understand," Dad continued calmly. "But this is important. My name is Fletcher Kwirk. This is my family. I'm afraid we might have left something inside your museum. Something important. And I was wondering if you could just let us have a look."

The old man's eyebrows shifted. "Kwirk?" he repeated. The whole family nodded in unison. "Hmph." I wasn't sure if it was an I-should-have-known kind of hmph or a that-name-means-nothing-to-me kind. Whichever it was, Mr. Oglesby didn't open the door any farther, and I suspected my dad—the stand-in-the-back, avoid-conflict-at-all-costs science geek—was about to muscle his way in, knocking this poor old man over like an NFL linebacker, but my mother had a softer approach.

"What war were you in, if you don't mind my asking, Mr. Oglesby?" Mom pointed to his arm. The sleeves of the old man's shirt were rolled up, revealing the words *Semper Fidelis* tattooed in fancy blue script. I had no idea what that meant, but obviously Mom did. "That *is* the Marines, isn't it?"

"Yes, ma'am. Third Battalion," the curator said in a manner that made it sound like we should be impressed. "Though I'm afraid I never got the opportunity to serve my country on the battlefield. My service ended abruptly two years before I would have been sent to Vietnam. An accident during a live-fire field test put me out of action." Mr. Oglesby reached down with his right arm, the one with the tattoo, and tugged at his pant leg, pulling it up to reveal a rather complicated contraption attached to his calf. His black sock concealed most of it, but you could tell by the scar tissue, white and ragged, that Mr. Oglesby's real leg stopped above the ankle. "At least when I'm told to put my best foot forward, it's an easy decision."

I snorted. Judging by the not-so-subtle elbow nudge I got from Cass, maybe this wasn't meant to be funny, but the smile on Mr. Oglesby's face suggested a little snort was okay.

"Sorry you lost your foot," Lyra said.

"This one suits me fine," the curator replied with a shrug. "And it's five fewer toenails I have to clip. *I'm* sorry for your loss," he said first to Lyra, then eyeing the rest of us. "I knew Frank. And I liked him—even if he did call me Old Splinterfoot."

I snorted again, but this time I got a cross look from Old Splinterfoot himself, and I snapped to attention, shutting my trap. Probably best not to mess with a marine.

"If you knew my father," Dad said, "then you should know

that he's actually the reason we're here. He asked us to come, as a way of honoring him, of paying our respects before we leave town. By letting us in, you wouldn't just be doing us a favor, you'd be doing him one too."

The curator stood there, jaw working back and forth as he took each one of us in. When he looked at me, I gave him my we're-really-not-as-crazy-as-we-look smile.

"Please. Just fifteen minutes," Dad pleaded. "We won't cause any trouble."

I noticed he didn't say "I promise." I thought about the mess we'd made in the ice-cream parlor bathroom, the hole we'd left in some poor lady's backyard, the shards of glass skittering across the table at Bailey's Pub. Beside me, Cass had her hands clasped together as if she were pleading for her life.

After a suspenseful pause, Mr. Oglesby nodded, stepping back and opening the door the rest of the way. "Fifteen minutes," he echoed. "After that I'm kicking you out, under-stood?"

We all nodded obediently.

"And don't think I can't kick either. This baby packs a wal-lop," he added, tapping his prosthetic foot against the tiled floor. "And I'm not too old to fight."

As far as museums go, the Museum of Modern Warfare was the first one I'd ever been to that I would want to spend an hour in.

So of course we had only a quarter of that.

The place had high ceilings and a polished green marble floor that I could see my reflection in. The exhibits started in the front vestibule with a display showing the history of America's involvement in armed conflict, starting with the American Revolution and going clear up to operations still going on in places like Afghanistan. The sign above the main entry into the museum displayed a quote from some guy named H. G. Wells: *If we don't end war, war will end us.* Deep, I guess, though you could probably say the same thing about global warming or fast food or the flu.

Mr. Oglesby corralled us in the center of the atrium. I couldn't help but notice how straight he stood. He had better posture than any of us.

"You'll have to look around yourselves; I'm not giving you the tour. Don't touch anything. Don't sit on anything. And don't smudge the glass. None of the guns or bombs in here are functional, but the knives and swords are sharp, so don't mess with them. I'll be in the front office if you need me." Mr. Oglesby moved toward the door behind the welcome desk, then turned and put up a crooked finger. "But don't need me," he said before shutting himself inside.

Dad got right down to business. "All right. We don't have much time. I think it's best if we split up."

Cass and I shared a nervous look. I figured she was having a total Scooby Doo moment like I was. Terrible things always happen when the gang splits up.

"What are we looking for?" Lyra asked.

"I'm not sure," Dad said. "Another clue. A hint. Anything with your grandfather's name or face or even just something that reminds you of him."

Papa Kwirk was a former soldier who got me crossbows and knives for Christmas, and I was standing in a museum full of deadly weapons. I was pretty sure *everything* was going to remind me of him.

"Just keep your eyes peeled and call out if you find something."

Dad clapped his hands and urged us onward, and armed with only the vaguest idea of what we were doing, we crossed under the arch with H. G. Wells's words of wisdom and were instantly transported back a hundred years, to 1914 and the start of World War I. According to the news articles on the wall, some guy named Franz got shot and triggered what was supposed to be the "war to end all wars."

"This Franz character must have been a pretty big deal to cause the whole world to go to war over his death," I remarked. Then again, people do some pretty wacko stuff when somebody close to them dies.

The moment we went back in time, we fanned out to cover more ground. The exhibits seemed to be in chronological order and mostly consisted of cabinets full of tools and uniforms and weapons, plus the placards used to identify them. I scanned everything, skimmed every line, inspected every artifact, looking for clues. The guns grew more high tech the farther you went, firing more bullets faster, though it still only took one to do the job. Bombs got bigger. Uniforms got more pockets. Only the boots didn't seem to change that much. I paused on a gas mask, thinking about all the times I'd pulled Papa Kwirk's finger. I doubted this was what he had in mind, but it made me smile thinking about it; he always lifted his leg when he farted to, as he put it, "ensure maximum particle dispersion."

I passed a hundred-year-old torpedo and a grenade called a potato masher for the way it was shaped. I supposed you could use it for that, provided it didn't explode in your face and ruin your Thanksgiving, which reminded me of the time our Thanksgiving was ruined because mashed potatoes and lasagna—like dads and grandfathers—didn't always go well together. Though now, at least, I had some idea why.

After what seemed like ten minutes of fruitless searching through the years 1914 to 1918, I turned a corner and jumped forward in time. I spotted Lyra in the middle of the World War II room, standing near a big display called Troop Transport through the Years. There were pictures of trucks and tanks and planes and boats, all with descriptions of how they'd evolved and been adapted to each new conflict, designed to get soldiers to places most of them were in no hurry to get to.

At the center of the exhibit sat a motorcycle, complete with sidecar. Lyra was admiring it. "It's a Harley. Papa Kwirk's is a Harley."

"They're called hogs," I said.

"I prefer to call them Harleys. Hogs sounds uncivilized."

It was a cool-looking bike. Papa Kwirk would have liked it. I could picture him, wearing a pair of those old-fashioned goggles, riding across the French countryside, delivering urgent stolen documents to High Command. That's when I noticed Lyra stepping over the velvet rope that was supposed to keep meddlesome kids like us from sitting on the bike and pretending they were fighting the Nazis. "What are you doing?" I hissed.

"C'mon, Rion. It's a bike just like his. Maybe he left a clue here or something," she said, starting to explore. She looked in the sidecar and even felt around in the leather satchels that hung from the bike's rear. "Nothing," she said after two minutes of looking, plopping down on the edge of the sidecar.

"Maybe that's because Papa Kwirk didn't *fight* in World War II," I told her. He was a Vietnam vet. We were a few decades behind.

Which probably meant . . .

I heard my father call out from around the corner.

"Guys, hurry up! In here!"

Lyra leaped over the velvet rope and ran ahead of me as we turned down a corridor into another large room. A massive map of Vietnam greeted us, the country divided into a green part and a red part with arrows scattered all around. Mom and Dad both stood in front of a large glass display near the back of the room. The sign beside it said *A Soldier's Story: Vietnam 1967–1975.*

I came up beside Dad, whose hands were pressed to the

glass. "In there," he said, almost breathless.

Inside the case was a collection of framed letters, all of them handwritten, some creased or weather-beaten or barely legible. Each letter was accompanied by an artifact: a combat knife, much like the one waiting for me in my attic at home. A rusted lighter. A deck of cards. A dog-eared novel (*Stranger in a Strange Land*—never heard of it). A Purple Heart medal displayed in its box.

The letters were all written by soldiers, most of them to family members or to high school sweethearts. To My Dearest Lisa. To My Brother Bill. Dear Mom and Dad.

And one to Shelley.

"Go ahead. Read it," Dad said. I could tell by the catch in his voice that he already had. I pressed my nose to the glass, my cheek close to Lyra's, who was on her tippy-toes, doing the same.

Dear Shelley,

Thank you for the last letter. And for the picture. The guys are jealous and giving me a hard time, but it's worth it to see your face. I'm back at base after an S&D and had my first real shower in six days—soap and all. I swear I scrubbed off seven layers before I found my own skin.

Not much to report, thankfully. Got more men down from diarrhea and heat exhaustion than Charlie lately. Bugs and heat. It's almost like the land itself wants us to leave. Last night Big Mac killed a spider that was big around

292

as my hand. Stabbed it with his Ka-Bar like he was going to roast it on a spit, then started chasing the rest of the squad around the barracks with it. I suspect one of us will find its shriveled-up body in our cot tonight. Big Mac's crazy like that. Though between the heat and the bugs and the bombs and the boredom, it's a wonder any of us are still sane.

I am ready to come home.

I can't stop thinking about that shell, the one I told you about in my last letter. I've still got it. Sarge said I could keep it 'cause it was a dud and because it's evidence that nobody in this war knows how to do a damn thing right. By all accounts, I should be dead. I know it. Sometimes I think maybe you had something to do with that. I figure it was either you or God or both. Everything happens for a reason, right? PFC Griggs says that's dangerous thinking, says you should assume that every round fired has your name on it and that the next shell that hits will blow your you-know-whats to you-know-where, but what does he know? He's from Kentucky and thinks <u>Bonanza</u>'s the best show ever made. He hums the theme song as he's falling asleep.

I miss you, Shel. You're pretty much the only thing that keeps me going out here. I can't wait for us to get married as soon as I get back. We'll find a nice house near the woods with a big backyard where you can plant your flowers and a good tree for climbing. We'll have a couple of kids and I can teach them how to fish and you can read them your *favorite books and we will have Sunday picnics and stuff them full of sweets and spoil them with all the stuff we never had growing up. It will be perfect. I just have to make it through this hell.*

I think about you all the time. I think about us growing old together. I would climb a mountain for you, but you know that already.

Wait for me. I'll be home soon.

Love,

Frank

I read the whole letter twice. As I read it the second time, the whole crazy puzzle of a day slowly started to piece itself together. A good tree for climbing. Learning how to fish. Favorite books. A perfect life. It was all there, in one form or another. Everything Papa Kwirk ever wanted.

Except for the growing old together.

It made my heart ache.

"Did you see this?"

Mom pointed. Next to the letter, lying on its side because it was too tall to stand upright, was an artillary shell.

No, not *a* shell. *The* shell. The one Sarge said Papa Kwirk could keep. My grandfather had somehow smuggled it all the way back home. It was his souvenir, his constant reminder of how close he'd come, just how lucky he was. It was olive green with yellow markings and a tarnished silver tip. The word "INERT" had been painted in white block letters across it. I hoped INERT meant "no longer blowupable." No doubt Lyra would know, but she had something else on her mind.

"Shell," she said, reciting from her dictionary or maybe just making up a definition on the spot. "A projectile containing an explosive charge. But also, more generally, a hard outer casing designed to protect or hold something."

I was about to suggest that she should give us some credit for not being *total* idiots when Dad's eyes lit up. *"Of course,"* he said, kissing the top of her head. I wasn't sure what caused my father's lightbulb to blink on, but apparently Mom did.

"Oh, Fletcher—you don't really think?"

"What? What is it?" I asked.

Dad nodded toward the cabinet.

"I think we found him," he said.

I looked at the glass cabinet, at my father, back at the cabinet. "Wait. You're telling me that Papa Kwirk is *inside* that shell?"

Dad nodded. "Something's in there," he said. "Has to be."

There was only one way to find out. Unfortunately, the glass cabinet containing the letter and dud artillery shell was locked. The door didn't even seem to have a latch or a handle of any kind on the front. There wasn't anywhere to put a key.

"It must have *some* kind of release," Dad said. He got on his tiptoes and reached to the top, running his hand along the edge until it stopped. I heard a click, and then the lock holding the door gave way. A secret trigger. Just like in a Scooby Doo cartoon.

Dad carefully slid the door open and took out the shell with both hands. The tip, where the fuse would have been, was only loosely screwed into the top. Probably somebody had dismantled it to remove its innards, just to be sure it was safe. Dad was still careful with it, though, handing the pointy top first to Mom, who shook her head vehemently, then giving it to me instead.

Dad peered inside the shell.

His breath hitched. He blinked, like, twenty times. Then, with two fingers, he reached inside and pulled out a small plastic bag, much like the one that had held Dad's childhood book back in the magic tree, the one that I'd almost killed myself trying to get to. Except this bag looked to be filled with sand. Brownish-gray sand.

But I knew what it really was. I knew in my gut.

Dad tucked the artillery shell under his armpit and carefully pried apart the seal, dipping a sweaty finger into the bag, a film of coarse brown dust clinging to the tip of it. He rubbed his thumb and finger together. He grunted and shook his head. And then, for the first time since this whole thing started, my father's eyes glossed over with tears.

"It's okay," he whispered. "I've got you."

I stood there, staring at the bag of dust in my father's hands. I didn't know what to say or even how to feel. Sad? Relieved? Confused? A little grossed out? I think it was all of those. But mostly I felt this weird sense of accomplishment, watching my dad hold his dad, knowing what we'd been through. What he'd been through.

Mom broke the silence, sniffing and wiping away her own tears. "Wait a minute, where's Cass? She needs to be here."

I glanced around the otherwise empty room. I wondered if she'd gotten lost. "We'll find her," I said. I handed the tip of the artillery shell back to Dad and gave Lyra a nudge toward the Gulf War while I headed back toward Korea. I was rounding the corner to the next room when I thought I heard footsteps.

"Cass, you'll never believe this. Guess where we found Papa Kw—"

But it wasn't Cass who appeared in the archway bridging the gap between two wars.

It was Broomstache. The guy from the pub. He was holding a baseball bat. And right behind him was Freckles with a knife.

That was suddenly pointed at my chin.

You know that moment when you've just discovered your bananapants grandpa's ashes hiding inside a fifty-year-old artillery shell in the middle of a war museum in his hometown, and you turn the corner to find yourself face-to-face with a couple of armed thugs who have, apparently, been stalking you for most of the weekend?

That's the moment when you should act on instinct,

letting your fight-or-who-are-we-kidding-it's-really-just-flight reflexes kick in, making you turn and run back to your parents rather than just stand there, staring dumbly at a man with more freckles on his cheeks than a planetarium has stars, giving him the one second he needs to get two beefy arms around you in a chest-crushing hug.

I could feel the point of the knife just tickling beneath my chin as Freckles pushed me around the corner back into the room where we'd found Papa Kwirk.

Mom gasped and Dad started forward the moment they saw me, but he froze when Broomstache snarled.

"If you know what's good for your family, you won't take another step, Mr. Kwirk. And you won't try anything stupid. We don't *want* to hurt you or your kid. But we're not opposed to the idea. So just stay right where you are and give us what we want."

Broomstache bumped his aluminum baseball bat against his leg. *Thump thump thump.* He had a cockeyed kind of smile. Smug and sinister all at once. Freckles held me tight, so close I could smell the stale cigarette smoke in his clothes. His arms were extremely hairy. Yeti hairy. And muscular. I felt like my ribs were about to break. The more I struggled, the harder he squeezed.

Dad's hands went up again, the same as they had with Mr. Oglesby, except what had worked with the old curator wasn't going to work this time. "Please," he pleaded, still holding

Papa Kwirk's artillery shell in one of those hands and the bag of ashes in the other. "We'll give you whatever you want. Is it money? I'll give you everything I've got. Just let my boy go."

Dad's face drained of color. I'd never seen him this scared before. Of course, I'd never *been* this scared before either. My eyes darted across the room, looking for some sign of either of my sisters. My hope was that they knew what was happening, that they were already going to get help, circling back to the front of the museum to warn Mr. Oglesby and call the police.

"We don't want your money," Freckles barked in my ear, his voice huskier than his companion's. "We want the formula."

If I hadn't been held at knifepoint, I probably would have given Freckles a puzzled look. *Formula?* Formula for *what*?

Then it dawned on me. No. Freaking Way. It couldn't be.

Dad shook his head. "Formula? You mean for the *jelly beans*?"

With the hand not holding the bat, Broomstache reached in his back pocket and pulled out a small notebook, the kind Lyra would copy unfamiliar words in to look up later. He tossed it across the tiled floor, where it skidded next to my father's feet. "Write it down," he growled. "All of it."

In that moment, a flash of anger masked the fear that I'd seen on my father's face. "You're from Garvadill, aren't you? They hired you to come and find me?"

"We don't need you to talk, Mr. Kwirk," Freckles insisted. "Just give us the formula so nobody gets hurt."

Yes, I thought. *Just give them the formula so I don't get hurt.* The man had a knife pressed to my Adam's apple. We were in no position to negotiate.

"Give them what they want, Fletcher," Mom urged. Her voice sounded desperate, but her eyes were steely, staring at the two men less than thirty feet away. She glanced sideways once, and then fixed those blue eyes back on me. *It will be all right,* her look seemed to say. *We won't let them hurt you.*

"Okay. Yes. Absolutely. Whatever you want," Dad said quickly. I tried not to swallow and struggled for a breath as Dad knelt and set Papa Kwirk's shell on the ground, placing the bag next to it and taking up the notebook instead. He removed a pencil from his back pocket—the same one we'd used to unscramble the fourth clue—and flipped the notebook open to the first blank page. "The formula is complicated. There are steps that I should explain. It will take time to write it out, and even if I do, I don't think you would understand it. If you just let my family go, we can talk this through. Let them leave, and then we can go somewhere, just the three of us, and I can give you the formulas for everything we've got."

"Or you can just shut up and write," Freckles snapped. "Before we lose our patience." The point of the knife pressed a little deeper.

"All right!" Dad said. He started to scrawl something in a hurried hand. In my head, I begged him to write faster. To just jot down some random chemical equations. Surely these two goons wouldn't know the difference between the formula for fried-chicken jelly beans and the formula for baby aspirin. Next to Dad, my mother started to ever so slowly dip her hand into her purse.

Beside me, Broomstache pounded the head of his bat into his open palm. "Come on, Mr. Kwirk. We ain't got all day," he warned.

"Ain't is *not* a proper contraction" came a salty voice from the corner of the room.

Freckles twisted me around in his giant monkey arms to confront the voice, only to find my pigtailed little sister with her hands on her hips.

"But I guess *you* wouldn't know that, you bumbling, backwater, boorish buffoon!"

"What did you call me?" Freckles spat. In that moment, I really thought he was going to let go of me and go for her instead. Except he didn't realize that Lyra was only providing a distraction.

So that he wouldn't see the other girl sneaking up on us from behind.

It would have worked, too, if it wasn't for his partner. But Broomstache's "What the—" gave Freckles just enough warning to spin me back around to find Cass standing less than ten feet away.

Armed with a sword.

It wasn't the kind she practiced with all the time, with the pencil-thin blade and the rounded, cuplike guard. This one looked more like something a military officer would carry, with a long, curved blade and a more ornate handle. But Cass still held it confidently in one hand, its tip pointed in our direction.

"Unhand my brother, you vile fiend," she said between clenched teeth, no doubt channeling her inner Elsalore. For once, I didn't mind.

Freckles dragged me backward, pressing his back to one of the glass cases that lined the wall as Broomstache took up his bat in both hands and stepped toward my sister. "Put that down, little girl, before you hurt yourself," he said.

Cass gave the sword her customary flourishing twirl. I knew what was coming. I'd been through this before. My sister narrowed her eyes.

"En garde," she said.

What happened next was pure Kwirk.

Cass's first lunge was parried easily off Broomstache's bat, but it was followed so quickly by a second that he barely had time to recover, just knocking the sword out of the way, but losing his balance in the process. Stumbling back, he couldn't manage to deflect Cass's third stroke—a hard blow across his right arm. The old saber must not have been as sharp as Mr. Oglesby promised, judging by the thin scratch it left, but it was still enough to send Broomstache's baseball bat clattering to the ground.

Freckles, meanwhile, momentarily shocked by the

appearance of my blade-twirling sister, suddenly cried out in pain as Lyra rushed out of her corner and sank her teeth into his forearm, causing the knife to slip from his hands. I felt the iron grip on my chest loosen as he tried to shake off my vicious little sister, giving me just enough room to maneuver and drive my elbow as hard as I could into his gut. I slipped free just as a voice called out.

"Rion! Duck!"

I crouched and spun to see my mother with her purse in one hand and a canister of pepper spray in the other. She kept just about anything you could ever need in that bag.

Freckles took a full shot of fiery spray to the face, temporarily blinding him. The bumbling, backwater, boorish buffoon screamed and pressed his fists into his eyes, turning and running face-first into a glass display of army helmets, smashing his nose bloody and sending him crumpling to the floor.

I looked just in time to see Broomstache stagger as another of Cass's expert slashes found his cheek, slicing a bubbly red cut that ran clear down to his chin. He cursed and fumbled toward her, stretching out his arms, no doubt ready to tackle her or choke her to death, when Dad grabbed him by his shoulder and spun him around.

The last thing Broomstache saw was the bottom of Papa Kwirk's shell clonking him right between the eyes, sending him crumpling beside his partner.

Dad stood over the brute's body, the inert shell in his hands, ready to deliver another shot if necessary. But even though it had been a dud during the war, the artillery shell was still good for something. Broomstache and Freckles were both out cold.

The sound of more footfalls echoed from around the corner, and all five of us looked up to see Mr. Oglesby in the entryway, wide-eyed and gasping.

"What in General George S. Patton's name is going on here?" he shouted.

We stood there, my older sister wielding a sword borrowed from an exhibit, my father holding the artillery shell, and my mother looking all too trigger-happy with her pepper spray. Two men lay unconscious on the floor, one with tooth marks on his arms and two swollen puffy eyes, the other with a red welt on his forehead and a couple of bloody scratches to boot. It probably defied explanation, but Dad tried anyway, like always.

"They broke in," he said. "They were trying to steal something. But we stopped them."

The curator shot my father a skeptical look, then quickly scanned the room to see what else was broken or missing. The glass case with the letters from Vietnam was the only one open, but only the one shell had been removed. There was a knife and a baseball bat on the ground, neither of them part of the museum's collection.

"You say they were trying to steal something?"

All five of us nodded. Mom tucked her pepper spray discreetly back into her purse. Lyra smiled real big. Cass set her borrowed sword gently on the floor.

Mr. Oglesby reached out with his wooden foot and gave Broomstache a little nudge, just to make certain he was unconscious. He looked back up at Dad.

"Oorah, then," he said.

And he left to call the police.

THE TEST OF MEN

In war there really are no winners, only losers. That was a quote I remembered seeing posted somewhere in the museum. Or something close. It's possible I got it a little mixed up because I also remember that the words were attributed to Neville Longbottom, and I know that can't be right.

It may be true in war, but in the battle for the secret jellybean formula, on the hallowed grounds of the Greenburg Museum of Modern Warfare, the good guys definitely won.

It honestly didn't take much to get the curator on our side; he believed our story from the start. The Greenburg County Sheriff's Department, however, was a little harder to convince. It helped that we had Mr. Oglesby's support, though he seemed a little miffed at us for using museum artifacts in self-defense and thanked Cass for not cutting anyone's limbs off, because it probably would have driven up the cost of insurance. He blamed himself for not relocking the door after letting us in, and blamed the other two men for the rest.

It really helped that those other two men, whose names apparently were *not* Broomstache and Freckles, both had criminal records and were wanted in connection with a string of robberies in Pennsylvania. Authorities had been hunting them for months. We Kwirks, on the other hand, had one unpaid parking ticket between us, for which my mother apologized profusely.

There was no evidence that the two intruders were connected to Garvadill in any way, and neither would admit to anything without first talking to a lawyer, but the detective in charge said she would investigate my father's claim that this was not a random armed robbery but a case of corporate espionage.

"No doubt in my mind. They were hired thugs. Those jerks will stoop to anything to get my secrets," Dad said.

"And by 'jerks' you mean the other candy company," the detective, who was blessed with the name Alicia Strong, confirmed.

"They are *not* a candy company. *I* work for a candy company," Dad insisted. "*They* are an artificial flavor manufacturer. And I'm telling you, they have to be the ones behind this." Unfortunately, there were no security cameras in the Museum of Modern Warfare save the one in the gift shop, so the detective had only our family's word to go on.

"We will look into it," Detective Strong said. She had short, black, no-nonsense hair and a matching no-nonsense expression, and she stood over six feet tall. I know I wouldn't have tried to argue with her, but Dad was too angry not to. "It's just . . . it's a little hard to swallow, Mr. Kwirk. You said you were in the museum—after hours—on some kind of scavenger hunt? And these two guys must have been following you around our little town where you don't even live?"

Honestly, we didn't know how they found us or how long they'd been stalking us. Since the park at least. Maybe long before that. Just biding their time, waiting to ambush us when there were no witnesses around. They hadn't counted on Cass having to take an emergency potty break and sneaking up on them, saber in hand. They hadn't counted on my mother being armed and dangerous.

They didn't know what the Kwirks were capable of.

"It wasn't a scavenger hunt, exactly. It's hard to explain," Dad said. "The point is, we didn't know who these guys were until they attacked us and demanded my formula."

"For the fried-chicken-flavored jelly beans that I'm not supposed to tell anyone about?" The detective seemed to be struggling to keep a straight face.

"They really do taste exactly like fried chicken," I said.

"It's uncanny," Lyra added.

"Uh-huh," Detective Strong said. You could tell she was ready to go home. Or at least to get away from us. "Sooo I think I've got everything I need for the time being, but I'm going to want you all to stick around town, if you don't mind, just for another day. I'm sure I'll have more questions. Could be a *lot* more questions. But for now, how about you and Mrs. Kwirk take your kids back to your aunt's house, and I'll take these two wanted felons down to the station. I'll give you a call if I need anything else."

"But you promise you'll look into it?" Dad prodded. "You wrote it down. Garvadill. That's G-A-R-V-A—"

"Yes. I got it, Mr. Kwirk. Corporate espionage and chicken-flavored beans."

"Jelly beans."

"Right," Detective Strong said. "'Cause what the world needs is some chicken-flavored candy." She made a few more notes in her notebook, probably doodles of my father in a straitjacket being led away to the funny farm. Then she headed toward the squad car where Jamie Trendall and Gavin Blane, aka Freckles and Broomstache, were conscious, cuffed, and complaining that they had done nothing wrong and that they were the ones who had been assaulted. I could see where it might look that way, judging by their bruises, bloody lips, and swollen eyes. I had scratches all over me, but that was the magic tree's fault; Freckles's knife hadn't even left a mark.

Detective Strong looked back over her shoulder. "And one more thing, Mr. Kwirk."

"Yes?"

"Just want to say that I'm sorry for your loss. I knew Frank. We all did. He was a good man."

Dad nodded. He'd heard that same thing a hundred times since we'd been here.

I wondered if he was finally starting to believe it.

The ride back to Aunt Gertie's was quiet, but a different kind of quiet than before. The kind of quiet that every now and then gets interrupted by a snort or a sigh, but not an unhappy one. More like the sigh you give when you've finished off the last bite of peanut butter pie and you're sort of sorry to see the empty plate, but your belly's too full anyway and you've still got the taste of peanut butter on your tongue to remind you of just how great it was.

Any other time, if one of us had broken the silence with a laugh or a knowing grunt, somebody else would have asked, "What?" demanding to be in on it. But this time we were all in on it already. So when Lyra giggled or Dad whistled or Mom said, "Huh," softly, to herself and shook her head, I didn't have to ask. I didn't even try to guess exactly what was going through each of their heads. I just let the evening's cool slip through the crack in the window, teasing my hair, and laughed quietly to myself as I thought about mountains of ice cream and Garbage Pail Kids and girls in flower dresses.

And Papa Kwirk. Stuffed in a shell and hidden away in a museum. Waiting for us to solve the puzzle and come find him. Though now that we had, I still felt like I was missing something.

Then again, maybe there was no one right answer. Maybe

Papa Kwirk's last wish was like a scatter of stars in the sky, a collection of moments and memories that you traced your own pattern over, making your own story from the connected dots.

"Vile fiend," Lyra whispered in front of me, stretching so she could rest her head on Cass's arm. "Good one."

I looked up at the sky—just dark enough that you could start to see the stars if you looked hard, starting to wink at you, as if they've just whispered a secret—and thought about the grandmother I never knew and how she didn't have to wait for Papa Kwirk any longer. He'd come home at last.

When we pulled up to the house, Aunt Gertie was waiting for us, sitting on the front porch in the dark, in different color yoga pants with a shawl draped over her shoulders and a phone in hand. "I heard what happened!" she yelled as we spilled from the car like clumsy circus clowns. "Got a call from a Detective Strong just a few minutes ago. She told me everything. Are you okay?"

"We're fine, Aunt Gertie," Mom said, putting her arm around Cass as we all trudged up to the house. My legs were like Slinkys. I could still probably pick bits of sticks and leaves out of my hair. My ribs hurt from where Freckles had squeezed me. But Mom was right. I was fine. Maybe even a little better than fine.

Aunt Gertie wasn't convinced. "She said two hooligans tried to *rob* you?"

That was one way to put it. It was probably what Detective Strong would write in the report, at least. I was ready to launch into a full retelling, but Lyra cut me off, running up to the porch with more energy than I could muster. "It was wild, Aunt Gertie. These two guys accosted us and took Rion hostage, and one of them was armed with a knife, and the other had a baseball bat, and they were demanding Dad give up his formula, right, but then I distracted them with my verbal prowess, and Cass showed up with a sword, and Mom blasted them with pepper spray and Rion . . . well, I'm not really sure what Rion did . . ."

"Thanks, Ly," I muttered, but she just ignored me and kept going.

"And then Dad knocked one of them unconscious with Papa Kwirk's old shell and then the police came. It was *intense*."

Lyra probably could have kept going, but at the mention of Papa Kwirk, Aunt Gertie raised a finger to shush her and looked at Dad, now leaning against the porch rail.

"You found him, then?" she asked.

"We found him," he said with a nod.

Aunt Gertie smiled her own peculiar smile. I'd seen that same smile before: right after the service, the first time Dad had tried to say goodbye to Papa Kwirk. I didn't trust it.

"In that case, there's something else you need to see," Aunt Gertie said, already sounding guilty. But before any of us could even get inside, she made Dad promise not to be mad— probably the most frequently broken promise in history. He did anyway, and she opened the door.

It was time, she said, to read the will.

When I was younger, like seven or eight, I didn't know what the word "testament" meant. I didn't even know it *was* a word. I wasn't like Lyra. I thought the thing everybody read out loud when you died was called a Last Will and Test of Men. And with a name like that, I sort of imagined it was a list of trials you had to go through in order to inherit the dead person's leftovers. If you could pass the Test of Men, you got your late rich uncle's house on the beach and his collection of pink porcelain pelicans, or whatever strange thing your family was bound to leave behind. To make matters worse, I also had been told that there was both a "new" and an "old" Test of Men, which just confused me further.

Eventually I figured it out. Sometimes it takes me a while.

Papa Kwirk's last will and *testament* was only two pages long, single-spaced, which struck me as odd. Aunt Gertie had been keeping it on top of the fridge, of all places, at the bottom of a bowl of three-year-old Halloween candy. It had been right there, right next to us, all along. She blew off a dust bunny and handed the document to Dad.

"Go ahead," she said. "Read it. But remember . . . you promised."

He wasn't angry yet, but he did look confused. "It's so short," he said, echoing my thoughts. After all, this was the will that not only outlined the kind of memorial service Papa

Kwirk wanted (the infamous *fun*neral), but everything that came after: from the frowning clown to the Museum of Modern Warfare. The empty casket. The clues. The quest. The whole crazy day. It was all in there somewhere. We'd done it all for him.

That's what Aunt Gertie had told us, anyway. And she was the executor of the will.

We all stood behind Dad—who sat across from Gertie at the table, like two foreign leaders negotiating a treaty—and waited for him to read through it. It didn't take long. When he finished, he flipped back and forth between the two pages, shaking his head.

"This is it? *This* is his will?" Dad slapped the pages with the back of his hand. "All *this* says is that he grants you power of attorney as executor, and that his body should be cremated and his family should 'dispose of his ashes in a manner that brings them peace and understanding.'"

Aunt Gertie leaned back in her chair, clutching a cup of coffee in both hands. "Yes. Well. I might have read into that last part a little bit," she admitted.

Dad's jaw dropped. Cass's eyeballs bulged. Lyra's face folded into a look of confusion.

In a manner that brings them peace and understanding. It took a hot minute to fully process what Aunt Gertie was saying, what all of this meant, but like I said, I get there eventually.

"Oh," I said. *"Oh."*

Aunt Gertie winked at me.

What it meant was that all of it, from the bottom of the bottle to the top of the mountain, everything we had been through that day—it hadn't been Papa Kwirk's idea at all. It hadn't been written into his will. He hadn't sent us on some harebrained scavenger hunt around town to find him.

Aunt Gertie had. She had masterminded the whole thing.

"Wait . . . so *you* did this?" Mom asked.

Aunt Gertie wrapped her blue shawl tighter around her shoulders. "Well, if we are being completely honest, I had some help from Jimmy's friends and acquaintances. And I wouldn't say it was all my idea, either. He did say that it would be funny if singing clowns were the bearers of bad news. And he absolutely *insisted* he didn't want people crying and carrying on at his funeral. He wanted it to be a celebration of his life, with singing and dancing and everyone having a good time. And tacos, he was adamant about the tacos. The rest, I suppose, was up for interpretation."

"Up for interpretation?" Mom repeated. "Gertrude, stashing Frank's remains in a museum is not an interpretation. Making his family traipse all the way across the city looking for them is not an interpretation. I mean, come on. A marching band? At a funeral? Who does that?"

"Actually," Lyra chirped, "the jazz funerals in New Orleans are famous for their marching processionals."

"*Fun*neral, dear," Aunt Gertie reminded her, casually taking a sip of coffee.

"We almost died!" Mom snapped.

It sounded like an exaggeration, except it really wasn't, though the almost dying part wasn't really Aunt Gertie's fault; Broomstache and Freckles weren't part of her plan. Though I guess I *could* have broken my neck falling out of the tree.

"I'm sorry," Aunt Gertie said. "It was never my intention to hurt you."

"And what was your intention, exactly?" Dad asked, leaning across the table, his temper still somehow in check, though I noticed his hands were trembling again, just as they had been when he'd held Papa Kwirk's shell in the museum. "If it wasn't set out like that in Frank's will, then why do it?"

Aunt Gertie sighed as she reached across the table and put hers on top of his. And for the first time I realized just how old her hands looked. The knobble-boned fingers and creased skin. Liver spots marching straight up her arms. She had found some time in the day to get her nails done, though; they shone a pearly pink.

"I didn't do it for him," she said. "And I didn't do it for you either. Not just for you, anyway. I did it for me."

Dad tried to pull his hands back, but Aunt Gertie clamped down on them, wrapping those bony fingers around his wrists. Like my sister, she was a lot stronger than she looked. Maybe it was a Kwirk thing. "Jimmy had a plan for what his life was going to be. He had it all mapped out, all the dots connected. But all of it—his whole entire world—it all revolved around Shelley. It absolutely shattered him, losing her. For a time, I think, he just didn't see the point in trying.

And, unfortunately, you were the one who paid for it."

I looked at Dad and saw, in that moment, the little boy who had lost his mom. Who woke up and got himself fed and out the door to catch the school bus. Who spent his Saturday mornings alone in the living room watching cartoons while his father slept. Who grew up the rest of the way with what seemed like only half a parent, as if the death of Grandma Shelley had split Papa Kwirk in two.

"It took him a long time to crawl out of that hole, Fletcher," Aunt Gertie continued. "And when he finally did, you were gone."

"I wasn't that far away," Dad said.

"Not in miles, maybe," Aunt Gertie replied, arching a sculpted eyebrow at him. "For twenty years I watched you two circle around each other, holding it all in. He was too stubborn or too scared to say he was sorry. And you were too proud and too hurt to forgive him. And I get it, Fletcher. I do. There's no excuse for the kind of father he was." She shook her head but kept her eyes fixed on Dad's. "But I'm not getting any younger, and I'm not about to keel over being the only one who knew how much your father loved you. And how it broke his heart that you two grew so far apart. I needed you to at least try and see him the way *I* see him. The way the people in this town that you never wanted to come back to see him. For the man he *wanted* to be. That way, maybe . . . just maybe . . . you'd forgive him. And yourself."

Aunt Gertie took a deep breath, and the room suddenly got

hear-your-heartbeat quiet. Dad's hands were still locked up in hers. The rest of us still huddled behind him.

"So then why didn't you just *tell* me these things?" Dad said, finally breaking the silence. "Wouldn't it have been easier?"

"Sure it would have." Aunt Gertie smirked. "But we Kwirks never believed in doing anything the easy way."

I watched Dad's face, waiting for him to finally break one of his promises. Waited for him to start yelling, to storm out of the room and stomp up the stairs, or to pick up Papa Kwirk's too-short will and tear it in half right in front of Aunt Gertie's face. That's probably what I would have done.

Instead he grunted. He shook his head and grunted again.

And then, like a train building steam, chugging out of the station, the grunts turned to chuckles, and the chuckles exploded into startling uncontrollable laughter so loud it filled the whole kitchen. Both Cass and Lyra looked at him like he was possessed, and Mom put her hands on his shaking shoulders, but Dad just kept going, squeezing Aunt Gertie's hands now, tears trickling from the corners of his eyes.

Then it spread. First to Aunt Gertie, then over to Cass, who couldn't help herself and caught the giggle bug whenever it struck anyone around her. Cass laughing made Lyra laugh, which got Mom going. All five of them now, doubled over in the kitchen, squealing and howling like lunatics.

And I tried to resist, because it seemed wrong to be laughing at a time like this, but I couldn't't. They sucked me in. I wasn't even entirely sure what we were laughing about. Maybe just the ridiculousness of it all—because it was ridiculous—but it was also perfect in its own way. A perfectly ridiculous Kwirky day. Tears coursed down Dad's cheeks. Aunt Gertie was moaning, leaning back in her chair, clutching her stomach. I laughed so hard my nose ran. Lyra was cross-legged on the kitchen tiles, rocking back and forth.

Finally, after a minute Dad stopped and took a deep breath. The giggles slowly petered out, though Lyra was still on the floor. We all wiped our wet cheeks on our sleeves, save for Aunt Gertie, who used her scarf. A final guffaw from Cass threatened to send us off again, but our insides hurt too much.

"I have so many things I want to ask you," Dad said to Aunt Gertie, his face ruddy and shiny with smeared tears. "But there's this one thing that's really nagging me. There was only a small bag of ashes in the museum. I know that's not all of it. So where's the rest? And please, just tell me this time. No more ghosts. No more clues. Where is my father?"

Aunt Gertie got this look on her face, somehow horrified and amused at once. She pointed behind us into the dining room.

At the vacuum cleaner resting in the corner.

SYMPATHY FOR THE DEVIL

Turns out, Papa Kwirk had been with us all along.

Or most of him, anyway.

Aunt Gertie owned nine vacuum cleaners, five of which were operational. But only one of them held the remains of our recently departed grandfather. She told us how she'd accidentally spilled him all over the dining-room carpet trying to fill the ziplock baggie that would eventually stuff a shell in a museum. She'd decided to just keep him in the vacuum because, as she put it, "Jimmy was always ragging on me to be a little neater around the house."

It was one of several stories that Aunt Gertie shared with us that night, though they were mostly stories that Papa Kwirk had shared with her. About things he'd held on to and things that haunted him. Garbage Pail Kids cards and the books Fletcher used to read as a kid. His own war medals and the letters from Vietnam that Grandma Shelley had kept in a drawer of her nightstand. Memories of love and of loss and the many bottles of bourbon he'd nearly drowned himself in. Over the years, it seemed, he'd told Aunt Gertie everything he couldn't bring himself to tell Dad—the apologies and explanations, the hopes and regrets.

When he died, she said, the weight of all that passed on to her. So she had to find a way to pass on the message. Hence the scavenger hunt, inspired by the Easter-basket adventures of Dad's youth, a tradition passed down from Kwirk to Kwirk. It was the best way she could think of to preserve his memory.

I still had some trouble picturing Aunt Gertie burying a box of trading cards in a stranger's lawn. And I couldn't imagine how she'd managed to get that book forty feet up that tree. But the rest was easy enough. Aunt Gertie knew almost everyone in town. All it took was a few phone calls. A few favors. She knew the owner of the ice-cream parlor, of course, and was friends with the manager at Bailey's Pub. And, as it turned out, she and Mr. Oglesby were scheduled to go on their first date this Thursday.

She'd even given us a push when we needed it—sending us to Mallory's so we could climb the Mountain. After all, you don't hide the Easter basket from your kid so well that he never finds it.

And just like the basket full of candy I could have gotten just as easily elsewhere, it wasn't about what was stuffed inside that shell at the museum. It was the finding it that mattered.

We sat for another hour around the table, the whole family, trading stories with Aunt Gertie, laughing and crying and remembering, until Cass asked if she could be excused to text her friends and Lyra asked if she could hunt for Beelzebub one last time.

"Can I go call Manny?"

I suddenly felt an overwhelming need to tell somebody what had happened, somebody not named Kwirk. Mom said I could, but that I had to leave out the part about the hired thugs—or at least what they had been hired for. I was just supposed to say that we were almost mugged. "We don't want to say anything else until the police have had a chance to investigate," she warned.

Getting mugged didn't sound nearly as cool as being blackmailed in an act of corporate espionage, but I nodded, grabbed Aunt Gertie's phone, and headed up to the Vault. I found a box big enough to sit on, glancing suspiciously at another vacuum cleaner sitting in the corner.

As soon as Manny picked up, I erupted, spouting like my dad after an ice-cream binge. I started with "Dude, you're not going to believe this: I was just held at knifepoint," then started over at the beginning, telling him all about the search for Grandpa's ashes, from digging holes in the dark to the showdown in the museum.

"And get this," I finished. "It turns out it wasn't even my

grandfather's idea. My aunt Gertie was behind it all. How incredible is that?"

I waited for him to say something.

"Manny? You still there?"

When he finally spoke, I could almost hear his head shaking. "You know what? I take it all back. All those times you complained about how your family was crazy and I was, like, 'All families are like that' and tried to get you to shut up about it? I was wrong, dude. Your family *is* psycho. Like full-on straitjacket."

"Yeah, but—" I started to say, but Manny wasn't finished.

"I mean, a scavenger hunt? For his body? And not even all of his body? Just the part that wasn't sucked up by the vacuum cleaner?"

"Well, she did spill him on the carpet. I'm sure if it had been the linoleum—"

"And who hides somebody's ashes in a museum?"

"Yeah, it's a little weird," I admitted. "But then if you stop and think about it—"

"A *little* weird?" Manny insisted. "Dude, I will never doubt you again. Your family is certifiably bonkers."

He was finally finished. I sat on my box surrounded by Aunt Gertie's treasures—her toothbrushes and toasters and bags of aluminum foil—the phone pressed to my ear, struggling to come up with a response. I'd been waiting years for Manny to agree with me, to say this exact thing, and now that he finally had, I suddenly felt the urge to tell him he was wrong. Or that he was right, but that it didn't matter, because, certifiable or not, they were still my family. I couldn't change them, even if I wanted to. Or maybe it was wouldn't, even if I could.

I was about to tell him so when a heart-stopping scream echoed through the giant house, reaching me from downstairs. It was the kind of scream only my drama queen sister could produce. But this didn't sound like acting; this sounded like she was in real trouble.

"Sorry, Manny. Gotta go. I'll call ya later."

I hung up quickly and stuck my head out the door. I could hear my sister from the far side of the house. "Mom! Dad! Hurry! Get in here!"

What now? As I barreled down the stairs, I could see everyone else running to the garage, all of us following the sound of my sister's hysterical voice.

"Delilah, *no*! Bad snake! *Bad* snake!"

I had a pretty good guess what had gone down.

It hadn't actually gone down. Not all the way, at least. In fact, it was still sticking halfway out of the snake's mouth.

Poor Beelzebub.

There had been no sightings. No sock nibblings. No streaks of fur slipping around the corner or under the couch. Lyra had spent most of Saturday and part of Sunday fruitlessly looking for Papa Kwirk's fuzzy little weasel. Apparently she hadn't thought to look in the garage. Or if she had, she hadn't looked hard enough. There were a hundred places for a ferret to hide in there.

Delilah had found him, though. And then Cass found them both.

We all stood there in the entry, shocked speechless, looking at the python coiled on the concrete. I felt like we'd been striking that pose a lot lately. One glance at the terrarium told part of the story. In her rush to get out of the house the morning of the funneral, Cass had clearly forgotten to secure the latch on the top. Delilah, no doubt sensing warm blood in the air, had managed to push up one corner enough to climb up and out of her enclosure and drop over the side. Suddenly the whole garage was her playground. Or her cafeteria.

There was no telling how long the python had been loose, but it was obvious that her encounter with Beelzebub was a recent event: she'd barely managed to swallow his head.

"You put that ferret down right this second!" Cass screeched, scolding the snake with a wagging finger. Delilah's head turned slightly, taking in the six humans scrunched in the doorway. I swear she looked embarrassed—like her mom had just yelled at her for chewing with her mouth open. But it was too late now; the ferret hung limp from Delilah's unhinged jaws. She'd given him the "big hug," even more crushing than the one Freckles had given me.

"Your stupid snake murdered Beelzebub!" Lyra shouted, glaring at Cass before burying her face in Mom's shirt. With a look from Dad, Mom escorted my little sister back into the house; she seemed happy to have the excuse to leave the scene of the crime.

"I'm so, *so* sorry," Cass mumbled, apologizing to nobody in particular. Dad draped an arm across her shoulders.

"It's all right, dear," Aunt Gertie said with a shrug. "We all gotta eat." Cass let out another squeal. I imagine it was something close to the sound Beelzebub made when the python got her coils around him.

"Yeeah . . . I'm not sure a whole ferret's such a good idea, though," Dad speculated. "She's used to eating mice."

Delilah did seem to be struggling; she couldn't quite get past Beelzebub's front feet, which dangled just beneath her chin. Her head looked like a water balloon about to bust. Cass pleaded with Dad to do something.

Dad turned and asked Aunt Gertie if she had a pair of gloves he could borrow.

And maybe a set of salad tongs.

I don't think anything good ever follows the words "in retrospect."

Nobody ever says, "In retrospect, climbing that steel ladder in a lightning storm was a great idea." Or, "In retrospect, forgetting the dinner rolls in the oven was a fantastic way to test the batteries in the smoke alarm." Most of what we see in retrospect we regret.

In retrospect, it might have been better to let Delilah try to finish her meal. After all, if the Kwirks could conquer the

Mountain, it's possible the snake could have swallowed the rest of that ferret. She didn't seem at all thankful to have it taken away from her, hissing and striking at Dad the moment Beelzebub was disgorged. Dad fell backward, just out of reach, holding the limp, wet weasel by its hind legs.

Cass managed to sneak around and grab the snake behind her head, and I held the terrarium lid up while my sister dropped Delilah in. I shut it quickly and made darn sure it was locked. I had visions of that angry python breaking out again, now with an even bigger appetite, slithering upstairs to get her revenge on those who'd snatched her dinner right out of her mouth. For some reason, I suspected she would come for me first.

With the snake secured and the ferret's body recovered, Aunt Gertie went upstairs to find a shoebox—she only had about two hundred of them—to make a suitable-sized coffin. Mom had managed to calm Lyra down, and my little sister wiped her nose as she helped make a comfortable final resting spot using cotton balls and Kleenex. Dad, still wearing Aunt Gertie's ski gloves, settled Beelzebub's body gently in his makeshift casket; then Lyra added a couple of the toys from the box marked *Ferret Crap*, arranging them just so.

The Kwirks put on their jackets and sweatshirts. It was getting dark outside and there was a chill to the night air, but we had no choice. We had a funeral to attend. A real one this time.

Cass went and got the dirt-crusted shovel from Aunt Gertie's shed and Dad let us all take turns digging this time. Apparently there was some law regarding how deep to bury animals in your yard.

I guess there are all sorts of rules when it comes to honoring the dead.

When it was finally deep enough, we let Lyra lower the box into the hole we'd made. Aunt Gertie excused herself and went back to the house, returning with a carnation from one of the many arrangements that had been given to her in memory of Papa Kwirk, its frilled petals white as a mound of whipped cream. She gave it to Lyra to lay on top of the box.

"Would you like to say something?" Dad asked.

"One eulogy in a week is enough for me," Aunt Gertie said. "How about you take this one?"

Dad nodded and cleared his throat. When he bowed his head, we all followed suit.

"We, uh . . . we gather this evening to mourn the passing of, *ahem*, Beelzebub Kwirk—please excuse the name—whose sudden, tragic end both saddens us and gives us cause to reflect." Dad took a deep breath and I opened my eyes, mostly to see if anyone else was looking. I couldn't be sure because it was so dark, but I thought I could see Aunt Gertie trying not to laugh.

"Honestly, I didn't get the chance to know Beelzebub very well," Dad continued. "He was Frank's pet, after all, so I didn't see him much, and the few times he *was* around, I basically ignored him. But now I wish I hadn't. I wish I'd spent more time with him, even though he was annoying. When he'd bite your ankles. Or steal your socks—"

"Or crap in your shoes," Aunt Gertie added. Cass giggled.

"Right. And that. But still. Even though there were things about Beelzebub that frustrated us," Dad said, "he was still a member of this family. And for that we loved him. He may have been a weasel, but he was also a Kwirk. So goodbye, Beelzebub. May you rest in peace. And may ferret heaven be full of empty paper bags. Amen."

"Amen," the rest of us mumbled. All except for Lyra, who said something that sounded like "See monumentum rera queries sir come a speecha."

"What's that mean, sweetie?" Mom asked.

"It's Latin. It means, 'If you seek his monument, look around.'"

Of course my little sister would know Latin. "And what does *that* mean?" I asked.

"It means we live on in those we leave behind," Aunt Gertie said.

Lyra shrugged. "I just saw it in a superhero movie and thought it was cool," she admitted.

Without thinking too hard about it, I leaned over and gave my little sister a hug.

Dad grabbed the shovel and started to fill the hole.

Hours later, it seemed—long after Beelzebub had been laid to rest—I decided to put an end to the longest day of my life before anything else could happen. I started making my rounds, telling everyone good night.

Cass was in the garage consoling Delilah, who had been robbed of her dinner; I found her leaning over the terrarium, whispering. I waved to my sister from the doorway and she waved back, which was how we usually said good night. I started to leave but then turned.

"Hey, I just wanted to say thanks, you know, for saving my life and all. You're, um . . . you're pretty good with a sword." I looked down at my feet as I said it. When I glanced back up, I noticed Cass smiling at me.

"Wow. That was hard for you, wasn't it?"

"A little bit," I admitted.

"Well, you did okay yourself back there," she said. "I mean, at least you didn't faint. Which must have been tough given what a big swooner you are."

"Swoonster."

"Swoonmeister."

Swoonmeister. I guess I could handle being a swoonmeister. I could also let her have the last word. Just this once. I waved again, leaving her in the garage with a cold-blooded killer.

Dad and Aunt Gertie were back at the dining-room table, still talking about Papa Kwirk. I was tempted to join them, to just sit and listen and take it all in, but I'd learned enough about my grandfather for one day. Dad gave me a long hug, the kind I'd normally try to wriggle out of. "Get some sleep," he said. They didn't look like they were going to bed anytime too soon. I said good night and went to find Mom.

She was sitting on the back porch. Lyra was curled up beside her, cocooned in Mom's jacket, her head resting on Mom's lap. The girl was out. Thwarting a band of formula-filching criminals during your quest to find your grandpa's ashes drains a person.

My mother sensed it was me without even looking around. She could tell by my footsteps, I guess. Or maybe it was just motherly sixth sense. Out in the yard, the fireflies blinked on and off.

"It really is beautiful out here, isn't it?" She was looking up at the stars, the universe's light show on full display now. There were thousands of them. So many it was nearly impossible to focus and pick out the shapes. *Find the belt and you find the man.* I went and stood beside her, careful not to nudge my sister and wake her.

"That's the funny thing about stars," Mom continued, her voice barely above a whisper. "They burn so bright, with such intensity, and yet you can't even see them most of the time. It's only when everything gets dark, the darker the better. Then you realize—they were out here all along."

I knew what she meant. When something's always there, always around, it's easy to take it for granted. I bent down to let my mother kiss me good night like she always did. Lyra squirmed a little, readjusting.

"I'm proud of you, Rion," Mom said. "You did good today."

"Well," came my sister's husky little voice, talking without even opening her eyes. "He did *well*."

I smiled and patted Lyra's head and started back to the kitchen door, rubbing the imprint of Mom's kiss from my cheek. I had my hand on the knob when she called out, "There you are!"

I turned to see her pointing at the sky.

THE NECKLACE AND THE HOG

On the detective's orders, we were told to stick around Aunt Gertie's one more day. One more day in Greenburg, Illinois, population: one less ferret. It wasn't that much to ask. Just stay close by in case Detective Strong wanted us to come into the station. And don't get into any more trouble.

Maybe it *was* asking a lot.

We didn't have much planned for the day. We'd completed Aunt Gertie's quest and found—I suppose—whatever it was she'd wanted us to find, though I think it was something a little different for each of us. At Mom's earnest request, the rest of Papa Kwirk's ashes had been transferred from the vacuum cleaner to an old cigar box, which seemed slightly more normal in the grand scheme of things. At least we weren't mixing him with bananas and having him for breakfast.

Afterward, Dad insisted on taking us fishing on the pond

near where he grew up as a sort of tribute to Papa Kwirk, even though none of us really liked to fish. Mom came along this time, though we had to promise to bait her hooks for her because she couldn't bear to hurt the worms. Aunt Gertie declined, saying that the only kind of fishing she liked to do was for men who were ten years younger than her and ripped, or ten years older than her and rich. I doubted poor Mr. Oglesby fit either of those categories.

We took all four of Papa Kwirk's old fishing poles and dug for worms close by the water this time, staying a fair distance from Dad's old house, just to be safe. It was a good day for fishing: bright and crisp, the kind of spring morning when you could count the dew drops on the grass stems and everything hummed around you. We sat in a row, with Lyra and Mom sharing a pole, Cass in the center, Dad and me on the other end. Of course Cass caught a fish in the first five minutes—a bluegill she christened Captain Hooked before throwing it back.

I didn't catch a thing, but I wasn't trying too hard either. I sat at the edge of the pond with my bare toes skimming the surface and watched the sunlight shimmer across the water and thought about Papa Kwirk. About the difference between living hard and having a hard life. Papa Kwirk had done both, I guess. When somebody dies, you try to only remember the good parts, but nobody's life is made up of only good parts.

One thing could be said for my grandfather, though: he was

one of a kind. And there was a whole town full of people who would never forget him.

I was lost in my own head, mulling over all these things, when Dad bumped my shoulder with his. "Is fishing really *that* boring?" he asked. He seemed to be back to his old self again, smiling and cracking jokes. Even his bow tie was back, this one patterened with multicolored jelly beans. It was perfect for him.

I smiled back as best I could. "It's not that," I said.

"Wanna talk about it?"

I glanced down the bank to make sure my sisters weren't paying any attention; Cass was busy rebaiting her hook and Lyra and Mom were whispering to each other. I looked back at the pond. The sparkles on the water reminded me of the shards of shattered glass scattered across the table at Bailey's Pub. I wouldn't have thought to just shatter the bottle like that.

"You ever feel like you don't quite belong?" I began, making it a point to keep my eyes focused on the orange float bobbing up and down in the water, because I knew if I looked at Dad I might freeze up and not say what was on my mind. "I mean, Papa Kwirk lived this extraordinary life. He had all these friends and did all this stuff. And Aunt Gertie is, like, sixty-something years old and still does yoga at six a.m. And you and Mom are, like, both these genius scientists. Cass is freakin' Zorro and seems to know exactly what she wants out of life, and Lyra's like this ten-year-old Shakespeare, and I'm just so . . . you know . . ."

Dad shook his head, waiting, silent. He wasn't going to finish the sentence for me. I just had to spit it out.

"You know . . . I'm just so . . . *ordinary.*"

There. Finally. It was the same thing I'd been saying to Manny for years. *"They're so weird."* Except *they* weren't the problem.

I looked over at Dad, who was frowning now, and I figured I must have disappointed him somehow.

"Rion Kwirk . . . you are anything but ordinary."

"You have to say that," I mumbled. "You're my father."

Dad set his pole down in the grass beside him, never taking his eyes off me. "That's not true. If I've learned anything from your grandfather, it's that you don't *have* to say anything. You can go through your whole life keeping it all bottled up. I'm saying it because it's true. You're smart. You're funny. You're terrific with numbers. You've got your father's crazy good looks," he joked, running a hand through his hair. "And you're a helluva tree climber."

"I fell," I reminded him.

"Yeah, but *you* didn't break anything," Dad countered.

Only because you *caught me,* I thought.

Dad's glasses had slipped down his nose. He drew in his knees and wrapped his arms around them, resting his chin on top. Sitting there, by the edge of the pond, he looked like a kid. "Remember that story about the milk and cookies?"

"You mean graham crackers and Gatorade?"

Dad nodded. "Yeah, those too. It turns out I was wrong.

Aunt Gertie told me last night. It wasn't your grandmother who left them outside my door, it was Frank. It was him every time. I just always assumed it was my mother because . . . well, you can probably guess why."

I could guess. Because of all the times he woke up to an empty house. Because sometimes we remember only what we want to remember, or we let one memory cloud over all the others. But I *could* picture Papa Kwirk standing outside Dad's door with a plate of Oreos in his hand, contemplating if he should walk in and say something, then talking himself out of it, knocking, and leaving the plate and glass on the floor. That was his way. I wondered if he did it the day Dad broke his arm. If he thought about doing it any of those nights after Grandma Shelley died—nights that he spent at the pub instead, drinking two fingers of bourbon at a time. I wondered how different things would have been if he'd just opened the door, just once.

"Here's the thing," Dad continued. "You don't always get the chance to say it. Or maybe you have chances, but for one reason or another, you let them slip by until, before you know it, you've run out of time. So no matter what—no matter what you think of me, or I think of you, or whatever happens between us—I don't want you to ever, *ever* think that I don't love you for exactly who you are."

Dad blinked at me, waiting for confirmation like he always did.

"I know," I said.

I did. I knew without him saying it, because he'd said it a million times already. Because he wasn't the kind of dad who just left the plate by the door.

My father cocked an eyebrow. "Wait a sec, did you just Han Solo me?"

I cracked a smile. I couldn't help it.

"You did. You totally just Soloed me, you little stinker."

Dad shook his head and smiled too. Then he took his pole back up, and for the next hour we sat shoulder to shoulder and hummed as many cartoon theme songs as we both could remember. There was nobody around to hear us, of course, but I wouldn't have cared either way.

We quit in time for lunch, having caught a total of three fish between us, and after ten minutes trying to figure out how the photo timer worked on Mom's phone, we managed to get a halfway decent picture of the five of us: Fishin' Fletcher and His Equally Fishy Family. Dad said he was going to print it out and frame it alongside the old Polaroid we'd dug up when he got back home.

He also said that his collection of old Garbage Pail Kids cards were mine if I wanted them. They might be collectors' items worth a lot of money by now. I suggested maybe we should just hang on to them, maybe bury them in our backyard for future Kwirks to find someday. Like a family heirloom.

"So does that mean you want to have kids when you grow up?" Dad asked.

"They're called progeny," I told him.

Only boring people have kids.

The Garbage Pail cards weren't the only thing my father was ready to part with.

Before we left for home, we also had to decide what to do with the rest of Papa Kwirk's stuff. According to his surprisingly short will, Francis T. Kwirk left nearly everything "to my son, Fletcher," with the exception of a few minor possessions of sentimental value. All his old LPs were to be distributed among the members of his beloved barbershop quartet, the Salty Shakers. His poker table—which he'd also eaten off for the last five years, according to Aunt Gertie—went to Larry Demotte, who still owed him sixty-five dollars from their last game. His bowling ball went to Pastor Mike. Apparently, they'd been in a league together.

For her part, Aunt Gertie got Papa Kwirk's old biker jacket, the black leather faded and cracked from too much sun and snow, though she just called it "broken in." She also inherited a set of earrings that had once been Grandma Shelley's, a sugar and creamer set that was shaped like spotted cows, and Grandpa's old vacuum cleaner to add to her collection, bringing her operational total up to six. I would have thought he would have left her more—she was his best friend, after all—but when I said something about it, Aunt Gertie huffed. "I told Jimmy I didn't need any more junk."

"That's good," Mom said, overhearing the conversation. "The first step is admitting you have a problem."

"Says the woman with a sixteen-ounce bottle of hand sanitizer in her purse," Aunt Gertie fired back.

Yet even with the bowling ball and spotted-cow creamer accounted for, it still left us with a storage unit full of furniture, several boxes of clothes, and, of course, a motorcycle that nobody in our family knew how to ride. Dad declared his intention to let Gertie sell most of the stuff and give the money to charity. Something local. Something Papa Kwirk would be proud of.

"We could donate it to the museum," I suggested. "As a thank-you to Mr. Oglesby." I wasn't sure how much Papa Kwirk's stuff was worth—his Salty Shakers vest did have some pretty fly sequins—but it might be enough for the curator to buy another rusty sword to put on display. You never knew when something like that would come in handy.

"You don't want to keep any of it?" Aunt Gertie asked. "What about the pictures? Or the books? There's at least three boxes of books."

"We'll take the pictures," Dad said. "But I've still got a book I need to finish."

We were packing the boxes of photo albums up in the Tank when a black sedan drove up the road to Aunt Gertie's house. I froze, first thinking maybe it was Freckles and Broomstache, somehow escaped from the county jail and here to finish the job. Or worse still, Garvadill had upped their game and hired members of the Mafia to come rub us out. Then I thought it might be Detective Strong, come to interrogate us some more about yesterday's events. Maybe she'd discovered that we'd been trespassing in the Bur-somethings' backyard and come to arrest us.

What I didn't expect to see was Tasha Meeks getting out of the car, followed by her father.

Mr. Meeks waved hello to Aunt Gertie, who was standing on the porch, smoking one of Papa Kwirk's old cigars. It was a habit she'd taken up only yesterday, her own personal way of carrying on Jimmy's legacy, she said.

"Hey there, Gertrude. Hello, Kwirk family," Mr. Meeks called out. The owner of Mallory's ice-cream parlor shook hands with my parents in the driveway. He was wearing a T-shirt that said *Scream for It* and had a drawing of an ice-cream cone. It was perfect. "Just wanted to come say farewell," Mr. Meeks said. "I missed you at the restaurant yesterday."

"Yeah. We had no idea you owned it," Mom said. "That place is fantastic!"

Mr. Meeks shook his head, embarrassed by the compliment. "Believe it or not, it was actually Frank's idea. He had fond memories of Mallory's as a kid. Told me I should fix it up and bring it back, just like it was. You know, for nostalgia's sake. I'm just sorry I wasn't there when you all tackled the Mountain." The breathless way Mr. Meeks said it—*the Mountain*—made it sound like conquering it was some kind of death-defying feat. Maybe it was.

"Thirty-six scoops is a lot of ice cream," Dad said.

"Don't look at me. That was all her idea," Mr. Meeks said, pointing at Aunt Gertie, who smiled behind a waft of cigar smoke. "She wanted me to make you work for it, so I told my manager on duty extra whipped cream and don't go easy on the sauce."

While Mr. Meeks and my parents continued to talk, I shuffled to stand next to Tasha. In the last twenty-four hours I'd climbed a giant tree, faced a couple of armed hooligans, and helped extract a dead ferret from a python's mouth, but I think I was more nervous walking up to her.

"All packed up?" she asked, looking at the Tank, which was one hungry snake away from being full. She was wearing a bright yellow sweater. It reminded me of dandelions.

"Pretty much . . . yeah," I said, smooth as sandpaper.

"I heard about what happened last night. All that crazy stuff at the museum. I'm glad you're okay."

You, plural, like my whole family? Or you, singular, like me specifically? "Oh, you know. Just a couple of jerks looking for money," I said, repeating the half lie Mom had instructed me to tell. "It was really no big deal."

I could tell by the look on her face that she didn't believe me. "Well, it must have been scary. I know *I* would have freaked out."

"Yeah, I mean, it scared me a *little*, but what are you going to do? My whole family was in danger." I didn't bother to tell her that I was the one everyone else had saved.

"It had to take some guts to climb that tree too," she added.

I tilted my head. "Wait a minute. How do you know about the tree?"

Tasha pursed her lips and rolled her eyes. "Puh-lease. You don't really think your sixty-year-old aunt climbed forty feet to put that book there, do you? I mean, she's crazy, but she ain't *that* crazy."

Of course. It had all been Aunt Gertie's idea. But she'd had help. Including from the girl who used to get rides on Papa Kwirk's motorcycle. Which meant Tasha Meeks and I had both climbed up the only magic tree in all of Greenburg, Illinois. That seemed significant somehow.

Mr. Meeks glanced over at us and gave his daughter the one-minute warning sign. Which meant that in one minute, she woud disappear, and soon there would be two hundred miles between us.

I thought about Papa Kwirk, stationed over in Vietnam, which was like ten *thousand* miles away, and all his letters to Grandma Shelley. All that distance, all that time spent apart, not knowing for sure when they would see each other again, or even *if.* And yet they still found a way to be together. He still found his way back home to her.

I could almost hear Papa Kwirk's voice inside my head. *What are you waiting for, kid, an invitation?*

Even rejection's better than regret.

"So, I don't actually have my own phone yet," I began hesitantly, "but I do have a computer. We could, like, Skype or something. You know. If you wanted to." I glanced over at her, bracing myself for the what-planet-are-*you*-from look. The same look I gave my family all too often, I realized.

Tasha Meeks smiled her turquoise smile. "Yeah."

"Yeah?" I repeated, sounding surprised. Papa Kwirk wouldn't have sounded surprised.

"Yeah. That sounds good," she said. "I'll get your email from your aunt."

"Time to go, Tosh," Mr. Meeks said.

I rejoined the family circle just as Mr. Meeks and my father were shaking hands goodbye. Then the owner of Mallory's reached into his pocket and brought out something concealed in his fist. "Before I go, there's something I want you to have. I meant to give it to you at the service but never got around to it."

His fingers peeled back to reveal a necklace—a medallion or coin of some kind, suspended on a leather string. Not exactly fine jewelry, but still cool looking. The coin had a triangle in the center, with the letter I, and around the triangle were engraved the words *To Thine Own Self Be True.*

"It was Frank's," Mr. Meeks explained. "He gave it to me the year after I had my accident. He was my sponsor at AA. By that time, he'd already been sober for eight years. He helped me get my act together. And he looked out for my little girl. He was almost like family to us." Mr. Meeks draped one arm around Tasha, pulling her against him. She smiled, partly

344

embarrassed but mostly proud. I could tell. "As his real family, you all should have it."

Dad—normally an ask-are-you-sure-three-times kind of guy—took the medallion without question. This wasn't the kind of gift you said no to, I guess.

"Thank you," he said. Then he got an idea. I could see the flash of inspiration behind his glasses, as if he'd finally unlocked the formula for armpits. "Turns out I've got something for you too," he said, and turned and started walking toward the garage.

Stopping right beside Jack Nicholson.

Before they left, Mr. Meeks told us how nice it was to meet us all again and to stop by the parlor anytime we were in town—"Just don't expect thirty-six free scoops." He also told Aunt Gertie he'd come back and get the bike later—after he'd convinced Mrs. Meeks that a motorcycle was also the kind of gift you just didn't say no to.

I stood close by their car on the off chance that the movie music would kick in, and Tasha would swoop in for the goodbye kiss. But it didn't happen. Instead she just waved and smiled, which, somehow, was even better. Besides, if she *had* kissed me, out there, with everyone watching, I'd have had to listen to Cass and Lyra tease me about it all the way home. No doubt Ly knew at least fourteen different synonyms for smooching.

I watched their car disappear down the long dirt road, only hearing Mom call my name on the third try, asking me to help my sister with the snake.

Once Delilah was safely inside the Tank, the top of her aquarium securely fastened (double-checked by yours truly), it was time for us to say goodbye to Aunt Gertie. We had a basket full of brownies and peanut butter sandwiches to see us across the Indiana border. The old tackle box full of cards was in the back seat for me to sort through. Dad's Thunder-cats toothbrush was tucked under his arm, along with his dog-eared copy of *Bridge to Terabithia*. He'd already decided he would just start over from the beginning. Sometimes that's just what you have to do.

He and Aunt Gertie faced each other, squaring off like they were preparing for another duel, though I think they were both just trying to find the right thing to say. Aunt Gertie got there first.

"Jimmy hated jelly beans," she said.

Dad looked confused. "What?"

"Jelly beans," she said, pointing at Dad's tie. "He didn't like them. Didn't like how they always got stuck in his dentures. But he ate them anyway. And not just when he came to visit you, either. He'd buy them here and take them to the Legion or to his Saturday-night card game and make all the other old farts try them. And he said that whenever they got an unusual one, they'd make the most hilarious faces and say things like 'How do they do that?' and 'Who thinks of such things?' and then Jimmy would say, proudly, 'My son, that's who.'"

"He never told me he didn't like jelly beans."

"Add it to the list," Aunt Gertie replied.

She then went down the line of Kwirks, whispering something in each of our ears, some little bit of Kwirk wisdom, starting with Cass. When she got to me, she leaned in close, and I could smell the acrid combination of her perfume mixed with Papa Kwirk's cigar smoke. She looked deathly serious all of a sudden. Her breath tickled the hairs in my ear.

"Be nice to your sisters. They're good to you. And who knows, they might just end up being your best friends someday. Got it?"

"I got it," I said. After everything I'd experienced this weekend, I supposed anything was possible.

"Good." Her stern look softened. She gave me a pat on the cheek and then looked me in the eyes. "And don't forget to floss."

Once Aunt Gertie had gotten her hug from Lyra, we all piled into the Tank, my sisters sharing the middle this time, me lording over the back. I had to admit I was a little sorry to go. And not just because of Tasha Meeks—though my left eyebrow still twitched whenever I thought about her. Turns out Greenburg wasn't entirely terrible. It had its good parts. Like everything else.

"Everyone buckle up," Dad said, beating Mom to the punch, though she still twisted around to make visual confirmation.

"Did we get all the toiletries?" she asked.

347

"Yup."

"And the phone chargers?"

"Yes."

"And you gave your aunt the check to help cover the memorial expenses?"

"She refused. Again. But I snuck it into her purse. It seemed like the least I could do, after all the sneaky stuff she pulled on us."

"You checked the tire pressure?"

"Actually, hon, the car has an onboard computer that monitors tire pressure," Dad said. "But yes. I checked it manually as well. We're all good."

Mom turned to us. "Did everyone use the restroom—numbers one *and* two?"

The collective groaning should have been answer enough, but she waited for us all to say yes. "Okay." My mother took a deep breath and placed her purse in her lap, then nodded to my father, who put the Tank in reverse.

He'd made it three feet down the driveway when she told him to stop. "My sunglasses," she said, digging frantically through the Bag of Holding. "They're not in here. I must have left them on the kitchen counter."

Dad reached into his inside jacket pocket and pulled them out with a flourish. "Ta-da," he said.

"What would I ever do without you?" Mom kissed him on the cheek.

Dad finished backing out of the driveway, and we all waved

goodbye to Aunt Gertie standing on the lawn. Her last words, shouted out to us, were "Drive safe!"

"It's safely," Lyra mumbled.

When we were on the road, Mom turned on the radio and started flipping through stations. "What should we listen to?"

"Stuff You Should Know," Lyra suggested.

"Wicked," Cass said emphatically. "No. No. *Into the Woods.* But only the first act. The second act is such a downer."

"Anything other than what these two want," I pleaded. Being nice to my sisters didn't mean having to like everything they did.

"I'm the driver," Dad proclaimed, "which means I get to decide."

He gave my mother an almost Aunt Gertieish grin and cued up something he'd loaded onto his phone.

Three seconds later, I heard the four-part harmony kick in. I looked at Cass and rolled my eyes, but I couldn't help smiling, and neither could she, as the Salty Shakers, led by their golden-voiced tenor, Francis T. Kwirk, started singing us home.

FINDING PAPA KWIRK

You probably want me to tell you what happened after that. Whether or not Freckles and Broomstache went to jail. If they were ever tied to Garvadill Food Supplies. If my father managed to produce his fried-chicken jelly beans and if the company made a fortune off them. Some of you are probably more interested in whether or not a certain girl got a certain email from a certain aunt and wrote a certain boy, who may or may not have lied to his best friend about that whole good-bye kiss business just to make it sound like he was cooler than he was.

I guess I could tell you, but that's not really what this story is about.

This is a story about remembering. First dates and fishing trips. Easter-basket hunts and magic trees. Empty bottles and boxes full of treasures. Things we choose to forget because it's easier, because remembering them might make us see everything a little differently. It's a story about fathers, the ones who catch you and the ones who don't, and about being lucky enough to take things for granted.

It's a story about coming home.

I will tell you what happened to Papa Kwirk, though, since it's mostly his story anyway. Some of him was taken to the Greenburg Cemetery and sprinkled in the grass over the grave of Michelle "Shelley" Kwirk, devoted wife and mother, who passed away on May 14 at the age of thirty-three. Some of him was taken back to Indiana with us and planted with a new sycamore tree, much like the one that overlooked the butterfly garden where Dad would dig for worms. And believe it or not, some of him still sits in an old cigar box on my great-aunt's mantel above her fireplace, flanked on both sides by a dozen porcelain cats. One day, I suspect, they will turn Aunt Gertie's house into a museum, and that cigar box will be just one of many oddities to see on your way to the world's biggest toothbrush exhibit upstairs.

And speaking of museums, if you're ever in the town of Greenburg, Illinois, you might pay a visit to the Museum of Modern Warfare. There you might see a little display in the Vietnam section about a man named Francis T. Kwirk, or Jimmy, as only one person in the world ever called him. You can read the letter that he wrote to his then-girlfriend, soon-to-be wife. You can also see the 105mm artillery shell that nearly landed in his lap. Don't worry. Its dud explosives were taken out long ago, though if you could get your hands on it, you might swear there was still a little something inside.

Afterward, you should head over to Polk Park and take a spin on the rusty roundabout, or find a good tree to climb. Or if you're hungry, go to Mallory's and try to conquer Mount Everest. They don't call it Mount Everest anymore, but the people who work there will know what you're talking about. Just don't forget to bring loose-fitting pants. And maybe a bucket.

Whether you reach the summit or not, be sure to check out the wall in the back. You can look for the picture of my family. The Kwirks.

I'm the one in the middle, rolling my eyes and shaking my head, trying way too hard to act normal.

Surrounded by something extraordinary.

ACKNOWLEDGMENTS

An oddball family goes on a scavenger hunt to recover their grand-father's dead body. It takes a special (crazy?) group of people to think that's a good idea for a children's book, starting with the dynamic duo at Adams Literary (thanks, Josh and Tracy) and extending to the equally talented group at HarperCollins: Tiara Kittrell, Katie Fitch, Amy Ryan, Megan Barlog, Ann Dye, and Meghan Pettit—thank you all for all your contributions. To Renée Cafiero and Laaren Brown, thanks for making my messy manuscript readable. Much gratitude to Deb Kovaks and Donna Bray for continuing to believe in me—you are the Masters of the Universe. Special thanks goes to my partner in crime, the Broomstache to my Freckles, Jordan Brown, who knows more about ThunderCats than I do, proving, once again, that I will never be as cool as him.

To my incredible family: This is a work of fiction. Any similarity to actual events or persons, living or dead, is purely coincidental. And even if you should happen to catch a glimpse of your personalities or eccentricates in any of the characters, it's not my fault. You raised me, encouraged me, supported me, loved me, and inspired me. You are the reason I write, so really you have only yourselves to blame.

Finally, to all the oddballs out there—the kooky, nutty, wackadoodles who dance to their own special tune—remember this: being out of the ordinary only makes you extraordinary. So keep dancing.

ONE
LAST
SHOT

Author of *Ms. Bixby's Last Day* and *Posted*
JOHN DAVID ANDERSON

HOLE #1

<u>Par 2</u>

A gentle downhill slope leads to a solitary stone hazard blocking the cup, which is located just behind the rock and out of view. Your average golfer will settle for two, but with the proper angle and appropriate force, you can make it in one.

And everyone knows one is better.

It's a beautiful, sunny day here in Williams Bay, Wisconsin, where twenty-four talented young golfers are getting ready to tackle this monster of a course.

That's right, Bill. This one is a killer. Each hole more challenging than the last. Expect to see some serious bogeys on the cards today. We've got sand. We've got water. But this ain't no day at the beach.

You said it, Jim. And here we have the underdog: twelve-year-old Malcolm Greeley in the dark blue polo. What do you make of him?

Well, his ears are a little big, Bill. They're just not in proportion to his face. Sort of like a Mr. Potato Head. And those shorts his mother picked out for him are hideous. He looks like he just waded waist deep through Mustard Creek. A little yellow goes a long way out here on the green, Mrs. Greeley.

No, Jim. I mean what do you think of the kid's chances? Do you *think he has what it takes to bring home the Morris-Hirschfield Trophy this afternoon?*

"Malcolm."

Well, it's a challenging field, Bill. A lot of talented golfers out here today. But the odds-on favorite has to be returning champion Jamie Tran, who has dominated just about every mini golf competition he's played in this year.

"Malcolm."

No question, Tran has the skills, Jim. I suspect he's going to annihilate the likes of Malcolm Greeley. Really rub his face in the—

"Malcolm!"

Mom snaps her fingers. Her freckled face is only inches from mine. I can smell her perfume, the stuff Dad puts in her stocking at Christmas every year. It's flowery but also sort of sweet smelling. Like rose petals and vanilla frosting.

"You okay?"

I lick chapped lips and give her two nods. Normally two's enough to convince her, but not today. I could nod until my head snapped off and she would still know better. Given everything that's going on, how could either of us be okay?

"You're up," she says, touching me softly on the shoulder. "Don't be nervous. Just relax. Visualize." My mother takes a series of deep, cleansing breaths—in through the nose, out through the mouth. She probably learned that in yoga class. I don't understand the point of paying someone to teach you how to stand like a tree, but she likes going. It relaxes her, she says. I'm pretty sure I don't relax her. She places her hand over

3

her heart as if she's about to recite the Pledge. "You're going to do great."

I know she thinks so. But not everybody's definition of *great* is the same.

I scan the crowd—the hundred or so people who have turned out for the tournament, most of them parents or grandparents. A few hold up poster-board signs with colorful bubble names and drawings of golf clubs. Many more hold Starbucks cups. Most of the siblings who have been dragged along already have their faces in their phones. I've seen some of them before. Heard these same parents telling their respective kids to take their time, to relax their elbows, to focus. They've probably never tried to relax their elbows. It's harder than it sounds.

Mom scans the crowd too. She looks disappointed. Or maybe I just *want* her to look disappointed. The announcer comes on over the PA system. His voice muffled and mechanical, nothing like the voices in my head.

"Up next on hole one, Malcolm Greeley, age twelve, from Falls Point, Illinois."

"That's you," Mom says. I know it's me, even if I'm not always crazy about the fact. Out of the corner of my eye, I spot Jamie Tran talking to his coach by the Coke machine that's really a Pepsi machine. Jamie's coach whispers something and both he and Jamie look my way. I look down at my feet and wonder what I've done to get their attention. Not that it matters. I can only assume today will end the same way as last time. There's no way I can win. And at this point I'm not even sure if it matters.

He's not coming.

That's what the voice inside my head says.

He's not coming.

Which sucks. Because this was maybe my last chance to fix things. To make him happy. To convince them both that this is all worth it, the three of us together. It's foolish, I know—it's just miniature golf—but I figured it was worth a shot.

Except the voice in my head is right. He's *not* coming.

And I still can't help but feel like it's somehow my fault.

I've heard voices ever since I can remember. But I didn't hear *that* voice until one night a little over three years ago.

The night I almost died.

Dad says it's an exaggeration. He says I would have had to sustain some sort of physical trauma. A car accident. A heart attack. A mauling by a mountain lion. You need to pass out, or at least be bleeding from your ears and eyeballs, as my salty old Granny Allison would say. *Then* you can say you've almost died. Dad says you can't almost die of freaking out, which was what *I* was doing.

I know he's right. I know I just panicked. But at the time, I felt like I'd lost everything.

It was buy-one-admission-get-one-free day at the fair. Also the day of the big horse race, although that part didn't interest me; those horses always look like they want to trample me, snorting and pawing the ground, just like some of the bigger kids at school. Going to the county fair was a Greeley family tradition. Every year for as long as I can remember. I mostly went for the ice cream, though that year I had another prize in mind.

I needed a goldfish.

At school, Susan Stottlemeyer was always bragging about the goldfish she'd won at the same fair two years ago, playing that game where you have to toss the Ping-Pong ball into the bowl with the colored rim. Her fish's name was Willy McGilly, and she'd managed to keep it alive for two years already. She said that proved she would make an excellent mother someday. Susan wasn't exactly a friend—I didn't have a lot of those—but she had awesome scented markers that she shared and orange hair that reminded me of a campfire.

"Fish are marvelous," she informed everyone at our table. "They listen to everything you have to say and never talk back, and they always give you something to watch when you've used up your screen time." I was always maxing out my screen time, so I figured I could use a fish. Besides, it might be nice to have someone else to talk to besides myself.

After two weeks, I'd almost convinced Mom and Dad through a delicate mixture of nagging and begging. I figured if I were to win one at the fair, they'd have no choice but to let me keep it. Dad weighed in, saying the last thing we needed in the house was another mouth to feed, until I informed him that a goldfish's mouth is about the size of a freckle and promised I'd buy the food with my allowance.

Dad frowned. Mom said, "We'll see." They left it at that.

For the ten days leading up to the fair, I practiced the carnival game in the kitchen, using a Ping-Pong ball and whatever containers I could find—mixing bowls, flower vases, empty orange juice cartons—the ball click-clacking across the linoleum. Mom watched silently, smiling whether I made it or not. I knew better than to practice when Dad was around; I didn't need that much advice.

By the time Saturday arrived, I could sink my shot from ten feet away more than half the time, which meant, with three balls per try, I was destined to make at least one shot in the bowl. I would be the Steph Curry of the Allen County Fair goldfish game. I overheard the kids on the bus talking about Steph Curry a lot, so I figured he must be good.

We gave the grumpy lady at the entrance our coupons, and she asked us if we were coming to see the pigs. "Not unless they are slow-roasted and smothered in barbecue sauce," Dad said. The lady smiled politely, but her eyebrow twitched. I notice these kinds of things. We grabbed a program with a picture of a dancing cow on the front and entered the fairgrounds, and I was instantly reminded of what I *didn't* like about the fair. It had nothing to do with the pigs—roasted or otherwise.

It was the people.

There were always way too many of them. You couldn't help but bump shoulders as you walked, and there were places where everyone was pushed together, noses to necks, sweaty and musky, jostling to get a look at something—the fattest sow, or the longest cucumber, or the most accurate butter sculpture of Abraham Lincoln. Bodies against bodies. And because I was too busy navigating around those bodies, I always ended up stepping in something brown and gooey that caused my shoes to stick to the pavement so that every step made a little ticky-tack sound. Disgusting.

But it was still worth it to see my parents having a good time.

We worked our way slowly along the road, dodging the golf carts and the little kids dueling with balloon swords. We bunched up against the fence to see the baby goats. Mom grew up in the country, three doors down from a farm, and she used to spend her afternoons helping her neighbors. She missed those days, so she insisted on petting every four-legged creature she saw. "Aren't they just adorable, Malcolm?"

"Their eyes are creepy," I said. The goats had hyphens for pupils, like cyborgs. They looked like they were planning to take over the world.

"He's right. They do look kind of demonic," Dad seconded, making little horns on top of his head.

"Well, *I* think they're cute." Mom stuck her hand between the slats of the fencing to pet the closest baby goat; it nipped at her fingers and she jerked back.

"Adorable," Dad said.

We moved through the rest of the animal pens quickly after that. My mother kept her hands at her sides. I kept mine in my pockets. I almost always keep my hands in my pockets. Not because I'm afraid to touch stuff—though that's true too—but because there's always something in them to fiddle with. A gum wrapper. A paper clip. A chewed-on eraser. Usually, though, it was a lucky nickel given to me by my grandfather, Grandpa Ellis, before he passed away. A Denver-minted 1929 buffalo head worth about fifty bucks. It was supposed to be good luck; I brought it to help with the goldfish getting. Mr. Curry probably had a special pair of lucky socks or something that he wore for big games too.

"Smell that?" Dad inhaled deeply, which seemed like a dangerous thing to do considering we'd just exited the cow barn. I took a tentative whiff as we stepped beneath the flashing sign for the midway. Sure enough, the smell of manure was quickly overpowered by a bouquet of buttered popcorn and caramel apples. It was like sniffing all of Susan Stottlemeyer's scented markers at once. "Smells like destiny."

The midway was even more crowded than the rest of the fair. People were roped into lines, waiting to ride the Himalayan and the Whirligig. Rock oldies blared out of unseen speakers. I watched every step I took like a minesweeper, wary of the brown glop that was waiting to swallow my shoes, and kept my distance from the cardboard-box trash cans that were swamped with bees.

"Let's ride until we puke," Mom said.

Dad bought a strip of twenty tickets without even complaining about the price, and the three of us tackled a few of the tamer rides. Dad couldn't do anything that went up and down or spun around real fast—they gave him a headache—so I picked rides all three of us liked. I didn't bother to ask about the goldfish game yet, even though I could see it in the center of the midway next to the Bottle Toss. My parents always insisted on doing the games last on the off chance we'd actually win something; no sense lugging around a giant Pikachu all night.

A half hour later we stepped out of the Fun House, which was neither fun nor a house, and Dad rubbed his belly. "Think I'm going to go get a funnel cake. You could help me tackle a funnel cake, couldn't you?" I nodded, hoping that splitting a funnel cake didn't exclude me from getting ice cream later.

Mom frowned. "Do you know how much grease is in those things?"

I held my breath. Grease was one of the things my parents didn't agree on. It ranked somewhere in the middle of a very long list, alongside which brand of toilet paper to buy and whether opera was beautiful or boring. The list was so long, I sometimes lost track of who stood where on what, but this one was obvious. Dad was pro grease.

"That's what makes them taste so good," he countered.

I watched my parents' faces carefully, waiting to see if this would turn into something bigger. I knew all of their cues. The sudden crease of my mother's mouth. The pinch of my father's eyebrows. The way she cleared her throat before she said something that would make him mad, as if priming her vocal cords for battle. I'd catalogued all my father's sighs. The exasperated sigh—huffy and pronounced. The dismissive sigh—which was really more of a snort, a nasal sound that meant "you're wrong, but it's just not worth telling you why you're wrong because it's just *so* obvious." The defeated sigh—long and drawn out, usually punctuated by a head sag.

This time he delivered a combination, a little huff and a little snort. "Malcolm wants one, don't you, bub?"

Bub was one of the things my dad sometimes called me. *Bub* and *buddy* and *little man*. It wasn't just me. He called everybody by some nickname or another, neighbors, coworkers, friends. Except my mother. He called her Nicole. Not Nickie, or Nic, like everybody else. Not honey or sweetie or babe. And she called him Matt. Matt and Nicole.

Mom and Dad.

And me.

Mom rolled her eyes, conceding the point, but she wanted the eye roll down for the record, to let him know that he only won because she *let* him win. I knew all of this about my parents. I'd been watching them for years. Triumphant, Dad took off, following the scent of fried batter, my mother watching after him. Then, as if she'd just realized I was standing right next to her, she looked at me and smiled. "Come on," she said. "Let's go try *that* thing."

She pointed to the Wild Mouse, a kind of multitiered coaster that reminded me of a human-size Rube Goldberg machine. It was the biggest ride at the fair next to the Ferris wheel. Definitely not the sort of thing we could do with Dad. Mom took my hand as we stepped in line. The woman in front of us had a tattoo of a bleeding heart with a knife sticking out of it covering her shoulder. I wondered what it was supposed to mean. Love hurts? Judging by the size of the knife, it must hurt a lot. The guy with her had a tattoo of Mickey Mouse on his neck. I liked his better.

Beside me, Mom hissed a bad word then immediately apologized. "Sorry. Pretend you didn't hear that." She didn't realize that I already knew at least thirty curse words, including three in Russian that I learned from the school custodian, Mr. Popov. I gave her a what's-wrong? look and she held up five tickets. The Wild Mouse ride cost three each. "Do you think you could ride it without me?"

I shook my head emphatically. If I rode by myself, there was a chance they would stick me with a stranger. Better to not ride it at all. Of course, Mom knew the answer before she even asked. She spun in place. "Do you notice how your father is always gone when you need him?" The line inched forward. We were still a ways from the loading platform. She pointed to a booth with a bright yellow sign. "See there? I'm just going to run over and get us a few more tickets. You hold our place, 'kay?"

I glanced around, hoping to spot Dad in the crowd. I didn't like this idea. We could always just jump out of line and jump back in. But the ticket booth was close. Less than fifty feet away. I almost said no. Almost.

"I won't be gone but a second," Mom said. "Keep me in your sights."

She made a pair of pretend binoculars with her hands and put them up to her hazel eyes. I imitated the gesture. It was one of our things, just hers and mine, something we'd done since I was little and she would take me to the playground. *Go play with the other kids,* she'd say. *They won't bite, I promise. Besides, I've got you in my sights.* Then she'd put her fingers in circles. Circles to eyes. Always on the lookout.

I watched her hurry over and get in line behind one other couple, fishing her credit card out of her wallet and turning and waving it at me. I still had my binocular hands pressed to my face.

"Hey, kid. . . ."

My hands darted back into my pockets, and I looked at the two teenage boys standing behind me, clearly older, the top of my head barely coming up to their necks. The one who had called out to me had a White Sox ball cap on and an annoyed look on his face. I wondered what I'd done. Maybe I was wearing the wrong brand of shoes. Or maybe it was just because I was suddenly by myself, unprotected. He pointed, and I could see his frustration growing, jabbing his finger at me like he was about to stab me with it. "The line, idiot," he said.

I spun to see the gap I'd made. The line had moved up while I'd been staring after Mom. "Sorry," I said, and stumbled forward, glancing back over my shoulder, trying to look past the two boys laughing and shaking their heads at me. The mouse-shaped cars ahead filled quickly, taking on passengers and zipping along the track. I could hear the *cachick, cachick, cachick*

13

of the chain hefting them up the lift hill, the screams of the riders sliding into each other on the hairpin turns. There were only eight or so people in line ahead of me now. I could feel the two boys start to press closer, and I twisted back around, expecting to see my mother walking toward me, tickets in hand.

My eyes darted to the bright yellow sign, to the window where she'd been standing only seconds ago.

Gone.

There was a man standing at the booth instead. I quickly scanned the crowd, looking for the navy blue coat, the chestnut hair that was already turning gray at forty—*Partially your fault,* she joked, *but mostly your father's*—expecting to see her pushing her way through, apologizing for cutting back in.

Nothing. I froze, staring at a dozen strange faces in line behind me. Two dozen more filling the street between me and the ticket booth. All of them older than me. Bigger than me. Crowding around me. Unbreathably close.

"Next."

My hands jerked out of my pockets, making circles, binoculars up to my eyes, but I couldn't spot her anywhere.

"Next," the voice said again, less patient this time, though I could barely hear it over the rush of blood in my ears. I felt dizzy. I reached out with one hand and grabbed the railing that led into the ride, eyes leapfrogging, face to face to face.

"C'mon, kid, are you riding or not?"

I looked at the teenage boy with the ball cap, pointing

again, not at me, but at the empty car. I turned to see the man at the ticket booth, heavy mustache barely hiding a scowl. I shook my head dumbly. The two boys brushed past me, tickets in hand, and I stumbled out of line, spinning with each step, looking everywhere now for the blue coat, for my father's white shirt and broad smile, listening for my name being called, but there was too much buzzing and clanking and screaming. I clutched my hands to my stomach, suddenly feeling ill.

I reached the ticket booth with the yellow sign and spun around again. She was right here a minute ago, standing right in this spot. Where could she be?

That's when I heard it. The voice. Coming from somewhere deep inside.

They're gone, it said.

My throat closed. I struggled for a breath.

They left you.

This voice sounded like me, like my own voice, except with an edge, the words cutting and cruel.

You're alone.

I started to walk, eyes darting, hands over my ears to block out the noise of the crowd, but I could still hear that voice muttering the same thing over and over.

Alone, it said. *Alone. Alone.*

Something touched me on the shoulder. A hand, dark skinned, grown-up. Lots of rings. Coat, not blue. Shirt, not white. Face, unknown.

"Hey, sweetie, you all right? You look a little sick."

Her hand still on my shoulder. Holding me. Trapping me. It was too much.

I bolted. Back into the crowd. Away from the hand. Away from the Wild Mouse ride. Toward the center of the midway with all the games. I called out for Mom and Dad, but my mouth was dry, and it came out as a squeak, impossible to hear over the music. I turned with every other step, trying to look in every direction at once, afraid I would miss them, certain I'd missed them already, that every time I looked left, they'd already passed by on the right.

They're gone, the voice said again. *They left you.*

An explosive sound from behind. Bells screeching, like the fire alarm at school. The man who'd just won the Test Your Strength game held the sledgehammer high above his head like Hercules. Everywhere I looked, lights blinked and blazed. I felt dizzy again, the whole world spinning like a teacup car. I took another step and backed into a girl holding a drink, knocking it out of her hands. It splashed across the front of her jeans, down onto her shoes, onto my shoes.

"Jesus! Watch where you're going!"

The girl glared at me with murder in her eyes. She had rainbow-colored braces crisscrossing her bared teeth. I didn't stop to apologize, I just ran, pushing back into the crowd, the sticky soda soaking through the tops of my sneakers into my socks. I tried to talk over the voice in my head. "They're here. They have to be here."

They left you.

"They would never do that."

You don't know that.

"Stop it!" I shouted. "Stop it! Stop it!" I stumbled from the busy center street and pressed my back against the side of the nearest booth. I closed my eyes and wished it all away. The crowds. The music. The rides. The voice. Wished I was back home, back in my living room, curled onto our couch with my parents sitting on either side. Warm and secure. I dropped into a crouch and wrapped my arms over my head, burying my face between my knees, squeezing out hot, stinging tears.

I wanted to go home.

Alone.

Stop.

Alone.

Don't say that.

Alone. Alone. Alo—

"Malcolm!"

I blinked through the blur. Navy blue coat. Frizzy hair. Purse tucked under her arm. She broke through the crowd and knelt down in front of me, pulling me tight against her. I leaked snot all over her collar. She grabbed my shoulders and held me at arm's length.

"Malcolm. Malcolm, I'm so sorry. The man at the booth— their credit card machine was down. But he said there was another ticket booth right around the corner. I wasn't thinking."

I wiped tears on the back of my sleeve. I didn't say anything.

I didn't know what to say.

"I came back to the ride and couldn't find you. Why didn't you wait there for me?"

See? It was your fault.

It was all my fault. My cheeks continued to burn. Before I could answer, I saw Dad appear over Mom's shoulder, a partially eaten funnel cake in one hand, his phone in the other. "You found him. Where was he?" He turned his eyes on me. "Where were you?"

They were both looking at me, waiting for an answer.

"I'm sorry. I didn't mean to . . ."

Dad shook his head. "You've got nothing to be sorry for," he said, giving my mother a sideways glance, the kind that said, *I left him with you,* but Mom didn't even look at him. Instead she helped me stand up and fished in her purse for a tissue.

"It's all right," she whispered. "You're all right now. Calm down."

I pulled my jacket tight around me. The top of my sock was soaked through with soda. Warm snot smeared across my lip.

"C'mon," Mom said. "Deep breath."

I did my best, my breaths long and shuddering. I nodded twice to let her know I was okay. I was safe. They were here. I wasn't alone. Dad held out the paper plate with oil spots soaking through the bottom.

"I saved you the half with the most sugar," he said; then he pointed to the booth we were all standing next to. "And look where we are."

I hadn't even realized where I'd ended up, where I'd gone to hide. I could see now the picture of the goldfish painted on the side.

"You okay?" Mom asked, but before I could respond, Dad chipped in.

"Of course he's okay. Aren't you, sport?"

I nodded. Sniffed. Nodded again.

I wasn't, though. I could still hear him. Way down, little more than a whisper. That new voice inside of me. The one I hadn't invented, that didn't have a name. The one I couldn't control or ignore like all the others. That sharp, insistent voice, telling me that I was the one responsible. That I was the one to blame.

Dad put his arm around me, strong and heavy. He and Mom exchanged a glance, and I realized the look that I thought was anger before could just be worry. "Let's go play some games, huh?" he said.

I nodded again. Dad kept his arm around my shoulders, Mom took my hand, and I let them lead me back into the crowd, the whisper in my head now drowned out by the sounds of the fair. I was okay. I wasn't bleeding. I hadn't died. I'd just freaked out.

I kept the voice to myself.

That night I came home with two goldfish. My father won the first for me on his first bounce. "See, Malcolm. Now *that's* how it's done." I won the second, though it took me four tries. I named the first fish Nemo and the second one Jaws. Dad said two fish were good because now they would each have a friend, and friends were important. He was always saying things like that.

Nemo died the next day. I found him floating belly up, Jaws circling underneath him like he was waiting for his mouth to get big enough to swallow his dear friend whole. Mom fished the dead fish out with a slotted spoon and flushed him down the toilet.

That was three years ago.

Jaws is still happily swimming in his bowl on my dresser, all by himself, which maybe means I will grow up to be a good father someday. I still feel bad whenever I have to leave my room, though, knowing I'm leaving him all alone, so I always promise him that I'm coming back.

I don't want him to freak out.